Brian Stableford

THE TRUTHS OF DARKNESS

Brian Stableford has been writing for fifty years. His fiction includes include eleven novels and seven short story collections in a series of "tales of the biotech revolution"; a series of metaphysical fantasies set in Paris in the 1840s, featuring Edgar Poe's Auguste Dupin, most recently *Yesterday Never Dies* (2012); and a series of supernatural mysteries set in an artist's colony, most recently *The Pool of Mnemosyne* (2018). Recent novels independent of any series include *Vampires of Atlantis* (2016) and *The Tangled Web of Time* (2016). He also translates antique works from the French, with particular interests in the Symbolist and Decadent Movements, *roman scientifique* and the *fantastique*. The current volume is the third in his Morgan's Fork series, being a sequel to *Spirits of the Vasty Deep* (2018), and *The Insubstantial Pageant* (2018).

BRIAN STABLEFORD

THE TRUTHS OF DARKNESS

THIS IS A SNUGGLY BOOK

Copyright © 2019 by Brian Stableford.
All rights reserved.

ISBN: 978-1-64525-005-0

THE TRUTHS OF DARKNESS

Oftentimes, to win us to our harm,
The instruments of darkness tell us truths,
Win us with honest trifles, to betray us
In deepest consequence.
    Shakespeare, *Macbeth* Act 1 Scene 3

Quod est inferius est sicut quod est superius,
et quod est superius est sicut quod est inferius,
as perpetranda miracula rei unius.
    Tabula Smaradgina, Chryosodorus Polydorus, 1541

[As it is below,
so it is above,
 the wonder of the whole being thus
procured and perfected.]

I
In the Kitchen

When Simon was sure that Felicia was finally sleeping peacefully, he stood up from the chair, a trifle unsteadily, and made his way along the corridor to the head of the stairs. He didn't switch on the light, because he knew the way by now, and didn't even have to put his hand on the

. . . the music abruptly took possession of his memory, of him, not as something heard, or as something played, any more than the darkness that took possession of him at the same time was something seen, or nothing seen, but as him, as himself, his true self, his deep self . . .

wall.

He tried to mutter an oath but couldn't. All he could do was stop dead, and wait for the moment to pass. It was not the first such alarm, and he had no expectation that it would be the last. His rational consciousness told him that because he was sleeping so little nowadays, his mind was suffering a dream drought, so he was getting flashes of dreams while awake, which only interrupted the movement of consciousness momentarily, and permitted its resumption without any substantial loss of continuity in action, or even in speech, but which nevertheless delivered a jolt to his psyche, a disruption that his conscious mind, when he tried to capture the elusive moment in memory, usually construed as music or as darkness, although he knew that that was only a matter of retrospective imaging, and that what he actually experienced was as indescribable as it was ungraspable.

Indescribable, that is, except by means of words that he did not want to apply, primarily "madness."

He shook himself, literally as well as metaphorically, and went downstairs to the kitchen. In order to steady his self-confidence, he checked his watch on the way down; the luminous hands told him that it was a few minutes after five. He already knew that, but the confirmation was nevertheless welcome, giving him confidence that, even if everything was not right with the world, it was still there, and sufficiently stable, in space and time, to make continued existence possible.

He expected to find the kitchen dark and empty, but it wasn't. The light was on, and Edith was sitting quietly in the corner, in her rocking chair, moving very gently back and forth. She made as if to rise to her feet but Simon raised his arms, almost pleading with her not to get up.

He sat down himself, in one of the plain wooden chairs neatly arranged around the wooden table, which must have been even older than the rocking-chair, although all the appliances surrounding it were relatively recent, James Murden having had the entire kitchen refitted and scrupulously modernized less than twenty years ago, perhaps to celebrate the advent of the twenty-first century but more likely to capitulate reluctantly with the relentless march of time and technological progress. Somehow, though, Edith and the table did not seem out of place. They belonged, part of the essential matter of the location, reassuringly solid. The only thing that didn't belong in the kitchen, it seemed to him, was him, whose solidity, identity and propriety all seemed anxiously precarious.

But he suppressed that thought. He had to get a grip, on himself and the world, and keep it, if he could.

He knew that Edith was waiting for him to say something, that she wasn't going to ask how Felicia was or whether, for once, she would be permitted to make him breakfast, given that the house now had a guest and circumstances had shifted yet again. She would simply wait. It was his responsibility to make things clear, to determine what was to be done.

"Felicia's asleep," he told her. "The fever is gone and she seems to be much better; at any rate, she should be all right for a couple of hours. I'll check in on her again before I go out, but I'll have to leave before nine. It's a terrible nuisance, but I have to go; the solicitor was quite insistent. I might not be back until mid-afternoon. Please, can you check on her at regular intervals while I'm away, and sit with her, if it seems necessary?"

"Yes, sir," said Edith. She didn't add *of course*, but the phrase seemed somehow to be suspended in mid-air, un-voiced but implicitly reassuring. A great many things had been hanging in the air of late, infinitely less reassuring for the most part.

"You don't have to call me 'sir'," Simon said, in a slight fit of petulance brought on by nerves as much as lack of sleep. "I'm not your employer—and I won't be, even if I do inherit the Abbey when James's will is finally proved."

Technically, Simon knew, none of the Abbey's three remaining servants was an employee. The payments that they were still receiving from the estate were a pension, not a salary, additional to the pension that each of them had been receiving from the State for at least fifteen years. James had offered all three of them the option of moving into cottages on the mainland, but they had refused—horrified by the prospect, according to Felicia. Not only did the idea of leaving the Abbey horrify them, but also the prospect of leaving the roles that they had within the household. Even the prospect of hiring "assistants" had not pleased them—although if James had ever got to the point of insisting, they would naturally have accepted the decision meekly, because it wouldn't have been their place to object. They had lived all their adult lives in the Abbey, and they wanted to die there, just like Ceridwen and James . . . and Felicia, perhaps not too far in the future.

Please God, not yet, thought Simon, and then cursed himself silently for blaspheming his atheism, especially on a day when he had an appointment to meet an agent of the Holy Office in less than six hours' time.

He was not so exhausted that his native pedantry did not kick in. "The Congregation of the Doctrine of the Faith," he murmured—aloud, without meaning to.

"Sorry, sir?" said Edith, whose hearing was nowhere near sharp enough to have made out the words.

"Nothing," he said, in a more robust tone. "Talking to myself." *Creeping senile dementia*, he thought but didn't add, thinking that he had no right, having not yet reached his seventieth birthday, to lay claim to senility while addressing a woman in her eighties, while another more than a decade older than her was lying in a double bed upstairs, perhaps suffering from nothing worse than a trivial virus or bouts of fever brought on by bad dreams, and definitely, Simon insisted *in petto*, whether she eventually consented to seek medical help or not, *not dying*.

Edith stopped the rocking chair from rocking and stood up, in a fashion that made Simon know that no gesture of which he had command could have stopped her. She switched on the electric kettle and took hold of a pewter teapot that had evidently done decades of loyal service, though not quite as many as her. Simon judged from the number of spoonfuls of tea that she put into the pot that she intended to fill it up, and knew even before she took three cups and three saucers from the dresser that she had no intention of simply making tea for herself.

"Will you be wanting to take a cup up to Miss Marianne, sir?" she asked. Her voice was very soft, but that didn't make the question any less of a challenge.

"I doubt that she keeps the same hours as you and I, Edith," he said. "It's probably too early." He had no idea what hours Marianne usually kept, and because it was the first night that she had spent as a guest in the Abbey, neither had Edith.

Simon's original invitation to his sister had been to come and stay for a few days in Raven Cottage, but he had casually extended the invitation to her daughter and granddaughter too, and they had arrived two days before her. Given that Krysten had a baby only a few months old, the cottage wasn't really big enough to accommodate all of them comfortably. Marianne, Zoe and Krysten were all now living in the same house in Bristol—Simon's former residence—but each in a separate flat, with plenty of space of their own. Crowding all three of them into Raven would have been, Simon was by now all-too-uncomfortably aware, a recipe for severe abrasion. Ergo, Marianne had been given a bedroom in the Abbey—as Felicia's guest, obviously not his, since he was still a guest himself, heir presumptive at best to the building and the island.

Edith poured hot water into the teapot, and then waited. Simon had a strong suspicion that the old woman had very fixed ideas about the exact length of time required to allow tea leaves to brew, and was certain that he couldn't stand a pregnant silence that long—but the responsibility for breaking it was his.

"How long have you lived in the Abbey, Edith?" he asked.

"Seventy-one years, sir."

"You arrived not long after the end of the war, then?" he prompted, with the aid of rapid arithmetic. He didn't know exactly how old Edith was, but he assumed that she must have been in her early teens at the time.

"Yes sir," she said, and darted a glance at him that presumably allowed her to infer that he would appreciate it if she would take the strain off him by taking on at least a share of the conversational burden. She added, in an atypical fit of garrulity: "I was on a farm the other side of Morpen before that, evacuated during the Blitz. Couldn't go back to Stepney—no house, no parents. Big bomb brought down the whole block. Mum and Dad were sheltering in the cellar, with the babe, so I was told, all buried by rubble. Dug out, but only to be buried again."

"I'm sorry," Simon said, reflexively.

"I was one of the lucky ones," said Edith, but added, equally reflexively: "So I was told."

"It must have been very hard," said Simon.

"The farm?" she queried, although he had meant losing her family to a bomb-blast. "Not so bad. From what I see on TV, they'd call it child abuse nowadays, but in those days it was just the way things were and nobody thought anything much of it. When they found me the position here, though

. . . that was like going to heaven. Maid-of-all-work, it was called, though it was old-fashioned even then, but it hardly seemed like work after the farm. Everything clean, my own little room, a real bed, and no one laid a finger on me that I didn't want them to. Miss Murden and Mr. James wouldn't stand for that. The butler, Mr. Bullen, had been in the army too, like Mr. James, and he was a great one for discipline, but no punishment. The only punishment here was exile to the mainland, and believe me, sir, nobody wanted that, not then . . ." *Or now*, she conspicuously didn't add.

"So long as it depends on Felicia or me," Simon told her, "you're not going to be exiled to the mainland. This is your house far more than it'll ever be mine."

"Thank you, sir," she said, dully. He realized that that wasn't what was worrying her. She wasn't worried about losing her little room under the eaves and her real bed. What was worrying her was losing her function in the household, the possibility of no longer being "the cook," and she wasn't worried about it because she thought that "Mr. James's" replacement might replace her, but because old age might make it impossible for her to do the job the way it needed to be done. She wasn't a Murden. She was a child of London's East End. She didn't have whatever enabled so many of the Murdens to live to be a hundred and remain reasonably healthy, and had enabled one of them to live to be nearly two hundred, even once bed-ridden. By way of compensation, she presumably didn't have the downside of that particular family trait either—except that, she seemed, in more ways than one, to have "gone native."

"Did you never want to leave?" Simon asked, and added, even though he knew that it showed a distinct lack of tact: "You never wanted to get married, have a family of your own?"

She didn't seem offended. "No sir," she said. She could have left it at that, but perhaps she decided that he had just licensed a modicum of tactlessness. "Never saw anything that made it look like something attractive," she said.

Simon could understand that. There was no TV during Edith's formative years, and she had probably not been much of a reader, so she could only derive her ideas from what she saw around her. And what she had seen around her, once she escaped from the slums and farmyard hell, was Murdens and domestic servants.

"Did many people get exiled to the mainland back then?" he asked, proud of what he thought was cunning obliquity—but she knew exactly what train of thought he was following.

"No," she said, bluntly. "And if Gwyneth Harwyn had had an ounce of common sense or common decency, it wouldn't have happened to her either. Whatever you might have heard elsewhere, sir, Mr. James was a saint. They would never have thrown Gwyneth out if she hadn't made it impossible for them to let her stay. If you trust my arithmetic, sir, there was only one chance in four that child was his, but even if she was, she had no call to make demands the way she did. I don't hold it against little Megan, mind, that her mind was poisoned. Gwyneth was the devil's child—and I don't mean the one in the . . ."

She stopped, abruptly.

"That's all right," Simon said, glad that it offered a way to turn the suddenly discomfiting conversation away from Megan Harwyn's mother. "You've been living here for seventy-one years. You must know far more about the family secret than I do, even though James took the trouble to initiate me officially."

"I don't, sir," Edith was quick to assure him. "I've never been down there, and I don't pry, sir. And I'm not so foolish as to think it really is a devil, or any of the devil's works. I've been living with it long enough to believe that it doesn't have any intention of hurting people—quite the reverse. I know it kept Miss Murden alive long after her time. She always told me not to be afraid, that even if the morgen and the neider came back, they wouldn't mean us any harm, any more than the ghosts do."

"You've seen the ghosts?" Simon queried.

"*Everybody* has seen the ghosts," Edith assured him, finally deeming that the tea was ready and pouring two cups, adding milk to both of them without asking, presumably because she thought it was a decision she was entitled to make, just as she felt entitled to assume that he had seen the ghosts too.

"But Ceridwen—Miss Murden—told you not to be afraid of them?" Simon queried.

"Yes, sir. She said it was a secret, that she wasn't supposed to tell us about it, but she told us anyway. She told us—me, at any rate—not to be afraid because the Black Monk doesn't have a face, because it was just too difficult for him to put one on. Appearance is easy enough, she said, in dim light, but even becoming vapor is hard, and solidity is almost impossible. Even the neider finds it hard, she said, and even what it can do, it can really only do under water. But it doesn't want to hurt anyone, even if it drags them under and through the water, Miss Murden said. And I never saw anything to make me think she was wrong."

Her slight emphasis of the word *never* rang slightly false to Simon, and he couldn't help adding a mental Gilbert-and-Sullivanesque *Well, hardly ever*.

"Until I arrived," he observed, almost absent-mindedly, and took a sip of tea.

The cook looked at him then, sharply, as if she had just had a sudden revelation. She hesitated, but then let her tongue off the bridle. "You're not to blame for anything, sir." Her tone said clearly that she wasn't just being polite, and certainly not hypocritical. That puzzled him slightly.

"A lot of bad things have happened since I turned up," he said. "I know, rationally, that I'm not responsible for them, but I can't help feeling like a walking disaster area. How can you possibly think of me in any other way, with Ceridwen and James dead, Melusine having disappeared, and Felicia suffering nightmares and fevers . . . for which I might, in fact, be at least partly responsible . . ." He frowned as he dwelt momentarily on that thought.

"No, sir," said the cook, her voice suddenly becoming insistent, in a fashion that reminded him distantly of Ceridwen. "Please don't think that. I was with Miss Felicia, sir, before you came, the morning after Mr. James died. I was sure that she was going to die too—that she was never going to wake up. I was *sure*. And then you came. Miss Cerys sent me back down here, but I know that you held her hands, and went to sleep with her, and I know that by the time I saw her again, things had changed. You kept her alive, sir, I know that . . . and you ought to know it too. And you went into that horrible darkness to fetch Miss Cerys back. She hasn't said a word about what happened down there, but Rhodri took that gun out of her hand and he told me that it had been fired, so I know that something happened, and I know that you brought her back safe and sound. So from where I'm sitting, sir"—she sat down in the rocking-chair, as if to dramatize what he was saying—"it seems to me that if you've walked into a disaster area, you've come to save people. You're what the TV calls the emergency services, not the bomb."

It occurred to Simon that the emergency services back in 1940 or 1941 hadn't been able to excavate anything from the rubble of Edith's former life but dead bodies, but he certainly wasn't about to say so, for his own sake as well as hers.

Instead, he said: "You saw the darkness in the crypt. That must have frightened you, at least."

"Yes, it did," she agreed, conspicuously dropping the reflexive "sir". "But I knew it would be all right. Miss Felicia sent us away, but I could see that she knew that it was going to be all right."

She hadn't, Simon knew. Nor had he. Felicia, he felt sure, had been terrified—for Cerys, for him, and for all the dark possibilities that the uncanny transmogrification of the underworld beneath the house might imply. He had been terrified himself . . . but perhaps it wouldn't be tactful to admit that to Edith. He could hardly blame her for casting him as a hero, since he had cast himself, quite deliberately, in that role . . . except that he had never thought for an instant that he was genuinely fitted for it. If God had existed, Simon thought, he would have to be deemed a lousy casting director.

"Has anything like that ever happened before, Edith?" he asked. He had asked Felicia the same question, obviously, but Felicia's negative answer had been tinged by doubt. He thought that a second opinion, taken from a different viewpoint, might be useful.

"I wouldn't know about what happens underneath the trapdoor," the cook told him. "I've hardly ever seen it open. But the special darkness in the air . . . yes, sir, I've experienced that before, over the years, enough times to lose count. Maybe six, maybe seven."

"Special darkness?" he queried.

"I don't know what else to call it," she said. "Gas, maybe . . . but it didn't feel like a gas, just *something*. Something in the air. I've never seen the thing down there, but I know some people call it a cauldron, as if it gives off fumes, or odors, but Miss Murden always told me that it wasn't really a cauldron, and that nothing was really cooking down there. It was more like a crack in a wall, she said, but just a hairline crack, too thin to let in anything solid, but which sometimes oozes something that can make your head buzz, so that you think you can hear music, or see things. It helps the ghosts, she said, and not just our familiar spirits. Maybe it's more like electricity than gas, but not our kind of electricity . . . more like what's in the air before a storm, lightning that hasn't flashed yet. That's happened sometimes, just as real storms have . . . I don't known what to call it, but it seems to me that it's just another kind of weather. As for whether that other darkness ever escaped from the trapdoor . . . well, in the dark I wouldn't have been able to see it if it had, would I?"

"No," Simon admitted, "I don't suppose you would."

"But the special darkness never did me any harm," she said, a trifle insistently. "Everything that ever did me any harm was *out there*, bright and solid. It can't do solid very well, Miss Murden said, and being dark, it can't do bright at all. Everything that ever harmed me could do both."

Nowadays, Simon thought, *they would call it child abuse, but back then, it had just been the way things were.* For Edith, the Abbey had been a kind of heaven, even in the utterly humble role of maid-of-all-work, let alone that of cook, which was practically archangelic. And James Murden had been a saint, who had never laid a finger on her, and had had to be seduced into falling from grace with Gwyneth Harwyn, the apprentice Whore of Babylon.

Fundamentally, Simon was convinced, Edith was right. The "thing" underneath the crypt didn't seem to mean anyone any harm, and nor did the neider. Quite the reverse: they seemed to be more interested in doing what little they could to try to keep people alive, even if it meant bringing them back from the dead. They were surely not *bad*; but that didn't mean that they weren't dangerous to know . . . or, for that matter, mad. Byronically mad, at least, and also contagiously mad. Their telepathic influence belonged more to the realm of the unconscious and dream experience than that of consciousness and real experience, but that was dangerous in itself.

Simon was still trying to drag himself back from that whimsical train of thought in order to investigate Edith's second opinion when Marianne appeared in the doorway, hesitating there as if she wasn't sure whether it was a threshold she ought to cross. Evidently, she didn't keep the same late hours that Simon had casually assumed . . . either that, or she hadn't been able to sleep in a strange house . . . a very strange house, which, despite James's denial, warranted the name of Nightmare Abbey far better than Simon would have liked, even as a guest, let alone its Heir Presumptive.

Simon leapt to his feet. "Edith's just made a pot of tea," he said. He grabbed the pot and the third cup that Edith had taken down from the dresser, and started pouring before Edith was able to reclaim the privilege.

The cook had her retaliation all ready. "May I make you some breakfast, Miss?" she said. "We have plenty of everything, with Miss Cerys being away and Mr. Simon having no appetite at all. Bacon? Sausages? Eggs? Tomatoes? The bread's not fresh-baked, I fear, but it'll fry, or make toast."

Slightly startled by the barrage of alternatives, Marianne demonstrated that she was a true Murden by her careful retrenchment. "Could I possibly have some scrambled egg on toast?" she asked, warily.

That counted as a victory in Edith's scorebook, and the cook didn't try to press her any harder. Nor did she let the triumph show in her face as she turned to Simon and said: "You too, sir? You'll need a good breakfast if you're going all the way to Carmarthen to see your churchman."

Simon capitulated, accepting that he no longer had any alternative but to "play lord of the manor," no matter how uncomfortable he found the role or how miscast he was therein. "Scrambled eggs on toast will be ideal," he told her. As he pushed the cup and saucer over to the place where Marianne had sat down, however, he said: "Or would you prefer coffee?"

"Tea is fine," she assured him. "How's Felicia?"

"Much better, I think," he said. "Sleeping peacefully, at any rate. It was probably just a virus. I'll look in on her when we've had breakfast, just to make sure."

"You won't need to call a doctor, then? That must be difficult, way out here. Ten miles to the nearest town, Zoe says—and I got the impression driving here yesterday that she wasn't exaggerating."

"I wanted to call one," Simon, said, defensively, "but Felicia wouldn't hear of it. I don't think she's even registered with a GP. When I suggested that I might have brought back a virus from one of my various excursions, to which she'd never been exposed, she said: 'Murdens don't catch viruses,' but she was exaggerating. I do, occasionally."

"So do I," Marianne confirmed.

"But it's true here, sir," Edith put in, her tongue having apparently been thoroughly loosened now. "Miss Murden never saw a doctor in her life, and wouldn't have seen one dead either if Mr. James hadn't needed the certificate. He didn't see one himself in the seventy-one years I've known him, although I expect the army didn't give him a choice, when he was wounded. Miss Felicia is the same."

"I don't like doctors much myself," Marianne said, "but you can't avoid them if you have children."

"Did you sleep well?" Simon asked his half-sister, knowing that it was the conventional thing to do.

"Yes, thank you," Marianne replied, presumably because it was the conventional thing to do rather than because it was true, and added, as if by way of apology, addressing Edith: "I don't usually get up this early, but I knew that Simon does."

Simon had explained his working habits to Marianne, but had not had an opportunity to bring her up to date by admitting that the routine he had maintained so religiously for so many years had been shot to hell by the confusion of recent events, and he had no intention of trying to explain to her why he no longer seemed to be able to sleep at all, except in short and troubled bursts. That was just one item in a long list of things he had no intention of explaining to her, in fact, although he wasn't at all confident that he could ring-fence her awareness of what was going on in his life to the extent that might be ideal.

Not for the first time, he suggested to himself mentally that it had been a bad idea to invite her to come and stay when they had met for the first time and a very bad idea indeed to extend that invitation to Zoe during their deeply embarrassing first meeting. In a spirit of fairness, however, he reminded himself that Zoe and Krysten had really seemed to be enjoying themselves yesterday, while he had been tied up all afternoon with the solicitor, and most of the rest of the day with poor Felicia.

Perhaps, he thought, a trifle bitterly, *the fact that I wasn't able to put on a show of playing host made the time all the more enjoyable for them.*

Marianne, probably feeling that she wasn't pulling her weight in the conversation, broke the silence that had formed during his distraction by saying: "I could drive you to Carmarthen if you like, and save Miss Harwyn the bother."

"No, that's all right," he was quick to say. "It's already arranged. I'm truly sorry that I have to leave you alone on your first day here, all the more so as I really don't want to see this fellow, no matter what he has to say, but the solicitor insists that the situation needs handling with kid gloves. 'Never irritate the Church,' he said—I won't attempt to imitate his accent—'especially a Church that probably thinks it still owns your Abbey, let alone the relics in its crypt. They can't take it off you without overturning five hundred years of English property law, but if they take the trouble to register some kind of official interest with the probate court, and ask for an injunction, it could tie up the process for months or years.' You know what bureaucrats are like—scared half to death by headed notepaper."

"I can see why Vatican-headed notepaper might be a trifle intimidating," said Marianne, mildly.

"If he has the Pope's backing, it's only very distantly," Simon said, trying to sound scornful but not quite succeeding. "The Congregation for the Doctrine of the Faith sounds very imposing, but it's just a fancy title, and although the notepaper was from the Palace of the Holy Office, next door to the Vatican, the postmark on the envelope was London. I thought it was a joke when I first saw the signature—Thomas Mallory, O.P., I ask you!—but it turns out that there really is an expert in Canon Law called Thomas Mallory-with-two-ells. Ninety per cent of his work seems to be internal to the Church, but he's appeared in the European Court of Justice more than once to give opinions on tricky questions of the relationships between the Church and various member States."

"But I can't see what interest the Catholic Church could possibly register in James Murden's will," Marianne said.

"Neither can I," said Simon. "That's why the solicitor says that I have to go to the meeting, in order to find out. He's completely in the dark, but he has a solicitor's imagination.

He thinks they might want to reclaim the bones of their saint, for want of any practical possibility of being able to reclaim the Abbey itself."

"But you don't think that?"

"I don't know what to think—but the fact that Thomas Mallory O.P. wrote to the solicitor, as the person in charge of the execution of James's will, rather than to me, in order to request that I meet him, at the Ivy Bush of all places, seems distinctly eccentric, not to say enigmatic."

"What does this O.P. you keep stressing stand for?" Marianne asked.

"Do I keep stressing it? I suppose that's because it worries me a little. It stands for *Ordo Praedicatorum*, the Order of Preachers. It means that he's a member of the Dominican Order, known in England as a Black Friar."

"Like the ghostly monk Mother asked you about? The one you admitted having seen?"

"Not exactly—but the reason it worries me a little is that I wrote a book not so long ago about the legendry of the Albigensian crusade, in the course of which St. Dominic founded his order. I wasn't very complimentary about him. In fact, I suggested, in so many words, that the mythologists of the crusade might have had some justification for considering the original Dominican Order as a gang of murderous thugs led by a vicious psychopath. Needless to say, that's not the Church's view of their saint and his works. I did, in my usual scrupulous fashion, admit that there's another side to the argument, by which the historical stigmatization of Dominic, the Order, and the Inquisition, with which they were heavily involved, is an aspect of the so-called Black Legend, the attempted demonization of the Catholic Church by Protestant propaganda, but I think a Dominican reading my book, especially one attached to the Holy Office, might well think that my account was insufficiently balanced."

"So you think this O.P. might be prejudiced against you?"

"I suspect that might be putting it mildly."

"But the world is full of heretics, and the Catholic Church can't persecute them any longer, in any practical way. Not in England, anyway, or Wales. Surely this Mallory fellow wouldn't try to interfere with the proving of the will just because he didn't like something you wrote about the founder of his order, out of simple vindictiveness?"

"One would hope not," Simon agreed, by no means entirely convinced.

"Didn't you mention at Mum's funeral, though, that you'd had an argument with another clergyman, some college chaplain from Bristol?"

"That's right. Alexander Usher, with one ess, likewise no relation to the notorious one. A man who, when I enquired as to whether he might have a hidden agenda in his surprisingly intense interest in the architecture and legendry of the Abbey, immediately replied: 'I'm C-of-E, not a Dominican Inquisitor'—which seemed like idle flippancy at the time, but now seems a trifle ironic, to the point where I'm almost inclined to wonder whether he might know any Dominicans, or whether they might know him. Call me paranoid if you like, but I'm not entirely unsympathetic to people who argue that there's no such thing as coincidence."

Edith chose that moment to place two plates of scrambled eggs on toast in front of Simon and Marianne, and came back a few moments later with a toast rack containing four more slices and the butter dish. "Strawberry jam or marmalade?" she enquired, and added, before listening to any answer either of them might give: "I'll make a fresh pot of tea." She met Simon's eyes before turning away, and said: "You'll need a good breakfast if you're going to face the Spanish Inquisition."

Simon was almost tempted to explain to her that the Spanish Inquisition had been a separate institution, from which the modern Holy Office did not claim any descent, established by the King and Queen of Spain, not the Papacy, but he refrained.

When Edith brought both the jam and the marmalade, no one having proclaimed a preference swiftly enough, she took further advantage of her reinforced authority to say: "May I make a suggestion, sir?"

"Of course," said Simon, aware that he was now on trial before his sister.

"As I said, sir, the larder is a trifle overstocked at the moment, with the supermarket having made the usual delivery and Miss Cerys having gone away and Miss Felicia being ill. As we have a guest in the house, perhaps you might like me to make a proper dinner this evening, for Miss Marianne, her daughter and granddaughter, you and Miss Felicia, and Miss Harwyn too, if you'd care to invite her. Margaret can help me to serve, and . . . well, sir, it will be almost like old times." Her voice was almost pleading by the time she finished the speech.

"That's extremely kind of you, Edith," Simon said, after the most minimal of pauses. "I'll ask Miss Harwyn when I see her, and Marianne can warn Zoe and Krysten. Shall we say seven for seven-thirty?"

Edith brightened visibly.

"Yes, sir," she said.

Simon didn't bother to remind her that she was not really a servant and that he really would prefer it if she didn't call him *sir*. He accepted that sometimes, things simply were the way they were. He couldn't resist saying: "I'm not sure that we can manage formal dress, though. I don't actually possess a dinner jacket, and I only own one suit, which I never wear, except at funerals."

"No one has dressed for dinner in this house since December 1957, sir," said Edith, mildly, with what was either a frightening precision of memory or a cavalier bluff. Then she turned away again, to make another pot of tea.

II

On the Headland

Felicia was still asleep, seemingly very peacefully. Simon couldn't help wondering whether that might have something to do with his absence from the bed. Although the quasi-empathic link by means of which they had been trying to share their dreams before the invasion of the dark seemed to have been somewhat disrupted when Cerys might or might not have shot him in the back—he was still not entirely sure whether the bullet and the injury had been real, in spite of Edith's casual revelation that Rhodri had ascertained that the gun really had been fired—he still wondered whether his own mental disorientation might be partly responsible, by contagion, for Felicia's bad dreams.

"Has she really never seen a doctor?" Marianne asked, as they made their way quietly downstairs. The sun had risen, and the weather was authentically spring-like, so Simon automatically headed for the back door, thinking that they could walk through Rhodri's vegetable plots and out to the extremity of the tine, to savor the sea breeze. He picked up his leather jacket on the way, though, thinking that there might still be a chill in the wind. Marianne collected a thick cardigan, which seemed to Simon to have an insistent dowdiness about it that was overdone even for a school secretary in her late fifties.

"So far as I know," he said, when he got round to answering Marianne's question. "I gather that the Murden philosophy has always been a matter of letting things get better on their own, although now that the holiday season is beginning and St. Madoc and Morpen are both becoming populated again, I dare say there'll be some kind of medical help close at hand until September. It's a facility of which members of the family have probably taken routine advantage in the past."

"Is that the door to the famous chapel?" she asked, as they passed it.

"Yes," said Simon. "Would you like to see the morgen and the ouroboros?"

"Yes, please," said Marianne. "Krysten showed me the picture she took with her phone, but it's not like seeing the real thing, is it?"

They turned into the chapel—an insignificant detour, since it also had a door to the headland—and Simon showed her the image set in the wall of the morgen surrounded by a circle that might or might not be an image of a sea-serpent swallowing its own tail: a notion that Simon no longer had any reason to find implausible.

"Kyrsten took a picture of it, you say?" he said. "When?"

"Yesterday. She and Zoe did a lot of exploring yesterday, apparently, while you were shut away in the house with the solicitor. They seemed quite excited about it. Zoe says that you gave her a key to the lock on the gate to the bridge?"

"Yes. I thought they ought at least to have the run of the place while I couldn't show them round. It really isn't very exciting, though; there's nothing much to explore except for the two caves, and there's no way down to Nyder's Cave at present except by ladder. There are a few rock pools at low tide, but the tide was in all yesterday afternoon. The wildlife on the plateau of the tine is primitive, the tine being treeless, and you'd have to be an expert botanist to determine whether there are any rare plants. To me it's all just green stuff."

"Well, they seemed quite excited about something. I was amazed to see them getting along so well for once, given that Zoe practically disowned her when she found out that she was pregnant. Since Mum's funeral, though, it all seems to have been patched up. I'm almost envious, in a way. I know you gave Zoe the same lecture you gave me about how nice it would be for all of us if we could all make an effort to get on, but I never expected it to work. I never expected her to move into Gran's old flat, either, but so far, so good. That had something to do with you as well, I gather? It's because of the money you gave her when she got into trouble, isn't it? It's the saving on her rent that she's using to pay you back?"

"I'm glad things are working out," said Simon, in a tone as neutral as he could contrive, carefully avoiding answering any of the questions that had been put to him, as he closed the door of the chapel behind him and led the way past Pamphile's stable and the vegetable plots on to the path that went past the hole above Nyder's Cave. "I can't claim any credit for it, though. As you say, I think it was your mother dying that put things into a different perspective—that long deathbed vigil, and then the funeral. I think Angela gave Zoe a lecture as well, from her deathbed, before I arrived."

"She certainly driveled on at me at extraordinary length— you too, when you eventually turned up. It was decidedly late, if you ask me, for her to start getting sentimental about family, long after all the damage had been done, but if it did have an effect on Zoe, I suppose I ought to be grateful. Her new addiction is bound to be a lot safer than the drugs, and infinitely better to share with Krysten."

"What new addiction is that?" Simon asked, having lost the thread, filling his lungs with the sea breeze that was blowing in their faces, and appreciating the tangy chill after the closeness of the kitchen.

"You," said Marianne, in a curt fashion that seemed to have a curious hint of resentment about it, as if Simon was somehow her own property, not because of their belatedly discovered blood relationship but because he had once taught her A-level English, and that the privilege of being interested in him was something that her daughter was somehow steal-ing from her.

"Me?" said Simon. "You mean she's reading my books?"

Marianne laughed. "You wish. No, that's not fair, yes she is, some of them. But she's not a fan the way I once was."

That, Simon knew, was an overstatement, but he took the claim as a compliment. "What way, then?" genuinely puz-zled, unable to think of any way in which he could qualify as an object of addiction, except in his prolific writings.

"I put it badly," Marianne said. "It's not you personally that she seems to have become obsessed with, but the Murden family curse, of which she now thinks that you're the expert and the interpreter, and of which she naturally thinks she's a victim. Didn't she badger you about it at the funeral?"

"She asked me questions about incidents in the family history of the birth of children genetically identical to their mothers, but I wasn't able to tell her very much, and I was careful to stress that the ideas of rebirth and the apparent instances of children taking over their mothers' identities was all speculation. I thought she was interested in it because she was an instance of it, but she did ask about other things that ran in the family, and about the Murdens' supposed relationship with the bardic Myrddin and the morgens. I couldn't go into detail about that, though—we were at your mother's funeral, after all."

"Well, she's been getting more information from somewhere," Marianne told him without bothering to challenge his employment of *your* rather than *our* in respect of Angela Richardson's maternity. "I think she's been exchanging emails with your friend Megan."

"Oh," said Simon, thinking, on the one hand, that there were other reasons than curiosity about Murden family history for Zoe to be keeping in touch with Megan, given that it was Megan, rather than him, who had given Zoe the money to pay her drug-dealing friends for the consignment she had mislaid in a police trap, and, on the other hand, wondering how much Megan might have told her about matters about which it might have been wiser to remain discreet.

"What's wrong?" asked Marianne. She had been looking out at Cardigan Bay, watching the gentle play of the distant waves, but now she turned to look at Simon with an appraising gaze, as if the bright morning sunlight had changed his appearance sufficiently to reveal flaws and faults that had not been obvious inside the Abbey or in its shadow.

"Nothing," said Simon, although he knew that she was unlikely to take that at face value. Swiftly, he added: "I'm slightly under the weather, that's all. I can't seem to sleep any more, except in short doses. It's just stress and anxiety, I think—or perhaps a touch of the virus that Felicia doesn't believe in. I'm sorry. Perhaps it was too soon to invite you all out here, and perhaps I should have asked you to postpone, when Felicia fell ill. This dinner of Edith's might not be such a good idea . . ."

"She backed you into a bit of a corner there," Marianne observed, "although I can't really see why she had to. Obviously, you're uncomfortable taking advantage of her, but given that she seems delighted with the opportunity, and Felicia would surely have thought of it if she hadn't been laid up in bed, I can't see why you would think that it might not be a good idea to get us all round the same table. I thought that's exactly what you wanted, in fact: one big happy family?"

There was an irony in her tone, which suggested that she had stopped believing in the possibility of happy families at about the time she had stopped believing in Santa Claus—to the extent that it even made her feel envious to see her clone-daughter getting along, for once, with her granddaughter.

She was still examining him, but Simon had no idea what that inquisitive gaze might be telling her. This was only the fourth time that the two of them had met since the 1970s, and the other three had been in such fraught circumstances that he hadn't been able to make any guess about what her attitude to him was, or how it might be shifting as she got to know him. He had no idea what she expected to come of this visit, or this walk on the tine. He looked away, out to sea, cursing the fact that there never seemed to be a seal in sight at times when one wanted to say, "Look, there's a seal." There were seabirds aplenty, but Simon wasn't much of an ornithologist either, and wouldn't have been able to recognize a stormy petrel if he saw one. He had no alternative but to face up to the provocative question.

"Well," he said, "given that I've suddenly found not one but two families, after a lifetime of isolation, why wouldn't I want to find a little comfort therein? Thus far, I've watched Eve die slowly, and I've watched Angela complete her slow dying, and I've been in the vicinity when Ceridwen and James died, and quite frankly, all the mourning is getting to be a bit much. I can't help hoping, at least, that there might be a little comfort and joy to be found among the survivors.

I don't know much about any of you, but I know that your mother and your grandmother were both mortally afraid of their own loneliness, and regretful of having brought it on themselves, no longer thinking that it was simply a matter of thankless children being sharper than serpent's teeth. If you and I can still spare ourselves a little of that, even at our age, don't you think that it's worth a try? And if we can do something—anything—to spare Zoe and Krysten from it, don't you think that would qualify as a good deed?"

They had reached the westerly limit of the tine and had stopped, automatically, staring out at the marine horizon, behind which Ireland lay to the north and the vast extent of the Atlantic to the south. Reading thoughts—even the thoughts of other Murdens—had never been Simon's forte, but making up stories had, and it was easy to imagine that Marianne might be fighting an impulse to say that Zoe and Krysten were her affair, not his, and that he had no business criticizing or interfering, but that she couldn't possibly say that because she too, not even secretly, hoped that there might be potential for something positive in the fact of finding a brother she had never known she had: perhaps comfort, and perhaps joy, and perhaps something to which she could not even put a name, but *something*.

Simon suspected, though, that she couldn't even begin to believe it, that she was already thinking of it as a cause already lost, and that she was wondering what on earth she was doing here, on this bleak Welsh headland, without a single seal as yet in sight.

"As science fiction writers go," she remarked, making a sarcastic joke of it, by means of a tactic that he recognized only too well, "you're quite an Agony Aunt, aren't you?" Immediately, though, she concluded that she's said the wrong thing—another reaction that he recognized only too well. "Oh shit!" she added. "Forget I said that, will you? I'm supposed to have put the spikes away for the duration."

"It's fine," he said. "We're siblings, after all—we ought to be able to say anything that comes to mind without fear of giving offense."

"Really? That's not the way it works in your novels."

"Novels thrive on dramatic tension," Simon said. "Life imitates them, alas, but that might be unwise. A little winding down and loosening up can only be good. But the spikiness, and awkward friction is something else that runs in the family. I do understand."

"Do you?" she queried, with a regretful skepticism. "I'm not sure that you can."

If the vegetation hadn't been damp, or if one of the Murden ancestors had ever bothered to install a bench at what was, after all, one of the tine's few viewpoints, Simon would have sat down, and invited Marianne to sit beside him, so that they could put on a show of comfort that they couldn't yet feel, but as things were, they could only remain standing, trying to relax by absorbing the placidity of the patient sea.

"Because I never had children, you mean?" he said, keeping his voice deliberately soft, devoid of any hint of aggression or sharpness. "Or because I never met my biological mother until she was out of mind with pain, and only once after that, when she was tripping because the very process of dying had freed her from the pain for a few brief hours? Yes, you're right; that's not experience on which I can build any sound judgment of family life, and as a writer, I know better than anyone that everything you read or see in fiction about the necessity and invincibility of family is just so much starry-eyed crap. But I have lived a life, of sorts. I've been human, or at least a Murden. I do have at least that slight existential qualification. I know what it's like not to be able get along with people, either because I rub them up the wrong way, without meaning to, or because they rub me up the wrong way, probably without meaning to. I know what it's like to want to like people, even to want to love people, and not to be able to do it, and to retreat defensively into myself, into my own obsessions, and to hide there.

"Given that, whether I *know* or not, I think I can at least begin to speculate rationally what it might have been like to be a woman like me and to have had a child like me—not necessarily genetically identical, although I can see how that extra twist might make it even worse, but just another human being, or another Murden—and to find, in that most intimate of relationships, the most abrasive of frictions . . . that even though I really wanted to love the child, and even though I *would* love her, in my own foolish way, it would have become increasingly difficult, as she grew older and more like me, just to be in the same room, and to know that she found it just as hard, and to wonder why on earth I was the only person in the world who felt like that, when all the others seem to have no difficulty at all in not only loving one another but finding that love rewarding—except, of course, when my own child repeated the patterns with her child, and I almost started to believe in family curses, or I contemplated the divorce statistics, and began to wonder whether all those appearances can really be trusted, and whether I was quite as absolutely alone as I thought . . . except, of course, that I would be alone, and so might they.

"You're right: I don't know, and I can't. But that doesn't mean that I can't imagine, can't sympathize, and can't wonder whether, if I—or, if not me, someone else—could try a bit harder, I, or she, could eventually get the hang of it, at least sufficiently to ease the pain

. . . and the music whined, as if the bow were running through his soul, and the tentacles of the darkness caressed his crwth, and he fell into the chain of wombs, back, back and further back, albeit in an instant that was just the tiniest fraction of eternity made space and wanted to cry fiat lux but had no voice and knew that light was, in any case impossible, because . . .

a little, or if not that, at least enough to be able to say, eventually, to myself or herself, as our mother said to Zoe with her dying breath, perhaps because she didn't dare say it to you: *I can cope.*"

Then he shook himself, literally. *Mid-sentence?* he thought. *The bloody thing couldn't wait for the pause, but had to hit me in mid-sentence? And not just any sentence, but in the home stretch of my big speech. And it had to leave fragments available to memory that will only make more puzzles, if I even contrive to remember them?*

After a long moment's pause, Marianne, who had been carefully not looking at him, and probably had not seen him shake himself in order to rid himself of the dream-fragment, any more than she had noticed any interruption in his speech, said: "Bloody hell, Simon." He was disappointed not to be able to find any admiration in her tone, but there was no anger or resentment in it either. The metaphorical spikes hadn't come into play. She knew that he was trying to sympathize, trying to connect.

"That pretty much sums it up," he agreed, feeling that his grip was firm. "So, was it a mistake, do you think?"

"Was what a mistake?"

"To write to one another, after Eve's will was sorted. To think that it might be interesting to meet, for each of us to measure the other, and measure ourselves in the process. To see if anything might come of the contact, in spite of all our miserable experience of past contacts that produced nothing, in the end, but nothing."

"Oh," she said. "That. This." After another pause, with due contemplation of the western horizon, which gave the optical illusion that the earth was flat, even though the most elementary logic proved that it couldn't be, because if it hadn't been curved, Ireland would have been visible, she said: "No, I don't think it was a mistake. Do you?"

"Not for me," he said. "I just worry that getting to know me might not be doing you any good."

"That's a coincidence," she said. "Or would be, if there were any such thing. I've wondered the same thing myself—about knowing us not doing you any good, that is, not vice versa. And in spite of all that bullshit you just poured out, like a character in one of your books, I know full well, because I've heard you say so, that you had adoptive parents who were definitely on the plus side of okay, and that you must have hoped, in making contact with your biological family, that we were more like them than us, or more like the people here, since, again in spite of all that bullshit you just spouted, you don't seem to be having any trouble at all loving Felicia, and sleeping with her, even though she's old enough to be your mother. Forget I said that, by the way. Oops again." The tone of her voice was genuinely mild, not spiky, with at least a hint of the lightly insulting humor in which siblings confident of their common cause ought to be able to indulge without giving offense.

"It's okay," he told her, "you can mock my taste in women. We're family, after all. And you're absolutely right again; for longer than a month, now, Felicia and I have needed one another, desperately, like two shipwrecked mariners clinging to the same plank, and it's probably brought us closer to a kind of love that isn't just lust or fakery than either of us has ever been before, or ever expected to be. But it seems to me, looking round at the world, that lots of people, even Murdens, find that kind of intense mutual need possible for a month, or a year, or even seven years . . . but that not many can sustain it for life. Mercifully, as you say, Felicia's old enough to be my mother, and she might not last the week, let alone a year, and I feel as if I've already died once, so there's no need for us to have any unrealizable expectations of our mutual need maturing into true and eternal love."

"I did say *forget it*," she pointed out. "Also *oops*. But it's good to be able to let things like that out without getting the usual blowback. It's not enough just to be family, though, to get that effect—quite the contrary, in fact. When I try it with Zoe, it . . . well, I believe you've heard her remarks about me going off the deep end. She's no better—but she wouldn't be, would she?"

"But she is making an effort, you say? With Krysten . . . and with you?"

"Not to mention you. Speaking as a writer who thinks about such things in his own quirky fashion, do you know what the absolute worst story in the world is?"

"No, I don't," said Simon. "There are far too many candidates to pick just one."

"The story of bloody Narcissus: the fool who could look at himself in a pool of water, fall in love with himself and drown. Has anything more ludicrous ever been imagined? To look into the pool and hate himself and drown, I could believe, no problem: utterly banal, in fact, but the idea of someone looking at themselves, seeing an accurate reflection, and falling in love? I don't know about you, but it makes me want to vomit."

"It's not a reaction I could imagine," Simon admitted, trying to match the eccentric flippancy of her tone, with which he felt comfortable, and which he was oddly delighted to recognize in his sister, "but I have a very limited imagination. There are all sorts of things that other people claim to have no difficulty imagining, that I never could. God, for instance. The idea has always seemed so ludicrous to me that it has always seemed obvious that nobody could possibly believe it, and that all the people who say that they do are just pretending."

"Including Black Friars?"

"Especially Black Friars. Who could possibly become a heresy-hunter except a secret heretic hateful of his own heresy?"

"This meeting you've got to go to is really preying on your mind, isn't it?" She checked her watch, reflexively, to make sure that he didn't have to rush off just yet.

"A little," Simon admitted.

"But it's not because you're afraid that the Catholic Church might stick a spoke in the wheel of probate court justice, is it?" she said, perceptively. "Because you don't actually give a damn about the Murden inheritance, do you? In fact, you'd rather the burden got taken off your shoulders, including the seven million pounds?"

"Right again," Simon admitted. "It has occurred to me more than once that if I hadn't been so quick off the mark throwing in the towel when Eve's solicitor told me that the execution of the will made it necessary for him to give me notice to quit the flat, if I'd just been pig-headed enough to hang on for another couple of weeks, we'd have met there, and you'd have told me that I didn't have to go. Then James Murden wouldn't have changed his will before he died; in fact, he wouldn't have died, because he wouldn't have been trying to phone me when the thunderbolt hit the lightning rod, and he wouldn't have had his heart attack. And I'd still be working peacefully for twelve hours a day on books that hardly anybody reads, and nothing would have changed, except that I'd have a new sister and a niece . . ."

"A niece who would probably be in jail by now, if she hadn't been able to run to St. Madoc when she panicked," Marianne interjected.

"Not necessarily. It could still have been sorted out. But we can't turn the clock back, alas."

"That's not what it says in your book on dark matter and dark mind," she said, amiably.

For a few moments, Simon had no idea what she was talking about, even though the book in question was relatively recent, and he had been reminded of it several times by Cerys, who had been reading it before she went down into the darkness and shot him in the back. Then he realized what she meant.

"That was purely hypothetical argument," he said, "and it didn't say that *we* can turn the clock back."

"It said that God could, if he wanted to—except that you didn't think he'd want to, although it seems a trifle presumptuous to psychoanalyze him when you don't actually believe in him."

It seemed to Simon that Marianne was now becoming a trifle presumptuous herself, perhaps on the basis that he had told her three times that she was absolutely right, and had given her a license to mock his choice of girlfriends. It was, however, no time to let the spikes bristle.

"You're missing the point slightly," he said, breezily. "That passage was a response to an anecdote about a dialogue between a skeptic and a priest. The priest, if you remember, says that God can do anything. The skeptic picks up a ball and says: 'Could God make it so that this ball wasn't round any more?' and the priest says: 'Yes, of course.' And the skeptic says: 'And could God make it so that the ball had never been round?' And in the anecdote, that argument confounds the priest. Except that it wouldn't, in reality, because the priest could simply say, again: 'Yes, of course.' But my argument goes on to point out that if a hypothetical God were to rearrange the universe so that the ball had never been round, it would involve turning the clock backwards, effectively undoing creation. And my argument was that, even if God could do that, he wouldn't, because undoing creation would undermine the purpose, and the very concept, of creation.

"What I was trying to demonstrate, or at least to illustrate, is that creators—including secondary creators like writers and artists—have to accept the consequences of their creation, including the unintended, unanticipated and unwanted consequences, or they undermine the very idea of creation. Yes, a creator can turn the clock back within a plot, but only by undoing the text, by obliterating the creation. And he shouldn't do that, if he ever hopes to get to the end of the process. At some point, even if he rips up his text and starts again, once, or twice or a thousand times, if creation is actually to be completed, and to mean something, he has to accept the consequences of what he has created, including the unintended ones imposed by logic, and accept the roundness of the ball—or, if you decode the parable in terms of theodicy, the existence of evil in the world."

Marianne sighed, only partly by contrivance. "I think I liked your earlier books better, when they were about stranded spaceship captains being beguiled by the gardens of some alien Armida and didn't need explanations like that. That argument is a little too cerebral for me."

"'When I hear the word theodicy,' as the philosopher said," Simon quipped, with unrestrained esotericism, "'I reach for my gun.' You're far from alone in that sentiment, alas," said Simon, "But what can I do? Once I started thinking, unthinking was out of the question. Maybe I've retreated so far into the circumvolutions of my own twisted mind that I'm out of touch with all my potential readers, but that's just an accurate reflection of where I'm up to in life: almost alone. Aren't we all, eventually?"

"Touché," she said, appreciatively. "Are you sure you wouldn't like me to drive you to Carmarthen—I'd rather like to sit in on your discussion with the heresy-hunting preacher."

"So will Megan, I suspect, but the way I feel at present, I fear that she might be direly disappointed by my performance. I'll give you a blow-by-blow account when we get back, win or lose. I'll still need to take my daily two-mile walk. You could come with me, if you like. Unless you want to spend the whole afternoon with Zoe and Krysten?"

"And ruin their mysterious new-found harmony with my abrasive presence? That would hardly be kind. And I'll forgive you for not having simply invited me to go with you and Megan. Three's a crowd, after all. Or is it because there are secrets you might have to discuss with the Dominican that you don't want to mention in front of me?"

Simon couldn't quite bring himself to issue a flat denial of that, and knew that he wouldn't have been convincing if he had.

"I thought so," his sister said, now surfing the tide of her intuition confidently. "You practically admitted it to Mother in the nursing home, but it wasn't until Zoe contracted her new obsession and started quizzing me about it that the penny dropped."

"Exactly what penny are we talking about?" Simon queried, slightly annoyed at not being able to keep up.

"The family secret. The mystery of the Murdens. Whatever is hidden in Merlin's Cave underneath the Abbey. To be honest, if you gave Zoe the run of the place yesterday, I'm surprised that she and Krysten haven't been down there with their phones to take pictures. Still, it's given Krysten something to write about instead of the agonies of teenage single motherhood—which, believe me, was almost as painful for me as it must have been for Zoe. I suspect, in fact, that the whole basis of their new chumminess is the fact that Krysten is no longer slandering her every day on Facebook."

Simon suddenly felt the blood draining from his face, as he realized the awful margin by which he had not been able to keep up.

"Facebook?" he echoed. "Krysten keeps some kind of diary on Facebook?"

"She's a teenager, of course she does. Didn't you know?"

"No. I'm a technophobe, remember. I'm not on Facebook. I don't even have a mobile phone. And you say that Krysten, who has been telling the world about the agonies of her teenage motherhood, has now switched, with Zoe's aid, to writing about the so-called mystery of the Murdens? That's why she was taking pictures yesterday of the morgen in the chapel?"

"Yes, of course. Why did you think she was doing it?"

The simple answer to that, obviously, was that Simon hadn't thought. "And she's going to post it?" he queried.

"I assume so, although they never tell me anything. My guess is that as soon as she and Zoe have put the story together, as melodramatically as they can, they'll upload it—if that's the right term, I can't keep up any more. The dream of every teenage girl nowadays is to post something online that has enough friend-appeal to go viral. If the prospect scares you, though, you probably have nothing to worry about. She doesn't have very many followers, in spite of all the soul-baring that went with the tragic tale of her teenage baby blues. I suspect that the North Koreans will land a man on the moon before Krysten posts anything that will go viral—and why would you worry even if she did? Unless the family secret involves mass murder or pedophilia. Pacts with the devil and the Holy Grail are small beer nowadays. Does it?"

"Does what?" Simon repeated, mechanically, lost in distraction, contemplating the illusory simplicity of the horizon, beyond the curve of which all kinds of things might be lurking. Almost unconsciously, he had started walking again, veering to follow the southern edge of the tine, heading back toward the mainland. Marianne moved with him, matching stride for stride, seemingly moving quite comfortably, in spite of the unevenness of the turf.

"Involve mass murder or pedophilia?" she elaborated. "The family secret."

"Not recently," was all Simon could say to that. "But that doesn't mean that I want anyone poking around underneath the Abbey, least of all Zoe . . . no, I take that back, least of all Thomas Mallory, O.P., who, if he has been in contact with Alexander Usher, in spite of their doctrinal differences, might want to do exactly that, and might not be as easy to put off as a C-of-E college chaplain. Zoe can't get down there without the keys to both padlocks, mercifully . . . but I'll have a word with her at dinner, and Megan will help. Maybe we can talk them out of posting anything that might cause embarrassment. Can we, do you think?"

"You might be able to; if I tried, I'm sure it would only make her more likely to go ahead. But I can't see how it could cause trouble, even if you really do have the Holy Grail down there . . . you haven't, have you?"

"Of course not," said Simon. "What I mean by embarrassment is the possibility that, even though I haven't, there might be some people crazy enough to believe that I have . . . and if not the grail, the diabolical pact."

"So what if there are? Are you afraid of burglars, or fanatical assassins?" Marianne laughed politely, to make it clear that it was a joke—but even as she laughed, he saw that the certainty that it really was something unthinkable, merely because it was so ludicrous, had begun to ebb away in her mind. She looked out over the calm waves, as if scanning for seals.

"I'll have a word with them," Simon said, decisively. "This afternoon, in fact. I'll explain to them that it might cause some awkward embarrassment, to Felicia, if not to me, and that I really would like to keep the mystery of the Murdens in the family, until I can solve it, if it can be solved. They need to give me some time, until . . ."

"Until what?" Marianne queried.

"Until I know more," Simon parried, weakly, unable to say: *until Melusine comes back*, not merely because that would be letting the cat out of the bag, but because he really didn't have the slightest idea what might happen if or when Melusine did come back. In spite of all his tortuous brain-racking, he had little or no idea of what she might have to say, if she were capable of saying anything at all. In fact, he was beginning to think that it was stupidly over-optimistic to think that the neider would even try to speak to him, to explain itself to him in words, in the substance of his own writerly consciousness, instead of its own consciousness, which, if it resembled anything human was far more like music than speech.

Then he thought back, momentarily, to the flash of dream consciousness that he had had himself while he was making his big speech to Marianne—or, more accurately, to the memory he had tried to form of it immediately afterwards, reflexively, in order to try to capture and preserve something of it, even though he had been in the middle of something else entirely.

"Crwth," he muttered.

"What?" said Marianne.

"Sorry?" said Simon, startled.

"You drifted away for a moment—not the first time you've done it . . . probably lack of sleep. But you said something. *Crude?*"

"Oh," said Simon. "Not crude, *crwth*. It's Welsh. It's a kind of ancient musical instrument, like a lyre or a harp, played with a bow or plucked. The sacred instrument of the bards, of Myrddin Wyllt, Taliesin and their mystic kin. The idea has been preying on my mind a little lately, for some reason. Lack of sleep, as you say. I keep switching off momentarily. It's not deliberate. I'm sorry."

"I do it myself, sometimes," she admitted. "It's the weirdest feeling. I read somewhere, or saw on TV, that dolphins don't sleep all at once, but that they switch one half of their brain into sleep-mode at a time, so that they're dreaming with one hemisphere while the other is still awake and conscious—dolphin-conscious, obviously, not the kind of talky consciousness we have. And I wonder, sometimes, whether the same thing doesn't happen to us occasionally, so that one part of our brain is dreaming while the other is just carrying on with normal business. Does that make any sense?"

"I'm not sure that sense is what it's supposed to make," Simon said, pensively, "or whether it ever can—but I'm sure that it's true. I've never put it to myself in those terms, but what I've felt is surely the same thing."

He met her eyes then—or she met his—and just for a moment, for the first time, he felt a connection, a true relationship.

"It must run in the family," she said, perhaps speaking more accurately than she knew.

III

On the Road

When Simon rang Megan's doorbell, the answer was immediate. He had been tempted to call in at Raven on his way to Sanderling to have a word with Zoe and Krysten about the immense value of discretion, but he didn't have time for a substantial lecture, let alone to answer the inevitable protests and even more inevitable questions. It seemed better to handle his problems one by one, if only they would avoid crowding and form an orderly queue.

"You're not going dressed like that are you?" was the first thing Megan said, as she set her burglar alarm and stepped across the threshold. Although they were only distant cousins, and had only known one another for a matter of weeks, circumstances had thrust them together sufficiently for them to reach the stage in their relationship where casual insults were not merely licensed but had come to form part of its ordinary cement.

"I always dress like this," Simon retorted, "except for funerals."

Megan always dressed elegantly and expensively, but Simon could see that she had made a particular effort for the occasion of meeting a legally qualified priest. Even if he had wanted to do likewise—and he had not—his limited wardrobe would not have facilitated it, given that his one and only suit was a trifle threadbare, and really only fit for funerals because it was black.

"How long have you had that leather jacket?" Megan queried, with a sigh that was only partly contrived, as they moved off along St. Madoc's only street, walking down the middle because of the unusual number of cars parked to either side, several of which were infringing the sidewalk.

"Twenty-nine years," Simon said, thinking that it would be inappropriate to be outmatched in arithmetical accuracy by the Abbey's cook. "It's good quality. It was a fortieth birthday present."

"From your wife?"

"Yes, of course."

"And she let you keep it in the divorce settlement? I suppose it didn't suit her. At least it wasn't a gift from your adoptive mother. It's not exactly the right image to offer to Thomas Mallory O.P., though, is it?"

"Honesty is the second-best policy," Simon said. "I am what I am—no point in trying to conceal it from a man of God."

"Is that your subtle way of telling me that I look like whoremistress mutton dressed like holy lamb?"

"Certainly not," Simon assured her. "In fact, I'm very relieved that one of us is taking the matter of image seriously."

"You don't want me to wait in the car, then, while you and the inquisitor talk man-to-man?"

"Absolutely not. I need the moral support—and no, before you make the joke, I don't mean immoral support. We're in this together now, defenders of the Murden inheritance, in all its aspects."

"Pity you couldn't arrange the meeting for a deserted crossroads at the dead of night. We could have recruited the Black Monk and put on a convincing show of unity." There was a slight edge to Megan's voice, although the humor was entirely in her style: a hint of some underlying anxiety, presumably occasioned by the impending meeting.

"He wouldn't have come," Simon answered, trying to keep the parallel anxiety from subverting his own attempt to maintain a light and breezy tone. "Too much risk of being exorcised, especially as he was never really a monk. I must try to get used to calling him the Black Bard. Where the hell have all these cars come from? I didn't think the holidaymakers were due to flock back to the cottages for another week?"

"They're just day trippers," said Megan. "It's the first really nice day of spring; it always brings people out, after months of being cooped up. It'll be like this all along the coast, from Milford Haven to Aberystwyth, and probably from there to Holyhead. You've been lulled into a false sense of security taking your daily walk along deserted paths at the tail end of winter. From now on you'll have to cope with the hiker brigade in full battle array. Dai will have to suppress his natural parsimony and take on extra bar staff at the Mermaid. You have no idea what a transformation the place will undergo in the course of the next fortnight."

"You mean that St. Madoc's going to be a glorified car park for the next six months?"

"Pretty much. What do you care, snug in the Abbey behind your iron grille?"

Simon knew that there was no point in protesting that he was still resident in Raven Cottage, all the more so as he was in temporary exile from it.

"Have you seen much of Zoe?" he asked, as they climbed into the BMW and Megan started the engine.

"Not much. She was on the tine with her daughter all day yesterday. I saw them briefly in the evening, but they seemed engrossed. They didn't come to the Mermaid, but I suppose they couldn't, with the baby."

"I thought Zoe had been pestering you with questions about family history?" Simon queried.

"Did Marianne tell you that? You know perfectly well that we've had other reasons for communicating—which, by the way, she's attending to very conscientiously thus far, having moved into her grandmother's old flat in order to free up a bigger slice of her income to pay off her debts. It's early days, but, as I told you before, I think she's okay, and that my initial skepticism was mistaken. As to how long she'll stay clean, I wouldn't like to bet, but she does seem to be trying."

"Marianne thinks that she's replaced her old addiction with a new fascination with what she calls the mystery of the Murdens."

"Does she? Well, perhaps she's right—but if you're worried that I've spilled too many beans in her direction, don't. I haven't given her anything that isn't in the public domain. Most of it, in fact, is stuff I got from Alexander Usher, which he'll doubtless be publishing any day now."

"Unless Krysten beats him to it."

"What do you mean?"

"Apparently, she's an addict herself—Facebook, not synthetic cannabinoids. You didn't know?"

"Why would I? So far as the world wide web is concerned, I'm the Black Nun, remember, all my activity under the Google radar, mostly on the dark web. I'm not on Facebook, and I have no more intention of joining it than you do. So what has she been posting?"

"All I know is what Marianne told me, and I don't think she's on it either. But Krysten took a picture of the morgen in the chapel yesterday, and she and Zoe spent the rest of the afternoon on the tine poking around, so she was probably down in Morgan's Cave, and maybe Nyder's Cave too, if Rhodri lent them his ladder. We might need to have a serious word with them at dinner tonight, if not before, about boundaries. Speaking of which, you're expected at the Abbey at seven for seven-thirty, so that Edith can put on a show to prove to us all that she's still up to the job. You don't have other plans, I assume?"

"Do I ever? I thought Felicia was still in bed with geriatric flu."

"She seems to be much better this morning—and it really isn't a joking matter."

"No, I know—sorry. Old reflexes. You were up all night again, I presume? Did I mention that you look terrible? Even worse than the leather jacket."

"No, you didn't. I expect you were being diplomatic. I haven't been quite myself for some time now, as you know, but thanks for the update, and for at least not saying that I look like death warmed up."

"Sorry, again. How's Cerys bearing up under the strain of being an accidental murderess?"

"Fine, given that she probably believes that it was all a bad dream—understandably, given that I'm still walking around, albeit a trifle awkwardly—and she might well have thought that I looked like death warmed up even beforehand. Edith confirmed, though, that she had really had fired the gun, and she must know that."

"So that isn't why she's gone over to the opposition?"

"She hasn't gone over to the opposition. I agreed with her, when she consulted me, that she couldn't possibly turn down Douglas Jefferson's offer once he'd spelled it out in full: a two-year contract as a management trainee in his company with a fat salary, a company car, a flat in Swansea, and funding to do an MBA at Swansea University while she's learning the tricks of his particular trade in-house. It will set her up for life, whether she stays with him, comes back to work for the Estate, or moves elsewhere. Cousin Douglas might think of it as recruiting a spy in our camp, but she definitely thinks of it as our having a spy in his."

"And how do you think of it?"

"I'm trying to think of it as having a potentially valuable liaison between the Estate and Jefferson's organization, which might be all the more valuable if the truce in Jefferson's old feud with Bernard Pallister turns into a genuine pact—which, according to Cerys, Cousin Douglas is trying hard to achieve, in spite of Bernard's instinctive paranoia. I don't see any reason to disbelieve her."

"You wouldn't," Megan said, sourly. Again there was an edge to her voice, but Simon knew that Megan's long-standing dislike of Douglas Jefferson had acquired a savage twist when he had slyly revealed that Megan had once given away a child—a secret that she had never even suspected that he knew. She seemed to be about to say something damning, but changed her mind, and said, quite mildly: "You do realize, don't you, that in his own mind, Dougie has already cast himself in the role of puppet-master, with the rest of us as marionettes who are going to dance to the pull of his strings?"

"I realize that's the way he sees it. It doesn't mean that it's the way it will be. But I am acutely aware that I haven't actually qualified as a puppet yet, let alone a potential puppeteer, so I'm not really in a position to put up much opposition to his maneuvering. He's still on the outside, though—still a distant relative."

"That's what you think," Megan said, the edge in her voice becoming more distinct. She was about to say something else,

. . . the darkness seethed, expanding, and crwth sang red, sang warning, sang the dawn of time, and facelessness of the bard was his own facelessness, because he was the bard, bowed by the crwth and born of the crwth and Melusine was laughing and teasing, and offering a kiss, and he felt, although he had no business feeling, that she had never really gone away, because the song, like everything else, never really died, but only faded into the depths, the velvet depths, the underworld . . .

but Simon thought it politic to interrupt rather than allow Megan to spin out her hymn of hate, and he shook himself in order to pull himself together and focus at least the part of his mind that was taking care of business.

"Jefferson's future relationship with the Estate is a distant problem," he said, glad that she wasn't looking at him, that she hadn't seen him shiver. "I have more urgent ones to think about, to the extent that I can still think at all. Given that I'm still more than half-convinced, in spite of the obvious implausibility, that I'm kin to Lazarus, I might be a candidate for a straitjacket before the will clears probate, and if you think I look terrible on the outside, you should see the horizons of my mental landscape. I can't shake the conviction that my trying to build up a unique rapport with Felicia is actually causing her illness, and that if she's able to get up and come downstairs for Edith's dinner tonight, it will be because I've been out of the Abbey all day. In fact, I suspect my madness is so contagious that it's affecting Marianne, Zoe and even poor Krysten and Monique. I'm not sure you're doing yourself any favors by joining me in a *folie à deux*, although I'm certainly grateful to you."

"Well, you might change your mind about that in a minute," Megan muttered, but raised her voice to say: "I drive this road a lot, but I don't think I've ever seen so many cars heading in the opposite direction. I know the spring sun brings out the coastal path walkers in droves, but this is ridiculous."

It seemed obvious to Simon that the half-hearted attempt to change the subject was papering over a deep crack in what was actually on her mind, and regretted his own attempt to deflect her from it — and regretted, too, having shaken himself up and tried to firm up his grip of the real situation, when he was sure that the momentary dream had somehow been important, that the upsurge from the unconscious was not mere froth, best forgotten and disregarded.

Except, of course, that reality was reality, not merely solid but forceful, a constant, insistent pressure, and he knew that the one thing that he mustn't do was let it slip away. That way madness lay.

"What do you mean, I might change my mind about being glad of your help?" he asked, suddenly concerned. "Has something happened to make you change your mind about declaring an interest of your own in the estate?"

"No," she said, "it's not that. But I've been digging, as you know, ever since that night in Fishguard, for any sort of relevant information recoverable via the web, and I've found a couple of items that gave me . . . well, pause for thought. As you warned me back then, and again just now, the madness really is contagious, and my imagination has been running away with me in some very weird directions. Most of it, to borrow your favorite phrase, was just playing with ideas, but as you've just pointed out, sometimes they stick, and you can't shake them . . . and sometimes, they turn dark."

"What ideas?" Simon asked, warily.

"Well, two in particular. I'll give you the innocuous one first, because it's definite. You were wrong about the impossibility of the second Rhys the Engineer being a clone of the first."

"You're saying that the Murdens discovered some kind of cloning technology in the mid-nineteenth century?"

"No, of course not. I'm saying that it's not impossible for natural births to occur in which the child is a genetic duplicate of the father rather than the mother. It's rare, but it's almost certainly been happening occasionally for thousands of years, without anyone noticing, because they didn't have the conceptual framework to allow it to be noticed and properly evaluated. Now they have, and in the same way that the phenomenon that affected Marianne and Zoe and the various Ceridwens has made it belatedly into the medical textbooks, the other has been spotted, reported, and will be incorporated into a corner of the standard medical literature in due course."

"But I don't see how . . ."

"Then you must be off your game. The Simon Cannick I met on that memorable evening in the Mermaid would have worked it out while I was talking. The birth of identical daughters requires an anomalous diploid ovum, so that when the moment of contact that would usually by the prelude to fertilization occurs, the development of the ovum is triggered, but the sperm's chromosomes, being superfluous, don't integrate with the ovum's; they're atrophied and wither away. But there are also anomalous diploid sperm, which compete in the fertilization race with all their haploid fellows, perhaps on level terms, perhaps at a slight advantage or disadvantage. Presumably, most of the contacts they achieve with ova produce no result, but every now and again—hardly ever, but not never—the sperm's chromosomes are injected into the ovum intact, and it's the ovum's haploid set of chromosomes that wither away. The clone isn't perfect, because the child still gets his mitochondrial DNA from his mother, but that's a very tiny difference by comparison with the difference between a normal father and his son. So, it's theoretically possible that Rhys Two really was a duplicate of Rhys One—a rebirth, in terms of Murden legendry. They wouldn't have understood what had happened, of course, but they, unlike the medical establishment, had a conceptual framework that allowed them to perceive it, and to see more than a simple resemblance between father and son."

"Okay," said Simon, having caught up, and retaining a slight annoyance at not only having been so slow to do so but having had his slowness pointed out to him. "So what?

"So nothing, except that it's one more detail to add to your picture of the history of the weird cult that was centered on the Abbey for hundreds of years and was still exerting an influence over the family while the old lady was ruling the roost there, and which might not be irrelevant to the neider's subtle interference with Murden heredity. Isn't that enough?"

"I guess. So what's the story that isn't innocuous?"

"I need to ask you some questions before I spring that one on you, and there's also another little matter that I'd like to clear up, if I can, while we have the time. You remember what happened when we left the restaurant in Fishguard a few weeks back?"

"How could I forget it?"

"Ditto. It's been preying on my mind, as you can probably imagine, and I've been racking my brains trying to make sense of it, because at first, it didn't seem to make any. I had to take the pieces of the puzzle you'd given me and fit them together in a slightly different way before I began to get a glimpse. According to you, if I understand you correctly, the neider, or at least the part of it composed of ordinary matter and not some bizarre other kind that we can't see and can't grasp, is something like a giant hydra that is rooted way beneath the seabed somewhere between the central and northern tines of Morgan's Fork, right?"

"That seems the likeliest hypothesis."

"You could have just said yes. So, the thing that appeared to us in Fishguard was either a second neider, or a tentacle broken away from the parent to become a kind of sea serpent?"

"Probably. The latter seems far more likely."

"Again, a simple yes would have done. At any rate, it seems so to me too. So what was it doing in Fishguard?"

"I don't know. I've thought about it, obviously, but the best story I can come up with is that it probably followed the boat that brought me down to Fishguard from Morgan's Fork, and might even have hitched a ride on its keel."

"That's what I figured. Why?"

"Again, I don't know, but it has occurred to me that if whatever was interfering with the vitreous cocoons at the time made it difficult or undesirable for the neider to get a message to me while I was in the Abbey, it might have taken the opportunity of my trip to deliver it elsewhere—all the more so as Angela Richardson also claimed to have a message for me."

"We'll get to that in a minute. In the car, though, after the event, you also suggested that what you initially assumed to be a message might not actually have been intended that way: that the reason the tentacle had an eye was simply in order to look at us, seeking information rather than wanting to deliver it. You said that the impressions we got, filtered differently through our unconscious minds, might just have been an unintended consequence of the neider trying to look into us."

"Yes, I did," Simon agreed. "Again, it's occurred to me that most, if not all of the contacts I've had with the neider, even including my first game-changing encounter with Lenore, might not have been attempts to give me information at all, but attempts to obtain information, which simply had the unavoidable consequence of allowing me a counter-perception. That certainly seems to have been the case with the most crucial encounter, when Melusine dragged me down to the seabed and into an exotic space beneath it. I've wondered whether the first, and perhaps the only, deliberate message that the neider has actually tried to transmit to me, thus far, was the one it sent me in duplicate before I went down into the alien darkness: *Don't go*. Perhaps I should have listened to that one, instead of trying to decipher all the others, which might have been more sanely conceived as garbled echoes from my own personal unconscious."

"Good—we're on the same wavelength."

"As I remember it, you hated the suggestion at the time."

"Yes, because I didn't like the idea that the illusory rape was something that I was doing to myself. I still don't—but I can live with it, and even excuse it. It's just a matter of perspective. Now, when you saw your mother in Southmead before the creeping destruction of her nervous system shut her down completely, you talked to her for some time."

"That's right, but I don't see . . ."

"You will. Now, this might be important: did she say anything to you about your father?"

"Not a word."

"Nor when you saw her in the nursing home?"

"No, nothing. The only person who ever told me anything about my father was the Black Monk— I mean the Black Bard—if you can call him a person, and I'm pretty sure that everything he said to me was a by-product of my own hyperstimulated unconscious."

"Probably. But what your mother did say to you in the nursing home was that she had a message from hell: *As above, so below*."

"Yes."

"And you construed Hell as possibly referring to the hot core of the earth, where the dark minds that created the neider live, or the literal and figurative underworld of the portal under the crypt?"

"Yes."

"But what if it wasn't? What if it came from her own personal unconscious, because it was something that, unconsciously, *she* wanted you to know?"

"Okay—but I still don't see . . ."

"That's because you don't know that the Jefferson family branch of the Murdens has a kind of imitation coat of arms, which has a Latin motto in it: *Sicut superius sic inferius . . .*"

"Actually, I did know that," Simon said, interrupting swiftly. "I saw it on the business card that Douglas Jefferson gave me before I rushed off in response to Felicia's urgent phone call. Even though I'm no Latinist, by comparison with James, I noticed that it was a misquotation from the emerald tablet, although it conserves part of the meaning . . ."

Thus far, Megan had kept her eyes religiously in the road ahead, but now she turned her head to give Simon a long stare. Eventually, she looked back at the road again and said: "You're unbelievable. You must surely be the only man in the entire world who would have noticed that motto in order to pick up a stupid, quibbling, pedantic detail instead of making what might be an infinitely more important connection."

"But it's a common cliché," Simon objected. "It's all over the place in the kind of literature I deal with every day. Coming across it twice like that didn't seem in the least surprising to me. It was just . . ." He remembered in time how much sympathy he had with people who believed that there was no such thing as coincidence. "What are you getting at?" he asked, instead, although he had a horrible sinking feeling that the Simon Cannick that Megan Harwyn had met in the Mermaid on that epoch-making night would have pieced it together while she was still talking—unlike the confused, overloaded, oft-interrupted, feverish wreck of a mind he was well on the way to becoming, if he wasn't there already.

"It occurred to me that when Evelyne's mother, Lilith, left the Abbey," Megan said, speaking quietly but firmly, "although she cut off all communication with James's father and the parents of Felicia and Melusine, she probably didn't cut off all communication with the distant relatives. It occurred to me—although it was just playing with ideas at the time—that she probably went to them for help to establish herself elsewhere, and received it. At a price, naturally, given that they were such good businessmen, and there was so much rancor in the air, hung over from the schism. At any rate, it occurred to me that a connection might have been maintained, perhaps reluctantly on Lilith's part, and warily on Evelyne's. And maybe this was just a symptom of your contagious madness, but I began to mull over the possibility that Angela didn't actually know the identity of your father—not by name, anyhow, or not consciously—and didn't know, either, why her mother was so desperate to get rid of the baby to whom she gave birth. And perhaps there was no way on earth that your Eve was ever going to explain that to you, when she worked out who you were . . ."

"Stop!" said Simon, unable to help remembering what Edith—who might very easily have been evacuated to a farm owned by the Jefferson family—had said only a few hours before, that what was nowadays called child abuse had simply been the way things were in those days. "This is all pure conjecture, just a fantasy."

"It was, when it first occurred to me," Megan agreed. "Just playing with ideas, just like you. Contagion, as I say. I would probably have discarded it out of hand—if it hadn't been a testable hypothesis."

Where are flashes of dream-semiconsciousness when you need them? Simon thought, feeling that a break with reality, however transient, might be just what the moment called for. But whether his grip on reality was solid or not, reality's grip on him wasn't letting him go, for the moment. But he tried very hard to think: *So what? Even if it were true, crazy as it is, what difference would it make?*

Carefully, he said: "Are you telling me that you've actually compared my DNA with Dougie's father's DNA, the way you contrived to do with Angela's?"

"Not exactly. I couldn't get a sample of Ranald Jefferson's DNA, obviously—but yours was on file at the lab, and Dougie's was easy enough to get. I got the results back this morning."

Simon felt a strange chill somewhere in his inner being, which he couldn't quite locate in his stomach, his heart or his crwth. "You're telling me that the test confirmed that I'm Douglas Jefferson's illegitimate half-brother?" he queried, even though he knew that he was now only stating the obvious.

"Not exactly, given the measure of uncertainty inevitably in a half-sibling match, but it confirmed that the two gene-maps have a lot more alleles in common than would be expected in cousins as distant as you and Dougie—exactly the number, in fact, that would be expected if . . ."

"But there's a measure of uncertainty?" Simon interjected, as if grasping for a straw.

"Inevitably. But that's not all."

"What more could there possibly be?"

"In terms of the gene-analyses, one of the rare alleles you and Dougie have in common is a peculiar one, because it's on the Y-chromosome, which means that it can only have come from your father. In terms of circumstantial evidence, Dougie has already told you that he gained access to the result of the DNA comparison I made between you and your mother, and had it double-checked. At the time, that just seemed like Dougie being thorough, sly and quick off the mark . . . but it's possible that he didn't need the samples I took, or the analysis I paid for, because he'd already obtained a sample of your DNA, maybe only a couple of weeks before, or maybe years."

Wishing that his mind was not in such turmoil, Simon tried hard to remember his first conversation with Douglas Jefferson, which has taken him so completely by surprise—

not least because Jefferson had seemed so oddly preoccupied with the subsequent inheritance of the Murden estate, given that Simon had no natural heir, whereas he, Dougie, had a son . . .

"How could he possibly have had my DNA years ago?" he said, although even the Simon Cannick he was now had already worked it out.

"Well, this really is playing with ideas, pure speculation . . . but it's addictive, isn't it? Once you start, it's hard to stop. So I asked myself, what if . . . ? What if he knew your Eve, as he might well have done if the Jeffersons helped her when she left the Abbey? What if he knew her quite well . . . and Angela too. Do you think that any attempt to hide the birth and the fate of a child could possibly have defeated the resources of a man like Ranald Jefferson? And if Ranald told his son Dougie that there was a candidate for the Murden inheritance living quietly in Bristol, blissfully ignorant of who and what he was, what plans might Dougie have made, in the light of that knowledge . . . ?"

"This is all fantasy."

"Agreed. But if Dougie did find out, one way or another, that there was a possible Murden heir, even one unrelated to him, we can be sure that he wouldn't even have given a thought to the possibility of letting you in on the secret. You already know about one secret he kept for more than forty years without letting the interested parties know that he knew, and how he produced it with a flourish when he thought that the right moment had come. But he would have made his own inquiries, and maybe that's how and why he obtained your DNA. And when he got your DNA profile back from the lab, with a report comparing it to the control sample of Murden DNA he'd provided—which is to say, his own—well, his analyst would have seen exactly what the analyst who did my test saw: the Y-chromosome anomaly."

So what? Simon tried hard to think. *So what if he did? So what if he jumped to the same crazy conclusion that Megan has? I don't have anything against him. It's Megan who hates him, not me.*

Aloud, he said: "You didn't think to mention this before today?"

"Of course not. While it was just playing with ideas, it would have been tactless in the extreme. But once I got the comparison result, I had to tell you, didn't I? I'm not like Dougie—and nor, thank God, are you, even if you are Abel to his Cain."

"That's a bit strong. I know you don't like him, but do you really think he's the kind of man whose immediate reaction, on discovering that he might have an illegitimate half-brother, would be to hate him?"

"Yes. Your stubborn attempts to love Marianne are another case entirely, not comparable—and you're a saint, which Dougie definitely isn't. But anyway, that took far longer than I hoped, because I found it so difficult to spit it out, heartless bitch though I am. Carmarthen's not far off. How are we going to handle this importunate churchman?"

This time, the attempt to change the subject wasn't in the least half-hearted; in fact, it was crude, brutal almost desperate. Simon thought that it was probably a good idea, though, and he made a stern effort to pull himself together, to put the strange quasi-revelation to one side for future contemplation and concentrate on the imminent problem.

"God only knows," he said, without managing to inject a tokenistic hint of humor into his tone. "We don't even know what he wants yet, unless you definitely haven't hacked his email account the way you definitely didn't hack Alexander Usher's."

"I haven't—really haven't, not euphemistically haven't—but I do know that he hasn't exchanged any emails with Usher. That doesn't necessarily mean, though, that he doesn't know everything that Usher knows, and even what he fantasizes. But there is one thing I noticed while looking at the sparse online data that might conceivably be relevant. Thomas Mallory is interested in palimpsests."

"Palimpsests?" As changes of subjects went, Simon thought, that was certainly quite a leap.

"Yes—they're pieces of parchment which have been re-used and overwritten, but from which the original texts can be recovered by means of various special techniques. It's been going on for centuries, but multispectral imaging has recently made the methods of recovery much more powerful and precise."

"I know what palimpsests are," said Simon, taking slight offense at the implication that he might have needed that enlightenment. "Why on earth would an expert on church law be interested in them?"

"Because he's an expert in church law, of course—in general, but with a particular interest, obviously, in the rules and organization of the Dominican Order. By the time the Order was founded, paper was becoming more common, but official documents were still mostly written on parchment, and sometimes overwritten. What do you think all the texts underneath the overwritten manuscripts in the Dominican archives are?"

"Earlier Dominican documents," Simon guessed, without any exceptional stretch of the imagination. "Especially if the new texts were designed to replace the older ones. So, the old parchments in his Order's archives might be able to do double duty in tracing the legal history of the Order."

"Just as the documents in the Abbey library might, with the aid of sophisticated modern equipment, do double duty in tracing the history of St. Madoc's community . . . and might perhaps be especially revealing with regard to its secret history. And one of the few things we know about Thomas Mallory is that he has ready access to equipment and technical expertise about which Alexander Usher could only dream."

"I see," Simon conceded. "But why would he have an interest in our archives? There's no overlap between the Dominicans and St. Madoc's community, except . . . ah!"

"There's the Simon Cannick I know. *Ah*, indeed."

"The Abbey was under investigation because of denunciations of heresy," Simon thought aloud, "before Henry

VIII's takeover made the results of the investigations redundant. That investigation was presumably carried out by Dominican inquisitors, whose report was presumably sent back to their base in Rome. There, it would have been filed away and forgotten . . . or overwritten. Lost, at any rate . . . but not irrevocably. It's possible, I suppose, that the document in question has been recovered. But it can't possibly have any relevance in the twenty-first century . . . no practical relevance, anyhow."

"Alexander Usher didn't think so, did he? He thought—and he still thinks, as we speak—that whatever was hidden under the Abbey back in St. Madoc's day is still there, and might be something seriously weird. And he's not wrong, is he? I'm sure, just as you are, that he sets rumors of the Holy Grail scrupulously aside as so much legendary fantasy, but he still thinks that there must be something there that helped to give rise to them. His curiosity was piqued, and piqued even more surely by your refusal to let him take a look, when he'd been so sure that you'd play ball. We have to assume don't we, that Thomas Mallory's curiosity has also been piqued, one way or another, and that he too wants to take a look. I'm assuming, of course, that at least some of those old documents in the Abbey library are parchments that have been overwritten."

"Almost certainly," Simon agreed. "And I guess that, although no Welsh court would admit that the Catholic Church has any legally enforceable claim to ownership of the Abbey, the same argument might not apply to the manuscripts. And even if they don't have any legal claim, if the Vatican has a fully operative scanning system and research program in place, they can make out a persuasive case on academic grounds for the Estate to allow them at least temporary custody of the parchments for analysis, especially if they have documentation of their own suggesting that there might be something of interest therein. And just like Usher, Mallory would at least start with the gentle approach, with a friendly meeting in a pub . . . but unlike Usher, he might have further persuasive resources if I simply decided to say no. *Merde.*"

"And that, I fear, might be the best-case scenario. I was up late into the night on this—although you'll note that it didn't stop me putting on my make-up with consummate expertise and power-dressing to kill the morning after—so I can't claim to have finished the job, given the enormous number of loose ends and possibilities there are, but I'm not altogether convinced that you're correct in saying that the Church couldn't mount a claim to ownership of the Abbey that would stand up in a Welsh court, precisely because St. Madoc's Abbey is unique, and any judgment rendered in respect of it wouldn't necessarily create a dangerous precedent. I can't go into it now, because I need to do a lot more work to get my head round it, and we're almost in Carmarthen, but I just wanted to warn you that if the Black Friar mentions Owain Myrddin, it might be a danger signal."

Simon took due note of the fact that Megan, aided by her natural accent, but with extra emphasis, had pronounce the name of the courtier to Henry VIII recorded in English documents as Owen Murden as if the central consonant were a *th*, like the Welsh *dd*, respectful of the fact that the Murdens claimed descent, rather fancifully, from Myrddin Wyllt."

"According to James, there was hardly any recorded information about Owen Murden except for his name," Simon observed.

"Yesterday, that was true," Megan admitted. "But in exactly the same way that medical knowledge is expanding far faster than anyone can keep up with it, with respect to such eccentricities as diploid sperm, all kinds of other ongoing scientific projects, including some scanning projects using multispectral analysis to excavate hidden text from palimpsests, are dumping new data on to the web every day. Ninety-nine per cent of it is ditchwater, of course, and it would take an expert eye and a first-rate Latinist even to perceive a few nuggets of interesting data. So the fact that Owain Myrddin doesn't show up on your search engine today doesn't mean that he won't tomorrow—and it certainly doesn't mean that a man with Thomas Mallory's interests, expertise and connections isn't way ahead of the game. There are, of course, a great many projects that *aren't* publishing on to the web on a daily basis—and you can guess which category the Vatican programs fall into. But we're here now. Let's find out what the fellow wants before making any more stabs in the dark, shall we?"

As she spoke, she pulled the car round into the car park of the Ivy Bush Hotel, and veered smoothly into an empty spot with an elegance almost matching her outfit.

Simon unfastened his seat belt, opened the door and stepped out of the car, having so much on his confused mind that he was paying no heed at all to his surroundings—until a seemingly gigantic shadow

. . . the angry darkness . . .

suddenly loomed over him, and a vituperative voice spat down into his face: "What the *hell* are you doing here?"

IV
In the Hotel Lounge

Simon was so surprised by the virtual assault, and the momentary glitch in his consciousness of it, that he was literally dumbstruck. He shrank back against the BMW, direly intimidated by the fact that a man several inches taller than he was, and a good deal balder and broader, was invading his personal space, already restricted by the exiguity of the gap between the BMW and the Renault parked in the next bay.

It took him a full thirty seconds to realize that the man was not actually going to hit him, and that the tall man had actually stepped back a little, as if anxious for his own personal space, or perhaps frustrated by the unthinkability of actually seizing his victim violently.

By that time, Megan Harwyn had moved around the back of the car in order to confront the tall man and say to him, in a voice dripping with contempt and sarcasm: "We hadn't realized that we needed your permission to be here, Bernard."

Bernard Pallister rounded on Megan. Somehow, although it was surely metrologically impossible, he did not appear to Simon to be nearly as tall by comparison with her as he had appeared by comparison with himself. Indeed, the big man was the one who now seemed intimidated, and he took a further step back. "I'll kill the little rat," he muttered.

Megan raised an eyebrow. "Should I infer from that, Bernard, that you're here to meet Douglas Jefferson?"

"Yes, of course," said Pallister. "Aren't you?"

"No," said Megan, flatly.

Simon was delighted to see that it was now the would-be-aggressor who was defensive and confused. "Oh," he said. "When I saw Cannick, I assumed it was one of Dougie's tricks—that he'd invited him without telling me to what I'd assumed to be a private meeting. What *are* you doing here, then?" His tone was considerably more polite than when he had first posed the question, but it seemed still something of an affront to Simon.

"That's none of your business, Bernard," snapped Megan. "And it seems to me that you now owe Simon two apologies."

"Two?" queried Pallister.

"Have you forgotten that you broke into his house and tried to steal the data from his computer? You'll recall, I think, that I advised him to call the police and charge you with home invasion with intent to commit murder, which he very kindly refrained from doing, because you're his cousin and he's a saint. So that makes a big thank you as well as two apologies that you owe him, don't you agree?"

"I was the one who was nearly murdered!" Pallister protested. "That bitch of a niece of his hit me over the head."

"You're confused Bernard. You fell over your own enormous feet when you saw the Black Monk, while in the process of committing a crime. And by my count, you're still two apologies and a thank you in the red. But if you still want to kill cousin Dougie, we won't stand in your way, given that I assume that it was him who decided the time and place of this meeting."

"We always meet here," said Bernard. "We've been doing it for twenty years. It's convenient."

"Maybe so, but it was Dougie who set the time and date, wasn't it?

Slow on the uptake as he was, Pallister caught the implication. "You mean he set the time because he knew you'd be here. So it *is* one of his tricks?"

"Yes, Bernard, but he's not playing it on you, he's playing it on us. He wants to know what our meeting is about. He might even want to buttonhole the person with whom we're meeting, in order to offer his services—hypocritically, of course—in pursuing whatever quest he has against the Estate."

"And who are you meeting with?" Pallister asked, having failed to learn from experience.

"That really is none of your business, Bernard," Megan repeated. "And Simon is still waiting for his apologies."

It was patently obvious that Pallister wanted to tell his persecutor to go to hell and storm away, but he thought better of it. "I made a mistake, all right?" he said. "Sorry."

"How many mistakes, Bernard?" said Megan, with a smile of which, in Simon's judgment, Mephistopheles would have been proud.

"Two," conceded the big man. "But I'm damned if I'm saying thank you because he didn't call the police after his niece gave me a concussion."

"In view of your obvious confusion," Megan said, "I'm sure that Simon will be gracious enough not to insist. On the other hand, since you're prepared to be more generous in the matter of apologies, perhaps you'll remember that you owe one to me for the ludicrous accusations you made against me while you were bleeding all over Simon's chair and carpet."

Again, it was obvious that Pallister wanted to vomit an obscenity, but again, he controlled himself, and turned to Simon, as the safer option. "Dougie wants us all to be friends," he said, sullenly. "*Catch more flies with honey than vinegar,* he says, in his usual mealy-mouthed fashion. I can't see it working myself—but he says that you really are who you say you are, and that he has the DNA to prove it, so I guess we'll have to live with one another. I was wrong, okay—wrong, wrong and wrong again. Satisfied?"

Megan, evidently, was far from satisfied, but Simon decided that it was time to stop playing dead, all the more so as Pallister was deliberately addressing him in preference to Megan. He stepped forward and offered his hand to the tall man. "Perfectly satisfied," he said. "Can we forget it and start again, given that it probably will be in all our interests to work together, or at least not in opposition, if I do inherit the Murden Estate?"

Pallister looked startled, but he took the hand, and shook it. "Fair enough," he said, apparently ungrudgingly, still refusing to glance at Megan. "Clean slate?"

"Clean slate," Simon confirmed. "Shall we go in, now? Our man will probably be waiting for us, and Douglas will probably be waiting for you."

Megan made no objection, and even looked at Simon with apparent approval of his tactics. Simon led the way, but when he reached the door of the hotel he stepped aside politely to let Megan go in first, followed by Bernard. When he asked at reception for Father Thomas Mallory he was directed to the lounge.

He scanned the room quickly from the threshold. Douglas Jefferson was not there, having apparently decided that it would be diplomatically wise to be fashionably late for his meeting with Bernard Pallister. Thomas Mallory would have been easily identifiable even if the lounge hadn't been almost deserted. He was seated in an armchair in front of a small coffee table, on which a tray was already placed, with a large coffee pot, three cups and saucers, and a milk jug. He was a small man, shorter than Simon or Megan, but he did not give the impression of being weak or meek. He was not wearing a monk's habit or a clerical collar, but he was clad completely in black—with far more austerity, elegance and assurance than Simon—and he had a neat tonsure excavated in his black hair that left no doubt as to his vocation. He stood up as his guests arrived, and bowed politely to both of them before inviting them to take the two armchairs facing his own. He had blue eyes, suggestive in association with the black hair, of Celtic descent—but Simon already knew, thanks to his search engine, that Mallory had been born in Ireland.

Simon remembered that he had not actually said, in the reply to the invitation that the solicitor had passed on to him, that he would not be coming alone, but he was not surprised by the fact that his host had prepared chairs and cups for three.

"I took the liberty of ordering coffee," said the Dominican, blandly, once the formal introductions were complete, "but you're very welcome to have tea, if you prefer, or something stronger."

"Coffee's fine for me," said Simon.

"And me," said Megan, adding, as if her sobriety needed explanation, even at eleven o'clock in the morning: "I'm driving."

The Dominican unscrewed the cap that was sealing the pot to keep the coffee hot, and filled three cups, with a precision of movement that seemed to Simon to be symptomatic of an infinite self-confidence, or perhaps of faith in Providence.

"I'm sorry that you had to come such a long way," said the Dominican, his mild voice exhibiting the same careful precision as his movements, "but the Diocese of Menevia is far from replete with church premises, as you're probably aware. I thought, though, that we ought to meet on secular ground; given the nature of the requests I have to make to you and the subsequent discussion they might necessitate, the Deanery of St. Mary's wouldn't have been ideal."

Before Simon could make any response to that, he was conscious of Megan suddenly looking round, and he turned his own head. Douglas Jefferson had just come into the lounge. He went swiftly to join Bernard Pallister in the far corner of the room, as if he had not noticed Simon and Megan sitting with a man with a clearly visible tonsure, although he could not plausibly have failed to do so.

Thomas Mallory obviously noticed their attention and looked in the same direction, but made no comment. Instead, he continued his own introductory speech. "I realize that you are not yet the legal custodian of St. Madoc's Abbey and its Estate, Mr. Cannick, but the executor referred me to you, not only as the designated heir and *de facto* custodian of the documents, but as the late James Murden's confidant. I ought to make it clear right away that I am not here in my capacity as a lawyer, but as a historian, and I hope that we can talk frankly as one scholar to another. I have only read a little of your work, the abundance of which would defeat braver men than me, but what I have read leads me to think that we ought to be able to achieve a sympathetic understanding."

"Really?" said Simon, very warily.

Mallory smiled. "I can understand your skepticism. In fact, I'd like to think that I understand your skepticism better than you do, but that would be hazardous vanity. At any rate, what I have read of your work suggests to me that you are conscientious in trying to see both sides of an argument and that you do not rush to judgment—that you are capable of setting your prejudices aside temporarily, while not letting go of your convictions. You will understand, therefore, that as a lawyer, I routinely have to do exactly the same. While I hold certain unshakably firm beliefs, I have to be able to set them temporarily aside in order to look at all the arguments surrounding a case, and to measure their strength as seen from other viewpoints. Long ago, in the seminary, I was inevitably nicknamed 'Doubting Thomas' and sometimes 'the Devil's Advocate,' merely in the routinely banal spirit of such establishments, but I took the designations as compliments anyway. So, while not necessarily agreeing with some of your conclusions, I am not unappreciative of their occasional elegance and the frequent enterprise of your arguments. I am entering into this conversation with an open mind, and I hope that I can assume the same of you. I honestly do not think that we need to be adversaries or competitors, and I believe that our communication might be mutually profitable."

"I hope you're right," said Simon. "What is it, exactly, that you want from me?"

"Well, since you ask so directly, I'll answer directly, although I do want to give you a more elaborate explanation of the reasons for my requests. First of all, and most importantly, as you might well have guessed, I would like to make some arrangement with the Estate for the parchments in the Abbey library to be subjected to scrupulous examination, including examination by means of X-ray imaging, in order to determine what there is within them of interest to the history of the Church, including any overwritten texts that do not meet the naked eye. I would, of course, make all my findings available to you, on the assumption that there might be material there, both overt and covert, of interest to you and other members of the Murden family.

"Secondly, I would like a copy of any summary notes that James Murden might have made regarding his own investigations of the Abbey archives, in order to aid that research.

"Thirdly, I would like you and Miss Felicia Murden, and also the other residents of the Abbey, if possible, to provide a full and accurate account of any unusual events that have occurred in and around the Abbey while they have been resident there, and what they have observed in the cave beneath the crypt, as a possible result of visual or physical contact with the entity contained there."

The third request was the only one that surprised Simon, after having been primed by Megan in the car regarding Mallory's interest in palimpsests, but the surprise of the third was considerable, and he hesitated for some time before saying: "You just want statements? You're not asking to see the Abbey's subterrains for yourself?"

Mallory's smile was a trifle wary. "No," he said, "I'm not asking for that at present. I realize, however, that you might consider that I'm asking too much. I have never met Alexander Usher, but I do know that you have already refused him access to James Murden's documents, as well as to the cave. I'm hoping that you might find my request more acceptable."

"Why?" countered Simon, uncomfortably aware of the fact that the bluntness might seem rude, while the Churchman was being so carefully long-winded and pedantic. He added: "Why are you hopeful, I mean?" although he was well aware that it did not lessen the effect.

"Because I believe that you and I have exactly the same interests," said the Dominican, "even though we are approaching the problem from different directions. I believe that our best hope of success in our quest for understanding is to pool our resources. You seem to have custody of a good deal of information that I do not, and I certainly have custody of a good deal that you do not. I hope that by fitting all the various pieces together we might both get a much clearer idea of the whole picture."

"With all due respect," said Simon, "I'm not at all sure that we have the same interests, and I suspect strongly that the different directions from which we're bound to approach the problem will prevent our ever fitting any of the pieces together."

The little man took a very deliberate sip from his coffee cup and laid it down again in what seemed to Simon to be a remarkably elegant and expressive fashion that he could never hope to match. He was already feeling outclassed even in the competition of mannerisms, let alone the philosophical discussion that was about to ensue.

"You know that I am a member of the Order of Preachers," said Thomas Mallory, "and that has doubtless led you to make various assumptions, and invoke various prejudices, which I cannot simply deny. I do not want to debate dogma with you, Mr. Cannick. I know that you believe, mistakenly in my opinion, that you are an atheist, and that you have no sympathy with the institution of the Church, but I would like to suggest to you, on the basis of what I have read of your writings—just as hypotheses for consideration, if you wish— firstly, that you are not an atheist in any meaningful sense of the word, but that you merely employ a different vocabulary of terms in your account of metaphysical reality, and secondly, that whatever you think of the Church's methods, you are completely in sympathy with the fundamental message that it attempts to promote—I'm referring to the Sermon on the Mount, of course, not the Old Testament."

"I have no quarrel at all with Jesus's moral philosophy," Simon acquiesced, "but that's partly because Jesus loathed churchmen, and would have been utterly horrified by the very ideas of a Roman Church and an Order of Preachers, let alone an Inquisition."

Mallory did not even attempt a wry smile, but nor did he shake his head in false pity. "Well, doubtless you know your own ideas and opinions better than I do," he said. "Perhaps I should approach the matter from the other direction, by giving you a little more insight into my own ideas and opinions. I am, as you know, a man of law, specifically, of church law, and I'm sure you understand how enormously complicated the accumulated body of church law must be. You understand the reasons why English law is so complicated, as new laws have been overlaid on old ones, often without ever clearing away the lumber of obsolete statutes, and by the ever-increasing welter of precedents, of which no one can keep track efficiently. You will understand, therefore, that those problems are multiplied a hundredfold in the context of internal church law, even without taking into account the additional order of magnitude introduced by the intersections and confrontations of church law and secular law in different countries. Any competent lawyer has to be, to some extent, an active student of history, forever delving into the past in search of relevant precedents and forgotten statutes, but within the Roman Church that excavation necessarily goes far deeper and sometimes leads into stranger places.

"The Roman Church is sometimes seen as a monolithic and autocratic institution, but it is anything but that. It is a highly complex agglomeration of distinct institutions, many of which have their own rules and regulations, possessed of an enormously complicated bureaucracy and an intricately fragmented authority. It also provides an environment highly conducive to secrecy at every level. At the most fundamental level, the secrecy of the confessional is compulsory and sacrosanct, and forbids communication in any fashion of all kinds of discoveries. On a larger scale, there is not, and never has been, any institution more conducive to the formation of secret sects and secret societies, splinter groups and dissident parties. Precisely because of its determination to maintain its fundamental dogma, the church has always been a prolific generator of heresies, the organization of which has always been covert and conspiratorial.

"That is the intellectual environment in which I work, Mr. Cannick. That is the kind of world in which my personal endeavors move. And I love it. It fascinates me. It is an endless source of wonder to me. In practical terms, the expertise that I have cultivated allows me, very often, to settle cases, to deliver opinions, and to determine outcomes—but unlike many secular lawyers, if one can believe what one sees on TV, I have never been obsessed with winning, even in disputes which actually have some importance, rather than the petty squabbles that clutter all existing courts. What has always interested me is the process of exploration itself, the mechanisms of discovery, and the gradual attainment of revelation.

"Because of that, and although I am only speaking for myself and not as an official representative of the Church, it does not matter to me in the least whether you or someone else inherits St. Madoc's Abbey and the money associated with that inheritance. But what does matter to me, personally, is the mystery of the particular heresy of the monks of St. Madoc, and the implications of the investigation carried out by my forebears into the beliefs and conduct of Owain Myrddin,

. . . red darkness and discord, but not warning, not alien, a link in the chain, the unsolid chain, the bow drawn across the gut of the crwth, the bowels of the music of time, the soul of souls and the harmony, not of spheres but of chimeras and metamorphosites, of chrysalides and far, far travelers, of the great, great darkness beneath the sea and beneath the void, and the sheer aggression, the awful usurpation of the WORD . . .

the renegade prior who persuaded Henry VIII to allow him to keep his Abbey and its Estate, seemingly in recompense for promises that might or might not have been kept, and then to hold on to it even during the reign of Queen Mary. Were I a saint, especially one akin to the founder of my order, I suppose that I might only be interested in the entity beneath the Abbey as something in need of exorcism or destruction, but the world has changed since the thirteenth century, and so has the Order."

Simon was certain that the Dominican had seen him shiver, but it didn't interrupt the flow of his speech at all. He just continued his train of thought, with his own agenda, with perfect, almost unctuous smoothness: business as usual.

"Even if I had lived in the remote past, I believe," Mallory continued, "I would have been a scholar, perhaps what is nowadays called a mystic, far more interested in understanding than reaction. If I had ever been confronted by the Devil, as Martin Luther and many others claimed to have been, I hope that I would not have assaulted him with a deluge of holy water or told him sententiously to get behind me. I hope that I would have had the courage to look him in the face, not hatefully, or aggressively, but sympathetically, and that I would have asked him calmly whether we could discuss our differences as two sane and civilized intellects, with a view to improving our understanding of one another, even if, in the end, we had to agree to disagree about our fundamental beliefs and objectives. And I would have done that, if I could, because I would have known that there were many interesting things that the Devil could tell me, and might be willing to do so, even though my soul was not for sale, and I could not make any pact with him that would imperil my salvation."

Simon glanced at Megan, who seemed amused—which did not surprise him in the least. He couldn't help envying her, wishing that he too could find amusement in what was happening. "You're likening this meeting to an encounter with the Devil?" he said to the Dominican.

"No," said Mallory, "I'm explaining that even if it were, I would not refuse it. I'm almost convinced that you're not an agent of the Devil, Mr. Cannick, not even the pettiest of Antichrists, even though your pride might lead you to assert otherwise . . ."

Almost convinced? Simon thought. *But not entirely . . .*

"I truly believe you to be on the side of the angels, as I am," the Dominican went on, "but even if you were not, I would still hope and believe that communication between us might be mutually beneficial. There is one analogy, however, that I am tempted to draw that you and Miss Harwyn might find amusing, and perhaps informative. May I put it to you?"

"Of course," said Simon.

"Thank you. The Church is often likened, metaphorically, to a giant hydra with many tentacles. It is not an inapt analogy, except that many of those tentacles are detachable, producing fragments capable not only of independent life but of metamorphosis, the relationship of which to the parent hydra can easily become problematic, even frankly opposed. But while imagining the church in that way, as if it were a simple living organism, one ought not to forget that it also has a mind, and a will, and that the mind in question is enthusiastic to interact with other minds,

. . . like minds, minds of music, morgen minds, divided between morgen dreams and morgen consciousness, which never speak and can never be fully human, no matter how hard they strive, but in the dark, in the deep, beyond the void, are capable of hearing other instruments, other songs, other aspirations . . .

and thus to spread the fruits of its own mentality. It is, essentially, an organism dedicated to the ideal of conversion, ideally by persuasion, but sometimes more insistently, being convinced of the necessity of its task. Do you understand what I mean, Mr. Cannick?"

Simon, having not even shuddered this time, understood only too well, not only what the Dominican meant to imply, but also what his implication might actually mean, unknown even to him. But the enlightenment was not a flash, not even a disturbance, because it was something he had known for a very long time, far longer than a human lifetime, and which, as soon as he remembered it, not only became obvious but *had always been obvious*. So, he had no difficulty at all in focusing on the reality of the situation.

What Thomas Mallory was telling him, with admirable indirection, was that he not only knew about the existence of the neider, but that he had his own view of the neider's purpose in its interaction with human beings.

"I hate to sound like a bargain-hunting Faust," said Simon, deciding that he had little alternative but to try and fight Jesuitical fire with fire, "but in order for me to decide to give you the documents you want, I'd like a little more clarification of what I might get in exchange—and you've also whetted my appetite considerably merely to know where you obtained the information you have about St. Madoc and its surroundings."

"But you already know where I obtain my information," said the Dominican, mildly. "I have access to all kinds of archives that you do not, many of them compiled in secret and maintained in secrecy for hundreds of years, by numerous organizations, large and small. We live in a glorious age of investigation, Mr. Cannick, where enormous amounts of information once held secretly, and much that was thought utterly lost, is now being revealed or recovered, on an enormous scale. I am a very small fish in that enormous pond, but I do have privileged access to all kinds of data, including data which is being revealed as we speak, by the cunning gaze of X-rays and other instruments of darkness."

"Like the instruments of darkness cited by Banquo in Macbeth?" Simon queried, promptly. "The ones that tell us little truths, only to deceive us with regard to the big picture?"

"That's a little too subtle for me," said Mallory, in what seemed to Simon to be an obvious untruth. "I was merely referring to the invisibility of X-rays, perhaps with an excessively poetic turn of phrase. As you clearly do not hate sounding like a bargain-hunting Faust, in spite of what you say, I suppose that I ought to be miserly in giving away too much of the information that I have in stock, but I would certainly hate you to think that I have any intention of playing Mephistopheles, and I don't want to indulge in pretty haggling, so I will tell you that I can shed light not only the history of the entity buried beneath St. Madoc's Abbey and the other terrestrial intelligence interested in its nature and function, but on the history of several other entities of similar kinds, especially the ones that were once buried near the cities of Toulouse and Jerusalem. My investigations of the one that apparently once existed at Delphi in Greece are still entirely at the speculative stage, and I cannot, as yet, even be certain of the past or present existence of others in Asia and the Americas, but if it is possible for us to collaborate in this endeavor, as I hope that it might be, I will certainly keep you abreast of my continuing research."

There were too many revelations in that brief speech even for an experienced idea-juggler like Simon to keep in the air simultaneously, and it was by no means obvious which one he ought to tackle first. He grabbed the one that seemed most significant.

"*Once* existed?" he echoed. "You mean that the entities at Toulouse and Jerusalem no longer exist?"

"Without splitting hairs regarding the definition of existence, they certainly do not seem to be accessible any longer. You'll understand, of course, that St. Madoc's successors might have been exceptional, once having discovered the entity and having eventually accumulated an understanding of its dangers, in trying with all their might to preserve it, not least by preserving its secrecy. The eventual, if not the initial, response of almost all other discoverers, in all times and places, seems to have been to try to destroy the entities, or, at the very least, to make it impossible for anyone to approach them. I presume, although I might be wrong, that the fact that all those whose historical existence I have been able to ascertain were located in deep caves, already carefully secreted, before human beings were able to stumble over them, was a conscious protective measure on the part of whatever placed them—but I might be wrong about that."

"And the Church has known about this for hundreds of years?"

"In a manner of speaking. Various individuals and collectives under the umbrella of the Church have certainly known something about the entities, just as various individuals and organizations did before the advent of Christ, but they have used various vocabularies of representation, and have filtered their publicity in different ways. It is only very recently, in fact, that the intellectual and technological means for the collation of the relevant information and the commencement of a coherent analysis has become available. There is a long way to go, as you know. We are still at an early stage, only just emerging from what your writings tend to call 'scholarly fantasy.'"

"Forgive me for interrupting," said Megan, "but might I pick up on a different observation that you made in your sales pitch: the assertion that the entities are so dangerous that the eventual reaction of their discoverers has always been to try to destroy them, or at least to bury them. *How* dangerous, exactly?"

"Very dangerous, I fear," said Thomas Mallory, flatly.

"And is that why you wanted to meet in Carmarthen rather than actually coming to St. Madoc?" she followed up, brutally. "And why you aren't asking to see the entity in question?"

"I can't deny a certain apprehension," the Dominican conceded. "As I said, if I were a saint, I might feel obliged to that confrontation, but I'm a man of law, and no hero—but as I also said, I'd like to think that I would have the courage to confront the Devil, if I thought useful communication were possible. The Dominican archives suggest otherwise, but they might be a trifle naïve."

Megan had more urgent concerns than subtleties of suggestion in ancient archives. "But we're living on top of the thing," she said, "and the *various individuals* within the Church who know about these entities never thought to warn us?"

"On the contrary," said Mallory, smoothly. "The Church has always, throughout its history, issued continual and urgent warnings about the dangers of temptation and trafficking with the Devil. The warnings have generally been crude and vague, because the vocabularies of understanding employed have been crude and vague, but the one thing of which you cannot possibly accuse the Church is not having issued sufficient warnings against the dangers of insidious evil. With specific reference to the community of St. Madoc, you must know that my Order was instructed to mount an investigation of the Abbey community in the early sixteenth century, in order to ascertain the extent and nature of its diabolism, which might well have resulted in its excommunication.

"At the risk of seeming impolite, Miss Harwyn, if you have been unaware of the nature and extent of the threat you face in living in St. Madoc, the fault lies not with the Church but with your ancestors, and, more specifically, with your father. And although I can give the two of you much fuller information, I suspect that what Mr. Cannick has recently been able to learn, and communicate to you, has made you both fully aware of both the nature and the extent of the danger you are in. Before criticizing the publicity of the Church, and my own, you might care to examine your own a little more conscientiously. The most recent examples of it, I must admit, seem to me to be rather peculiar, and distinctly unwise."

Simon had almost been bursting to react to the accusations of diabolism leveled at the vitreous cocoons and his own dealings with them, but the Dominican's last remark threw him completely off his intellectual stride. "What recent examples?" he said, utterly confused.

For the first time, the priest seemed surprised, as if he were astonished by Simon's failure to take his meaning. His gaze immediately switched to Megan Harwyn, as if inviting her to explain.

"Don't look at me," she said. "I haven't done any publicity at all."

Without a word, the Churchman took a smartphone out of his jacket pocket, and started tapping away at the screen. Simon, never having owned such a device, had no idea what the dance of the fingertips might signify, or might be trying to achieve, but after a matter of seconds, Mallory turned the device around and offered the screen for their simultaneous contemplation.

Immediately, a brief video clip began to play, obviously recorded on a mobile phone. There was no soundtrack, and the quality was poor. The fakery was blatantly obvious, especially to Simon, who not only recognized the background of the southern tine of Morgan's Fork, as seen from Morgan's Cave, but also the supposed mermaid, the upper part of whose body, including her naked breasts, was above the intervening water, while the lower part, enclosed in some kind of gray sheath crudely modeled on the sign outside the Mermaid, was below it.

Once again, Simon was literally dumbstruck, while all Megan Harwyn could say, very inappropriately, in the presence of a man of God, was: "Oh, hell!"

The fake mermaid was Krysten. Presumably, the person shooting the scene was Zoe. And evidently, Simon had failed dismally to appreciate the speed at which things moved in the world of the internet. While he had been imagining his niece and grandniece sitting down patiently together to draft a mini-essay about the "mystery of the Murdens" with a view to posting it on Facebook, which would have produced no substantial result until tomorrow, at the earliest, they had shot a micro-movie yesterday afternoon on a vulgar mobile phone and had already posted it on YouTube in the evening. And even if it had not "gone viral," it had already attracted enough attention to help turn the central street of St. Madoc into an improvised car park and boost the traffic heading for the village to levels that longtime resident Megan Harwyn had never seen before.

IV
In Mental Limbo

"It's titled *The Mermaid of Morgan's Fork*," said Thomas Mallory O.P. "That's why my search engine picked it up last night while I was preparing for this meeting. You didn't know?" His voice had a hint of what seemed like genuine sympathy.

"No," said Simon, hoarsely. "I didn't."

The Dominican turned the phone round again and looked briefly at the fake mermaid before shutting off the image, presumably not wanting to be thought to be savoring pornography. "You know her?" he queried.

"She's my great-niece," Simon admitted. "This is my fault. When I first invited Zoe to come and visit, I told her about the local legends as a kind of teaser. I had no idea that she'd even take an interest in it, let alone that she'd ever dream of taking her interest this far. She probably thinks that she's doing me and St. Madoc a favor. You're right, Father Mallory; I have no moral high ground whatsoever to criticize anybody's publicity, when I represented it to Zoe as harmless fun, knowing full well, as I already did, that there was some danger. I didn't know how much danger then, but I certainly can't claim ignorance any longer."

"Something has happened since then?" Thomas Mallory was quick to interject. "The entity is active?"

"It's *not* the Devil," Simon was equally quick to retort. "I don't know exactly what it is but it's not the Devil."

"A matter of vocabulary," Mallory said dismissively.

"*No it's not*," snapped Simon. "I don't believe that it's evil. It doesn't seem to me to have intention of harming anyone."

"That," suggested Thomas Mallory, "might depend on your definition of harm. But let's not get bogged down in quibbling. The girl, I assume, certainly didn't mean any harm—to her, it's just play. But even so, harm might come of it."

"How could her mother let her *do* that," murmured Megan, who seemed genuinely shocked. "She's got a baby, for Heaven's sake—you can even tell that by looking at her breasts. How could Zoe do that, actually holding the phone to take the picture?"

"Standards of decency have changed since our day," said Simon, weakly. "Teenagers are always swapping saucy pictures of themselves on the net."

"That's not the point!" Megan snapped. "You probably think that I'm the last person in the world to have any moral high ground from which to criticize a mother's handling of her child, but I would never have done *that*."

"I'm bound to agree with you, Miss Harwyn," said Mallory, presumably not realizing that he was siding with the ex-Whore of Babylon, "but in fairness to the other side of the argument, Mr. Cannick and I are right too. Her intentions are probably good, and they aren't so serious as to pave a road to Hell. It's nothing that can't be absolved with a little penitence, and I'm sure that Mr. Cannick will handle the matter with due kindness. But if I might make a recommendation, Mr. Cannick, it would probably be advisable not to stoke up the flames of that particular fire. If the entity is active, drawing crowds to St. Madoc might be a bad idea. If the archives can be trusted, the kind of madness that the blue honeycombs are able to distribute is contagious, and the contagion is all the more dangerous because it works below the level of rational consciousness."

Megan, meanwhile, had taken out her own mobile phone, but instead of making a connection to the internet, she tapped out a phone number. When the answer came she simply said: "Zoe? Hold on," and passed the phone to Simon, who looked at it as if it were a poisonous snake, and then looked at Thomas Mallory.

"It's perfectly all right," the Dominican assured him. "You might want to take it outside, though."

Simon took that advice, and hurried out into the car park, ashamed of himself for feeling slightly glad to take a few minutes' rest from a confrontation that was proving rather stressful, in more ways than one.

"Zoe?" he said. "Are you still there?"

"Oh, God, Simon," she said. "Mum phoned you, didn't she? I knew she'd go off the deep end, but I didn't realize how far. Look, it's no big deal, okay? It's not as if Krysten's Facebook friends haven't seen her tits before—she's been posting pictures of herself breast-feeding the brat ever since she was born. When she put the flag on her Facebook page she didn't know that anybody else was going to bother to look at the clip, and she knew they'd all recognize her and know it was a joke. We didn't think anybody would actually think it was *real*. How could they? And even if we had realized, we wouldn't have expected anyone to come all the way out here looking for mermaids. There must be nearly fifty cars clogging up the street and all the alleys—it's crazy! It was just a joke. You do understand, don't you? Mum doesn't, but you're cool." The last remark sounded more hopeful than convinced.

"It's okay, Zoe," Simon felt obliged to reassure her. "I'm not going off the deep end. And it wasn't your mother who brought it to my attention, but as things have worked out, it's been a little embarrassing. And it shocked Megan—which surprised me a little, but it evidently hit a sensitive spot. She was the one who dialed your number, and then handed the phone to me, but I really don't want to have a go at you. We will need to talk about it, though, later this afternoon, or this evening. I'll have a word with your mother beforehand, to see if I can smooth things over. But please will you do me a favor and not post anything more, until we've talked. I know you and Krysten didn't mean any harm, but it's turning out to be a bit of a disaster, for reasons beyond your control."

"I'm sorry," she said. "It was only supposed to be a bit of fun."

"I'll be back early this afternoon, and I've already suggested that your mother go for a walk with me. I'll try to calm her down. I have to go now, though. I know it sounds corny, but I really am in a meeting. I'll see you later, okay?"

"Okay," she said, sounding more than a little relieved. "Thanks."

Simon turned round in order to go back into the hotel, but nearly jumped out of his skin when he found Douglas Jefferson standing behind him, waiting patiently for him to finish the phone call, and by no means far enough away not to have heard every word that Simon had said. Simon frowned, but Jefferson, with the practiced ease of a doorstep salesman, seized the initiative with lightning rapidity.

"Bernard told me about the scene in the car park earlier," he said. "Entirely my fault, and I wanted to apologize. I should have told him why I'd chosen the time I did, but we were just exchanging texts, and you know what it's like—you have to be as economical as possible, and I don't have twenty-year-old thumbs any more. I know I shouldn't have seen the letter requesting the meeting, but I was in the solicitor's office for quite a while the evening before last, sorting out all the paperwork for Cerys's contract, and the letter was on a side-table in plain view. As I had a meeting with Bernard next on my to-do list after showing Cerys round the Swansea office yesterday and handing her over to my second-in-command to arrange today's site tour, I just texted him asking whether the time was okay, and when he texted back yes, I just left it at that. I knew you don't have a mobile, so I phoned Raven to ask if perhaps you'd like

. . . the truths of darkness telling lies, to win the bards to harm, and hypocritical trifles, the cold night that turns us all to darkness, cataracts and hurricanes and knaves and rascals, and evil instinctive evil of bastardy . . .

to have lunch with Bernard and myself once your meeting was over, but I got Zoe, who said you'd be at the Abbey until further notice, so I phoned the Abbey and got Margaret, who said that Felicia was ill and that you were looking after her and couldn't be disturbed, so I asked her to ask you to ring me back, and she said she would, but presumably she didn't, and I didn't follow up to check. As I said, entirely my fault— very busy, obviously, but no excuse, etc. Would you?"

"Would I what?" said Simon, having lost the thread yet again, just as he had momentarily lost *Macbeth* in fragments of *King Lear*, without even having to recall the quote about flies to wanton boys, although his dream-consciousness clearly knew it. He was convinced, however, this time, that it really wasn't his fault that he had lost the thread of what was being said, and that Douglas Jefferson had deliberately wrong-footed him.

"Like to have lunch with Bernard and me when your meeting with the inquisitor is over." Jefferson's voice was mild and warm, and friendly . . . and, Simon was now convinced, utterly false. But *so what?* he tried to say to himself. *I don't hate him. Why should I?*

"I can't," Simon said, gruffly, remembering all too painfully what Megan had said about Jefferson casting himself as a puppet-master and deeming him just one more marionette. "I have to get back to St. Madoc, Felicia's not well."

"Of course," said Jefferson, smoothly. "Rather inconsiderate of the Papist to drag you all the way out here. At least Alex had the grace to come to the Mermaid."

Simon made no comment on the fact that Jefferson had referred to the Reverend Usher as "Alex," although he was sure that it had been a subtle provocation.

"I have to get back," he said, and would have steered toward the door if Jefferson had not been in the way, showing no sign of stepping aside.

"There's no trouble, I hope?" Jefferson said, insincerely. "With the probate process, that is?"

"No," said Simon, shortly, seeing no reason to add anything further—but Jefferson was not to be put off so easily.

"Except that, while I was doing my research into the family history, it did occur to me that there was something distinctly dodgy about the way Owen Murden was given the Abbey by Henry VIII, and that it might conceivably give the Church grounds for some kind of objection to the Murdens' right of ownership."

Simon gritted his teeth, and lost his temper, but he stopped short of grabbing Jefferson by the shoulders and moving him out of the way bodily. He did, however, pick up the little man's right hand, the middle finger of which had a ring displaying an enamel shield with a tiny motto. The motto was unreadable, but Simon already knew what it said.

"Was that your father's ring?" he asked, bluntly.

For the first time in their admittedly brief relationship, Simon had the dubious pleasure of seeing shock and alarm painted all over the little man's face, and he saw—not guessed, but saw, quite plainly—that whether or not he had any reason to dislike Douglas Jefferson, simply because he had found out by strange means that there was a possibility that they had the same father, Douglas Jefferson thought differently. The other believed that the revelation in question—which his investigation of Simon's DNA had already suggested to him, just as it had been suggested to Megan—would be reason enough for a sort of hatred.

"As a matter of fact," the little man said, rallying. "It was. Why?"

"Antique, isn't it?" Simon said. "Eighty years old if it's a day."

"I believe so," Jefferson replied, but strangled the repetition of "Why?"

"The quotation is incorrect," Simon told him. "I suppose you could regard it as an abbreviation, but it's an offence even to the eye of a lousy Latinist who happens to be familiar with the original text. But as it's only a mock-escutcheon anyway, I don't suppose it really matters."

"I'm sorry it offends you," said the other, having recovered his unctuous veneer. "I hope you'll forgive me for not discarding it, but it is a family heirloom of sorts, and I really was very fond of my father, for all the old sinner's faults and their occasional unfortunate consequences. Don't let me keep you." As he pronounced the final phrase, he stepped aside. But as Simon reached the door of the hotel, the little man added, with false jocularity: "Better not leave the priest alone for too long with Megan in all her finery—it might put a strain on his vow of celibacy, even at her age."

Simon didn't even look back, but walked straight back into the lounge. He didn't deign to glance at Bernard Pallister.

"I'm sorry about that," he said to Thomas Mallory, as he handed the phone back to Megan. "I was delayed."

"It's all right," said Megan. "I've explained to Father Mallory who Dougie and Bernard are, and why they're spying on us."

"I'm the one who should apologize," said the Dominican. "Miss Harwyn has also explained that Felicia Murden is ill, that you've been under an unusual amount of stress lately, and that you haven't been able to sleep. I'm sorry that I've clearly inconvenienced you by dragging you all the way out here, but I think I've made the essential points of my position clear, and I realize that you'll need time to think about what I've said, and to discuss it with Miss Murden. I really would like to continue this discussion, though, when it's more convenient for you, at least to obtain answers to the requests I've made."

"I do feel that I need a little time to think over what you've told me," Simon agreed, after taking a swig of lukewarm coffee. "And I can't agree to anything without Felicia's consent. But for what it may be worth, I can see no objection to providing you with a copy of James's notes, although they're still somewhat disorganized, and the scans he's made of the documents in the library. Arranging for the examination of the parchments would be a lot trickier, though. Obviously, I'm as curious as you are to know whether there might be any recoverable text that was invisible to James's desktop scanner and the naked eye, but you'll have to explain to me exactly what's involved in *multispectral imagining*, and where you'd propose to carry out any such analysis. As for your third request, I'll put it to Felicia, but I'm not at all sure that she'll be able or willing to accede to it. As I've only been resident in Raven Cottage for a few weeks, and have only spent a very limited time at the Abbey, I'm sure that my own testimony wouldn't be of any value or interest."

"You'll forgive me, Mr. Cannick, if I suspect you of being slightly disingenuous," said the Dominican. "You might only have been in close proximity to the entity two or three times, but precisely because you must have been able to examine it with an educated, inquisitive and clinical eye, your impressions of it might be especially valuable. And I'm certain that you're capable of measuring any psychological effects the proximity might have had as accurately as any man—employing your own vocabulary, of course."

"I don't think it would be productive, or wise, to share any such measurements with you, if you're going to insist on interpreting them as intercourse with the Devil," Simon said, bluntly.

"Perhaps that's something else that you need to think about carefully," Thomas Mallory suggested. "If you can put your prejudices aside momentarily, in order to look at the matter with a genuinely open mind, I suspect that you might find it harder than you think to convince yourself that it isn't intercourse with the Devil. I'm perfectly capable of doing the same, however, and exploring very carefully the possibility that it's a purely natural phenomenon. You might appreciate the opportunity to convert me."

"I suppose I might," Simon agreed. "I'll be happy to continue this conversation tomorrow, if you wish, when I've had a chance to speak to Felicia, but I don't want to come all the way back here, as I don't drive, and have other pressures on my time. Would you be willing, in spite of your anxieties, at least to come as far as Morpen? There are cottages there that we could use for as long as necessary, and as often as necessary, in the next few days."

Mallory smiled. "In view of the progress that we've made and the bait you're laying down," he said, "I can't possibly refuse, can I? Very well; I don't drive myself, but I'm sure the Dean of St. Mary's will lend me a car and a driver. Let me know the exact address by text or phone—my mobile number is on this card—and whatever time suits you. I'll bring a memory stick with some documents that will certainly interest you; perhaps we can operate an exchange."

Simon accepted the card that Mallory handed to him, which contained no hint of any Latin mottoes apart from the letters O.P., and said: "Perhaps we can. May I ask you a personal question, Father Mallory?"

"Of course," said the Dominican.

"Do you ever worry that your research into these matters might be dangerous in itself, that merely knowing these things might expose a person to psychological hazards?"

Mallory nodded his head, as if he approved of the question. *"In much wisdom is much grief,"* he quoted, *"and he that increaseth knowledge increaseth sorrow.* Yes, I do, of course. I take very seriously the notions that there are things that man was not meant to know, even though the modern tendency is to scoff at the maxim. If I read your published comments about the defensive functions of consciousness correctly, you agree with me. But those hazards don't deter men like us, do they? The more we know, the more we want to know, even when we realize that we are looking into the abyss . . . and that the abyss is looking into us. Thankfully, I have armor that you have not." He made the sign of the cross, and added: "Should you ever decide that you want such armor, I shall be more than happy to hear your confession, and grant you such absolution as I can. May I, in turn, ask you a personal question?"

"Of course," said Simon, inevitably.

"Given that you know full well that what you are doing is exposing you to what you call *psychological hazards,* and that you have no armor of faith that might help to protect you, why are you continuing?"

"Because I've come too far to turn back," said Simon. "Because I'd lose far more if I did try to turn back than I could possibly lose by going on. And because, although I don't have faith in God, I do have faith in reason, and the scientific imagination."

"Not quite a difference in vocabulary, admittedly," the Dominican said, "but perhaps nearer than you think. At any rate, I approve. And now, perhaps we should leave it there until tomorrow. I shall pray for Felicia Murden, for your great-niece, and for both of you." He reached out with his hand toward Megan, and when she took it he brought his other hand round to clasp it. "Be kind to yourself, my dear," he said.

Then he shook Simon's hand, inclined his head slightly, displaying his tonsure, and made his way to the door of the lounge.

"Well," observed Megan, standing still for the moment, "that was unexpected."

"Him telling you to be kind to yourself?"

"No, that was just priestly unction. The rest of it. I've met some bullshitters in my time, but he's an ace."

"He's a Dominican lawyer attached to the Holy Office," Simon reminded her, as he followed in the priest's footsteps, at a respectful distance. "It's his job—and his vocation."

While following Simon's lead, Megan had already turned her attention to Doulas Jefferson and Bernard Pallister, who seemed to be deep in conversation, conspicuously not turning their heads to look at her, or Simon.

"What did Dougie say to you when he followed you out?" she asked, as they went into the car park, where the Dominican was nowhere to be seen, presumably having turned in the other direction inside the hotel.

"He apologized for not warning Bernard that he might bump into us, and claimed that he'd tried to contact me to warn me but failed. He nearly blew a gasket, though, when I asked him whether the ring he wears with his stupid mock escutcheon on it had belonged to his father."

Megan started with surprise. "Jesus!" she said. "So he does know who you are, in the fullest sense of the term—and now he knows that you know too?"

"It seems so. And I fear that you might also have been right about Cain and Abel. He certainly didn't throw his arms around me and say 'Brother!' although he might very well have been muttering 'Bastard!' under his breath, with a double layer of meaning and an arsenic filling. Then he pulled himself together and almost switched on the unction again—but he couldn't resist making a snide remark about you which rather spoiled the effect."

As Megan pressed the key to unlock the BMW, she frowned. "He's probably pissed because his previous attempt to drive a wedge between us didn't work. He'll certainly have other tricks up his sleeve, though. He hasn't given up on preventing, or at least slowing down, your inheritance. Do you think he'll try to have a word with the priest?"

"Probably," said Simon, as he fastened his seat belt, "but he'll meet his match there. What did you tell Father Mallory about the two cousins?"

"Just that they'd both fancied their chances of getting their hands on all or part of the inheritance, and are still looking for a chance to do you out of it, even though it will take a miracle."

"Father Mallory believes in miracles," Simon observed. "He might even be capable of working them."

"Maybe—but as he took the trouble to tell us, it's us he's going to pray for, not Bernard and Dougie. Did you tear a strip off Zoe?"

"No, I didn't. I tried to be kind to her, and I told her that I'd try to calm her mother down. Marianne, apparently, reacted the way you did. To be honest, though, I was slightly surprised that you reacted so fiercely."

"So was Mallory, it seems, even though he doesn't know that I was once a whore, let alone that I gave my own kid away. I suppose I ought to forgive you for being surprised, but there's a difference between selling yourself and selling your daughter, as your Eve seems to have known and felt, if what you've told me about her reaction to Angela's pregnancy is reliable. Having bailed Zoe out precisely because she seemed so desolate at the idea that she might be pressured to put Krysten in moral danger, I was deeply disappointed to find her doing just that. Maybe I overreacted, but on the websites I design, showing your tits is just a way of saying *come and get me*. Web traffic is full of pervs trying to persuade kids to prostitute themselves on their phones and webcams, and it sickens me. If you think that's hypocritical, tough, but nobody in my flock deals in kiddy porn."

"I'm not sure it qualifies as porn," Simon said, defensively, as he fastened his seat belt, although Megan had not yet shown any sign of an intention to start the engine. "And in spite of the reputation mermaids have, I can't really see that what they're offering can be an offer that can be construed as an attractive invitation to sexual intercourse, given that they're supposed to be fishy, or at last seal-like, below the waist."

"That's because you have a limited imagination," Megan snapped. "If you knew men like I do . . . but let's not go into that. You might not think that it's kiddy porn, but there are thousands who will. And don't tell me that Krysten's not a child, given that her mother's only thirty-eight going on sixteen. I certainly wouldn't give Marianne any award for mother of the year, and if you want to take offense at that because she's your sister and you're trying hard to love her, again, tough. You're the saint, not me."

"Not a very successful one, I fear."

"Not according to the Preacher. He's already got you marked down for martyrdom. Of course, according to you, the patron saint of his order was a vicious psychopath with a gang of pyromaniac thugs, so he probably doesn't have very high standards. Perhaps you ought to be worried that he thought you'd be so easy to get along with—although it didn't seem to me while we were in the hotel that he was wrong. You do realize, I suppose, that he didn't tell you anything you didn't already know, and only told you that much so he could score points by letting you know that he knew it too?" She started the engine and put the car into gear as she spoke, and backed out of the parking space as Simon began his answer.

"Yes, of course," said Simon. "Except that the fact that he knows it too isn't an irrelevant or uninteresting datum, especially the fact that he knows about the neider, and knows that it's a hydra rather than an Edenic serpent. Obviously, I've hypothesized that there might be other sets of vitreous cocoons elsewhere in the world, and if I'd had to guess where they might have been located, Delphi and Jerusalem would have been obvious candidates, but the interesting one he named is Toulouse. That can only have been a deliberate suggestion that the discovery in question, on the part of the Church, was made by St. Dominic or one of his associates, and that they were also responsible for its destruction or burial. It's tantamount to a suggestion that the vitreous cocoons of Toulouse were responsible for the origin and spread of the Albigensian heresy."

"But not, presumably, the corollary suggestion that the one in Jerusalem was responsible for the origin and spread of Christianity?"

"Why not? If the cocoons are just portals, through which good influences can pass as well as evil ones, they must be available to God as well as the Devil, in Father Mallory's terminology."

"It's not really surprising, though, that he didn't mention Mecca," Megan observed, putting her foot on the accelerator as she spoke, as if she were doing it for the sake of argumentative emphasis rather than because she had pulled out into the road and was now heading westwards. "But you don't really need to invent further sets of vitreous cocoons to explain the birth of religions. People are crazy enough to invent religions without any help. They do it all the time. And the ones we know about don't seem to have given birth to anything whose contagion expanded beyond the mad Murdens, or the mad Myrddins—a curse from which you and I obviously aren't immune, but which doesn't seem to have done any harm further afield."

"Perhaps not," said Simon.

"But they *are* dangerous," she added. "You and Mallory agree on that, even though he thinks the Devil's involved and you don't. Do you think that giving him James's scans and notes will keep him quiet, for the time being? At least until some further communication from the neider, presumably via Melusine? Assuming, that is, that you're not actually going to tell him your story, about Melusine, sleeping with the neider, going into the trap baited by Cerys and getting yourself killed and resurrected, whether in illusion or reality?"

"I have no plans, at present, to tell him that," Simon conceded.

"Not because he wouldn't believe you, but because he would, and would put his own diabolical spin on it?"

"Correct." Simon left it at that, feeling very tired and—unusually, for him, not really in the mood to discuss the mythology of the Devil and the harm that it had caused via the delusions of Churchmen.

In fact, that wasn't what Megan wanted. After a slight pause, she said: "Whereas you've told me everything—for reasons which, I admit, I can't quite fathom."

"True."

"That was supposed to be a prompt," she told him. "You were supposed to explain to me why, of all people, you picked me as a confidante. And don't tell me that it's because I asked. Mallory has just asked, and so did Alexander Usher, before him. Except, of course, that they're God-fearing, and bound to judge you, whereas I'm just an ex-whore, bound not to."

"It doesn't seem to stop you," Simon observed, dryly.

"No, I don't suppose it does," she admitted, with a sigh, although the sigh might have been caused by the fact that the BMW had just caught up with a tractor and had been forced to slow down. "I'm a very judgmental person. I have far more of my fair share of resentments and hatreds. But for your sake, I'll try to suppress them tonight. I'll be as kind as humanly possible to Marianne and Zoe."

"Don't forget yourself," Simon reminded her. "After all, you heard what the Inquisitor said."

"Yes, but he believes in miracles. You don't, mercifully. I can be kind to you and yours, I think, within reason, and Felicia, obviously. But me? Hardly. And don't try to be kind for me. You know as well as I do that you can't grant me absolution, any more than a priest can. You don't know how lucky you are, having nothing for which you need absolution."

"Thomas Mallory wouldn't agree with you."

"He's a prick. A clever prick, granted, but a prick just the same. Dougie in a dog collar. Or do you want me to be kind to Dougie now you know that he might well be as closely related to you as dear not-so-sweet Marianne?"

"No," said Simon, but didn't feel that he ought to leave it at that, even while he was too tired for long explanations so he added: "Even if it were true, I wouldn't feel protective toward him, the way I do toward Marianne and her offspring."

"And Felicia, and Cerys," Megan added on his behalf. "In fact, now I come to think of it, if it had been me who'd gone down into that impossibly dense darkness instead of Cerys, you'd even have come down after me, wouldn't you? Even though I'm older than you are, utterly morally derelict and have no intention of ever letting you screw me, you'd still have come to rescue me."

"What can I say?" he retorted. "If I said no, you wouldn't believe me. You think I'm a saint. Unbelievable, but a saint."

"I suppose so," she conceded. "But that still doesn't explain why you tell me all the things that you keep carefully secret from everyone else. Perhaps I ought to be flattered rather than worried, but I can't help thinking about that personal question you wanted to ask Mallory, and the answer he gave you. You told me right at the beginning that you thought telling me the family secret might do me harm, by driving me mad, but you did it anyway, and you're still doing it. Maybe I oughtn't to be taking it as a compliment. Maybe it would be sager, if not saner, to say *Vade retro me satanas*—forgive me if I'm misquoting, but I know even less Latin than you do."

Yet again, and still atypically, Simon didn't want to get into an intellectual debate about that issue, or even to respond with a witticism. He felt, in fact, that he had somehow drifted into a kind of mental limbo, as if the recent overloading of his conscious mind had finally stifled its ability to react and adapt. He struggled against the creeping psychic impotence.

"I tell Felicia everything too," he pointed out, "and maybe more, although neither of us is convinced any longer that we really can share our dreams. Our nightmares, maybe, but not our dreams."

His lazy tone probably made it obvious that he didn't really want to continue, and he tilted his head back and closed his eyes, even though he knew that he wouldn't be able to go to sleep, and also knew that if he consciously tried to invoke a slip into dreamspace, or even consciously waited for one, it was less likely to happen. Megan let it drop for a few minutes, but she couldn't suppress her own desire to talk for very long.

"Do you actually have a strategy in mind?" she said, eventually. "Do you actually have some kind of scenario planned out, however tentative, to produce a storyline in which all this works out for the best? If so, what is it? I really would like to know."

So would I, was what Simon subvocalized, but he knew that it wasn't adequate. Not only did Megan need more than that, but he needed more than that. He was in urgent need of a strategy that he didn't actually have, and in order to formulate such a strategy, he did, indeed, need to imagine some kind of storyline, in which the situation in which he found himself could reach some kind of conclusion. A conventional happy ending was obviously out of the question, but he still needed an ending that didn't culminate in hell and damnation. Even if he couldn't see how to contrive one, he needed at least to demonstrate to himself, and hopefully to Megan, that he could conceive such a terminus. There were, as always, too many possibilities—but he had to pretend to be a writer, even though he wasn't the one holding the metaphorical pen. He had to sift through the multitudinous possibilities, and search out the ones that might work out for the best.

"First of all," he said, eventually, "Melusine has to come back from the neider's lair, preferably articulate and able to spell out, more clearly than has so far been possible, what the neider wants and expects. Ideally, she'll be able to advise me on how to achieve it, or at least give me some suggestion as to what I might do. If Father Mallory can be trusted, the reflective reaction in the past has usually been to block the stairway leading down to the vitreous cocoons—to wall it up, one way or another, but that's not an ending I can approve of—or even one that Mallory could endorse, even though he thinks that we really are dealing with something diabolical."

"So what's the alternative?" Megan asked, challenging him.

"The alternative is to do what no one in Toulouse, Jerusalem and Delphi seems to have contrived, even though, if the lore of legend and mysticism can be trusted, thousands have tried, with all their mental might. The alternative is to secure and enhance a better communication between minds—between myself and the neider, between myself and whatever alien mind sent the abnormal darkness through the portal under the crypt, and perhaps with some kind of hypermind beyond that."

"What Mallory would call God, although we, as good atheists, wouldn't dream of so doing?"

"It's not that simple," Simon replied, realizing as he used the phrase—another of his favorites—that he was warming to his task in spite of his exhaustion. "Far from it, in fact. Remember what Mallory said about the Church: that it might look monolithic and autocratic, but in fact, it's a vast network of suborganizations, mostly working in secret and covert competition, with an intricately fragmented authority. Maybe the Church really is a reflection of God: an enormously complex bureaucratic God whose mysterious ways are worse than Byzantine; so complex and quasi-Byzantine, in fact, that it makes such nonsense of the idea of an omnipotent, omniscient, omnibenevolent supreme being that only a lunatic could think that the conventional idea of God can be applied to it. Whatever Thomas Mallory thinks, my toying with ideas like dark minds and hyperminds doesn't make me into a believer like him, who is simply employing a different vocabulary."

"Fair enough," said Megan equably. "So what? You still need an ending for your story. What is it?"

I still need a deus ex machina, *Simon thought. She's right. I can deny God as much as I like, but as a secondary creator, as a writer, I still need a substitute for the god from the machine. I still need to be able to imagine an ending that works, in narrative terms. And simply walling up the cave beneath the crypt won't do. It has to be better than that.*

"There's only one possibility," he said, after a moment's hesitation, reluctantly admitting to himself that it hadn't really been a pause for thought, given his present inability to think with any degree of elegance or aggression. "When you've eliminated the marriage, the inheritance and death, not because they aren't available but because you've already done them all, there's only one happy ending left, and that's enlightenment. One way or another, that's what I have to achieve, either by sleeping with the neider again, or going through the red portal again. Either of which would be direly dangerous, and from which I might not come back . . . but if that weren't the case, it wouldn't qualify as a satisfactory ending, would it? There's no drama without threat, no success without the possibility of failure."

"And what's my share of the ending?" Megan asked, reasonably. "Do you just come back and tell me what you've learned, at the peril of your life and sanity—no, cancel that, the sanity's already long gone, hasn't it? Do you just come back and make me even less sane than I am now?"

The honest answer would have been that Simon, selfishly, hadn't given that a moment's thought, but that didn't seem adequate. He struggled with his confusion and exhaustion, but to no great avail.

"You seem to have ruled out most of your own potential endings," he pointed out. "You're already rich, so you don't need an inheritance, and you've ruled out marriage with an unusual vehemence. What do you want, except enlightenment? What can you want?"

After a moment, Megan said: "If I'd actually thought it through, I'd have known you were going to say that. I've already had my ending, haven't I? I've wasted my life, stupidly, waiting for James Murden to acknowledge that I'm his daughter, thinking of that, foolishly, as some kind of climax, some kind of closure, and some kind of satisfaction. And now he has admitted it, in his testament, it isn't worth a handful of shit, and I've nothing left to put in its place. My subconscious was dead right, that night in Fishguard. I've fucked myself. All I have left is helping you in your crazy puzzle-solving, about which I can't even begin to care the way that you and Mallory and Alexander Usher can. The last thing I need is another ending. What I need is a beginning—but I'm seventy years old, and I'd already ruled out any kind of conventional beginning. I don't have any possibilities left in the locker. I really am up shit creek without a paddle, aren't I?"

Simon said nothing. He was not even sure that the Simon Cannick that Megan Harwyn had met in the Mermaid on the night of his arrival in St. Madoc could have thought of anything that would not have sounded so utterly lame as to be better left unsaid. *And she's right*, he thought. *At our age, nobody needs more endings than the one that's only looking at them with the facelessness of death. What they desperately need, if there's any possibility of finding one, is a beginning.*

"You do realize," she said, sardonically, "that that 'no comment' sounds more like a yes than a simple yes would have done?"

"No comment," Simon said.

"You could at least have argued that everyone else is in the same situation—that we're all just whiling away our time waiting for the Reaper to knock on the door, fooling ourselves into thinking that whatever we're doing in the interim is worthwhile and meaningful. But you couldn't, because even pathetic losers like Marianne, Zoe and Krysten, and poor bloody Felicia lying at death's door, still have possible new beginnings in mind, something to hope for, even if they don't have strategies to get there."

This time, Simon couldn't even muster a "No comment."

After a long pause, Megan said. "Sorry. No need to dump all that on you, especially when you don't seem to be in any fit state to respond, washed out and half-way to dreamland. But before I let you be, so that you can try to rest and recuperate before we get back to St. Madoc, can I ask you a personal question?"

"You've never bothered to ask permission before," Simon commented, dryly.

"Really? I thought I had. No matter. That story you just improvised, in which you get back into contact with the alien intelligences, and finally obtain some crucial conceptual breakthrough that will leave your triumphant mind bathed in intellectual bliss:

. . . but you can scream fiat lux all you want, and it won't help, because what's on the table here, what the neider can actually provide and even what the murderous jokers from beyond the stars are offering, isn't anything that can count as enlightenment for human consciousness, for wordy consciousness, because what was in their beginning wasn't the WORD at all but something else, as invisible and ungraspable as the dark matter of souls, as the dark intelligence of dark minds, from which humans have been expelled and excluded, because that's what human consciousness is: an exclusion and an isolation, whereas neider consciousness and stellar consciousness, and—who can tell?—maybe even dolphin consciousness is essentially wordless, and only musical by analogy, and you can never, ever grasp it, because you're just a poor, pathetic thing, all liquid and solid, with just sufficient darkness in you to enable human being, human mentality, human so-called intelligence, but not enough darkness to make any meaningful contact with the dark minds that make up the real mentality of the universe at every level, from the tiniest splinters of the hypermind of hyperminds, which definitely isn't God . . .

you don't actually believe that things are really going to work out that way, do you?"

"Not a snowball's chance in hell," Simon admitted.

"That's what I thought," she declared, although her tone suggested that the confirmation gave her no satisfaction at all.

VI
On the Coastal Path

Simon didn't feel that he had returned from spiritual limbo by the time he returned to the Abbey, but at least the return allowed him to focus on a close-range objective, and gave him a resource from which he could draw a little emotional energy. He didn't know how far he could trust the memory traces that he was now retaining from his spontaneous lapses into dreamspace, but he suspected that they were mostly fabulation: that the very effort of trying to remember them and import some sense into what he was remembering, was perverting and distorting them, and imposing his own conceptual framework—not to mention his own dark pessimism—on them.

When he reached the porch outside the front door—not without interruption—he had to pause before opening it, in order to pull himself together. He put his hands in his pockets, as if that might somehow help him to get a firmer grip on himself, and scanned the segment of the coastal path that was within his visual range, and all the people on it—not exactly a horde, by any means, but far more than he had ever encountered there before. He was not so far away that he could pretend that they were indistinguishable insects; they were far too obviously what they were: people drawn from the cocoons in which they had confined themselves for the winter, welcoming the return of the equinoctial sun and the knowledge of longer days to come, more light and less darkness.

A few of them, he knew, must have been prompted by Krysten's masquerade as the mermaid of Morgan's Fork. Not that they believed in mermaids, of course; they knew perfectly well that the video clip was a joke, even though they didn't know, as Simon did, that it was an escapade of two mothers regretful of the childhood they had left behind, caught up in the mood of a seaside holiday. None of them actually expected to see a mermaid, or a sea serpent. None of them thought that they were in any danger of being beguiled by a siren song, or swallowed whole by a marine monster; in being here, they were just responding to a quirky suggestion that, since they wanted to go somewhere to celebrate the sun's emergence, and there was no particular reason for selecting one place rather than another, why not take a trip to Morgan's Fork?

Except that there really was something lurking beneath the calm water between the tines, which really was dangerous, in its own exceedingly peculiar way, and something else lurking in a cave beneath the Abbey, which might be even more peculiar and even more dangerous . . .

It occurred to Simon that his present moment was the first pause for thought he had contrived all day, the first chance the flow of events had given him to try to pull himself together. He knew that he had to open the door and go upstairs, to see Felicia, to surrender yet again to conversation, communication and the flow of events, suffering the occasional momentary lapses into existential incoherence—but the need suddenly seemed urgent to give himself a break, to take a minute, even if it was literally only a minute, in order to try to recover his mental bearings, to bring his consciousness to bear on his situation.

But could he? And even if he could, could he trust his consciousness to get him out of mental trouble?

In the same way that he had to beware of actually believing anything that the Black Bard, or the neider, or the aliens from another galaxy seemed to be saying to him, because the mere fact that they seemed to be saying things had to be a distortion, he had to beware of his own trains of thought, which were doubtless constructed on fragments of truth, or honest trifles, but were bound to be treacherous in deepest consequence, because, in the final analysis, that was what human consciousness was: a mechanism lying to oneself, about what one was and what one could be. *Cogito ergo error*. I think, therefore I am deluded . . . because God didn't exist and he, Simon, was the Cartesian demon of the first meditation.

Consciousness, he reminded himself, remembering what he had written in one of his many rambling essays in supposed "non-fiction," is a defense mechanism: a means of creating a mental safe haven in which everything is orderly, and the pretence of rationality can be maintained. Perhaps, he had speculated, even before he had ever heard of the vitreous cocoons or the neider, the boundary separating consciousness from the dark expanses of the mind where dreams and delusions are born, is an essential defense mechanism, because if it were not possible to keep the sinister depths of collective unconscious at bay, they would drown us.

And that, he thought, *is why the vitreous cocoons and the neider are direly dangerous even though they don't mean to be. Their very existence, close at hand, constitutes an erosion capable of causing leaks in the dyke of human consciousness, which, if not swiftly blocked, can unleash the flood.*

But the problem didn't stop there, he knew. For a long time, the neider, at least, had been making deliberate attempts to intrude on the human consciousness of some of those most vulnerable to its probing. And recently—only very recently, but not for the first time—the vitreous cocoons, or something acting through them, had been making their own such attempts, perhaps in competition, or even conflict with the neider, but either way, adding to the confusion, and doubling the danger . . . or more than doubling it, since the combined effect was likely to be more than the mere sum of its parts.

I'm caught in the middle, Simon thought. *I'm the poor fool who has stumbled into the pitfall . . . or the poor moth drawn to the flame . . . or any one of a dozen other stupid metaphors, all as simple-minded as one another, all trying to apply the analogical reasoning of which consciousness is so fond. I'm buckling under the pressure, giving way. I need to fight. I need to step up and meet the challenge, because time is running out.*

But how?

If the integrity of his consciousness could not be preserved, he knew, if aspects of the unconscious—even the personal unconscious, let alone the collective unconscious or any kind of hypermind—were to break through, invade and occupy his mind, irresistibly . . . that would be quintessential madness, a poison from which sanity couldn't recover.

But what I said to Megan, in my stupid fashion, he thought, *was actually looking forward to that, and pretending that it could constitute a reward! Enlightenment! Dazzle at best, more likely blindness. What I ought to be hoping for, surely, is the opposite: friendly darkness, merciful darkness, the benevolent deception that tells you little lies, in order to hide the awful, intolerable whole truth . . . that, surely, is the only conclusion that I can possibly survive, let alone welcome . . .*

It was possible, he knew. It was possible to live in close proximity with the vitreous cocoons and the neider for more than half a century, as Edith and Rhodri had, and preserve the integrity of consciousness. Hundreds of people, before them, must have been able to do the same. The enlightened ones—the Black Bard, Owain Glyndwr, Owain Myrddin, probably Seymour Murden, Rhys Murden and Ceridwen, James and Melusine Murden, too—were the ones who had failed, who had allowed their minds be invaded, believing that they could control it, that they could cope, that it was a reward, that it was enlightenment, that it was some kind of fulfillment of the inevitable human desire to find a purpose in life . . . but which, when you got right down to it, was just madness.

And me too, he thought, *me too. But what the hell? It's not as if there were any possibility of turning back. It's too late. The hole in the dyke is already too big for a brave little boy like me to stick his finger in.*

It's too late . . .

He turned the door handle, went inside and went into the kitchen in order to obtain a report from Edith before going upstairs.

The news was good. Edith told Simon that Felicia had had something to eat, and had agreed that she would be able to come down at seven in order to have dinner in the dining room at seven-thirty, and had agreed that the gathering in question was a thoroughly good idea.

Simon was by no means sure of that, but he had no intention of letting on, either to Edith or Felicia.

Felicia was still in bed, but she was sitting up, chatting to Marianne, and she seemed to be in a positive mood. Simon kissed Felicia on the forehead, and then took her hand as he sat down beside the bed, Marianne having moved to another chair, a few feet away.

"You're feeling better?" he observed, gladly.

"Much," Felicia agreed. "In fact, I feel better than you look. Don't you think so, Marianne?"

"He's just a little tired," was Marianne's polite judgment. *If only*, Simon thought, before she added, addressing Simon directly: "Your meeting must have been stressful, especially with the interruption? Zoe told me you phoned her."

Before Simon could respond to that, Felicia chipped in. "Marianne has told me what Zoe and Krysten did. I've tried to assure her that it isn't serious, that all those people on the southern tine, staring at the water, are no real inconvenience to us, and that the fresh air will probably do them good, no matter how disappointed they'll be not to see any mermaids."

"And who knows?" said Simon. "Perhaps they will."

Felicia frowned slightly at that, and Marianne's contrived laughter was woefully unconvincing.

"You're going to be annoyed with me, I fear," Marianne said to Simon. "I lost my temper with Zoe. I couldn't believe that she'd taken that bit of video. I've been trying so hard, but I just couldn't keep it in."

"It's okay," Simon said. "Perfectly understandable, and you certainly don't have to apologize to me for it. It was just a mistake on Zoe's part. She realizes that now."

"She should have realized it before. She's thirty-eight years old, for God's sake. I know she spends all of her working life hanging out with five-year-olds and far too much of the rest of it getting stoned, but she's not a child any more. She's a grandmother, damn it."

"She does realize that, I'm sure," said Simon. "She just needs a little time to adjust to life beyond artificially altered states of consciousness. I'll have a word with her and Krysten before dinner, to explain why I'd rather the Abbey and the family didn't get that kind of publicity. I'm sure they'll both understand. I hope the two of you have managed to find more interesting things to talk about while I've been away than poor Zoe's misdemeanors?"

"Yes," said Felicia, "of course we have. Marianne's been very kind, and I feel a lot better. How did things go with your Dominican? Not too stressful, I hope, even with the complication."

"Not bad, all things considered," Simon said, judiciously. "He knows a lot more than I expected about our situation, but he doesn't seem to have any intention of creating difficulties for us, or even of being indiscreet. He seems to think that we can get along together without doctrinal difficulties causing too many problems, although I'm not so sure about that. He seems to be a thoroughly well-meaning fellow, though, as well as an intelligent one, which is a great relief, and I'll be very interested in what he has to tell me. I'm meeting him again tomorrow afternoon, in Morpen. Obviously, I said I'd have to check with you before I agreed to anything with regard to the Abbey archives, so we can have a chat about that tonight, before or after dinner, if you're not too tired."

"I'll be fine," Felicia assured him.

"I can leave, if you'd like to talk in private now," said Marianne, making as if to get up.

"No, no, dear," said Felicia, "you have first claim on Simon this afternoon. You're only here for a couple of days, and you must take full advantage of it. You have sixty years of separation to make up for, and the weather's so beautiful this afternoon, for the time of year, that you really ought to take advantage of it while it lasts. I only hope that the crowd won't inconvenience you. They seem to be mostly gathering on the far tine though, and the ones on the coastal path have plenty of room in which to spread out. There's no need to ask Edith to come and sit with me—she's busy, and I have a book to read. I may need another nap before dinner, in any case."

"Are *you* all right, though, Simon?" Marianne asked, evidently having noticed some deterioration since the morning in spite of the reassurance she had earlier hastened to give Felicia out of quasi-sisterly loyalty.

"Perfectly," Simon lied. "I've had a pleasant, relaxing time sitting in Megan's plush BMW, and what I need more than anything is some fresh air, if Felicia doesn't need me."

"Of course I need you, dear," said Felicia, "but I don't need you sitting by the bed looking at me as if you expected me to drop dead at any moment. I need you fit and well and content with your sister. I need you to take her out and make her feel better. Go, please, and leave me in peace, for a little while, so that I can pull myself together properly. You've been very kind, Marianne, and a great help, but for the moment, I need to be on my own, and you need to be with Simon. So go."

"If you're sure . . . ," Simon said.

"I'm sure," said Felicia. "We'll talk tonight. You can tell me exactly what Father Mallory wants, and we can decide exactly what we're prepared to give him. For now, the sun isn't getting any higher. Take advantage of it while it's still bright."

Simon kissed her again, and squeezed her frail hand, very gently. Marianne was already on her feet, backing away toward the door.

As they went downstairs, Marianne said: "She's an angel, and I can't believe that she's as old as a hundred and one. Even though she's under the weather, she looks thirty years younger than that."

"An angel, as you say," said Simon. "A godsend to me, at any rate."

As they made their way along the path toward the gate, Marianne looked slightly worried. "There are people there," she said.

"There were a lot more when I came in," Simon told her. "When they saw me with the key they tried to mob me, clamoring to be let in, but I told them politely that it's private property, and mentioned that the mermaid picture was so obviously kids on holiday having a laugh that no one but a moron could possibly think that it was anything else. They took it meekly, and dispersed. Megan had walked me to the gate, though, and when she puts on her intimidating face it's the next best thing to having a pet Medusa. The good thing is that there didn't seem to be any reporters in the crowd—it's presumably way too far for anyone to come, even from Swansea or Cardigan, let alone London, on the strength of a few seconds of bad phone footage. We're nowhere near the silly season yet, and Brexit and the chancellor's spring statement are producing comment-fodder by the yard. Just keep a straight face and don't even dignify any questions with a *no comment*."

The advice proved sound. Simon was able to lock the gate again and cross the bridge without being harassed, jostled or insulted.

"There you are," said Simon, as they turned left and started walking along the coastal path. "As long as the video doesn't clock up too many hits on YouTube during the next twenty-four hours, it will all dwindle away to nothing."

"What if the clicks keep mounting up, and it doesn't dwindle away?" Marianne queried.

"It will—and if it rains tomorrow, as it might, this place will be dead again. If it isn't, Dai Mermaid will simply order extra supplies of sandwiches and pies, take on temporary bar staff a little earlier than planned, and do a roaring trade in beer. If there's any hint of trouble, Megan will come out of Sanderling wearing her intimidating face, wielding a meta-phorical whip, and sort it. If they storm the gate wanting to get access to Morgan's Cave to see if we're hiding any mermaids there, Rhodri will be ready with his shotgun. There won't be any need for an armed response vehicle."

Marianne did not seem reassured by the jesting tone, but Simon continued with it anyway, adding: "If Krysten's worried about being recognized, she only has to dress up as the Black Monk. Nobody will even try to look at her face. And if the worst comes to the absolute worst, I'll summon the real thing, and he can scare them all away,"

Marianne gave him a long look, as if unsure whether the last comment was really as unserious as it sounded, although he had also tried to smile in a manner that suggested that it couldn't possibly be anything but a joke.

"Did your meeting with the actual Black Friar really go well," she asked, seizing the cue that allowed her to change the subject, "or were you just trying not to upset Felicia?"

"All in all, I think it went as well as could be expected," he said. "So far, it's all velvet glove, and he didn't give any hint of a hidden iron fist. Tomorrow's discussion might actually be very interesting, for both of us, as there seems to be plenty of scope for putting our cards on the table. He already knows so much that giving him the extra information he wants probably can't do us any harm, although he is the kind of person who gives the strong impression of possibly having a hidden agenda or two. I have to admit, though, that I was seriously embarrassed when he pulled out his smartphone and showed me that video, of which even Megan hadn't had an inkling, although she's usually well ahead of the rest of the world with internet scoops."

"I'm truly sorry . . . ," she began.

"I know," he said. "It just flustered me, that's all, coming on top of another shock I'd had, only half an hour previously."

"What was that?" Marianne asked, before adding, swiftly: "Not that it's any of my business."

"In fact, it's arguable that it might be," Simon told her. "It turns out that you might not be the only half-sibling I have . . . oh, don't look so horrified; your mother didn't give away any more children. Megan thinks that she might have contrived to identify my father, with a little bizarre conclusion-jumping, and, Megan being Megan, she immediately got a DNA sample to prove it, or at least to get supportive evidence—it's better not to ask how. So, if appearances can be trusted, I might have a half-brother as well as a half-sister. I just have to hope that half-siblings aren't like the proverbial buses that always arrive in threes."

"Are you going to write to him as well?" Marianne asked, curiously.

"Oh, I already know him," said Simon. "What's worse, he already knows me, and might have found out about me a long time ago. Unfortunately, he doesn't give the impression of having been delighted to discover that he might have a bastard brother, and although he's making every effort to be polite and full of bonhomie with regard to the Estate, because it's in his interest to do so, I'm certain that he's not sincere and is still frantically making plans to do me out of it, if possible."

Marianne performed a rapid mental calculation. "But he's not related to me at all," she said.

"That's one thing of which we can be certain—and probably something to be thankful for. All in all, I'd rather he weren't related to me, and I'm still hopeful that he isn't."

"But how do you know him, in order to dislike him that much? I thought you were a virtual recluse until a few weeks ago."

"Oh, I only met him for the first time a couple of days after I met you, but he came with baggage attached. Megan's known him all her life, and she loathes him; I suppose she's poisoned my mind a little . . . but not without justification, it seems to me."

"You seem to be very close to Megan," Marianne observed, in a carefully neutral voice.

"And you've just been talking to Felicia for the last couple of hours. Doubtless the subject came up. Felicia can't help wondering whether Megan might have what she calls *designs*.

If she has, they're not the sort that Felicia's afraid of. Megan's off men for life—bad experiences in the past."

"We've all had those," said Marianne, still in a carefully neutral tone, "but it doesn't necessarily deter us, no matter how we might slag men off. What we say and what we do are sometimes two different things—and Megan doesn't dress and apply her lipstick like someone who's off men for life."

"Well, she is, believe me—and even if she weren't, there still wouldn't be anything between us. I know that no one in the world, even Felicia, can actually believe that she and I might be together for good, but if it depends on me . . ." He left it there.

"And was your new half-brother one of Megan's bad experiences?" Marianne queried, apparently no longer sensitive to the diplomatic boundaries of what might not be her business.

"Yes," said Simon, but thought it necessary to add, lest he leave the wrong impression: "But that's not why I'd rather he wasn't related to me, and I don't actually hate him. I'm still perfectly prepared to get along with him, as he seemed very willing to do—and still does, although his mask slipped momentarily this morning, and gave me reason to be wary."

"I'm confused," Marianne admitted. "So, the only reason you'd rather not be related to him is because he seems to dislike you . . . because he's his father's legitimate son and you're not?"

"That's one reason," Simon said, realizing a second too late that it would have been far simpler just to say *yes*. Obviously, he was still nowhere near his A game.

"What's the other?" his sister asked, as he had carelessly made it inevitable that she would.

"It's not so much that I don't want to be related to *him* as that I'd much prefer not to be related to his branch of the family as well as ours. They're Murden-descended, like your mother, and for various reason to do with our eccentric family history, his ancestors and ours were probably very Murden indeed. There's been a lot of inbreeding in the family."

"Incest, you mean?"

"Maybe some—but certainly a lot of cousin marriages. That might be one reason for what you call the family curse. Intense inbreeding tends to be assisted with reduced fertility, even in the absence of the supplementary tendency to produce anomalous ova and sperm. There's as much superstition as reason in incest taboos, but even so, I'd like to think that I might have got the benefit of a little hybrid vigor from our mother's teenage escapade, just as you did from your marriage. Believe me, there's such a thing as being too Murden."

"But surely the old Murdens can't have been any more inbred than any other slightly pretentious family living in a relatively remote rural area?"

"Actually, they could, and seemingly made something of a fetish of it. The evidence is thin, but I'm beginning to suspect that it was all Owain Myrddin's fault. He was the Myrddin of what your mother called Merlin's cave, not the Arthurian wizard. He got the Abbey when Henry VIII dissolved the monasteries in the 1530s. There's no record of how, but Thomas Mallory knows that he was being investigated by Dominican Inquisitors, for heresy, probably for wizardry and perhaps for other sins too. Mallory called my attention to the fact that no one came after him, even when Bloody Mary came to the throne, perhaps because he was simply too far away, but perhaps because he still had covert influence in London, which might have increased again when Elizabeth came to the throne. At any rate, Owain Myrddin appears to have been the prior of the Abbey before the dissolution, although he was at least as much bard as priest, and after the dissolution removed the possibility of interference from the Dominicans and Rome, he appears to have founded his own little cult, with its own rules, norms and objectives, some of which survived at least into the nineteenth century."

"Which involved inbreeding?"

"Yes. Owain Myrddin's successors—perhaps including direct descendants, if he didn't take his Holy Orders very seriously—became obsessed with the idea of rebirth, a physical manifestation of which they saw in the ability of Murden women sometimes to give birth to identical children. They thought—not entirely without similar evidential grounds, it seems—that male rebirths could be produced as well as female ones, by inbred couples: mostly first cousins but perhaps siblings, or fathers and daughters. While I thought of my birth as the product of random statutory rape, I didn't think I could be regarded as a rebirth in terms of Murden mythology. Now . . . well, it seems that I might be."

"Rebirth of whom?"

"That depends on the shape of legends that have mostly been lost, but there's probably a sense in which all the sequences of rebirth were traced, imaginatively, back to two sources: a supposed enchantress known as Ceridwen, and the Myrddin Wyllt of Welsh legend, of whom Owain Myrddin probably considered himself to be a reincarnation."

"But it's all nonsense?"

"Genetically, yes, even with all the inbreeding and the consequent accumulation within the family of certain odd genes, but mystically . . . who can tell?"

"But at least you're not

. . . *music, dark but sweet, truthful and not deceptive, crythor and crwth as one, and also many, in the harmonious chain of wombs, owain well born, always well born, always musical, always in the well, audible in time, to the soul if not the ear . . .*

a wizard," Marianne observed, and then hesitated. "Although you are a bard, in a manner of speaking."

"I suppose I am," Simon agreed, pulling himself together yet again. "At least, I try. It's not easy . . . although it's not easy to avoid trying, either. It's a vocation one has to follow, if one's born to it . . . or reborn to it."

"And you've seen the Black Monk and the ghost of Owain Glyndwr?"

"I have," Simon confirmed.

"And you've seen whatever is in Merlin's cave: the mystery of the Murdens."

"That too," Simon confirmed.

"And you've shown it to Megan Harwyn." It wasn't a question. She and Felicia had been talking about Megan, and about the mystery of the Murdens.

When Simon didn't confirm the observation, Marianne went on: "But you don't want to show me, or tell me what it is, because you're afraid that it might put me in harm's way." Again, it wasn't a question, so Simon took the option of not answering.

"But you invited me to visit," she said. "You invited Zoe too . . . although you didn't think she'd accept, did you?"

"Not the next day, for sure," Simon admitted, "and I didn't expect my joking remarks about the ghosts and the morgens to seize her imagination the way they seem to have done. At the time, I really didn't think that any harm could come of it, given that the Murdens I met here had been living in company with the mysterious entity for a hundred years, without suffering any ill-effects . . . at least until I arrived. Now, though . . . I'm beginning to wonder if I haven't made a bad mistake. If I have, I'm truly sorry. The last thing I wanted was to put you, or your family, in danger."

"Are we in danger?" Marianne asked, with understandable bluntness.

"I don't know. I hope not."

She looked at him sharply. "But if we are," she guessed, "we wouldn't be out of it, even in Bristol. We never have been. There really is a family curse, as Felicia says?"

"Felicia said that?"

"Well, no, not in so many words. She just said that some things run in the family. She was doing what you did earlier, in fact: talking about herself but blatantly expecting me to apply it to myself. She told me about recurrent patterns, and observed in passing that Lilith leaving the Abbey and taking Evelyne away with her didn't seem to have made much difference to the fate of her descendants."

"And what else did Felicia tell you?" Simon enquired, warily.

"Well, among other things, not to tell you what she'd told me—but that is the kind of injunction that people can't really expect to be observed. She said that you're upset because you've begun to think that your coming here caused things to go wrong, but that you have it the wrong way round—that it was because things had begun to go wrong that you were drawn here. She said that her grandmother had been expecting someone for years, but that she and her brother had both assumed that the old lady had lost her mind a long time ago. When you arrived, though, she and Melusine, and even James, began to wonder. She also said that she would have died with James if you hadn't come—that you saved her life, and that you also saved Cerys from something bad. She said that she's trying hard to be enough for you, but that you probably need more. I got the impression that she was begging me to be nice to you . . . not that I was planning to be anything but, although . . ."

She left it at that. Simon inferred that she didn't mean that she'd changed her mind about being nice, but simply that she didn't think that it was her forte.

"As you say," Simon remarked, "she's an angel. So, where do we go from here? Do you want to pack your bags and your offspring, run back to Bristol and never set foot on any threshold of my door again, on the grounds that I'm a walking disaster area?"

"Good God, no," she said. "Anything but. You don't have to tell me the family secret, either, if you think it's better for me not to know it—but you might have difficulty putting a bridle on Zoe's curiosity. She thinks you're a saint too, but that won't stop her prying."

"I can't blame her for that, and I can't help feeling that both of you have a certain right to know why it might be dangerous to maintain my acquaintance, now that I'm beginning to glimpse the reason myself. It's complicated, though . . . hideously complicated. It's . . ."

He suddenly interrupted himself. They had just reached the point at which Simon usually turned round and went back toward Morgan's Fork in the course of his routine daily constitutional, and the day-trippers and hikers strung out along the path to either side of the Fork had thinned out almost to negligibility, but there was someone standing in the path in front of them, who showed no sign of standing aside for them, and who said, in fact: "Mr. Cannick?" in a tone redolent with embarrassment and awkwardness. "Might I have a word with you?"

Simon's instant assumption, when the woman spoke his name, had been that she was one of the curiosity-seekers attracted by the video of the fake mermaid, but by the time she reached the end of her query and he had focused his attention, he realized that he had jumped to the wrong conclusion.

The woman blocking the path was moderately tall, with a slightly Junoesque build. She had a woolen hat covering her hair and pulled down low over her forehead, almost overlapped by the huge dark glasses that were not merely covering her eyes but almost all of the top half of her face. As she finished speaking, however, she reached up, awkwardly but deliberately, and removed the spectacles with her right hand, and the woolen hat with her left.

Simon had already been rendered speechless by shock no less than three times in the course of the day, but it seemed that the three-at-a-time rule did not apply to surprises.

The woman standing in front of him bore a very close resemblance to Megan Harwyn, but Megan Harwyn rejuvenated, seemingly at least twenty-five, and perhaps as many as thirty, years younger, with dyed blonde hair.

She seemed almost relieved by the visibility of his surprise, as if it had cleared away an unwelcome lingering doubt.

"I believe you know a woman named Megan Harwyn," she added.

Marianne knew Megan Harwyn as well, and had no difficulty at all in recognizing her clone daughter, but she too was robbed momentarily of the power of speech, and in the end, it was Simon who recovered it first.

"Yes," he said, keeping his voice as calm as he could, "I do."

"Mr. Jefferson suggested that I speak to you," she said. "He telephoned me a little while ago to say that you had just left the Abbey and turned left, at a leisurely pace. He'd already told me that if I cut across country and walked briskly I could catch up with you at the point where you usually turned back."

Simon made a rapid calculation. "You were in Blackbird Cottage I assume?"

"That's right. It belongs to one of Mr. Jefferson's friends. I realize that the distance from that cottage to Sanderling Cottage is a lot shorter than the distance from there to here, but Mr. Jefferson suggested that it would be far better if an introduction to Miss Harwyn came from you rather than him. She doesn't like him, it seems."

While speaking, Megan Harwyn's daughter glanced more than once at Marianne. Evidently, Douglas Jefferson had not told her that anyone was with Simon, let alone who she was.

"This is my sister, Marianne," Simon explained. "Like me, she's a distant cousin of Megan Harwyn—and she has a daughter who is her identical twin, one generation removed."

The blonde woman's attention switched entirely to Marianne. "Mr. Jefferson did say that intergenerational doubles were common in the family, but . . . you have a daughter identical to you, you say? A twin of sorts? How is that possible? She's definitely your daughter? You actually gave birth to her?"

The sudden flurry of blurted questions evidently surprised Marianne as much as they surprised Simon, causing her to frown at the slight hint of surreality. Unable to respond to all the questions at once, she settled for answering the last one, which was certainly far easier than one or two of the others. "Oh yes," she said. "I definitely gave birth to Zoe. They say you don't remember the pain afterwards, but I certainly haven't forgotten it."

The blonde woman was still confused, tripping over her own train of thought. "And now she looks exactly like you?" she persisted. "As if she were an identical twin, but younger?"

"That's right," said Marianne. "I suppose she is a twin, in a way. Identical twins are produced when an embryo divides in the womb. The division that produced Zoe was a trifle belated, but similar."

"Mr. Jefferson didn't explain that to you?" Simon put in, although it was a silly question, as the answer was perfectly obvious.

Megan Harwyn's clone was blushing now, in a fashion that Megan was not at all given to doing, to the best of Simon's knowledge—although he had not, of course, known her twenty-five years ago. She was ashamed of her confusion, although it was easily understandable, coming on top of the nervousness that she must have felt about accosting Simon in her deliberately dramatic manner.

She collected herself, visibly.

"Mr. Jefferson didn't explain anything much," she said. "He apologized, but he said that he didn't know how to explain it, but that Megan Harwyn might be able to—to explain the strange resemblance between us, that is. He showed me some old photographs of her. They looked exactly like photographs of me. He admitted that it might just be coincidence, but that there were family mysteries from which he'd always been excluded."

She looked at Marianne again, quizzically.

"Don't look at me," said Marianne. "The family mysteries are still a complete mystery to me. Simon understands, though."

The blonde woman's querulous and interrogative gaze switched back to Simon.

Simon had to collect himself too. The course of events kept throwing up the unexpected; he had been out of his depth ever since getting out of bed, and he felt as if he were floundering. "Mr. Jefferson didn't tell you that Megan Harwyn might be your mother?" he asked, putting it as delicately as he could.

"Oh yes," the mystery woman said. "He said that was the first idea that had popped into his head, but that so far as he knew, Megan Harwyn had never mentioned to anyone that she had ever had a child. He said that if anyone could explain the resemblance, though, it was her. So far as I know, she *could* be my mother—I was adopted, and my adoptive parents always told me that they knew nothing about my birth-mother. They admitted that the adoption had been arranged outside official procedures, so that there was no paperwork that might enable her to be identified. It's been a bit of an inconvenience, actually, having no birth certificate, but . . . that's immaterial. Anyway, I'd like to meet Megan Harwyn, if possible, and Mr. Jefferson said that it would be easier to achieve that if you were to introduce me to her. He didn't explain why . . ." Her embarrassment had deepened even further, and she seemed almost to be regretting having made the approach.

Simon couldn't fathom what Douglas Jefferson might be playing at, unless he simply wanted to cause as much embarrassment as possible for everyone concerned, while exacting a petty revenge on Megan.

"I'm sorry to have troubled you," Megan Harwyn's long-lost daughter said. "I didn't realize that it would be a problem. I shouldn't have . . ."

"That's all right," said Simon, trying to sound reassuring and to put the blonde woman at ease, although he didn't really feel at ease himself. "It's not your fault that you've been slightly misled. Mr. Jefferson has a habit of holding back relevant information for dramatic effect." Without really thinking about it, he added: "I don't suppose he told you, when he sent you to accost me, that he might be my half-brother?"

The surprise was renewed, this time supplemented by a start on the part of Marianne, because Simon hadn't identified Jefferson earlier as the possible half-brother. "No, he didn't," said the blonde woman. "He probably didn't think it was relevant."

In a pig's eye, thought Simon. Aloud, he said: "He hadn't told me that he was aware of the possibility, either, until he let it slip this morning. He could have told me then, presumably, that he had made contact with you and that he intended to bring you to St. Madoc this afternoon, but he didn't. Megan was with me at the time, and would certainly have been interested to know."

The woman's expression became apprehensive. "I think it's because Mr. Jefferson wasn't sure about her reaction that he suggested that I talk to you first," she said. "He warned me that there was a possibility that if I went to her cottage on my own, or with him, that she'd simply slam the door in my face and refuse to talk to me. He said that if anyone can persuade her to talk to me, and explain the resemblance between us, it's you. He didn't say why he thought so, but I assumed that it was simply because you were her friend and he wasn't. I suppose I should have realized that there were complications . . ."

Simon sighed. "In fact," he admitted, "Dougie might be right that if anyone can persuade Megan to see you, it's me—but even if I could, I'm not at all sure that I should, given that it's not really my place to intervene in private and personal affairs of a sensitive nature. May I know your name?"

The blonde woman started, realizing that perhaps she should have introduced herself as soon as she had completed her initial dramatic flourish. "Oh, sorry, yes—of course. I'm Jocasta, Jocasta Symonds." She put out her hand reflexively.

Simon shook it.

"How long have you known Dougie?" he asked, politely.

"Oh, not long. Only a few weeks."

"And how, exactly, did he introduce himself? What explanation did he give for his interest in the matter of your possible relationship with Megan?"

Jocasta Symonds blushed again. "He came into the shop where I work. He looked at me a few times while he was looking round, then apologized for his apparent rudeness, but said that he'd been struck by the striking resemblance I bore to someone he used to know. I thought it was just a chat-up line, but he showed me the photographs. He asked me whether I knew Megan Harwyn, and I said I didn't, and that it must be just a coincidence; I quoted the old saw about everyone having a double.

"He continued asking questions—very politely—and I didn't see any harm in answering. I admitted that I didn't know whether there might be a blood relationship, because I didn't know anything about my blood relatives, but that if the photograph was old as he said, it couldn't be a case of twins separated at birth, because the woman he'd known would be old enough to be my mother . . . and he agreed that might be a possibility, although, as I said, he told me that the woman he knew had never given any indication of having had a child. He said that if I wanted him to, he could make some discreet enquiries.

"He came back a few days later, and said that he hadn't been able to find out anything for certain, but that Megan Harwyn had just been officially recognized as the daughter of a man named James Murden, and that the Murden family was very mysterious. He said that there was a large inheritance involved, but that it wasn't clear as yet who would receive it. That didn't really interest me much—I was only working in the shop to give me something to do after the children had left home. I wasn't in financial need, in spite of the divorce, although I suppose you never know . . .

"Anyway, I was naturally curious about the possibility that Megan Harwyn might be related to me—especially, obviously, the possibility that she might be my mother—so that when Mr. Jefferson said that he had a friend who owned a cottage in the village where Megan Harwyn lived, and that it might be possible to arrange an introduction, we exchanged mobile numbers. He phoned yesterday, and I accepted his offer to meet me at Carmarthen railway station today—he said he had some kind of business lunch in the town—and to drive me out here. I didn't realize it was quite this remote, although it seems very crowded."

"And what did he tell you about me?" Simon asked.

"Not much, apart from the fact that you lived next door to Megan Harwyn. He told me your name, and mentioned that you were a writer—he said I could look you up online. I did, but it didn't tell me much except a long list of book titles. He said that you and she don't have many friends, but that you get along very well together. He also said that you're a kind person."

"That's a fine compliment, coming from Dougie," said Simon dryly, "given that he's such a kind person himself. Did he tell you why he was carrying old photographs of Megan around in his wallet?"

"He said that he was once very fond of her, but that his father hadn't approved of the relationship, and nothing had come of it."

"And that's all he said?"

"Just about," said the blonde woman, very warily, clearly becoming intimidated by the barrage of questions. "He gave the impression that he didn't like to talk about it. Obviously, there's a lot of background to this of which I'm unaware, and you're obviously upset about my putting you on the spot like this. I'm sorry if I've offended you somehow. That wasn't my intention. I'll go back to the village and I'll ring Mr. Jefferson from there to ask him whether there's another way to obtain the introduction."

Simon had not expected to feel so sympathetic to Bernard Pallister so soon, but he now understood perfectly why Cousin Bernard's semi-automatic reaction to hearing Dougie's name or having the idea of him pop into his head was to say: "I'll kill the little rat." He couldn't help feeling sorry for Megan's daughter, though—and couldn't help feeling, too, that he was being unreasonably churlish, and that a refusal to involve himself might well make the situation worse for her, and perhaps for Megan too.

"No," he said, "don't go. I'll talk to Megan, to give her fair warning, and try to persuade her to talk to you. I know there's no reason why you would believe me rather than Dougie, but you might be wise to be suspicious of his motives, and not to take anything he tells you at face value. As you say, there's a lot of background to this that you don't know."

"He's your brother, you say?" queried the woman, seemingly uncertain as to her entitlement to ask him questions, even though he'd fired so many at her.

"Half-brother, if that," Simon corrected, the dryness of his tone achieving Saharan standards. "Actually, I'm the product of a statutory rape, and he probably doesn't like the idea that it might have been committed by his father—a father of whom he was very fond, I gather, even though, to put it in his own words, 'the old sinner had his faults.'"

He stopped there, but he couldn't help his imagination running on—just playing with ideas, as he loved to put it, and remembering the family motto inscribed on the ring. He couldn't help fantasizing that Ranald Jefferson might have been wearing that ring at the time of his conception, and even wondering whether it might conceivably have made such a deep impression on poor Angela when he punched her in the face . . . but he knew that that idea was patently absurd, and he tried hard to expel it from his fragile, leaky consciousness.

Jocasta Symonds obviously had no idea what to say to such a revelation, so she said nothing, but she looked even more unhappy than she had before.

As gently as he could, Simon said: "Might I ask what, if I were able to obtain an introduction to your mother for you, you would hope to get out of such a meeting?"

There was no immediate answer to that question, either. Jocasta Symonds and Marianne were both looking at Simon with evident puzzlement, evidently unable to guess what he might be thinking and what his agenda in this strange situation might be. He wondered briefly whether he might have let something of his momentary fantasy show, but having checked back, he couldn't believe that he had. Even so, he said: "I'm sorry, I'm being insensitive. I fear that I have a few personal issues regarding contact with long-lost mothers that I haven't yet worked through myself."

"Are you sure, then, that Megan Harwyn *is* my mother?" Jocasta Symonds asked him, hesitantly.

The simple answer would have been yes, but it occurred to Simon that Megan might not be at all pleased if he made that admission before consulting her. He had no idea how she was going to react to the news that Douglas Jefferson had brought her daughter to St. Madoc, and had made such an absurdly elaborate plan to bring them together, for reasons that Simon couldn't fathom yet.

"It's not for me to say," he said, gritting his teeth slightly at the evasion. "As Mr. Jefferson says, it's probably best to consult her about the resemblance, and invite her to explain it, if she can. I have no right to jump to conclusions. I've only known her for a few weeks. As I say, I'm a little sensitive about the idea of meeting a mother after a long alienation because I met my own mother for the first time very recently, and only a few days afterwards, I had to go and sit by her deathbed. It was a rather harrowing experience."

Again, Jocasta Symonds had no idea what to say to that, and it was Marianne who stepped in.

"That's true, in fact," she said to the blonde woman. "Simon did have to do all that, and it must have been very hard. I was the one who acted as intermediary in that case, as you're asking him to do in this one. I had no idea what he was going to say to my mother, or she to him. I'd like to say that I was afraid that it might go badly, but I wasn't. It probably reflects badly on me, but I almost hoped that it would go badly, and that Simon would pay my mother back for decades of my own resentments by spitting in her face, metaphorically if not literally. But he didn't, and I'm very glad, in retrospect, that he didn't. He told her, very quietly and very persuasively, that he understood why she had been forced to abandon him, that he didn't bear her any grudge at all, and that he was glad to have had the chance to meet her before she died. And when she did die, he was the one she wanted to see before she passed. She refused point blank to see a priest, but she wanted to see Simon, to talk to him instead. And he's been very kind to me, and extremely kind to my daughter, so whatever faults Mr. Jefferson, whom I don't know, might have, he's absolutely right to say that Simon is a very kind person, and that there's probably no one on earth who could better act as an intermediary between you and your mother, if she is, in fact, your mother."

Simon looked at Marianne, glad to find that he was not particularly surprised by what she had said and done, and grateful to her for taking the trouble.

"Well," said Jocasta Symonds, her tongue finally loosened, "this isn't what I expected, but as I didn't know what to expect, I suppose that's only to be expected, if that make sense. And to answer your question, Mr. Cannick, I don't know what to expect to come of meeting Megan Harwyn. Even if she doesn't have anything to say about the resemblance between us, though, and even if it is just a matter of a coincidental double, it might allow me to see what I'll look like in twenty-five or thirty years' time. But if I ever do meet my mother, whether she turns out to be Megan Harwyn or someone else entirely, I wouldn't want any tears, and I wouldn't necessarily want an apology, although I would like to be able to say, as you apparently said to your mother, that I understood why she was forced to abandon me. I really would like to understand that, in order that there could be a possibility that I could say, to myself if not to her, that I didn't bear her any grudge. In spite of your evasion of the question, though, I can't help suspecting that you know more about this than you're telling me—just as Mr. Jefferson does, it now seems. I've obviously been caught in the middle of something. Is it something to do with this inheritance he mentioned?"

"I fear so," Simon said. "At present, I'm the heir named in the will. Mr. Jefferson is resentful of that—understandably, I have to admit, given that he seems to have long harbored hopes, if not expectations, that have been suddenly and rudely shattered."

"And Megan Harwyn is involved too?"

"Intricately."

"And where do I fit in?"

"I hate to sound evasive again, but it really would be far better if Megan explained that. As I say, I'll talk to her—but I can't make you any promises. I'm sorry."

Jocasta Symonds stared at him speculatively, presumably groping for a hint of fellow feeling. Eventually, she said: "Since you raised the issue, and asked me the question, perhaps you won't mind me asking why you made such an effort to be kind to the mother who abandoned you?"

"Her circumstances were difficult," Simon said, although he knew that he couldn't get away with that. He went on, before she could interrupt and press him: "My mother was very young—under the age of consent, as I mentioned, and perhaps, it now seems, related to her rapist. It was her mother, Eve, who actually abandoned me, by dumping me in a shop doorway in a cardboard box. My mother wasn't given a choice. My grandmother was a prostitute, you see, and she was absolutely determined to save her daughter from following her into that profession, and she thought that if my mother, Angela, kept me at home, she wouldn't have any alternative. So she got rid of me, because she thought it might save Angela. And it worked, after a fashion. Angela didn't become a prostitute, and she eventually got married— everyone's idea of a badge of respectability in those days— and had Marianne in wedlock. It wasn't a perfect solution, by any means, but it was a solution of sorts to a problem that Eve thought urgent, and to which she could see no other. That's what I understood, and that's why I wanted to be kind to her. Your mother's story might well be quite different, though."

"Or it might not," said Jocasta Symonds, cannily picking up the implication that Simon hadn't been able to help dangling. "Perhaps she was a prostitute, and Mr. Jefferson was one of her clients."

Simon had to make an effort to prevent himself congratulating her for her accurate guesswork. He already knew, though, that long distance conclusion-jumping ran in the family.

"I couldn't say," he replied. It was a lie, but he hoped it wasn't blatant.

The blonde woman gave the impression that she wanted to press him, but didn't dare, probably for complex reasons.

Instead, Jocasta Symonds turned back to Marianne. "You say that your daughter is also your twin? I didn't know that was possible. You think that I'm the result of a similar miracle birth?"

"I don't know," Marianne counted, effortlessly. "All I can say is that such things can and do happen, occasionally . . . and I've been told that it runs in the family. Megan Harwyn is my cousin, not so very distantly. So is Mr. Jefferson. Presumably, he knows that it runs in the family too. I'm surprised he didn't mention it to you."

Nice one, Simon thought, congratulating himself on having a sister capable of such subtle malice, although he really had no cause for any such congratulation—or, indeed, for any astonishment.

Jocasta Symonds, however, had other things on her mind than wondering why Douglas Jefferson hadn't mentioned that he was related to Megan—and hence, very probably, to her. Her thoughts were following a different track.

"And can you imagine abandoning a baby like that at birth, and never wanting to know what had become of her?" she asked Marianne.

Marianne laughed, bitterly. "I can imagine regretting later in life that I hadn't—no, disregard that. That's just flippancy, resulting from conventional mother/daughter frustration. Of course I don't regret it. But I wasn't in the same situation as Simon's mother. I had no need even to think about abandoning Zoe. If I'd been in the same situation as my mother, though, and had lost a child the way she did, I can't say how I might have felt if that child suddenly wanted to see me, when I was seventy years old. It would be complicated . . . and if I knew that she was like Zoe, a kind of second self, that would make it more complicated, and more terrifying. Maybe it's not my place to say anything about this, but if I had to guess, I'd imagine that you quite like what you see when you look in a mirror, that you quite like yourself, and perhaps that you even feel proud of being who and what you are. You might want to consider the possibility that your mother might not . . . as well as continuing to bear in mind the possibility that Megan Harwyn might not be your mother."

Jocasta Symonds seemed to accept that suggestion, and to give the possibility the consideration requested, even though she had to know by now that, as the cliché had it, that ship had sailed. Eventually, she said: "Obviously, I accept the possibility that Megan Harwyn might not want to see me, even if—perhaps especially if—she turns out to be my mother. I can understand, too, that in seeking to impose on you to help me, Mr. Cannick, I might be asking a great deal, but I hope you'll forgive me for persisting, since we're still talking about it, and you didn't let me go when you had the chance. If it turns out to be the case that your friend refuses to see me, I'll try not to take it too hard. It shouldn't be difficult. But I'd still like to try. I honestly don't know what to expect, or what I'm going to say to her, or what there might be to hope for as a result of whatever I do say, but I would like to see her, because everything you've said, on top of everything that Mr. Jefferson has said, has sharpened my curiosity extremely. I'd be very grateful to you, Mr. Cannick, if you can help me."

Simon sighed. "Since you put it like that," he said, "how could I possibly refuse? Please tell me, though, that you're not just following a script that Dougie Jefferson has provided."

Jocasta Symonds seemed surprised that such a thought could even have crossed Simon's mind. "No," she said. "This isn't a game, I assure you."

"I'm afraid that it might be," Simon said. "Not for you, or for me, certainly, but it might well be for Dougie. What he hopes to gain by it, I'm not sure, but he's surely not acting out of kindness. It might well be pure malice, and malevolence—but he has nothing against you, and if his unkindly action enables you to get something out of it that you think worthwhile, that's all to the good. If you get hurt instead . . . well, that's just one more thing Dougie will have to account for if he's the sort of person who decides to make a deathbed confession in the hope of absolution."

"Unlike Mother," observed Marianne. "But not for want of sins."

"Anyway," said Simon, to Jocasta, "whether or not it's a game, it's still a problem that will require a certain amount of strategic planning. How do you want me to go about it?"

"Might I make a suggestion?" said Marianne.

"Please do," said the blonde woman.

"Simon and I still have a little time in hand," Marianne said. "He needs to talk to my daughter about a separate matter before his saintly work for the day is done, but there should still be time before dinner, and if not, it seems to me that this is a more important matter, which ought to take precedence. So may I suggest that you and I, Mrs. Symonds, go back to the cottage where you're staying, while Simon goes to Sanderling Cottage to speak to Megan. Then, whatever the outcome of Simon's mission, he can come to the other cottage, in order to inform us of the result. Will that work?"

"It works for me," said Jocasta Symonds.

"Two questions," said Simon, swiftly. "Where is Douglas Jefferson at this moment?"

"So far as I know," said Jocasta, "he went back to a cottage that he owns in a place called Morpen. He said that he had things to do there, but that I should phone him on his mobile to let him know how things work out."

"At a guess," said Simon, "he'll be upstairs in the Mermaid with a pair of binoculars—but I might be wrong. Not that it matters—I'd rather he were doing that than trying to cozy up to Thomas Mallory, offering to sell him a barrowload of Medieval manuscripts, if he can only get his sticky fingers on them."

"And the other question?" the blonde woman asked, evidently not understanding a word of what Simon had just said.

"Have you introduced Douglas Jefferson to your son?"

"Anthony?" Jocasta was startled. "No. He has a place of his own, and a family of his own. He has nothing to do with this."

"You might find that he has. And you might want to warn your son that if he has encountered Dougie, or if he encounters him in future, he might want to be very careful of taking anything he says at face value."

Jocasta Symonds looked as if she might want to be very wary of taking anything that Simon said at face value too, but in the circumstances, she was not about to say so.

Simon took Marianne's hand, and said: "I'm sorry to dump this on you, Marianne, but thank you. You're an angel."

"I certainly never thought so," she said, "but it seems that it runs in the family, and I feel that I ought to try to live up to it."

They separated then, and while Jocasta and Marianne set off across country, Simon started back along the path, heading for what he suspected might be one of the most awkward conversations of his life, perhaps not even excluding the one he had had with something pretending to be Ceridwen, while he was temporarily dead.

VIII
In Sanderling Cottage

This time, when Simon rang the bell at Sanderling, the answer was considerably slower in arriving than it had been that morning.

"Come in," said Megan when she eventually opened the door. "We were just talking about you. I won't say talk of the devil and he shows his tail, though. Have you come to see Zoe?"

"I didn't know Zoe was here," said Simon. "Am I interrupting?"

"Of course you are. How can we continue dissecting your character in suitably clinical terms if you're here?"

"Is Krysten here too?"

"No, she's trying to get the baby to go to sleep in Raven. Zoe wanted to escape for a little while, and she didn't want to run the gauntlet that unlocking the gate to the tine would have necessitated, so she came here."

While speaking, she ushered Simon into her living room, where Zoe, sitting on the sofa, looked distinctly sheepish, and steeled herself visibly against a possible scolding.

"I'm sorry to interrupt you while you're busy singing my praises, Zoe," Simon said, "but I really need to talk to Megan very urgently, about a personal matter. I would like to talk to you and Krysten a little bit later, if there's time before we all have to be at the Abbey for dinner, but for now, can I ask you to go back to Raven?"

Zoe did not seem at all reluctant to postpone the expected remonstrations for a little longer, but she evidently felt a trifle resentful about being asked to go away while her uncle and her new best friend discussed matters that might have to do with the mystery of the Murdens. After a momentary struggle, apprehension regarding the fallout from her mermaid-filming exploit prevailed, and she left meekly.

"That sounds ominous," said Megan, when she had gone. "I thought you were out with Marianne, bonding. Has something happened?"

"Yes, it has," said Simon "Douglas Jefferson has just made the latest move in his weird game, and it seems to me to be a nasty one, although, as is his wont, he's pretending to be the very soul of kindness and generosity. At any rate, you're not going to like it—but I'd really be most obliged if you wouldn't kill the messenger."

Megan's lips tightened. "Do we need to sit down?" she asked.

"It might be advisable," said Simon, and waited for Megan to settle into an armchair before taking the place the Zoe had just vacated, on the sofa.

There was no point in beating around the bush, so Simon put his cards straight on the table.

"Jefferson has brought your daughter to St. Madoc," he said. "He sent her to intercept me on the path, telling her that I was the best person to act as an intermediary, who might be able to persuade you to see her if she asked me nicely. So she did."

Megan was sitting upright, slightly rigid, but showed no sign of astonishment or anger. Simon judged that she had known that this would be a possibility as soon as she heard that Douglas Jefferson was aware of the fact that she had had a child. After a few seconds, she said: "Where is she?"

"In Blackbird Cottage, with Marianne. But there's more. Dougie introduced himself to her by showing her an old photograph of you, posing as an old flame and asking if you might be related. Naturally, she didn't know, and he volunteered to make enquiries. He hasn't told her straight out that she's your daughter, just dangled the possibility like live bait. I've no idea why he's playing it this way—maybe for the convenience of his approach to her, but more likely out of malice, leaving it to you to provide all the explanations . . . and tacitly leaving you an opportunity to deny it, if you want to. You still have the option of looking at her photograph, expressing surprise, and telling her that it must be a coincidence, trotting out the old saw about everybody having a double."

"And will she believe that, if that's what I tell her?"

"Probably not, especially as Marianne and I might have blown that possibility out of the water by saying too much about such things running in the family—but she can't prove any different, barring a DNA test, and she might decide that it's in her interest to pretend to believe it, and accept it at face value, in order that the two of you can just shake hands and part as chance acquaintances."

"Do you think that's what Dougie wants? That he wants me to deny my daughter?"

"I think he probably wants to put you in a no-win situation and see how the screw turns. As you've never missed an opportunity to warn me, underneath his superficial bonhomie, he's malevolent and nasty-minded. And he couldn't resist the temptation to rope me into the scheme, perhaps in the hope that you'd shoot the messenger, but at the very least in order to thrust us into a situation embarrassing for both of us."

"And where's Dougie now?"

"According to Jocasta, in Morpen. More probably upstairs in the Mermaid, with his binoculars trained on your front door."

"Shit," she said expressively. After a pause, she said: "What's his end game? Or is it just simple malice, stirring for the sake of stirring?"

"I have no idea. I dare say that he'd be over the moon if you got thoroughly pissed off with me for even coming to you with the proposition, and never spoke to me again, but he can't really expect that to happen. On the other hand, he might be equally delighted if you were to come clean, and you and Jocasta were to hug and make up for all the lost years, and Jocasta were then to say to you: 'What's all this about an inheritance of which my darling Anthony might be entitled to a share?'"

"Has he said that to her?"

"Not in so many words, obviously—he's dangling that as teasing bait, just as he's dangling the likelihood that you're her long-lost mother. I gather that she's divorced, and although she made a point of saying that she's only gone back to work in order to fill in time now that the nest is empty, she's probably feeling the pinch in more ways than one. If you do kiss and make up, she might well want you to help

Anthony make a bid for a share of the loot. It wouldn't put any money directly into Dougie's pocket, but he'd probably be content to take it out of mine, all the more so as you'd virtually be forced to help remove it."

"The bastard," Megan opined.

"No, that's me," said Simon. "He's the legitimate son, if we are, in fact, more closely related than either of us would prefer to believe. Needless to say, I'm hoping that this visit doesn't have the effect of driving a wedge between us, but as I've told you before, I wouldn't have any objection to your grandson putting in a claim for a slice of the estate. He has a good case."

"He has no case," Megan retorted, dryly. "He has nothing to do with the Abbey or the Estate. As for driving a wedge between us, if I had to receive this news—and I've been nursing the possibility that I might have to for more than a fortnight—I'd far rather receive it from you than Dougie, except for the fact that I could have strangled him if he'd had the brass neck to confront me himself. I still might. I suppose you didn't even consider the possibility of just telling her to go away and never, ever to darken my doorstep?"

"Of course I considered it. I just couldn't bring myself to do it—quite apart from the fact that, if she's her mother's daughter, let alone her clone, she probably isn't the kind of person to take that kind of no for an answer. In any case, I couldn't imagine that Dougie would let the matter rest. All in all, it seemed better to play ball, at least for the opening gambit. This way, if I have to say no to her on your behalf, I can do my best to console her, and conserve all my moral purity. I hope you can understand and sympathize with my reasoning. But you still have the option of claiming that it's all a big coincidence. Even though a DNA test would prove otherwise, she might be ready and willing to accept it."

She reflected for a moment, shook her head, and sighed. "Are you really ready and willing to go back to her and simply say no, if that's what I ask you to do?"

"Of course I am, if that's what you want. But as I said, getting her to take no for an answer might not be easy—and although I've done my level best to stick a few knives into Jefferson's back while chatting to her, I think we can take it for granted that, if you do refuse to see her, it will leave her in his web, looking to him to tell her what do next. If, on the other hand, you do see her, and come clean about her being your daughter . . ."

"I didn't ask for your advice, Simon," Megan snapped. "Not killing the messenger is one thing, but letting him call the shots is something else. This is my concern, and only mine. So shut up and let me think."

Obediently, Simon shut up.

After a minute or so, Megan said: "Sorry; I overreacted. You know me. As I said, far better to get the news from you than from someone else, partly because you're the only person on earth whose advice I might condescend to seek. Dougie doesn't know, of course, what kind of retaliation I'm capable of handing out in response to his shabby little tricks, or he wouldn't have dared."

"It might not be a good idea to escalate the feud," said Simon. "The ideal revenge, in my view, would be to act as if he'd done you an enormous favor, for which you're supremely thankful, and then substitute your puppet-strings for his . . . but I can see that it might be hard for you, especially as playing the coincidence card might still be a viable option."

"From which you're trying hard to steer me away, in your transparent fashion. You not only think that I ought to admit that I'm her mother, but that I ought to turn on the waterworks, beg her forgiveness and plead for a second chance."

"I think it might be wise, as well as honest, for you to avoid telling her any lies, although you might want to use a softer pedal with the truth than you used in explaining it to me. You don't need her forgiveness, and you probably aren't entitled to it, but a little understanding wouldn't hurt, on both sides."

"I'll put that down to your being a saint rather than wanting to try some bizarre reverse psychology on me," she said. "But my first choice would be to get rid of her, one way or another, and so far as I can see, my problem is just a matter of figuring out how."

"It might be insoluble—now that she's in the picture, getting rid of her might not be an option. It's probably better to think in terms of how you can keep her in the picture harmlessly."

Megan shook her head, still resistant, but the grimness of her expression suggested that she could see the logic of the argument. "How much does she know about me?" she asked.

"Hardly anything, for certain—but Dougie has dropped hints, and although I tried to leave everything as vague as possible, she's no fool. She guessed, without any prompting, that you were a prostitute back in the day, and that Dougie was one of your clients." Simon steeled himself for a possible backlash to that admission while adding, precipitately: "Obviously, I didn't confirm it, any more than I confirmed the suspicion that you're her mother. Mr. Discretion, that's me. But as you've pointed out to me more than once, a 'no comment' can sometimes be more revealing than a simple yes."

Megan looked at him sharply. "Did Dougie tell her that I used to be on the game?" she asked.

"I don't think so. That's not the way he's playing it—but she's an intelligent woman, and she must be trying to read between the lines. She's trying hard to figure out what she's walked into, and she'll make rapid headway as soon as she has a few more pieces of the puzzle. She's her mother's clone, after all."

"You don't have to keep reminding me," Megan snapped, letting her irritation show again. "You've made your point." After a pause, she sighed. "One way or another, though," she went on, "she won't be in the dark for long. It's just a matter of figuring out the best way to let the light in, and how best to angle it. I suppose it's better if it comes from me than from Dougie, no matter how awkward it will be. I have to see her, don't I? And I can't just fob her off with the story that it's just a coincidence that we look alike. She's never going to believe, now, that I'm not her mother, and, as you keep vindictively pointing out, she's probably enough like me not to be prepared to let the matter lie. She's going to want to know, and there isn't any realistic alternative, now, to confessing at least some of it. The one thing we mustn't do is let Dougie keep any cards up his sleeve."

Simon took note of her use of the plural pronoun. "That's true," he said, "but that's not the only problem. The more awkward problem will be that of keeping hold of the cards you have up your own sleeve. Gauging what to tell her and what to keep quiet might be very tricky, once she starts probing."

"I have no intention of letting the kid become Dougie's spy in Sanderling, whatever happens," she retorted. "You, I assume, think that I ought to play mummy to the hilt and fawn all over her, for my sake as well as hers?"

"Why do you assume that?" Simon asked, warily.

"Don't play the idiot. Because suddenly finding out after nearly seventy years that you have not one family but two has given you all kinds of starry-eyed notions about the possibilities. You're fawning over Marianne and Zoe exactly as you were fawning over Ceridwen, and even bloody James, and you're actually fucking Felicia. If you think it's part of your mission in life to patch things up between Marianne and Zoe, you presumably feel the same about me and what's-her-name."

"Come on, Megan," Simon said, quietly. "You know perfectly well what her name is, just as you know to the day how old she is, and know how absurd it is to refer to her as 'the kid.' You didn't tell me her name, but I'm not such an idiot as to think that it was because you didn't know."

Megan shrugged. "Okay, me and Jocasta. The argument stands, though. That's what you think—unless you're going to prove me wrong?"

"Who's playing reverse psychology now? Yes, I think you should see her, and yes, I think you should treat her as kindly as possible, but not because I have any starry-eyed illusions about the two of you becoming the best of friends. You're Murdens, remember, and so am I. You'll probably hate her, and she'll probably hate you. But that doesn't mean that you shouldn't meet, and look one another in the face, like civilized people, and be scrupulously polite. It might be an effort, on both sides, but it seems to me that, in the circumstances, it's far better than any of the alternatives. Isn't it?"

"I'm not so sure. My present feeling is that I should let her in and then freeze her out, as soon as I've put her straight about her Uncle Dougie and his underhand maneuvers. If I can't get rid of her, then the problem becomes a matter of keeping her at a reasonable distance—for her sake, as well as mine. It would have been better if she'd never been pointed in my direction, but since she has been, and aimed with careful prejudice, the optimum solution is to keep her from getting too close. I'm right, aren't I?"

It was probably a rhetorical question, but Simon preferred to construe it as a serious inquiry. "Well, I'm biased by my own experience, obviously. My mother not only agreed to see me, half-expecting me to spit in her face, but refused to take her morphine, to make sure that she'd feel it if I did. She had all kinds of excuses in stock that she could have employed in order to refuse to see me, to freeze me out, or to maximize the distance between us, but she took the other option—and I don't think she regretted it."

"The cases," said Megan, flatly, "are not similar."

"Aren't they? I told Jocasta about mine, by the way, and although I appended a note, dutifully, to observe that her case must be quite different, they're not without a few parallels."

"You mother didn't have a choice about dumping you, and she wasn't a whore. Given what we learned this morning, in fact, she must have been a hapless victim of a predator even nastier than you previously assumed. I got rid of Jocasta purely and simply because I didn't want her. Am I supposed to tell her that? What good could it possibly do either of us to let her know? Sometimes, not knowing is the best option.

You know that—unless you're planning to let Zoe in on the family secret, about which she was pumping me again before you turned up and got me off the hook. Or do you think I should just have told her everything I know, in a spirit of scrupulous honesty?"

"Fair point," Simon conceded, "and I certainly think there might be grounds for fudging the issue of your lack of desire to keep her, in order to spare her feelings a little. It's not as if you don't have other excuses in stock. In any case, she's a mature woman in her forties, who might not dress as well as you do but isn't that far off, and she certainly gave Marianne the impression of someone who feels moderately self-satisfied when she looks in a mirror. She isn't a delicate flower who's going to curl up and die just at the thought that her mother might be a heartless bitch—your description, not mine."

"She might not feel quite so good when she looks at her face in a mirror once she's seen me," said Megan, quietly. "She might never be able to look at a mirror again without being reminded of me."

"Which might make her feel even better, at the thought that she'll probably age just as well. Even Dougie Jefferson, who hates you, remarked this morning that you probably still had the wherewithal to make a Dominican lawyer a trifle wistful about his vow of celibacy."

"You know that's not what I meant."

"She's already guessed what you were, Megan, and what you were to Dougie. She must also have deduced that you aren't any more. For her, at least, I don't see that any harm can come of this, if you handle her with kid gloves. For you, I can't judge, and I confess that there are aspects of your personality that I don't understand—but whether you like it or not, Dougie has put you in a corner, and the only question left to ask yourself is how much dignity you can conserve in reaction. For myself, I'd rather you didn't give him the satisfaction of any kind of victory—but there's no need for you to take my feelings into account."

"You do remember that I've already volunteered to shaft the bastard good and hard if he lifted a finger against you?"

"Yes, I do, but he hasn't—at least, not yet. And I've already reminded you that he's the only one of the three of us who isn't a bastard, and I've told you that I'd rather play a waiting game. What you do on your own account is your own business, but if you do, don't try to excuse it by pretending that you're doing it for me."

Megan looked at him sharply, as if deeply offended by the implication that she was the kind of person who might need to give herself false excuses, but she simply shook her head. "He was playing a waiting game himself, until this morning, but you've blown that yourself by letting him know that you know his little family secret. The gloves are off now. Whatever happens today, it won't end here. Dougie will go after her son, if he hasn't already, with seven million pounds as illusory bait. And I wouldn't be at all surprised if, while we're all having a cozy dinner at the Abbey, he doesn't drive back to St. Mary's Deanery in Carmarthen to make friends with Thomas Mallory O.P."

"Good luck to him," said Simon, soberly.

"What do you mean?"

"I mean that if he can persuade the Roman Church to make a bid for the Murden inheritance, on the grounds that Owain Myrddin should never have been gifted the Abbey in the first place, and he can make it stick in court, I'll be glad to see the back of it."

"You can't mean that!"

"If you knew how I feel at this moment in time,

. . . dark music, but sweet, caressant, in a tentacular fashion, elegiac, perhaps funereal, but only music in spilling into consciousness and instantaneous memory, in itself, beyond grasp, beyond understanding, beyond utility . . .

you wouldn't say that."

Simon did not betray the momentary invasion of his consciousness by the slightest flinch or quiver, although he was fairly certain that Megan would not have noticed if he had.

"Well, if that's the case," Megan said, harshly, "there are definitely aspects of *your* personality that I don't understand—and can't believe. What would Felicia say if you said that to her?"

"Fair point," Simon admitted, once again. "She'd be disappointed, and that would make me feel terrible. Perhaps you're right to avoid any hint of fellow feeling like the plague. Sensing that one has a responsibility to others can be distinctly inconvenient, sometimes."

"Neat," she said, dryly. "I'm beginning to see the brotherly resemblance now—no, that's too much. Forget that one. We're on the same side, after all, and I know perfectly well that you have my best interests at heart, even if you might be mistaken about what they are. But if you're harboring any illusions about meeting my daughter somehow doing me some good, giving me an opportunity to save my soul from the morass of sin in which it's been wallowing all my life, forget it."

"Since you're so insistent," Simon said, "I'll try—but I won't be able to help remembering what you were saying in the car not three hours ago about your life-story having run into a writer's block, and not having any magnetic north any more to which you can point the compass-needle of your hopes. I'm paraphrasing, obviously, but you know what I mean."

"I know what you mean," she retorted, this time letting her resentment show, "but it's garbage. Believe me, a reunion with the daughter I gave away—the clone I gave away—is not going to provide my story with any sort of ending. Or any sort of new beginning. It's not that kind of story. I'm not that kind of character—so don't try to squeeze me into the mold. I know you can't help it, because you're a writer and you think you're my friend, but . . . well, just don't okay?"

Simon frowned. After a moment, he said: "Does that mean that you *don't* think I'm your friend?"

It seemed for a moment or two that a there was a cutting retort on the tip of her tongue—perhaps more than one, leaving her spoiled for choice, but after a brief hesitation, she said: "Dear God, I suppose you might be. Sorry—never had one before . . . not a man, anyway. It'll take some getting used to. But it doesn't affect the fact that I'm still a heartless bitch, and if I have a clone . . ."

She left the sentence dangling.

"Is that what you're afraid of?" Simon couldn't resist the temptation to ask. "Are you worried that if you find out that she's not a heartless bitch, that she's a nice, loving person . . . maybe even a happy person . . . that you'd have to wonder whether you might have been nice, loving and happy too, if only things had worked out differently?"

"Friends can always fall out," she observed, sardonically. "Not as easily as lovers, obviously, but they still need to be careful. But let's not, if only because it would make that rat Dougie think he'd won the round. And you're right; if I don't want that to happen, I have to grin and bear this. Okay, Saint Simon, you win. I'll not only see her, but I'll smile with feigned delight and I'll keep my kid gloves on at all times. If the pressure builds up, I'll just ask myself: 'What would Simon do?' and look at you for inspiration. You'll be here, I assume? You're not going to cut and run? I might need you, if only to play referee."

"Absolutely not. It's not a scene for three actors, and I have kid gloves of my own to put on. I've done my bit. I just want to walk over to Blackbird now, tell Jocasta that you've agreed to see her, and invite her to walk over here and ring the doorbell, perhaps blowing a kiss at the upstairs windows of the Mermaid as she goes past, just in case there's anyone there. After a decent interval of four to six minutes, I'll walk back to Raven with Marianne, and hold a family conference there, at which I shall do my very best to earn the blessing promised to the peacemakers in the Sermon on the Mount."

Megan shook her head. "You'll have to remind me," she said. "I was too far away to hear."

"For they shall be called the children of God," Simon quoted.

"Says the atheist."

"It's a metaphor. I'd rather be one of the pure in heart, obviously, but that ship, as the hated cliché has it, has sailed. Sometimes, you just have to settle for the more realistic target."

Megan didn't ask to be reminded that it was the pure in heart who would supposedly get to see God, perhaps because she remembered that one, and perhaps because she didn't care. "Okay, Peacemaker," she said. "You can go play messenger. I'll fix my face, in the faint hope of passing as her older sister. I'll let you know how it turns out tonight, although, if I appear at the Abbey at seven o'clock with scratches all over my face, you'll know."

"Thanks," said Simon.

"I'm not doing it for you."

"I know—but thanks anyway."

He left it at that. As he stepped out of Sanderling he looked up at the upstairs windows of the Mermaid. It was impossible to tell, with the ruddy light of the impending sunset shining obliquely over the façade, whether anyone might be lurking behind the blinds, with or without a pair of binoculars, but Simon made no attempt to hide the gaze, although he stopped short of adding any sort of gesture. He walked past the pub, forced to walk in the middle of the street because the parked cars were still there.

He gave Jocasta the good news, and then watched her retrace his steps in the reverse direction.

"She seems like a decent sort," Marianne commented, eventually. They were still standing outside the door of Blackbird Cottage, which Jocasta had locked conscientiously. "Exactly the sort of woman, in fact, that my mother would have liked me to turn out to be, except for being divorced—but that even happens to the most respectable people nowadays. We didn't have time to swap life stories properly, but I suspect that she could tell Megan exactly what you told Mum, if she had a mind to: that her adoptive parents did such a good job that she has no reason to bear a grudge."

"Maybe she will," said Simon. "But I can't quite see Megan as a candidate for a chocolate-box happy ending—and more to the point, nor can she. I advised her to try a little tenderness, but she probably hasn't got enough soul for that. I'll settle for politeness and no claws."

"Of course you will," said Marianne, as they started walking. "Except that it's not about you, is it? It's just between the two of them, mother and daughter."

"If only," Simon said. "If it gets screwed up, we could all feel the fall-out, and we can be absolutely certain that Dougie will do everything he possibly can to screw it up, if only just for fun."

"But you don't think he's doing it just for fun?"

"No. He wants Anthony Symonds to contest James's will, and because Megan had no intention of setting that process in motion, he's doing it himself, posing as the great benefactor while actually playing the part of the great manipulator. It's a lost cause, though. He has too much imagination by half. He's addicted to deceit, to the point that he long ago lost sight of the fact that he's a victim of his own machinations. And whatever false implication he's drawn from a comparison of a couple of gene-maps, he's not my brother . . . at least, I certainly hope he's not."

"But you don't mind me being your sister?" Marianne asked, with an uncertainty that suggested that she wasn't simply fishing for a fully expected compliment.

"After what we've been through together in the last few hours," he countered, "it's not a matter of not minding, more like sheer delight. Twin souls, to the extent that age and sex permit."

She smiled, partly to show that she was taking it as a joke, but partly out of simple pleasure. Simon wondered whether there was anyone else in the world who could feel pleased by the suggestion that they might be his twin soul. He suspected that there was not.

By the time they passed Sanderling, Jocasta Symonds had already been inside for at least three minutes.

"I presume this means that you and your possible half-brother Mr. Jefferson are at daggers drawn from now on," observed Marianne curiously, as Simon opened the gate of Raven and stood aside to let his sister precede him.

"Certainly not," said Simon. "I have no intention of drawing a dagger, and if I know Dougie—as I'm beginning to—he's going to behave exactly as if bringing Jocasta to St. Madoc was an act of selfless kindness, not only toward her but toward Megan, inspired by the saintliest of intentions. I have every intention of maintaining the same pretence. If we both pretend hard enough, and long enough, we might actually end up being friends—which is a far better outcome than anyone getting stabbed in the back. It's not the worst thing in the world to have to deal with a man who routinely does everything with an unctuous smile on his face, always pretending that his motives and his heart are utterly pure, even if his chances of ever seeing God, are less than zero."

IX

In Raven Cottage

Simon felt oddly awkward simply opening the door of Raven Cottage and going in, even though it was his house and his home, full of his possessions—almost all of his possessions, everything solid that he amounted to in the world. But the fact was that he had surrendered it, temporarily, to Zoe, Krysten and Monique, and it had become their space, an alien space, in which he was now an invader. And, like any invader, he knew that, from the point of view of the temporary custodians of the house, he had become ominous and intimidating, a subject of anxiety. He had not meant to be—indeed, it was the very opposite of what he had wanted, when he had blithely invited the strangers to come into his home, to take it over and drive him out, because it had somehow seemed to be not merely a good idea but a necessary idea.

What on earth had he been thinking? Had he been think-ing? Had he even been on earth? And what was he thinking now, wherever his head was at, if it could properly be said to be anywhere at all, given that he seemed to be continually slipping through the cracks in his own consciousness, falling into confusion, if not madness, as his private reality was be-ing repeatedly and insistently punctured by dreams: dreams that were undoubtedly his and undoubtedly meaningful, but over whose content, meaning and intrusion he had no control.

What was he actually going to say to Zoe and Krysten? He had no idea. He hadn't had time to make a plan, and he had no confidence that he would be able to make it up as he went along, even though he was now sitting down in his own swivel-chair, long since wiped clean of the blood that Zoe had spilled all over it, next to his own desk, surrounded by his own books. He was on the familiar ground of his life, in his own personal space, but he was not in familiar company. Marianne, his half-sister, did not seem so very alien, espe-cially as they had just gone through an awkward situation together, while tacitly on the same side, as a team. But Zoe? Zoe he could hardly begin to fathom; her experience of life, her existential situation, was simply too far away from his for him to be able to grasp it, for anything of her inner life of thoughts and emotions and desires to be graspable. And Krysten? Krysten, at eighteen, inhabited another universe, mentally, socially and in terms of its physical apparatus.

And yet, he had to try. He had to try to establish some kind of meaningful communication, not merely with each of them, but with all of them, simultaneously. And if that really was impossible, as it seemed to be, now that he was actually facing the situation, what chance could he possibly have of establishing any kind of meaningful communication with the neider, with the mysterious aliens who seemed to have tuned in briefly to the portal beneath the Abbey, and with the dark mind that seemed to be playing puppet-master to all of them, perhaps blindly and stupidly,

. . . and musically, and magically, and madly, middly, muddly, merling and skirling and churling, stringing ideas together blindly and blandly and bluntly, without rime or raisin, for the rum and the rhythm, just words, worms and warmth, because that was all his mind had and all his mind was except for darkness, and although there were truths in darkness they were only little truths, grains of sand in the hourglass of eternity, trickling and trickling, hypocritically, historically and hysterically but only hiding time, true time, in all its dimensions, squashing it flat and stretching it out, like a root groping in the soil, going down and down into a bottomless well of will and whole, hoping and hopping and hipping while the world ends and ends again, and never really was . . .

but certainly wasn't God in any of the conceptions that feeble humans had spent history trying to attach to the term.

Shit, he thought desperately. *I'm losing it completely. But I have to hang on, and not just for my own sake . . . .*

He thought it best, therefore, to start with something safe, secure and bound to be true, and see what he could build on that, so he said: "This is all my fault."

They didn't even have sufficient politeness to look surprised, let alone to leap in and say: "No, of course it isn't." They knew that it really was all his fault.

He scanned their faces. Just as the cottage wasn't really big enough to contain all four of them with sufficient psychological comfort, the study was manifestly cramped and crowded. Normally, he only kept one other armchair in there as well as the swivel-chair in which he worked, in the tacit expectation, or hope, that he would normally only have one visitor at a time. Now, two more chairs had had to be brought in from the kitchen. Krysten had the armchair, because she was holding the baby. Marianne and Zoe had taken the less comfortable perches, that being their duty as more elderly mothers.

"When I first told Zoe about the attractions of St. Madoc," he went on, "citing the legendary, the supernatural and the mysterious, I was trying to make it sound more interesting, because I knew only too well that without that sort of embellishment, the place is as dull as ditchwater, to employ the hated cliché. I wanted to make it sound attractive, because I liked the idea of being visited. I liked the idea of there being somebody in the world who might like to visit me, because it's one of those ideas that does seem vaguely attractive, in the abstract, although, like most ideas that seem vaguely attractive in the abstract, the reality is far more complex and far more challenging—like the idea of family.

"You've all grown up with the idea and the reality of family, so you know what it's vaguely supposed to be like and what it's actually like—except for Monique, who still has that dubious pleasure waiting for her, along with the dubious pleasures of learning to talk and think, which also seem, retrospectively, like marvelous gifts, although, if we ever sit down and ask ourselves what we've actually got out of them, personally, I suspect that most people find it hard to be anything other than bitterly disappointed. I know I do.

"Forgive me for talking like this, by the way—I know it's not the way most people talk, or the way that most people think, and it's bound to seem bizarre, but I've been a writer all my life, and for a long time now I haven't been anything but a writer; it's taken over my life and my mind, and even begun to seep down into my unconscious mind, to infect my dreams and my instincts, so I can no longer escape from it. It's the way I work,

   . . . the way I walk, and wake, and wreck . . .

in every sense of the phrase.

"But to get back to the point, it's my fault that you thought the things I mentioned to you by way of local color were just frivolous ideas, just, as Zoe puts it, very deftly and succinctly, a bit of fun. And it's my fault that I simply assumed that creating that idea would have no consequences. When Marianne first mentioned to me, only a few hours ago, that Krysten was writing about them on her Facebook page, I went slightly pale, because I could see vaguely ominous possibilities in that, but I also felt vaguely pleased by the idea of a member of my family writing, and writing about the kind of thing that I write about. My limited imagination couldn't see any further than that, because I don't live in the world of modern social media; I've shut all of that out of my own little world, except for scary news items that I can't help but see on TV, precisely because I find it too scary, too challenging, and too difficult.

"But here's the thing, as they seem to say on TV nowadays: to me, in my secret life, it isn't just a bit of fun. It used to be. In my life, in my work, everything I used to be or do, it was just fun, just amusement, just playing with ideas. And I continued to think that, or at least to hope that, even when the ideas began to bite. Suddenly, though, it wasn't fun any more, and in a matter of weeks—days, even—it not only wasn't fun, but became deadly.

"I've been a fool. Even before you and I exchanged letters, Marianne, I'd been down into Myrddin's cave and I'd seen the indescribable thing that's down there, and even though I didn't have a clue what it might be, I'd felt its effects. I'd seen ghosts; I'd been dragged under water by a real morgen, and I'd been shifted into a weird parallel space underneath the seabed by a giant hydra that people have been mistaking for centuries for a sea serpent because it usually only sticks one tentacle out of the water at a time. Naively, I thought they were all trying to tell me something, but I'm now almost

. . . all or most, all or nothing, all for one and all fall down . . .

sure that they weren't. They were just trying to learn something from me, and because of the way their kind of communication works, they couldn't pry into my mind without the intrusion being manifest. Anyway, I'd done all that, and I was still somehow able to think—perhaps I was even more inclined to think than before—that it might be a good idea for me to make contact with a few other human beings, who, because they were family, might actually like to make contact with me.

"If the weirdness had gone no further, it would probably have been all right, but I hadn't reached the end—in fact, I hadn't even really started. By the time I was summoned to my mother's bedside, because she too thought that it might be nice to make contact with another family member, since she had messed up the contacts she already had so thoroughly that they were beyond redemption, I had not only been back down into the underworld again, and through some weird kind of portal in the first underworld to a further one, but I actually thought that I had died and had been brought back to life, not quite the same as I was before, but recognizable—which is to say, close enough that nobody, including me, would recognize me as an alien doppelganger,

. . . double ganger, double goer, double gurgle, glug, glug, glug . . .

or as a madman. Although, come to think of it, I've probably blown that imposture now, simply by telling you about it, which I didn't really intend to do, but don't seem to have been able to help.

"Anyway, to cut a very long story very short, the reason I don't want to attract attention to the mystery of the Murdens is because there really *is* a mystery, which the Murdens have been trying to solve and hide for at least four hundred years, having inherited it from forebears who had been trying to solve it for two thousand, without any conspicuous success. And the reason that it distresses me to see day trippers flocking to St. Madoc because the local mermaids have been advertised on YouTube, even in an item of blatantly fake news, is because I've been waiting for weeks now for a real morgen to come back from her niche beneath the seabed, in order to reopen communication with me, and if the next video clip posted on YouTube depicts the real thing . . . well, again as they seem to say on TV nowadays, and although I hate to use clichés, the shit will really hit the fan."

When he finished, there was a moment's silence, caused entirely by the fact that he had been going on for so long that nobody realized immediately that he had finished.

Simon wiped his brow, expecting to find it covered with beads of cold sweat, but it was dry. He had lost himself so completely in the suddenly convoluted interstices of his consciousness that he couldn't even tell whether or not he was panicking.

Then, more-or-less simultaneously Krysten said: "I've taken it down," Zoe said "Cool!"—showing her age, because even Simon knew that people didn't say "Cool" any more—and Marianne said: "Thanks."

Although he was tempted to ask Marianne what she was thanking him for, it was Krysten that Simon thought he ought to address first. "I'm sorry, Krysten," he said.

"It's okay," she said. "I should never have posted it. I didn't think. I was desperate."

"Don't be silly," said her grandmother. "Desperate about what?"

Simon raised his hand, pleadingly rather than commandingly, to request that she let him take the point.

"I understand," he said.

"Do you?" said Krysten and Marianne, simultaneously, skeptically, but perhaps also hopefully.

"Of course," he said. "I was a professional writer for years, before it lapsed into a mere obsession. I had to write, because it was my living, not just in the sense that it was my source of income, but because it was what I did. I've avoided Facebook like the plague, but I can still understand how people who begin to document their lives on it can easily develop a kind of compulsion, and I understand only too well how urgent the thought *What on earth am I going to write today?* becomes. I've never had children, but I think I can imagine how a life-changing event like giving birth might look like an infinite source of copy, as well as something worth recording, demanding to be recorded—and I can imagine, too, the literal desperation that builds up, with frightening rapidity, when you find that there's nothing left to say except what you've already said, and the terrible fear that what you're going to write instead will seem meager and flat by comparison. You were desperate for something to keep the narrative momentum of your chronicle going—desperate enough to turn to your mother for help, and fortunate enough to find her desperate enough to hold the phone for you while you did your party piece."

"I wasn't desperate," protested Zoe. "I know you and half the world think I'm mad for making a video of my teenage daughter in fancy dress without a bra, but as I told you this morning, it really isn't that big a deal."

"Yes it is!" Marianne intervened. "And if you can't see that . . ." She stopped because she was lost for words rather than because of Simon's repeated pleading gesture.

"You're right, of course, Zoe," he said. "Desperate isn't the right word. For Krysten, maybe—certainly as good as any—but for you, no. I don't know what to suggest instead, but whatever I came up with, you'd probably think, and rightly so, that I'm just a boring old fart who thinks he's a writer, who hasn't realized that writing went the way of the dinosaurs ages ago, and who thinks that he understands everybody and everything better than they do, even though it's impossible . . . and believe me, I know how impossible it is, even while I'm trying to do it, obsessively . . . and desperately."

"It was just a bit of fun," Zoe insisted. "And it *is* your fault. You're the one who insisted on trying to stitch us all together again, because it hurt your feelings to find us falling apart at the seams. You're the one who demanded, as the price of getting me out of the stupid jam I'd got myself into, that I not only gave up on the one thing that had been making life tolerable for years but that I tried to be nice to Mum and Krys, and I'm so stupidly honest that I actually tried to meet your terms. So yes, when Krys asked me to hold the camera, I actually thought, in so many words: *Uncle Simon would want me to do it.* And I actually thought that was a reason, because I owe your fucking girlfriend five thousand quid. So shoot me—but don't forget to turn the gun on yourself afterwards."

"Five thousand pounds!" interjected Marianne, shocked to the core by the magnitude of the figure, before Simon could protest that Felicia, not Megan, was his girlfriend.

"God, Mum!" added Krysten, for no particular reason, loudly enough to startle Monique, who had been quiet thus far, presumably watching and learning, after a fashion, and though she didn't yet know how.

"Oh, sorry," said Zoe, sarcastically, "I thought it was confession time, that we didn't have any secrets any more, that we were letting it all hang out, *as they seem to say on TV nowadays*, God, you make me sick, the lot of you—and you can see now, can't you, Uncle Simon, why it was a really bad idea to tell me to stop taking Mother's Little Helper. I'd prescribe a strong dose of skunk for the lot of you, if I didn't know that even that wouldn't shut you up. I need some stuff—but would you believe, Uncle Simon, that your friend Megan claims that she doesn't have a stash? I practically begged her, but she says she never uses. Pigs might fly! Who the hell has five thousand quid in cash stuffed in her knicker-drawer except a drug dealer? What woman of her age has so many fancy knickers in her drawer except a drug-dealer or a . . ."

She stopped suddenly, as she hesitated to voice the alternative she had in mind.

"She designs websites," Simon put in, mildly. "She works on her computer. She's very good at it. And she's not my girlfriend. Felicia's my girlfriend. And if you have any snide comments to make about that, please make them now rather than at dinner. In fact, if you have any more snide comments to make at all, please make them now rather than at dinner. You can say anything you like to me, anywhere and any time, but I really would prefer it if you didn't upset Felicia, who is surely the one person who'll be in the room tonight against whom you don't have any resentments."

Having gone off the deep end, Zoe now swam precipitately for shallower conversational water. "I'm sorry," she said. "It's just the lack of drugs talking. I don't have any reason to feel resentful about anyone—certainly not you, Simon, or Megan, or Mum, or Krys, or even the brat. I'm a self-made mess, and all my faults are all my own fault. Maybe I did a stupid thing, but it's not because I'm stupid, okay? I can play the understanding game too, and I can look you in the eye, feigning sincerity and sympathy, and say that I can understand how distressing it must have been for you suddenly to start suffering from schizophrenic delusions at your age—although, let's be honest, it's probably your age that's brought it on. I can understand, because I know exactly what it's like to imagine that you've died and been replaced by someone who can pass for you, even in the intimacy of your own skull, but is actually an alien doppelganger—and before anybody wonders, I do know what a doppelganger is, I can even spell it,

. . . spill it, spool it and spoil it . . .

and use it in a sentence. So yes, I understand too. And I'll be as nice as pie at dinner, in spite of the lack of drugs, because I really wouldn't want to upset Felicia, not because you might kill me if I did, or even because Mum assures me that she's an angel, and fragile, but simply because I wouldn't want her to think badly of me . . . or any worse of me than she does already, as she's doubtless heard the horror story about my sensational debut as a movie director."

"I was the director," Krysten put in. "You were just the cameraperson. I even designed and sewed the costume. And they were my tits, so it's really me that everybody should be mad at, not Mum. She was only trying to help. And I'm eighteen, and a mother myself, so I'm responsible for my own irresponsibility, if that makes sense. Not that the rest of you are going to look good when I post all this on Facebook tomorrow."

That precipitated a sudden silence. Simon guessed that there wasn't anyone present—certainly not himself—who didn't suspect, and worry, that she might be serious.

"Joke," she said, after a decent interval—but couldn't resist added: "Pretending to be a mermaid is one thing, but reporting all the crap you've just spouted could get me committed."

Simon wondered whether it might not be a good thing that Zoe was prepared to believe that what he had told then was simply a tangle of schizophrenic delusions, and that Krysten was seemingly prepared to follow her lead, but he knew that Marianne, at least, believed every word of it, and he strongly suspected that where Zoe was concerned it was, as she said, simply the lack of drugs talking, and that her fascination with the mystery of the Murdens, and with him, would permit her, all too easily, to dive head first into the communal madness and love the insanity. Given that, was there any chance that Krysten could be spared? Probably not.

But I shouldn't have done it, he thought, too late. *Will I ever learn?*

Simon met Marianne's eyes, tacitly looking for support, but not really expecting to find any. Perhaps she understood; at least, she took advantage of the embarrassed gap in the conversation to say: "How do you suppose Jocasta's getting on with Megan?"

"Better than we are, I hope," said Simon, in a tone that was far from optimistic.

"Well," Marianne added, "I wish I could say that at least we've cleared the air, but it wouldn't be true and somebody would be bound to accuse me of talking in clichés. Unfortunately, because of the delay that Jocasta caused, we seem to have run out of time,

. . . or time has run out on us, alpha metamorphosing into omega, the word into the word, the worm ouroboros with nowhere else to go but down its own throat . . .

if we're going to tidy ourselves up a bit before dinner, so I suggest that we suspend the family council for the time being, and that Simon and I head back to the Abbey. I haven't been taking minutes, but can I assume that Krysten the mermaid has now been retired to wherever the ghosts of cyberspace go, and that she won't be making any more appearances?"

"Yes," said Krysten, succinctly.

"And that in future, the mystery of the Murdens will not be subjected to any further analysis on Facebook?"

"Absolute silence," Krysten promised. "Except . . ." She paused

"Except what?" said Marianne—and still, apparently, had sufficient maternal authority over the various generations of her offspring to have a quashing effect on their determination to know more, at least for the moment. Even Zoe said nothing, although Simon thought that he could read a distinct determination in the glint in her eyes to see what was in Merlin's Cave for herself, one way or another.

"Nothing," Krysten replied, for both of them, leaving the *for now* unspoken, and the family meeting broke up.

I've lost control, Simon thought. *Of everything, especially myself. If I can't pull myself together, and get a more stable grip on reality, I'm not even going to make it to the story-swapping session with the Dominican, let alone Melusine's return. Can I even get through dinner, and another sleepless night?*

As he and Marianne emerged from the gate of Raven on to the street, Simon looked reflexively at the silent mass of Sanderling, dark gray in the almost-extinct twilight, and expressed the hope, silently but sincerely, that things really were going better behind its walls.

"You did all you could," said Marianne. It wasn't obvious whether she was referring to Megan and Jocasta, or to Zoe and Krysten.

"I suppose so," said Simon. "It wasn't exactly enough, though, was it?"

"I'd say that you're only human, if I didn't want to avoid talking in clichés, and wasn't pedantic enough to worry about whether I might be wrong."

Simon looked at her sharply. "You do believe me, then? You're not going to take refuge in the idea that I'm just a senile old twat suffering from schizophrenic delusions?"

"Oh, I believe you," she said. "I've believed you ever since we were in the car on the way to Zoe's, and you convinced me that you really had seen ghosts. Since then, it's just been a matter of passing from one stepping stone to the next. And I've read your books. It's a sort of requisite, isn't it: the willing suspension of disbelief?"

"The phrase trips off the tongue nicely," admitted Simon, "but achieving it isn't so easy. And the alternative is so attractive—if it really were schizophrenic delusion, I could just take medication."

"You could take the medication anyway. Zoe does—although it really doesn't seem to make things any better, no matter what she says. Nothing works for long, so far as I can see—certainly not true love or motherhood, whatever the ads say. Or are you going to contradict me on that."

"No," said Simon, as he fastened the padlock on the gate again, although he felt as he said it that it was a small but significant treason against Felicia.

"So you really did die, and aliens of some sort really did bring you back to life?"

"I honestly don't know. Illusion and reality were overlapping at the time, in a complex and almost seamless fashion, so I could very easily be wrong, but even if it was just my dream-self that died, it made a real difference to me. I'm not quite the man I was before."

"Why? Why did the supposed aliens kill you and then bring you back to life, I mean?"

"That's a very good question. They seemed to claim that it was an accidental death, and they were just doing me a favor."

"Seemed to claim?"

"That's the most infuriating thing about this whole business. They can only communicate via suggestion and hallucination. Their minds aren't like ours; they don't have words, and there's no way to be sure that the words I supply, in response to their stimulation, really reflect meanings intended on their part rather than just groping for a story on mine. The neider seems to have tried, over a long period of time, to adapt its offspring in such a way as to be capable of speaking—that, in essence, are what morgens are, and ghosts too—but giving them a voice and enabling them to talk sense are very different things. The neider seems to feel that it's running out of time, and it's beginning to panic, because this sort of crisis has happened before, probably many times over, and it hasn't worked out well. Solidity always survives, but the rest—the intricacies of mind that make identity and ambition, intellect and purpose, have all been reduced to the intangible clay of chaos. I'm talking nonsense, aren't I? Sorry, I really must try to get a grip. The aliens might be able to do better, of course, if they're real and not just part of a delusion created by the vitreous cocoons, and that might have something to do with the reason why they killed me, if they actually did. I suspect that they're trying to contrive some way of being able to talk more coherently to human beings—but that it's bringing them into conflict with the neider."

"Why?"

Why? Simon thought. *All that and just* why? *Did I only think that I said it aloud?*

"I wish I knew. I'm tempted to say *creative differences*, precisely because it's an easy cliché. But what might come of the difference of opinion, if that's what it is, I can't tell. In all probability, the neider can't either. As for any other interested parties . . . I suspect that neither I nor the neider has begun to understand what they might be, what they might want, and what to do about it, if there's anything that we can do."

They had almost reached the front door of the Abbey. Naturally, that was the moment that Marianne asked the crucial question: "Why *you?*"

"The cliché says *why anybody?*" Simon replied. "Perhaps because I was simply convenient. Perhaps because they were desperate. Or perhaps . . ." He paused as he opened the door and stepped aside to let Marianne through. Then before the pause had had a chance to become dramatic, he continued: "perhaps because I really do have the optimum combination of Murden genes, enough to qualify as Owain Myrddin reborn, and hence Myrddin Wyllt reborn and hence . . . who can tell how far back it goes, and to where? But it isn't fun, I can tell you. It's madness, but it isn't fun."

This time, as they reached the bottom of the stairs, it really was for dramatic effect that he paused. Marianne was not overawed. She was a reader, if not a writer. She knew how to work an imagination. "You think you're the Murden Messiah?" she suggested. "Or the Alien Antichrist? Or some other snappy alliterative title?"

"Definitely some other title," Simon said. "But the work's still in progress. You never really know how these things ought to begin, or what label to stick on them, until you get to the end. I'm still a way off."

"But not that far, if time's running out?"

"Probably not. I might be able to learn more from Father Mallory tomorrow, if I can get past the God jargon to the actual facts. Then again, Felicia's fever dreams might yet bear fruit. And Melusine might return at any moment . . . although I'd prefer it if she'd leave it for a while, at least until after dinner, and preferably until tomorrow night."

"So would I," she said. Then she placed her slender hand on his arm, in a sisterly fashion, and said: "You know where I am, if I can be of any help."

And he thought, although he couldn't be absolutely certain even about that, that he did know where she was, if not quite what, or who, or why.

They separated then and she stepped away in order to go to her room—Melusine's room as it had once been—while he went to Felicia's. Before she disappeared, though, she added: "I have a million more questions, though, and so will Zoe, when she's calmed down. You might have opened Pandora's Box over there in Raven Cottage."

"I did that weeks ago," Simon said, with a sigh, "and if hope is lurking at the bottom, I haven't found her yet."

X

Dinner at the Abbey

"I could take offense at that," said Felicia, lightly, as Simon closed the bedroom door, having obviously heard the last remark. She was alone, out of bed, and dressed. She was still wearing mourning for Ceridwen and James, so the theme was black and severe, but it was not without elegance, or velvet softness.

"So you should," Simon conceded. "Forgive me, please. You know that I'm not the world's best arithmetician when it comes to counting my blessings—but you know, too, that you're my best hope, and the best I've ever had."

And simply for having said it, and having spelled it out, he felt more stable, as if he had dropped anchor in reality again.

"I know flattery when I hear it," she said, "although I can't say I've had much practice—but I'm grateful that you take the trouble. I lost my natural entitlement long ago. Have you had a pleasant time with Marianne?"

"Yes, and surprisingly eventful. We were interrupted in our amiable chatter by Megan Harwyn's long-lost daughter, who had been told by Douglas Jefferson that I was the ideal person to introduce her to her mother. It turns out that his father might also be my father and that he doesn't like the idea of possibly having a bastard half-brother in the least— although, perhaps paradoxically, it's making him try even harder to maintain a sugary surface in his dealings with me."

Felicia had been adjusting her tippet, with one eye in the mirror, but she turned to face Simon as if she had been stung. "Ranald Jefferson was your father?" she said.

"Might have been," said Simon, not having quite brought to the surface of his consciousness that Felicia must have known Dougie Jefferson's father at one time. "So Megan says—on the basis of a DNA comparison, but it's not even a full sibling match, so there's a wide margin of uncertainty. It seems that I have an overdose of Murden genes, at any rate."

"Ranald Jefferson might be your father?" she repeated, rephrasing the remark to match his correction. The emphasis was obviously symptomatic of something beyond casual surprise.

"Yes, it's possible," Simon repeated, and waited.

"Your mother was only fourteen," Felicia said, colorlessly.

"That's right," Simon confirmed.

Felicia bit her lip. "I once slept with Ranald Jefferson," she said, faintly and colorlessly, a trifle hesitantly, and perhaps reluctantly. She didn't specify exactly when, but it didn't require an expert mathematician to figure out that if she had been a teenager at the time he must have been much the same age, and could not possibly have been significantly older. Even so . . .

"Dougie did call him an *old sinner*," Simon observed. "I suppose it sounded better to him than *pervert*."

"How does Douglas Jefferson know that you might be his half-brother? Did Megan tell him?"

"No, certainly not. She thinks he might have known for some time—perhaps long before I came to St. Madoc. Even if his father had nothing to do with my conception, he probably knew Eve, and might have found out that I existed, and told his son, in connection with their discussions of the possible future of the Murden Estate."

"So he might also have told him that . . . ?" She left it at that.

"Possibly. Does it matter whether or not Dougie knows that you once slept with his father?"

"It does to me. But he hasn't said anything to you about it, even though he presumably knows by now that you and I . . . ?"

"No, he hasn't. But he only found out this morning that I now know that he might be my half-brother, and I suspect that he'd much rather I didn't know that, so he wouldn't have made any comment about my relationship with you that might have carried that implication. If he does in future, I think I probably still have the advantage in any insult competition. Did James know?"

Felicia blushed slightly. "Yes."

"And that's part of the reason why he didn't like the Jeffersons?"

"Yes."

Simon thought it best to change the subject. "I tried to smooth things over with Zoe and Krysten," he said. "It worked, after a fashion, but only after a fashion. Things might be a little tense at dinner—and I've no idea what kind of mood Megan will be in after her heart-to-heart with her clone-daughter."

Felicia didn't take the cue. "I don't want you jumping to conclusions," she said. "Ranald didn't rape me and I wasn't under age. We were both very young, though. It was . . . well, in retrospect, it was nothing. An experiment. A fumble. Does it make a difference?"

"Not to me," Simon said. "We both have history. It's in the past."

"Everything's in the past," she said. "Unfortunately, the past is still in the present."

"So is the future," Simon countered, putting his arms around her and kissing her on the forehead, feeling the anchor bite more clearly, steadying his psyche against the riptide. "Let's concentrate on that, shall we?"

"It's equally terrifying, alas," she said. "Even dinner is seeming more intimidating by the minute."

"Don't worry about that. I did go over the top at Raven, though, with regard to the family secret. It was an embarrassing situation, of a sort I'd never encountered before, and my tongue ran away with me. Some sharp questions might come up, if Zoe forgets her promise to be on her best behavior. She seems to be suffering some withdrawal symptoms."

"Shouldn't she be over that by now, if she really has stopped?"

"I don't know. Physically, maybe. Psychologically, probably not. Wine might help calm her down. On the other hand . . ."

"I get the picture. Damn—we have to go down now, and I've wasted the time that you could have spent telling me what the Inquisitor wants."

"I can do that later. It's not urgent. Do you want to go down now?"

"You're not going to change? You could probably find something in James's wardrobe that wouldn't be too awkward a fit, and would look much better than that old leather jacket. Edith said that she told you that it wouldn't be formal, but there's informal and there's . . . whatever you are."

"I'm sorry if you're ashamed of me," Simon said, "but I really don't think it would be appropriate to start rooting through James's wardrobe. I can leave the jacket off if you prefer; it'll be warm enough in the dining room to get by with a pullover."

Felicia sighed. "If I weren't so old," she murmured, "I could take you in hand, and if I weren't so paranoid I could ask Megan to drive you to Cardigan or Carmarthen and supervise the equipment of a whole new wardrobe, but from what I see on TV, it really doesn't matter any more, and propriety doesn't even enter into it, given that we'll be five women and only one man. Let's go down, then."

"You don't have to," Simon pointed out. "You have all the necessary excuses to hand. I can make your apologies. Everyone will understand."

"Everyone would," Felicia agreed. "That's exactly what I'm afraid of. If it gets to be too much, I'll faint diplomatically, but let's hope that it doesn't come to that."

Simon escorted her downstairs, at a suitably stately pace, and into the drawing room. Marianne was there, but she was alone. It was after seven, but Simon had no idea whether people still interpreted "seven for seven-thirty" as meaning quarter past, or even whether they ever really had.

"Megan will have to ring at the gate," he observed. "Unless she meets up with Zoe and Krysten so that she can take advantage of Zoe's key."

In the event, that was what happened. When the bell at the front door rang, Simon found all three of them standing on the step, Krysten and Zoe holding the straps of a carry-cot in which the baby, while not actually asleep, was serenely quiet. It was seven-twenty. Zoe knew the way to the drawing-room, so Simon was able to let her and Krysten go on ahead while he fell into step with Megan a couple of paces behind.

"All right?" he enquired.

"Why wouldn't I be?" she said, before adding, swiftly: "No, that sounds wrong. I mean yes, I'm fine. She was sweet, I was sweet. Everything is sweet. Don't worry your pretty little head about it. But if you can wrestle the dagger away from Dougie when he eventually tries to stab you in the back, give me a call and I'll take care of the castration. You haven't got the balls for it, anyway."

Simon didn't even have the time to say "Ouch." Everyone was in the drawing room now, all smiling. Felicia was busy telling Krysten how pretty Monique was, while Marianne and Zoe looked on—approvingly, if superficial appearances could be trusted. Megan, who retained notions of protocol, went to pay her respects to Felicia, while Zoe sidestepped into Simon's path.

"I'm sorry I lost my rag back there," she said. "No hard feelings?"

"None," Simon assured her.

"I saw Megan's daughter when she left and went up the street. I nearly ran after her to say 'Me too,' but it didn't seem appropriate. I can be discreet, you see. Two glasses of wine and I'll be less antsy—no need to worry."

"I'm not worried," Simon assured her, dishonestly. "Everything is sweet."

Mercifully, Edith hadn't put Margaret into a maid's uniform, or donned one herself although Simon would have wagered quite confidently that they both had more than one stashed away in their wardrobes, probably left over from the days when Harold Macmillan was prime minister and people had allegedly never had it so good.

Felicia had been placed at the head of the table, with Simon to her right and Marianne to her left. Zoe was next to Simon and Megan opposite her, next to Marianne, with Krysten opposite Felicia at the far end of the table, which seemed a little too large for six to sit intimately. Rhodri had dug a high chair out of one of the outhouses, which must have predated Neville Chamberlain, let alone Macmillan, and stationed it beside Kyrsten's chair, but Monique was still in the carry-cot on the floor, quiet and diffident, not even whimpering, let alone screaming.

Simon observed that Zoe, as she had forewarned him, had downed two glasses of wine before the soup was replaced by the fish course, but she slowed down then, dutifully.

"Will you be dining like this every night when you're the lord of the manor?" Zoe asked Simon, without a hint of malice.

"Probably," he said. "It might not be easy to fill all the seats, though, let alone recruit a fuller staff. It won't be like the days when Seymour Murden entertained Shelley and Thomas Love Peacock. He never got Byron, though. Chased into exile by scandal, and never saw Morgan's Fork, poor chap."

Oddly enough, Zoe seemed genuinely impressed. "You mean that Shelley might have sat where I'm sitting? *The* Shelley?"

"Yes. Not that chair, and not the same table, but he was certainly in the room, possibly on the same spot. And he was probably the last person before you to see a mermaid in the water from Morgan's Cave. He didn't have his mobile phone with him, alas, so the occasion is undocumented, except for Peacock's disguised reference to it in *Nightmare Abbey*. Peacock took it for granted that Shelley was dreaming, though. It's a common problem."

Zoe thought over the implications of that statement, but all she said was: "I've never read any Shelley. I don't like poetry."

"That's a common problem too."

"And you believe that Shelley really saw a mermaid?"

"A morgen. Maybe."

"And you definitely weren't dreaming when you were dragged down into the sea?"

"Oh, I was definitely dreaming—but I was also wide awake. The two aren't incompatible, whatever you might think."

"Preaching to the converted, Uncle Simon—connoisseur of designer drugs, remember. Shelley was a user too, I understand?"

"Medicinal opium, certainly. Humphry Davy is rumored to have supplied several of the Romantics with nitrous oxide for recreational purposes, as well."

"And you approve of them. But not of me?"

"I don't disapprove of you; I just worry about the dangers of overuse. It ruined Coleridge. If you write something comparable to *Prometheus Unbound* or *Kubla Khan*, I'll promise to approve a hell of a lot more, but I'll still worry."

"I'll bear it in

. . . Shelley in Morgan's Cave, at dead of night, with only a sliver of moon and bright stars to pale the darkness, with spray in the air, his clothes already damp, and a morgen hauling herself out of the choppy water on to the rocky ledge, her lower body dolphin-like, but with a ragged fluke, and her upper-body bare-breasted, but more delicately than Krysten's, not lactating, and her face recognizably Melusine's, not fierce, as on the night when she had grabbed Simon from the bridge, but seductive, and the song, the incredible, irresistible song, and Shelley disappearing into the roiling surf, without the slightest reluctance . . .

mind. What's wrong?"

Simon realized that, for the first time, someone else had noticed his reflexive shudder, not during the almost-timeless instant of the vision but afterwards, when his consciousness had reached out like an osprey's claw to seize it from beneath the surface of memory and draw it out, clear and crystalline.

Marianne, sitting opposite Simon, had been conversing with Felicia, while Krysten reached down to tease Monique and Megan sat silently, eating quasi-mechanically. But Marianne looked at Simon now, and so did Megan, and they both echoed Zoe's: "What's wrong," enabling Simon to recognize that the symptoms of his slip must not have been limited to a brief shudder this time. And, indeed, he felt a chill running down his sternum, and his head began to spin as his carotid arteries constricted, and the blood-flow to his face and his brain was interrupted.

Felicia reached out and seized his left wrist, half-rising to her feet, saying: "Simon!"

But Simon pulled himself together, stiffened his body, held his head up, and willed his blood to resume its normal flow—which, after three or four seconds of dizziness, it did.

He forced a smile. "It's nothing," he said. "Just a twinge." He reached for his wine-glass, which was still almost full, and took a swig.

All conversation had lapsed, and all eyes were on him, although the anxiety was ebbing out of them.

Feeling that some further comment was necessary, whether it counted as an explanation or not, he said: "I've had a long day. Just a twinge, as I say. I'm fine now, honestly."

"Was that my fault?" Zoe asked.

"No, of course not," said Simon.

"More like mine," Megan was quick to put in. "First I was the bearer of bad news, then I put him through the wringer when he brought me some."

"And mine," Krysten put in. "If I hadn't posted that clip . . ."

"It's nobody's fault," said Simon. "Not even mine, for once. Just a random flicker. I'm fine. Look." He held his hand out, horizontally, palm, downwards, intending to demonstrate that it was as steady as a rock—except that it wasn't. He watched the tremor for a second or two, and then brought all the force of his will to bear. The tremor stopped.

"See," he said, as if that was what he had intended to do all along—but all eyes were still on him.

Evidently feeling that he was in need of deflective assistance, Megan remarked, addressing no one in particular: "I met my daughter today, for the first time in seventy years, after I abandoned her. And you know what? She was exactly like Simon—not to look at, obviously, because she's almost attractive, and dresses well, and looks-wise, she's me all over again, and doubtless a heartless bitch to boot, when she isn't pretending to be sweet . . . but she was polite, and calm, and she told me in so many words that she didn't bear me any grudge. It was all fake, of course, but at least she took the trouble to make the effort. Civilization squared. I expect that was Simon's doing, given that she talked to him first.

"If the situation had been reversed, I suspect that I'd have given her an almighty slap, but I didn't have the option, let alone the right. So I cried instead. Can you imagine that, Felicia? James's bastard daughter cried. The old village whore, as hard as nails, shed tears. And I wasn't faking. Who'd have believed it? Not me, if I hadn't felt it—and not Jocasta, either, at a guess. But I don't know why. As Simon says, it was just a twinge. He and I have a lot in common, it turns out. I've even screwed his monster of a father—but at least the old bastard paid me . . . and he brought his son to me, so that I could pretend to be sweet and show him the ropes, and he gave me a tip on top of the standard fee, for treating him gently. People still did things like that, in those days. How times have changed."

"How indeed," murmured Felicia.

"Sorry," said Megan. "That isn't exactly appropriate dinner table conversation, is it? I should have remembered that there are ladies present. Sorry, Felicia."

"No need to apologize to me, dear," said Felicia. "I've heard far worse. Edith wanted it to be just like old times . . . and now it is."

"No need to worry about us, either," Zoe put in. "We know what it's like, Mum and I . . . and we haven't always held back with the slaps, although we've certainly shed the tears, with no fakery, even though we could probably both give you a run for your money, heartless bitchwise. So, Uncle Simon, you don't think the twinges are anything to do with your being an alien doppelganger?"

The question deflected Simon's attention away from the worry that even though Marianne and Zoe might have been able to take Megan's scabrous confession in their stride, Krysten might have been shocked—although, admittedly, she was not showing any sign of it. "I don't know," he said, in reply to the inquisition, trying his utmost to sound sarcastic.

"How did you die exactly?" Zoe asked, finishing her fourth glass of wine—although she had already finished her slice of Edith's beef Wellington, while everybody else had hardly started, so the wine had a substantial cushion to slow its absorption.

"I was shot in the back," Simon said, equably, carefully naming no names, "while trying to protect a stray fawn from a raging lion with my bare hands."

"But you really weren't dreaming?" Unsurprisingly, she sounded exceedingly skeptical.

"Oh yes," he repeated, "I was definitely dreaming—but the bullet wasn't. Then, for a little while, I was a ghost, and I chatted to a fake Ceridwen—all the Ceridwens rolled into one—while her colleagues conferred with the neider regarding the best way to repair my *corpus delicti*. After that they put me back in my body, only slightly the worse for wear."

"What happened to the fawn?" asked Krysten, equably.

"I don't know. I assume that it disappeared, like the figment of a dream that it was. The alien must have modeled it on my image of a fawn. I never realized that seeing *Bambi* as a child had made such a deep impression on me."

"Why would they do that?" Krysten asked. "Make a fawn, that is. And a lion to pounce on it? It's a very odd thing for aliens to do, surely?"

"Very," Simon agreed. "But aliens are odd, by definition. It would be odd if they weren't."

"Did they put the thing in Merlin's Cave?"

"No."

"Who did, then? And again, why?"

"I'm not sure that anyone put it there deliberately. I suspect that it might have grown from a tiny seed, a very long time ago. There were once more of them, in various caves underneath the earth's surface, perhaps many more. Perhaps there still are. Most of those that have been discovered, though, by humans or other intelligences, have disappeared, or have at least been sealed up, perhaps deliberately buried. I'm not sure that walling them up can stop their activity entirely, but it might damp their influence down to imperceptible levels. I hope to discover more about that tomorrow, when I see Father Mallory again. He knows what happened to at least one of the others."

"But he thinks they're the Devil's work," Felicia put in. "Ceridwen said that people had thought that before—of ours, of us."

"Mother thought there was a family pact with the Devil," Marianne put in.

"There wasn't," Simon said. "And I'm not convinced that even Father Mallory thinks that they're the Devil's work, in the sense that the Devil manufactured them. I'm not sure exactly how he conceptualizes the Devil, but does seem to think that diabolical entities or forces of some sort occasionally make use of the vitreous cocoons as portals of some sort. Again, I hope to find out more tomorrow."

"Why has he turned up now?" said Felicia. "If the Catholic Church has known that the vitreous cocoons were here since Owen Murden's day, why are they only taking an interest now?"

"Because the few members of the Church who knew about it in 1531 made a report that was shelved, and then lost or forgotten, along with countless other church documents, and it wasn't until we arrived in an era of relentless inquisitiveness, backed up by sophisticated techniques of information recovery and collation, that anyone could take an interest. And it isn't the Church, as such, and not even one of its Orders, but just one maverick historian, who, if he makes any kind of report to his careful superiors, will probably see it filed away and forgotten. A bad video clip of a fake bare-breasted mermaid is capable of attracting a flicker of public attention nowadays, in an era of cheap sensation, but the vitreous cocoons aren't as photogenic, and would only become newsworthy if some kind of story could be attached to them."

"It wasn't that bad," said Krysten, taking offense in her capacity as director and star.

"But why would anyone think that they were the Devil's work in the first place?" Marianne asked. "What is it they actually do that frightens people?"

Simon laughed. "They facilitate dreams," he said. "That's probably enough, but some of those dreams are seriously nasty, or at least seriously disturbing. Then again, it isn't just humans who are interested in the cocoons. Perhaps the most interesting thing I learned from Mallory is that he knows about the neider, singular or plural. Whether he thinks the neider is diabolical or not, he certainly seems to think that it, or they, are responsible for the association in legend between the Devil and serpents, or dragons."

"But the neider is benign," Felicia supplied. "Our neider is, at any rate. Ceridwen was absolutely certain about that—she believed that it was responsible for her longevity, James's, Melusine's and mine."

"I'm inclined to agree," Simon said. "It's probably much more limited in what it can do, and where, than I initially supposed, even though it can work certain kinds of what seems to us to be magic, but it could surely do a lot of harm very easily if it wanted to. In fact, it seems to be careful to avoid doing harm. It's not inconceivable that it's playing a subtly deceptive game, but I'm content to assume that it's benign, at least until I have evidence to the contrary."

"So," said Megan, "if, or when, Melusine comes back, if she wants to drag you down to the seabed again, you'll go gladly?"

"Yes," said Simon. "Obviously, I'd rather she came back able to talk—and walk, for that matter—but that might be too much to hope for. I'll settle for another session of collaborative dreaming with the neider, if that's all that's offered, hopeful that we might both get a bit more out of it than we contrived to do last time. Last time, the session was hastily improvised; this time, the neider has had time to prepare. And for what it's worth, I don't think that any of you have any need to worry about that particular possibility. It's me the neider will want, not just anybody."

"Just as it wanted Shelley?" Zoe asked. "Because you're a writer?"

"No," said Simon. "Because it knows me."

"Or did, before you were replaced by an alien doppelganger," suggested Zoe.

"It knows me too," murmured Megan. Simon suspected that she meant in a quasi-Biblical sense, although she was exaggerating, if so.

"Not the way it knows me," Simon said. "It was present during whatever was done to me down in the darkness, as a participant. Perhaps it wasn't a literal resurrection, but something certainly happened, and the neider was there, wrapped around my neck like Felicia's tippet, and inside my head. Believe me, it knows me better than any human being alive, and perhaps better than it has ever known anyone in the past."

"Or perhaps not," Felicia observed. "There has been more extensive collaboration in the past. We don't know how well the neider knew Owen Murden, Myrddin Wyllt, or St. Madoc himself."

"But we know that they weren't mentally equipped to understand the neider. Maybe I'm not, either, and nor is any human . . . but circumstances have thrust me into a position where I'm the best bet. The casting director might be an idiot, but that's the way it is . . . and surely will be, if the promise of Melusine's return is kept. But we also have to bear in mind that the neider's plan, at least, is long-term. If it takes me, it will surely send me back, and it will want our association to go on for a long time. The figure of another hundred years has been mentioned, and we know that Ceridwen lived for at least that long, even if she wasn't actually born in 1789. So long as the neider is calling the shots, everything might be all right."

"And if it's not?" asked Zoe.

"Who can tell?"

"At a guess," Megan ventured, "bad dreams all round. Contagious madness, perhaps local, perhaps universal—but nothing that hasn't happened before, perhaps a hundred times over, and isn't happening as we speak. Who, around this table, can put her hand on her heart and say that they're not a victim already?"

"Medication is available," Zoe put in. "More and better every day."

"So is rationality," Simon said. "I wish I could say that it works better, but the evidence is thin. Father Mallory has faith in faith, and also in the legacy of the Sermon on the Mount. He's probably a better man than I am, so who am I to challenge his judgment?"

"One has to admire the saintly modesty," said Megan, "hypocritical as one suspects it to be, and I'm just an old whore, but for what it's worth, my money's on you."

"And mine," said Felicia. She looked at Marianne.

"Do you actually need me to say it?" she said. She didn't look at Zoe or Krysten, who were therefore free not to make any declaration, and didn't—but Megan couldn't resist adding: "Unanimous, then, or as near as makes no difference. But you have to come back and supply the ending—or the beginning."

"I'll do my best," said Simon, setting down his dessert spoon, and looking round for Edith, who was standing quietly behind Felicia. "My compliments to the cook," he said. "That was first-rate."

Felicia turned round too. "Just like old times," she said. "James would have been very proud."

The old lady inclined her head, perhaps to hide a tear.

XI

Dreams of Rebirth and Bardic Music

At ten o'clock, Megan, Zoe and Krysten took the sleeping Monique back to Raven Cottage, and at half past ten, Marianne retired to bed, defeated in her attempts to lend Edith and Margaret a hand with the washing-up. Felicia and

Simon retired immediately afterwards, both exhausted but neither sufficiently relaxed to go to sleep immediately.

"Well," said Felicia, "everything's in the open now, at least within the family. We don't seem to have any more secrets from one another, unless I lost track of a few. Was that wise, do you think?"

"Can you imagine what the last three hours would have been like if we'd spent it avoiding issues that were on everyone's mind?"

"A trifle strained—but that might have been a small price to pay for keeping certain matters safely bottled up. I know it's not the fashion nowadays, according to TV, but I was born in a different era, when bottling everything up was *de rigueur*, and I can't help thinking that there are things to be said for it. I'm not sure that Megan Harwyn bragging about her shady past is a good show to put on for young Krysten, although Zoe seems to be a lost cause."

"What Megan said was hardly an advertisement for prostitution or child abandonment, and they've all had examples of both. I don't believe that Zoe's a lost cause—she's too intelligent and articulate—and Krysten could still make a success of life, with Zoe's support. I wouldn't bet on it, but the possibility is there, so I'm not going to write it off either. Whether I can do anything to help, except stay away from them, I don't know, but I haven't given up hope yet of being something other than a contagious disaster area, especially as you seem to have made a complete recovery."

"Do you think so? I'm not so sure. I'll see when I've tried to sleep. If the fever dreams come back . . ."

"Do you want me to leave you alone? I could sleep in James's old room?"

Felicia looked at him, with an injured expression. "Is that what you want?" she asked. "You're afraid that I might infect you?"

"Absolutely not," said Simon. "Quite the reverse, in fact. I worry that I'm the one who has been infecting you. Trying to share our dreams seemed like a good idea at first, even though the first attempt was direly depressing, and we don't seem to have made any great progress since—although it's been immensely valuable to me not to be alone, simply to have someone to hold."

"Someone," she echoed. "Anyone?"

"No," said Simon, "Not anyone. By no means just anyone. You know me better than that. You read me better than that. You know that it has to be you."

"I know that it hasn't. You're right—I read you far better than you read yourself. I was just any port in a storm—not that I'm not grateful for it. I don't think I could have made it without you. I needed you desperately, and I know that you knew that. I know that you responded to that, but I also know that you would have responded to someone else's need just as easily, just as wholeheartedly. You needed to be needed, and the reason you've needed me so much is that I needed you more than anyone else ever has . . . or hopefully, ever will. But your problem . . . actually, no, it's just my problem, not yours . . . is that you really are something of a saint, and if someone else's need for you was as great as mine . . . well, you wouldn't be able to help trying to accommodate both of us. And I don't think I could stand that. I'm too selfish."

"I don't think you realize how fortunate I am to have found someone who needs me at all, let alone as much as you do," said Simon. "I've been a spare wheel all my life; even my wife didn't need me, in preference to someone else—she just thought that I was sufficiently malleable to be molded into what she needed, and was stubborn enough to persist in that quest for longer than was reasonable. No one, in my entire life, has ever needed me, specifically, until you did, and I can't imagine circumstances in which anyone ever could. Which makes me very fortunate, because I don't think many people ever achieve that. To achieve it at my age, when I have absolutely nothing to offer in a conventional relationship, is a miracle."

"Don't be ridiculous, Simon. For one thing, you can still get it up, even for someone my age. For another, you're a writer, and not just any writer, but a thinking writer. I don't say that you're a great stylist, or a great philosopher, but you make the effort, and that's ninety per cent of the battle. And for a third, you're about to inherit seven million pounds, an Abbey, a private island and a mystery. You're the best catch in West Wales, bar none. If Melusine hadn't gone missing when she did, she'd have snapped you up, virgin or not, and I can't for the life of me imagine why Megan Harwyn doesn't want to, even if thirty-odd years of active prostitution has put her off the idea of ever having sex again. That's a mere matter of appetite, which could flip in a trice."

"Actually, I don't think it is a matter of appetite. It goes much deeper than that. Megan can get everything she needs from me without my laying a finger on her, and if I did try to lay a finger to her, I think I'd drop so far in her estimation — and for that matter, in mine — that I doubt that we'd ever speak to one another again."

"And Marianne?"

"She's my sister."

"Half-sister. And among the Murdens, if Megan's gene-alogies can be trusted, incest is practically a tradition."

"Well, it isn't among the Cannicks or the Richardsons, and I haven't seen the slightest sign of lust on her part for any-one, let alone me. I don't know what it was that put her off, as she seems to have been quite fond of her husband while the marriage lasted, but something has, and if her appetite were to flip, I'm absolutely certain that it wouldn't flip in my direction."

"Zoe?"

"That's even more absurd. I'm seventy years old, and she's thirty-eight — thirty-eight going on sixteen, as Megan puts it — and I don't have the slightest inclination in her direction. Why are you doing this? You know perfectly well that we're together, and that nothing is going to prize us apart."

"Says the man who wants to go and sleep in James's old room."

"Says the man who asked politely if you wanted him to, because he's afraid that his proximity is making you ill, but who would absolutely hate having to do it."

"Well, in that case, shut up, get undressed, come to bed, hold me, and for Heaven's sake try to think pleasant thoughts. Tonight, of all nights, you ought to be able to sleep, but if you can't, just shut up and let your mind drift, the way you did the first night I seduced you."

As she spoke, she finished undressing, but before she reached the end, before removing the last of her undergarments, she switched off the light and plunged the room into darkness, hiding the final removals that would leave her naked. Then he heard the slight rustle of the duvet as she slipped into bed.

He realized that he was almost naked himself, having obeyed her injunction automatically, unconsciously. He knew that they weren't going to have sex, in the sense of penetration, because, in spite of her complimenting him about his ability to get it up, at the present moment, he was in no fit condition. But he knew that it didn't matter, because what Felicia wanted, and needed, for the moment, was a softer, subtler kind of friction, more dream than brute physiology, and he knew that that was what he needed too, tonight of all nights. But they did need to be naked, unlike that first night, when she had, as she had asserted quite accurately, seduced him, because his train of thought then had been awkward, and inhibited, and although his thinking had been honest, in its way, it had only related to a part of him, of his life, and the most superficial part, not even delving into the more secret sectors of his adoptive history, let alone the deeper, more mysterious tentacles of the self, of the vasty deep of the unconscious . . .

Having joined Felicia under the duvet, he did exactly as she had asked, and held her, and tried to think pleasant thoughts, for Heaven's sake . . . although that wasn't easy, because it had never been easy, because he didn't have that degree of control over the mood of his thoughts, especially when he was trying, simultaneously and confusedly, to let his mind drift, to go with the gentle tide of time, over the surface of happenstance, stirred by the eddies of memory and the wavelets of vocabulary, under the lunar drag of dream . . .

And Felicia also held him, even more tightly than usual, even more insistently than she had the night after the one he had spent with the neider, and although there had always been a measure of desperation in her clinging, it seemed more intense now, almost as if she were suddenly afraid . . . again . . . of dying, or perhaps of being reborn . . . again . . . as if two frail arms and two slender legs, considerably shorter and less robust than his, were not enough to hold on to him, as if she would have liked to have—as if she needed—tentacles like a hydra, in order to enfold him completely, and engulf him, and smother him, while still feeding him oxygen to keep his blood red and the flame of life burning, but encompassing him nonetheless, swallowing his dreams as well as his flesh . . . primarily and essentially, in fact, his dreams rather than his flesh, because they were the more important aspect of him, of his conscious self and, quintessentially, his unconscious self . . .

She was still speaking to him, although she wasn't using her larynx, her tongue or her lips, and even though, he knew, or felt, or dreamed, that he was supplying the words himself, the way one had to do when one read someone, when one sensed and translated someone, when one grasped them properly, instead of just with clumsy fingers, and one made a mockery of the lovers' cliché that "we don't need words," because like all popular unwisdom, it missed the point completely, because what lovers actually didn't need, pedantically speaking, was *speech*, but they still needed words, because the WORD was not merely the beginning but, far more importantly, the end, and a world without words was a world without love, because love, however inarticulate it seemed and however difficult it was to voice, let alone to describe and to define, was not only a word itself but something that

174

only consisted of other words, of poetry, of further layers of symbolism, metaphor and meaning, and so *ad infinitum* . . .

And what Felicity was still saying, while she had him in her tentacular grasp, without speech, was:

"Don't worry about being depressed, or anxious, if you can't sustain the pleasant thoughts. With that kind of loneliness, that kind of hell, I can cope—and how. And don't worry, too, that you can't actually bring yourself to say that you love me, because I'm well aware of that measure of uncertainty, and I know that if you did say it, it would become a lie by virtue of being spoken—a white lie, a well-meaning lie, even a lie that wanted to be true, but still a lie, because it always is, because nobody ever really means it, because nobody ever can. Believe me, I know. And that's not just me speaking, or Ceridwen, or all the other people who are trying to be reborn in me, in my fits of fever, and all the things that aren't even people, because the chain of rebirth goes way beyond poor humankind, let alone poor fragmentary Felicia, and it isn't truly linear, because time isn't truly linear, and it isn't what keeps everything from happening at once, because it keeps everything, and everything does happen at once, if you have the tentacles to grasp it . . . so it doesn't matter that we can't love one another, because we want to love one another, and that's the important thing.

"It would be so much simpler if I were just me, isolated in my own consciousness, or even just mother, genetically identical to me, whose rebirth I am, physically . . . whose alien doppelganger I am, recognizably the same, but different . . . but it really isn't that simple. It would be simpler, too, if I were simply heir to Ceridwen, to all the Ceridwens, who have been lost in limbo since the storm, striving for an opportunity to be reborn in a new consciousness, or even as a ghost . . . but it isn't that simple. You have to remember that the hydra is plural as well as singular, that it might seem monolithic and autocratic, but when you look closer, it's anything but, it's fragmentary and disorganized, and it's secretive . . . even the poor individual walled-in consciousnesses that we are, that we strive and hope and fight desperately to be and to anchor and maintain, don't know what we're doing most of the time, and even when our right hands do, the cost of that knowledge, of that attention, of that focus, is that the left hand is going its own way, doing what comes naturally . . . because the mind, even as we imagine it, let alone as it really is, is a mess.

"As for how it is, well, it's a hydra, whose thousand right tentacles don't know what its left tentacles are doing, tentacles of which it's absurd, in any case to try to think in pairs, in terms of left and right, back and forth, up and down, when we know, even though we can't see, that the world has far more spatial dimensions than that, without even beginning to figure in the multiple dimensions of time, of which our poor conceptions can only handle one, and not even a line that extends in both directions, but one that only has a forwards and not a backwards, because even though the human mind, like God, could turn it back, it could only do so by destroying creation, by scratching out the self and starting again, and again, and again . . .

"And if you did that, you'd never get anywhere. You'd never be anything.

"Except that you can reply to that, because, after all, you're a writer, and you understand how these things work, and, perhaps as importantly, how they can work differently. You're familiar with the orgastic theory of plotting, the kind of story that builds up dramatic tension with more-or-less careful foreplay, and eventually reaches a climax, a metaphorical explosion that is really just a ritual repetition, symbolized in marriage or some other kind of narrative closure, and then says THE END because everything thereafter can only be a let-down, a *petit mort*, a post-coital *triste*. Because you're a thinking writer, no genius, not Shakespeare or Shelley, but at least a person who makes an effort, who is prepared to try, even in the unheeded darkness, to see what can be done, you realize that a greater intimacy is possible, a greater love, which might seem less instantly satisfactory because it

176

doesn't necessarily lead to the ritual climax, but which, in the long run, has the possibility of leaving a lasting impression, a love that isn't just a wordgame-playing sequence that goes lust-lost-lose-love, or *vice versa*.

"But it isn't just because you're a writer, is it, that you have possibilities of rebirth beyond the commonplace? And it's arrogance to think that that's all it takes. Is it even the better share to be the inheritor of Shelley and Shakespeare and Myrddin Wyllt, even if the bards are the truer legislators of the world than the unworldly legislators? You don't even have secure custody of the word, let alone the world, you're not the beginning and you're not the end, and even if you're the teller, you're not the tale. At the end of the day, you're just a self-delusion, not so much a dreamer as a dream . . ."

A schizophrenic delusion, Zoe had said, speaking as an explorer of technologically-assisted alternative states of consciousness, thirty-eight going on sixteen, who knew what a doppelganger was, could spell it—albeit without the umlaut, American style—and could use it in a sentence. Preaching to the converted, in her own words, but converted into what? And what did she mean by schizophrenia anyway, given that simply being able to put it in a sentence wasn't even the first step to an understanding? Did she mean anything by it but a stupid colloquial substitution for "split personality," for a dolphin brain that was half-asleep, or a right tentacle that had no idea what the left tentacle was doing, except that it was writhing round the twist, going gaga.

Once, Simon remembered, he had wondered whether he might be schizophrenic. He had read a book—hadn't he always?—about different modes of creativity, which, according to the author—a psychoanalyst—corresponded to, or at the very least were analogous too, different modes of mental abnormality, and the author in question had described "schizoid creativity" in terms of a tendency to create, maintain and develop imaginary universes, sometimes reconfiguring the real one, like Newton or Einstein, but more often building wholly imaginary ones, like Shakespeare, Spenser or Shelley.

And he had thought—as everybody is rumored by cliché to do, when they read quasi-medical textbooks—"I've got that."

It wasn't the first time he had thought that, or the last. He had read a lot of things, in his time, had tried a lot of explanations for himself on for size, some of which had looked good for one explosive moment and then had faded away into *triste*, had failed to make the Schopenhauerian transition from will to idea. It hadn't even been the only time that he had imagined himself to be schizophrenic, given that the word schizophrenia lent itself to so many interpretations. He had read R. D, Laing as well as Anthony Storr, perhaps even beforehand, and had been quite taken with the idea of the schizophrenic journey, the psychological ability to leave the real world behind, to switch from clock time to cosmic time, to launch oneself forth, inwardly, into a quest in possibility, an exploration of the wilderness of if . . .

But how many people remembered R. D. Laing nowadays? Briefly fashionable, he had been almost forgotten. And Simon's brief flirtation with the idea that science fiction, as a genre, with its escape from the mundane world, its substitutions of cosmic time for the leaden present, its explorations of the potentially infinite possibilities of the galactic empire, had been an inherently, gorgeously, grandiosely schizophrenic journey, of which he was one tiny, modest—but not *that* modest—particle had gone the way of all his other flirtations, romantic, Romantic or intellectual . . .

No, he was not schizophrenic, in any of the ways that Zoe might have meant it. Deluded, quite possibly, but deluded while not only awake but sane, mad while rational, a doppelganger but himself, Myrddin Wyllt reborn and born again . . . already reborn a billion times, and yet to be born a billion times more, whether he had literal offspring or not, by means of anomalous diploid sperms or the other kind, the kind that permitted chromosomal crossing-over and recombination, genetic exchange and variation, evolution and progress in the soma, the solid component of the self, while in the spirit, the soul, the dark mind, the ghost in the machine . . .

Except, of course, that it wasn't that simple . . .

It never was. There were always quibbles, always catches, always pedantic objections. Other people, Simon knew, didn't like that. They were resentful of quibbles and snags, hated contradictions, however tentative, and thought *pedant* was a dirty word, an insult, and a slur. Men like Thomas Mallory were rare, who could describe the intellectual world of the Church as a massive, chaotic hydra, enormously hospitable to misunderstanding, forgetfulness and secrecy, and do it lovingly, declare it fascinating, and feel at home therein, even if it did involve keeping imaginative company with God and the Devil, those two faces of the same conceptual coin, one smiling and one scowling . . . making it all the more difficult to tell which was which. Heads or tales?

Simon knew, though, that you have to quibble, that a pedant is someone who not only cares about whether what he is saying is true or not, but insists that others ought to care too, and he knew that in order to care like that, in order to love, if love is to be something more than a white lie, or a futile effort, you have to look for the catches, the contradictions, the things that don't make sense. Because, if you're going to make sense of things, you first have to realize that, at present, they don't. You have to see what's wrong before you can even think of correcting it, and you have to know exactly how and why it's wrong, if you're to stand a chance of recreating it, or turning back the clock and starting it again, from the right time, in all its dimensions, with the right time fully aware of what the left time is doing, and marching in step, flowing in harmony, crwth and not crude . . .

Because, after all, it's lousy theodicy—*crack! bang! boom!*—to say that the reason that evil exists in the world is because, if God could turn time backwards, he wouldn't, because he'd somehow be threatening the notion of creation. Because, if you were pedantic—genuinely pedantic—you'd turn the argument upside-down, and you'd say: but that's what the creative process really is; it isn't a matter of telling a lie and simply letting it run and run, and get bigger and bigger, and more and more complicated by virtue of secondary elaboration; the very essence of true creativity consists of doing exactly what the hypothetical priest says that God wouldn't do; it consists of unmaking mistakes, of seeing that things are wrong and putting them right. That's what an authentic creator, a genuinely good God, or storyteller, does. Never settle for the first draft, because it isn't until you get to the end of that initial creative process that you can see, practically and philosophically, how it ought to have begun . . .

And while you're at it, pedant, stop thinking of it, like some simple-minded moron, as "turning the clock back," as if time really were both linear and directional, when you know perfectly well, if you're any kind of philosopher or story-teller at all, that that time isn't really like that, and that any mind capable of thinking, of constructive self-delusion, can suspend that kind of time and set forth into cosmic time, without even having to go mad in order to achieve it, and preferably without, because, let's face it, going mad, like overdosing on medication, can really screw up your head . . .

Get a grip.

Why? Forget the grip, just let it drift, go with the flow, ride with the tide, dream with the stream. . . .

No, *get a grip,* because at some stage, you're going to have to wake up again, because you can't live here forever, in dream limbo, hugging your centenarian lover. You have to get a grip because, at some stage, you're going to have to let go. This is good, this is necessary, this is—let's be honest about it—love, but it's only a temporary relief from reality. And being awake is no excuse. It's good that you're awake, because it means that you'll remember the dream, that you'll retain the memory of all this and be able to reintegrate it all into the continuous remaking of your conscious self, but this is rest as well as recreation, and the essence of rest, of relief, of recovery, is that at some stage you have to wake up completely, get dressed again and go out into the world again, in order to act. And even though acting is ninety-nine per cent play-acting, following your script, playing your role, just pretending, it's nevertheless in the action that the proof of the pudding is contained. It doesn't have to be violent action—although you already know that getting shot or stabbed in the back is a possibility you can't rule out—but even if it only consists of talking things through, of negotiation and compromise, of signing on the dotted line or tearing up the contract, it has to end with action. So get a grip. Drift, by all means, but for God's sake hold the tiller, try to steer, to ply the helm. Can you ply a helm? Are helms pliable . . . ? Are elms liable . . . ?

Never mind that. There are quibbles and quibbles; the point is not to be pedantic but to use your pedantry, not simply to play with words but to play with the right words. Forget elms and lying, helms and plying, whelms and flexibility, worms and circumflexes, and concentrate . . . distill, filter, solidify . . .

Solidity, as Ceridwen once told Edith, is hard, pun probably intended. It's easy to be ghostly, not to mention ghastly, but not so easy to be liquid, to flow, to ooze, to seep, to trickle, to dissolve other substances, to be absorbed . . . all of which pose challenges to your existential status. But solidity . . . that's something else. Really, really hard. The very limit of the neider's capacity, the ultimate challenge of robust rebirth. Darkness is easy, that's plain to see.

The thing is—except that it's not really a thing, although it's certainly not nothing—the question is—a question, at any rate, there might be more—do you have to die in order to be reborn?

The simple answer is obviously no, even setting aside quibbles like the question of whether life itself is anything other than a continuous process of rebirth and recreation, self-repair and self-esteem. To put it as simply as possible, is it better to imagine rebirth in terms of classical reincarnation, a single, immortal, essentially immutable soul moving from one body to another, in an endless cycle of deaths and births, annihilations and conceptions, putrescence and gestation, or is it better to imagine it as a kind of cloning, of copying, of multiplication by division? Is Zoe Marianne reborn. Or, perhaps more interestingly, given the circumstances and the psychological hang-ups that seem to be involved, is Jocasta Symonds Megan Harwyn reborn?

In one sense, obviously, no, despite their genetic similarity. In another . . . but let's not get bogged down in thinking that the only, or even the simple, alternative to no is yes. What about not yet?

After all, if Megan is right and there were a whole series of Cerdiwens, beginning with Seymour Murden's second wife, a sequence of three more anomalous births, who succeeded one another in taking over a common documentary existence, the same civil estate, when did the handover take place? If the mother of a clone-child dies in childbirth, you could say that the rebirth and the birth take place at the same time—except, in the days before DNA tests, you wouldn't know for some time whether the baby that had just been born was a twin-daughter or not. And mostly, the mother and daughter would be alive simultaneously, perhaps for more than thirty years, as in Marianne and Zoe's case, or more than forty, as in Megan and Jocasta's. So when in the instances lost in the murky past, did such handovers take place? When was the identity of the first Ceridwen taken over by the second, the second by the third, and so on. When did Rhys Two take over from Rhys One? When the first one died, presumably. The clone is dead, long live the clone . . .

Things are different now, of course. Now we have DNA testing, you'd be able to tell immediately, if you did the test, whether or not a baby was a clone of her mother—Monique of Krysten, for example. Now, it can actually be proven, scientifically, that Jocasta is Megan's daughter, even though they haven't seen one another for twenty-some adult years, and never compared themselves with one another until today. Now, albeit only recently, the possibility no longer exists for Megan to deny her daughter, to claim that the resemblance is purely accidental, just a coincidence, like so many mother-daughter resemblances. DNA tests can now reveal and prove a lot of things that people would prefer to deny, if they could . . .

Brotherhood, for instance. And parenthood. DNA has become the ultimate evidence, the ultimate clincher: the deoxyribonucleic acid test, of identity, and hence of entitlement . . . provided that you could actually obtain the relevant samples . . . legally, if you wanted the allegation to stand up in court . . .

And that didn't begin to take in the other level of complication introduced by the fact that the Murdens had more dark matter and more dark mind in them than the human average, because they were a little bit neider or morgen themselves, and that too had to have its process of inheritance, probably more akin to mitochondrial DNA than chromosomal DNA, passed on through the maternal line, only divided or remixed in accordance with some other process of fusion meiosis and separation, mysteriously dark, and alien, like the process by which he had allegedly been copied after allegedly being shot, in order that he could be put back into his own body, perhaps more than once, perhaps multiplied a hundred times, stored away carefully in some kind of cocoon, awaiting rebirth or re-creation . . .

Which might, now he came to think about it, have been the whole point of what had happened to him down in the Underworld beyond the red, beyond the danger signal, beyond all the symbolic blood that had replaced the symbolic sky . . .

Get a grip.

Get a grip on something graspable, something down-to-earth, something umbilical, something ouroboros. Forget dark matter. Get back to DNA, and proof. Get back to solidity, to certainty.

Except that DNA comparisons weren't the kind of proof that they were sometimes taken to be. Even a parental match, as between himself and Angela Richardson, couldn't be completely reliable, given that he and his mother only had fifty per cent of their genes in common, and a semi-sibling match, like the one—allegedly—between himself and Douglas Jefferson, who would only be expected, logically, to have twenty-five per cent of their genes in common, had a far wider margin for error, especially if there were grounds for believing that one or both of them were descended from unusually inbred ancestral lines. It was perfectly possible . . . perhaps even highly probable . . . that he and Dougie had twenty-five per cent of their genes in common even if Ranald Jefferson were not, in fact, his father.

It was, after all, pure speculation that Ranald might have told Dougie, in a deathbed confession, that he had had a child by Lilith Murden's granddaughter. The probability was that Dougie had jumped to the conclusion based purely on the stolen results of Simon's DNA analysis, just as Megan had, without even bothering to wonder whether there might be alternatives. And it was beyond pure speculation that Angela might have seen Ranald's ring, might have been able to read the motto on it, and, even though she knew no Latin, translate it into English, and remember it seventy years later in order to convey it to her son as a message from Hell.

Absurd.

The supposed sibling match wouldn't, in any case, be sufficient to prove in a court of law that he and Dougie were related. There were grounds for reasonable doubt, even in the absence of the other considerations . . .

On the other hand, just as the existence of identical twins caused complications in the legal "beyond reasonable doubt" of DNA identification, once the existence of clone-daughters, let alone that of clone-sons, achieved promotion from medical reportage to citation in court, and hence to legal precedent . . .

"Oh shit," said Simon, aloud, suddenly waking up to the level of speech and action, as an idea occurred to him.

Felicia started. She was only shallowly asleep herself—but a single word was not enough to bring her all the way back to full consciousness, or even enough to make her say "What?" in her sleep.

Simon was still holding her, protectively, perhaps lovingly. She felt secure; she set herself adrift again, perhaps sharing his emotional undercurrent, the depression and anxiety to which she was accustomed, with which she could cope, but she couldn't actually "read his thoughts." The words were beyond the reach of the bond between the darker fraction of their minds, their particular collective unconscious *à deux*.

He let her sleep. He wanted her to feel protected and secure, even if it turned out be a lie, a delusion. But his own sense of security had just been shaken, because he had just thought of a possible reason why Douglas Jefferson might have invited Jocasta Symonds to stay at his cottage in Morpen, and why he might have sent the heartless bitch to see her heartless bitch of a mother, making use of him as an intermediary, to facilitate the confrontation.

It was pure speculation, of course, pure fantasy—but it was a story of sorts, and it might end, if Dougie had his way, with Simon being ousted, or at least convincingly challenged, as the heir apparent of the Murden inheritance.

His first thought in response to that possibility was: *Do I care?* And the answer to that was: *Not really.*

But it wasn't as simple as that. Felicia would care. And he had a responsibility to Felicia. He didn't know whether she loved him, but he knew that she wanted to. So he had to care.

And then, because the interval between dream-sleep and wakefulness is the point in linear time at which the brain is at its most inventive and most creative, Simon thought of another possible twist in the unfolding story of his strange and perhaps-mistaken relationship with Douglas Jefferson, and his strange and perhaps-mistaken relationship with the neider and the vitreous cocoons, and although it was pure speculation, it made him whisper—very quietly, so as not to disturb Felicia—"*Oh shit. Shit, shit, shit.*"

And he remembered Thomas Mallory's slightly smug remark that if he really thought about it hard, he might find it more difficult than he had previously assumed that the Devil was not involved.

And he fell asleep again. Or did he? He heard the music
. . . except that he didn't actually hear it, because, in some
strange sense, he *was* the music, not so much hearing as being
heard. And he got out of bed. Or, rather, he didn't, because
he was still in bed, lying down, asleep, holding Felicia in his
arms. He had a grip, an anchorage. He was solid. But he was
also split; he was also the music, the siren song, and he was
drawn . . .

He went downstairs, and out of the Abbey by the back
door, and past Pamphile's stable, and then he veered to the
left, and he went down the steps into Morgan's Cave, where
the Black Bard was waiting for him, holding the crwth, and
playing it, with a bow that bore a strong psychological resemblance to a magic wand, although it was perfectly natural, as
everything that exists is, by definition . . . although Simon
had to admit that the existence of the bow, the crwth, the
Bard and himself was a trifle precarious, not even gaseous,
let alone solid.

"About time," said the Black Bard. "For a while, there, we
thought we'd lost you."

The Bard was not actually speaking, in the sense of making a sound. Nor could Simon hear him—or, for that matter,
hear anything—because he was the speech, just as he was
the music. And there was a sense, too in which he was the
Bard—all the more so as the Bard, this time, was not Faceless
within his hood.

"Why do you have my face?" Simon asked the Bard.

"For the same reason that you have mine, obviously," the
Monk replied. "We're the same person, a little displaced in
time."

"Only a little?"

"Relatively speaking."

"I can't play music, and if I could, it wouldn't be on a
crwth."

"The music is inside you; it always has been. It's just a
matter of getting it out. You're flesh—usually, though not at
the moment—and I'm a ghost, but we're the same where it

186

counts, in the soul, in the song. When we collect ourselves—
really collect ourselves, that is—you'll hear the truth. It won't
be in words, but the real truth never is."

"I was hoping to see Melusine," Simon said.

"Aren't we all?" said the fake Monk. "These things take
time. Conception is moderately easy, gestation is moderately
hard, metamorphosis is even harder. They always take time.
Perhaps they always take too long. But a time will come . . .
this time, we hope, but if not . . . but that's not important.
You're right."

"About what?"

"In the deduction you just made—the guess you just
made. Frankly, I think you ought to have thought of it weeks
ago but you've been distracted, not entirely by virtue of your
own fault."

"And you brought me down here to tell me that?"

"No, you came of your own accord in order to obtain that
confirmation, because you don't have enough self-confidence
yet, being too confused by the words. You need to relax and
accept what you really are. By which I mean, since you need
me to spell it out, that you're the music, and the Bard—but
spelling things out distorts things, changes them. The words
are mostly yours and the thoughts are mostly yours; only the
inspiration is ours. You need a better connection. You need to
harmonize."

"If the words, the music and the speech are all mine, why
couldn't I simply stay in bed and dream them there?"

"You are in bed, fleshwise, dreaming them there—but
sometimes, you have to get away from the flesh a little, commit yourself to the soul—but only a little, because even you
don't yet have an inkling of how dangerous that can be. But
you're a storyteller. You know that you have to melodrama-
tize dreams to lend them emphasis, to give them clout. It goes
with the territory. But that's okay. We understand. We're on
your side. We're here for you."

"Who's we? I thought you were me?"

"I am, but no man is an island. We're part of something larger. Lots of somethings, actually—but you know that already. For the moment, the intimate *we* is me, Ceridwen and the neider."

"Does that mean you, Ceridwen *and* the neider, or that Ceridwen and you *are* the neider?"

The Black Bard sighed, and the sigh became part of the music he was playing, infusing it and enhancing its plaintive quality. "We're ambiguous," he said. "When you look at things closely, everything is. You know that too. Treasure that awareness; existence would be very dull without it. Treasure the pathos. Hear it, savor it, yield to it."

"I certainly feel ambiguous, at the moment," Simon admitted.

"You and me both, obviously. Joke."

"Obviously."

Simon tried to think, although he knew how difficult that was in a dream, and how dangerous it was to the integrity of dreams that were unthinking, and wanted and needed to be unthinking, to keep dangerous consciousness at bay—but the music seemed to be helping, as long as he could hear it, savor it and treasure its pathos.

"So," he thought aloud, "the reason that my dark mind is synthesizing this dream is simply to reinforce the idea that I just had, that while I was down in the darkness, for twelve hours longer than I originally thought, and Douglas Jefferson was keeping Felicia company, in spite of all prohibitions, and Felicia fell asleep, Jefferson went down the steps into the crypt feeling his way?"

"Simply? Oh, dear, Simon. *Simply?* Really? You know better than that. You know that this is far, far more complicated than that, that this is everything, everything in a nutshell, everything with a bullet. But if you need a straw to grasp, if you need to identify a trigger, a little spark of enlightenment that gives you a momentary sense of being able to see a pattern that was just a blur before, yes, Douglas Jefferson did go down into the dark."

"All the way down?"

"No, he didn't have enough guts for that. He convinced himself that he only needed to get the key: that if he had the key, that would count as an achievement, something solid, something graspable. People often think that about keys, not to mentioned marriages, inheritances and buried treasure. But they're only tokens—the truth lies beyond, and you have to go all the way down to get it. The real payoff, of course, is being able to come back without losing your mind. That's hard. For most people, it's safer to fool yourself, go no further than the crypt and come back with a key that really isn't of any much significance, in the greater scheme of things. Even to get that, though, you have to go down into the darkness, and that's dangerous. It makes you vulnerable."

"Vulnerable to what?"

"Possession. Among other things."

"Possession by whom? Or what?"

"Good question. Perhaps, in one sense, by you, as you provided the model for the parasite. In another sense, not you at all, nor even us. That's the worrying thing. Not the collaborators busy saving your soul, either, which might be worrying, or might be a relief. We can't tell yet. We don't know what the next move in the game might be. But we think that the key, trivial as it is in itself, might still be a significant link in the chain. That's the thing about chains, of course: every link is insignificant in itself, but take one away and the whole thing falls apart. Crack, bang, boom!"

"Crack, bang, boom?"

"Well, we hope not, obviously. But sometimes, hope isn't enough."

Simon's dream-self was lost. He had lost the thread, or the chain, or the tune. He wasn't feeling the pathos. Yet again, the words were confusing him, refusing to make sense. But he couldn't abandon them because they were not just the beginning and the end but the connection between them, the middle and the substance. He couldn't play the music; all he had was the words. If he couldn't make sense of this with words, what use was he, to himself, to the neider, or to the consciousness of the universe that was still in seed, let alone in bud, the God unborn, who might take billions of years yet to form a coherent thought, even though it was already billions of years since the dawn of light, the genesis of the blinding light . . .

He felt that he ought to ask a question while he had the chance, but he didn't know what it ought to be.

"This isn't just madness is it?" the queried, plaintively. "There is a plot here, a purpose and an intention?

"Certainly," said the Black Bard, as if offended that he could have doubted it.

"And is that intention?"

"If I could simply tell you, you'd already know, and we wouldn't be here. Play along, Simon, play along."

"For that matter," Simon said, a trifle peevishly, "what are *your* intentions?"

"We're trying to prevent the end of the world. You know that. You should have worked it out by now."

"To prevent the destruction of the world?"

"Of course. Not all of it. Hardly any of it, in fact, in crude physical terms. Solids always survive, liquids and gases might only be slightly compromised, and some—not us— might even call that progress rather than regress. The other phases of matter are endangered, but the real threat—the apocalyptic threat—is always to minds, more specifically, to the dynamics of dark energy."

"And how many times has the world ended before, in that sense?"

"Who can tell? But history is brief, and eternity long. Probably lots.

"Hundreds?"

"On Earth, yes. On a larger scale, more likely billions."

"But minds are reborn, at least sometimes?"

"Re-created, alas. Rebirth is salvation. Re-creation . . . perhaps best not to think about that, even if it were possible. It's discordant."

"And how many times has human race been saved from that kind of end?"

"Who can tell? Not as many times as it's been re-created. Probably far fewer. The odds must always be against entities of our kind, but we have to keep trying, What's the alternative."

"And there is a chance?"

"Of course. We exist, therefore we *can* exist. It's just a matter of figuring out how to do it."

"But we're running out of time?"

"There's never enough."

"And I'm important, somehow?"

"You are to us, as a link in our chain. In the great scheme of things, who can tell? Who can judge?"

"And I didn't foul up your plan by going down into the darkness when the neider told me not to go?"

"Of course you did. You fouled it up completely—but it's in the nature of plans that they have to be adapted. Errors have to be anticipated. Plans have to include contingencies. Sometimes, errors are productive and the adapted plans work better than the original ones. Sometimes, they don't. You never know until you reach the last page of the story, and whatever's there generally comes as a surprise, pleasant or otherwise. Of course, you have to get there first."

"I'll do my best. Is there anything else I need to know?"

"Of course there is. Far too many things. If we could tell you, we would, but we need to discover them first. We're trying, in spite of all the interruptions and all the distractions. We have high hopes of Melusine, though. If the darkness returns before she can get inside your head properly, we might be in deep trouble, but perhaps not. If that's the way it goes, keep trying anyway. We are. No alternative."

And with that, the crwth stopped playing; the phantom vanished, and Felicia said: "What?"

"Nothing," said Simon, sleepily, moving his arms in order to prevent them from going numb, and to hug Felicia in a slightly different physical configuration. "Go back to sleep. We need our sleep. Tomorrow is going to be a long day."

XII

The View from Morgan's Cave

"What are you doing?" Marianne asked.

It was, Simon thought, a good question.

In one sense, clearly, he was doing nothing, that being the sense in which he was sitting still, not moving, except for his eyes, which had been carelessly scanning the surface of the sea, appreciating its gray serenity—the sky was cloudy, and the breeze very light—and contemplating its depth, which couldn't be seen, as such, but could still impinge upon awareness, or at least imagination.

This morning, however, he had seen seals; they never seemed to be around when you wanted them to appear, but when you didn't care, up they popped from beneath the surface, from the depths. So he had the option, if he wanted to take it, of saying: *Watching the seals.*

A more honest answer, however, would have been: *Going mad.* He had been going mad all his life, of course, and perhaps had never been anything but, but not in the insistent, urgent, oppressive sense of the last couple of days. It couldn't go on the way it had the previous day and night, he knew. He couldn't hold himself together for much longer at that rate of disturbance. One more day, certainly, but one more night? One more night of last night's demands, with the pressure of his habitual circadian rhythms demanding that he sleep, dream, and lapse into the arms of Morpheus, the vasty deep of the unconscious? He could do it in the flesh, he presumed, but could he come back again mentally? Or might this morning have been the last time he would enjoy the sensation and genuinely returning to full, stable consciousness? Might today be the end of him, of the self that he had created so painstakingly within his inner world?

But that wasn't the kind of explanation that Marianne wanted. It wasn't the kind of answer that her question required.

"Just passing the time," he replied. "Felicia's sleeping peacefully again, and I couldn't . . . again. I didn't want to go to the kitchen, where Edith would probably have insisted on feeding me, so I came out here. I came down into the cave because . . . well, not for any particular reason. It just seemed to be too exposed up above. Too much sky."

"I made myself a little breakfast," Marianne said. "Edith seems to have overtaxed herself last night and she's still in bed this morning—Margaret's looking in on her regularly. She says that Edith keeps on insisting that it wasn't anything she ate. Margaret said that she ordered her to come down at five to make a pot of tea for you, but you'd already gone outside, apparently. Margaret didn't approve. 'No way to start the day,' she said. 'Mr. James never missed breakfast, not in the seventy-one years I've been here.' I suspect that she was exaggerating. I couldn't see you on the tine, so I assumed that you must be down here, looking out for morgens. No luck?"

She sat down beside him as she spoke, on the cold, exceedingly solid rock, and assumed the same idle stance, looking out over the sea, bounded by the gray and green ridge of the southern tine, extending from the mainland like a sullen, turgid tentacle.

"Only seals."

"Edith told me yesterday that you can see porpoises sometimes. They're like dolphins, she explained to me, but I don't think she meant that they can sleep and be awake at the same time, by dividing the business of living between the two halves of their brain."

"It must be nice to be that well-organized," said Simon.

"It must be nice to be content with being well-organized," she agreed. "My life's been very well-organized for years, now. That was easy, really—just a matter of paring it down, avoiding everything and everyone abrasive, subjecting home, workplace, time and life to order and routine. But then everything becomes dull and monotonous, and you start thinking you need a holiday, or, if the insanity really takes hold, a new relationship."

"Except that, whatever you were hoping to get from the holiday or the new relationship, it never delivers?" Simon suggested, in a questioning tone.

"I don't know," she said. "St. Madoc is, as your next-door neighbor says, the arse end of nowhere, but it has its charms. And a relationship with a half-brother isn't even half a relationship, in the full sense of the term, but it has . . . a lot of words. No sex, but a lot of words. Swings and roundabouts."

"It might be a good idea if you were to take Zoe and Krysten back to Bristol today," said Simon, bluntly.

There was brief silence before Marianne said: "Why?"

"Because I have a feeling in my gut that something bad is going to happen soon. It's possible—perhaps probable—that I'm just projecting, imagining that a purely personal disaster is something that's going to affect the surroundings, the Abbey, and the world—but even if that's the case, something bad might still be going to happen to me, and it might be better for you, Zoe and Krysten, if you weren't around."

"You're not dying," said Marianne, flatly.

"No," said Simon, "but I am losing my mind. I used to think that was just a careless turn of phrase, but it's not."

"I certainly noticed a certain amount of slippage yesterday," Marianne admitted, "but you're not dangerous, are you? All talk and no axes. I'd like to help, if I can. Can't I? I know you don't need anyone to hold your hand, or any other part of your anatomy, because you have Felicia, but you did write to me, and come to Bristol, and invite me here, so you must have thought that I might be useful for something. Or have I failed the test?"

"No, of course not," Simon assured her, sincerely. "In fact, I suspect that if anyone could bring me back from the inner dark, and surround me with sanity, it's you. Felicia, as you say, supplies my anatomy with necessary touches, and she has the words too; Megan has been a godsend, in her eccentric fashion; but neither of them can avoid feeding my imagination, nourishing my delusions."

"And you think I can avoid it? After what you told me yesterday?"

Simon pulled a wry face. "Probably not, no," he conceded "I shouldn't have done that. It was stupid."

"Perhaps," she agreed, "but I'm glad you did it. I won't say that I understand, but at least I have some idea now of what I don't understand. Even if it only equips me to feed your delusions . . . except that you and I both know that they're not entirely delusions, and that pretending that they are isn't going to solve anything."

"There you go," said Simon, lightly. "Surrounding me with sanity. As armor goes, alas, it's full of holes."

"So what terrible disaster is going to happen today?"

"I don't know. That's the trouble with gut feelings—they're inarticulate. They can't spell anything out."

"Maybe it's something you ate, in spite of what Edith says?"

"No, it's not that. I don't know what it is, but it's not that. Whatever it is, I'll face it . . . but you don't have to. You have options."

"And do you honestly think that after taking the lid off the can of worms, you can just send us all away? Do you think I'm the kind of person who could? Or Zoe?"

"There's Krysten, and Monique, to think about."

"True—but I don't want to be the one to suggest to Krysten that she isn't competent to make her own decisions. Zoe is always prepared to tell her that, but whenever she's done it before it's caused an almighty row. You might think she's terribly sweet, because she's got a nice face and breasts, but believe me, you don't want to get on the wrong side of her when she goes off the deep end. It runs in the family—but if you're really serious, I'll try to suggest subtly that it might not be such a good idea for them to stick around, even though I have no intention of going."

"Why not?"

"Because I've only just got here. Because I'm as mad as a hatter or as stubborn as a mule. Because I can't help hoping that I might be able to help, somehow. Take your pick. What are your plans for the day?"

Simon didn't bother to make the selection he'd been offered—not aloud, anyway. "I'm going over to Sanderling shortly," he said, "to find out what really happened between Megan and Jocasta yesterday, and bring her up to date with my most recent imaginings. Then I have to walk to Morpen to meet Father Mallory, in order to collect more crazy-fuel. The walk will do me good, I think—but when it comes to nourishing delusions, I suspect that Mallory might be a champion too."

"Don't go, then," Marianne suggested. "Stay here. I'm not the bastion of sanity you seem to suspect, but I'll do my best. Talking sense for a whole day might be way beyond my ability, but we could hang out with Krysten, if we can get rid of Zoe. Krysten's still relatively uncorrupted, and she has Monique to anchor her in vulgar reality, when she isn't pretending to be a mermaid."

"Thanks," said Simon. "I'm sure you'd both do me good—and Zoe isn't as bad as you think, it seems to me. But the problem is in me. I think I'm a corrupting influence on all of you. In relying on you to keep me nearly sane, I'd end up driving you mad. I honestly think you'd be better off going home."

"And if we don't want to?"

"You should want to—for Krysten's sake if not for Zoe's."

"Zoe has her car too. She drove Krysten here, so she can drive her back, if that's what Krysten wants. Zoe might see some advantages in that—all the wine she drank last night only blunted her appetite for oblivion temporarily, and alcohol doesn't really do it for her. Unless you're actually throwing me out. I'll stay, for all the reasons I listed. On the other hand, I wouldn't want to stay where I'm not wanted . . ."

Simon didn't rise to that bait. "Something is going to happen," he said, instead, a trifle dully. "I can feel it. And it's going to happen soon."

"Good," said Marianne.

"Good?" Simon queried.

"The best. I'm fifty-eight years old, Simon, and even if I hadn't lost the looks that Zoe still has—just—I don't think I could summon up the energy for any kind of romantic relationship. My mother's dead, but I hated her anyway, and my daughter can't stand me. My job is the ultimate in tedium, or would be, if there was no such thing as reality TV. I'm even beginning to lose my appetite for reading. Believe me, an apocalypse would be welcome. So, if your weird portal is threatening to turn into a door to hell, and the darkness is going to come rushing through, all I can say is, bring it on."

Simon laughed, a trifle bitterly. "I've already infected you, I see."

"You infected me forty years ago. I just didn't realize it at the time. It's been a long time incubating, but it's blossoming now. It started when you came to Bristol, but it didn't open fully until I came here . . . when I met Felicia that night before last. Don't you think we look similar—that there's a family resemblance?"

"There is," Simon confirmed. "I noticed it when I came to Bristol—in fact, it was the first thing I noticed about you."

"And do you know what I thought when you introduced me to her?"

"I can guess: *So that's what I'm going to look like when I'm a hundred.*"

"No. First I remembered what Zoe said to me when she eventually confessed that she'd been here, when she panicked after being caught ferrying drugs: 'He's got a girlfriend who's a hundred, and who looks like you, so maybe you'll still be able to pull when you're a hundred.' She didn't actually add *even though you can't now*, but she was thinking it. And I thought: *Zoe's right; she's a hundred and one, and an intelligent man is still willing to sleep with her, and to imagine that he loves her, and I look like her but forty years younger so someone ought to be willing to sleep with me too, and think he loves me.* And then I thought: *But not him; he's your brother, and he's probably one of a kind.* And then I thought: *What does that matter, nowadays? And anyway, it runs in the family.* And then I thought: *You're completely crazy, Mary Anne; you don't even want to, you just want somebody to be able to want to, for vanity's sake. If he actually did it, you'd end up hating it, just like you've always ended up hating it, and then you'd hate him, just like you've always hated all of them, and that's the last thing in the world you want, you stupid bitch.* So if you really are worried about the danger of my contracting some kind of contagious madness if I stay here, forget it. That ship has sailed, if you'll forgive the cliché."

Simon didn't know how to react to that, so he played safe and said: "You call yourself Mary Anne, not Marianne, when you're talking to yourself?"

"Usually. Sometimes Mary Jane. I don't know why. I suppose I've never felt like the person other people think of when they call me by my name. Don't tell Zoe. She used to call pot Mary Jane way back when, and she'd think it was funny. Perhaps I've always been mad. Can I stay, please?"

"Of course you can stay," Simon said. "I never wanted you to go. I just thought I ought to make the suggestion."

"Because you think you're a saint—or you think you ought to be."

"Actually," said Simon, "I wish people would stop saying that. I'm not virtuous, and never have been. I've just always been too lazy to be vicious. I can't understand where some people find the energy to be evil. I'm not a saint, I just have underactive adrenal glands."

"I think you might be worrying too much about losing your mind. You seem to be fully in possession of it now."

"I'm better in the mornings, and I think I exhausted my supply of dream-feed last night. I came down here then as well—not in the flesh, it was an out-of-body experience—to talk to myself . . . or, more accurately, an infinity of my other selves . . . while making sweet music on an obsolete musical instrument that I can't play. It seemed to go on for a long time, far longer than it could actually have taken, in hourglass time."

"I envy you that," said Marianne, quietly.

"Why?"

"What's not to envy? Out-of-body experiences, a miraculous ability to play a musical instrument without even having learned, the ability to stretch time, and having a self that's interesting enough not only to be infinitely replicated but able to hold a long conversation. Mary Anne has hardly anything to say to herself—she could bore for England, if you'll forgive the cliché."

"That's not true," Simon said. "I had a couple of opportunities to converse with you yesterday for some length of time and you didn't bore me for an instant."

"That's because the novelty hasn't worn off yet." She looked at her watch. "Can I walk over to the mainland with you? You need to go, if you're to have time to interrogate Megan and then walk to Morpen to meet your inquisitor friend."

"He's not an inquisitor," Simon corrected, with reflexive pedantry—and added, for much the same reason: "And he's not my friend, although he's hopefully not an enemy." His own wristwatch told him that she was correct in her estimation of the time, though, and he knew that it wouldn't be as elastic now as it had when he had left his body enlaced in Felicia's arms and gone a-wandering in the dark. He stood up, and made his way to the steps that would take him back to the naked sky.

Although he hadn't actually given her the formal permission she had requested, Marianne went with him.

"I'll call in at Raven," she said. "Zoe will still be in bed, but Krysten will probably be up with the baby. I'll be able to lend her a hand. A great-grandmother of fifty-eight has her uses, I suppose, but it's still absurd. I shouldn't envy your friend Megan, I know, but I can't help it. She's older than you, but she looks better than I do, and dresses far better. Trivia, I know, by comparison with finding herself in the situation she found herself in yesterday, and having so much hatred inside her, but you don't envy wholes, only parts."

"She doesn't seem to hate me," said Simon, pensively. "I can't help wondering why, sometimes. And please don't say it's because I'm a saint."

"Oh, don't worry. If I'm any judge—although I'm probably not—she hates you too, but she's declared a private truce with you because you're amusing. Hating everybody doesn't free you from the necessity of having to make occasional compromises. But don't worry that she'll stab you in the back one day; she's the kind of person who honors her truces. Do you think she calls herself Meg in the privacy of her own thoughts? I don't. Always Megan."

"Probably," Simon agreed. "Occasionally, she tries to come across as Megaera, but if I didn't hate clichés so much, I'd say that her bark is worse than her bite."

He locked the gate behind them conscientiously. There was no one hanging around on the other side of the bridge, and St. Madoc's one and only authentic street was still a navigable thoroughfare, for the time being.

"I'll try to get Zoe and Krysten to go home, if you think it's necessary," said Marianne, quietly, "but I'll have to use reverse psychology on Zoe to stand any chance at all, and it might not work. But I'll stay here, if you don't mind, no matter what might happen. Perhaps I can be useful, although I can't imagine how."

"Perhaps you can," Simon remarked, as he left her by the gate at Raven and went on to Sanderling. He looked back as he went, and added: "If things go really bad, Felicia might need help getting me into the straitjacket—metaphorically speaking."

She didn't make any reply, but he could tell by her slightly pitying expression that she thought that he was exaggerating wildly, and that she had every faith in his sanity, because he was a writer, and had a license to say odd things without being thought out of his mind. He was grateful for her confidence, even though he was direly afraid that it might be misplaced.

Before ringing the doorbell at Sanderling, he checked the sky. For now, it was brightening, and the sun would soon break through, but he had checked the weather forecast—it had become a habit of late—on the computer in the Abbey drawing room before going down to the cave. An Atlantic front was heading in from the west, scheduled to arrive at dusk or thereabouts. The day-trippers might turn out today in force, but tomorrow, things would be back to normal: drenched.

Megan let him in, but she escaped into the kitchen as soon as she had sat him down in order to make coffee, without bothering to ask whether he wanted any, simply in order to postpone the moment of truth.

"I suppose you want the whole story now," she said, when they were both seated.

"It is a matter in which I have some involvement," he suggested, "But not if it's too painful for you. Just give me the gist."

"You think you're involved because you think Dougie intends to cajole or blackmail her and her son into staking a claim to a share of your inheritance, I suppose, with or without my support?"

"No, I'm involved because I think that the confrontation might have upset you, and I wanted to lend you whatever moral support I can, just as you've lent me much-needed moral support over the last few weeks."

She laughed. "Unbelievable," she said. "Or it would be, coming from anyone else but you. Unlike me, you can actually do moral support—but it's okay, there's no need. I'm a big girl. Troubles bounce off me like hailstones off a roof. It's the other thing that bothers me. And yes, she does seem to be interested by the possibility of enriching her beloved Anthony, and questions of legal practicality seem to concern her far more than any hypothetical opposition I might put up. You'll never guess what Douglas has told her, which she was so careful not to pass on to you, for the time being."

"Actually," Simon told her, "I think I have."

"What?"

"He's told her that James Murden is her biological father—and that he has the DNA evidence to prove it."

"Oh. Okay, the *never* was obviously a gross exaggeration. You worked it out because he was so careful to preserve the potential for me to deny that I was her mother, I suppose—hoping that I'd stand aside in order to give his story free rein, at least with respect to her. Is that why you advised me to admit that I was her mother?"

"No, I hadn't worked it out then. But the admission only complicates the situation slightly; the evidence still proclaims a blood relationship, and perhaps an entitlement. I presume that what you've told her—everything you've told her—hasn't dented her readiness to make the claim?

"You presume correctly. Any suggestion I might make to the contrary would be futile at best, and perhaps counter-productive. As I said last night, everything was sweet—she was very polite, and she assured me that she didn't bear a grudge. But underneath the politeness, I can tell that she hates me, and that even though she puts on a better act than I ever could, even professionally, deep down, she's a heart-less bitch. I know, because she's me, a duplicate cut from the same cloth. Except that she's better than me, because she's never been a whore—at least, not on a pay-as-you-lay basis. She's respectable. And if you think that that ought to have prevented her from becoming a heartless bitch as she grew up, you have no understanding of female psychology."

"I think you're being a little hard on yourself," Simon said.

"On her, you mean."

"That too, but what I actually meant was what I said. If you were a little kinder to yourself, as Father Mallory ad-vised, you'd probably feel better about this whole situation."

"The greatest kindness I ever did myself—and her, for that matter—was giving her away. And whatever Dougie Jefferson might claim, to her or publicly, kindness had absolutely nothing to do with his assisting her to find me. Quite the opposite—but the bastard has no idea what I'm capable of doing in retaliation. I'll ruin him."

"I don't think that would be a good idea."

"Why not?"

"Because it would escalate a cold war into a hot one, which would only result in more people getting hurt without solving anything."

"You think I should just let it go?" She was incredulous.

"That's exactly what I think. Let it run it course. Fundamentally, Dougie hasn't done anything wrong—not in this instance, at any rate. You know, and I know, that kindness had nothing to do with his motivation in enabling Jocasta to find you, but it can pass for an act of kindness, in the eyes of the world—and in Jocasta's, for now although it probably won't take her long to figure out the truth. Let it pass."

She shook her head, still incredulous, but then frowned slightly. "Not in this instance, you said," she pointed out. "So you think he has done something wrong in another distance? You think he's attacking on two flanks at once—that he'll try to persuade Mallory to put in a claim against the Estate as well?"

"I wouldn't be at all surprised if he did that too, but even that wouldn't be wrong, and I doubt if Mallory would take the bait. In fact, now I come to think about it, even what I suspect him of having done might only count as a trivial sin, and it might only be my paranoia that makes me suspect him of it."

"Of what?"

"The night I went down into the darkness after Cerys, I was down there for fifteen hours, not three, as I originally thought. For at least twelve of those hours Dougie was in the chapel, uninvited, but pretending to be kind, keeping

Felicia company . . . and for several of those hours, Felicia was asleep."

"You think he went down the steps? But why, if he couldn't see anything? You said that the electric lamps didn't work down there."

"They didn't. He would have had to feel his way—but that was possible. I did it."

"But what could he achieve just by groping?"

"He could take an impression of the key to the padlock on the lower trapdoor, which was in the lock—having, of course, already taken an impression of the one used to secure the upper trapdoor, which was easy. He told me that he kept Felicia supplied with cups of tea and biscuits, so he obviously had free run of the kitchen and pantry. It would have been easy enough to find something in which to make the impression."

"So you think that he now has the means to get down, not just into the crypt, but into the cave where the vitreous cocoons are?"

"Yes—and to get into the house, obviously. He might have been down there already, but he's probably been too busy with his various other schemes. Eventually, though, he'll want to take a look. Probably soon, if he thinks it might give him an additional bargaining chip with Mallory. At the very least, he must be yearning to know exactly what all the fuss is about. He'll be disappointed, of course, to discover that it's something essentially incomprehensible—but he's a businessman; he'll want to figure out a way to profit from it, whoever actually obtains legal ownership of the cave when the legal dust settles."

"But if you can catch him in the act," said Megan, with sudden enthusiasm, "you can take him by surprise, as Zoe did with Bernard—and if you hit him hard enough, he won't wake up. And nobody will ever find the body, if you stuff it into one of the fissures in the crypt. That's genius!"

"It would be cold-blooded murder, which I have no intention whatsoever of committing."

"You can't mean that you're just going to let him do it—
no, obviously not. You'll settle for just changing the locks.
The wimpy option, but probably the wise one."

"That would be one alternative," Simon agreed, equably.

"You have another in mind?"

"Of course. It occurs to me that if he really does have the
keys—and all this is still pure speculation, remember—the
simplest thing would be to satisfy his curiosity without putting him to the trouble of using them surreptitiously. I should
probably have done it before, but Felicia wouldn't have approved. It might be time to talk her round. If showing the
cocoons to Dougie will help defuse the situation, it's worth
a shot."

Megan looked at him long and hard.

"I know," he said, in a world-weary fashion.
"Unbelievable."

"Actually," Megan said, "I was thinking—and you'll understand how hard it was for me—that you might be right. It
goes against my instincts to pander to Dougie, but as he told
Bernard, in his customary corny fashion, you catch more flies
with honey than vinegar. You really are thinking of institut-
ing a collaboration with him, aren't you? That won't stop him
hating you, you know. You're still his bastard half-brother."

"Possibly. But probably not."

"What do you mean? The DNA might not prove it, but it's
suggestive—and you said yourself that he obviously thinks
it too."

"Yes, but he probably doesn't understand DNA evidence
as well as you and I do. The semi-sibling match, combined
with the Y-chromosome anomaly, doesn't come anywhere
near to proving that Ranald Jefferson is my biological father;
it only proves that my father was someone with a certain accumulation of genes in common with Dougie Jefferson. Given
the degree of inbreeding within the Murden clan, prior to
the schism, that probably applies to several males. If Lilith
Murden maintained communication with the Jeffersons after
leaving St. Madoc, she might well have maintained contact

with other branches of the family, perhaps unknown to Jeffersons. The Pallisters, for instance."

"You think Bernard's father raped your mother?"

"I certainly hope not. The point is that the weak match you and Dougie have might have led you both to jump to the wrong conclusion prematurely. And if I were to point that out to Dougie, it would at least give him potential deniability, whatever other circumstantial evidence you and he might have. And unless I'm mistaken, Dougie's the kind of man who might well take that option. He strikes me as being a good deal kinder to himself than you are—inclined to err in the opposite direction, in fact."

"When did you work all this out?"

"This morning, sitting in Morgan's Cave, trying hard to fight the conviction that doom is hanging over me—although I got the inspiration last night, while I couldn't sleep but also couldn't help dreaming. I might well be in the process of going quietly mad, but there's still a little method in my madness, if I can forgive myself the cliché. It is Shakespeare, after all."

"And you're really going to do it? Have a heart-to-heart talk with Dougie about the exact degree of your relatedness—or not—and volunteer to give him a guided tour of the family secret?"

"I think so. It seems to me to be a better plan than setting an ambush in order to murder him, or launching an all-out cyberattack on his company and his personal finances. But I thought I'd better run it past you first—and Felicia, of course."

"You don't need my permission."

"I know, but it seemed only polite. You're an interested party, after all, and in spite of what you say, you have lent me a great deal of valuable moral support in recent weeks. I'd have been lost without you—and so would Zoe. I'm not about to start doing things behind your back."

"Wow. You know, I think that's literally the nicest thing anyone's ever said to me. I'd still rather ruin him—but then,

I'd still rather have slammed the door in Jocasta's face yesterday, and, in retrospect, even though it gave me a *really* bad couple of hours, you were probably right to persuade me not to do it. It's not going to be easy being in the same world with her, but I can cope. And at least she doesn't love me—polite hatred I can cope with. You really are a bloody saint, aren't you? You know that doesn't mean I have to like you, though, don't you? I'm the Whore of Babylon, after all, firmly committed to the opposition."

"I know. Polite hatred, I could cope with, if necessary, but I think we're on slightly friendlier terms than that. And I have to go see Father Mallory now, who must think that I belong to the Devil's party—and will probably be even more convinced when we've completed our information exchange."

"He was a trifle contemptuous yesterday—*not even the pettiest antichrist* was his judgment, if I recall."

"He was trying to reassure me. As a man of God, he presumed that he was doing me a favor by suggesting that I only think, mistakenly, that I'm an atheist. He's wrong—but I hope I can handle him gently enough to let him hang on to the potential deniability. I need to know what he knows about what happened in Toulouse before I face the neider again . . . or whatever might come through the red portal. And I have a horrible feeling in my gut that I'm running out of time."

"Do you want me to come to Morpen with you? I'll drive you if you like. I still think I'm only immoral support, but if it's of any use to you . . ."

"No, but thanks. Marianne offered too, but I think he'll speak more freely if I'm alone. I'll give you the full story, though, when I have it."

"Fair enough. I have work to do anyway—can't let the business languish. If you see Jocasta in Morpen, you can nod politely, but don't give her my love."

"You think she's still there? I assumed that she'd gone home last night, wherever home is."

"No—she had a meeting with Dougie scheduled after we parted company. I think she was intending to spend the night in Morpen—probably not in the same bed as Dougie, although I can't quite shake the skin-crawling suspicion, and he's old enough to be her father, even though he's definitely not—but who can fathom the mystery of the human heart?"

"If I see her, I'll be careful as well as polite—but I'll have to give my primary attention to the man with the information."

"Of course. Thanks for dropping in, and for the consultation. I appreciate it. And since you do seem to care, I'm perfectly all right; it isn't a happy ending, but whatever happens next, I can handle it, even if it involves a grandson and a granddaughter. At least she isn't still happily married—the Murden curse is still holding good to that extent. But I'm blethering—go and wring Father Mallory dry of all the information he's willing to leak. Good luck."

"Thanks. I wish I could say I didn't need it. But however this all works out, in the end, even if I end up still poor and Abbey-less, we'll still be next-door neighbors and friends, won't we?"

"Absolutely."

Unless, of course, Simon thought, as he stood up to make his exit. *I'm dead or in a straitjacket.*

XIII
In Morpen

The central street of St. Madoc was once again showing the initial signs of becoming an improvised car park by the time Simon left Sanderling and headed eastwards. Dai was not yet doing a roaring trade in the Mermaid, although the pub was open. Simon did not go inside to see whether he had taken on extra bar staff in order to cope with an anticipated rush. The salient point was that there seemed to be fewer day trippers in the village than there had been at the same time the day before. The fact of the video having been removed had presumably generated some comment and wonderment, but it had not blown up into widespread suspicion of a conspiratorial cover-up. There was still every possibility that online discussion of the mystery of the Murdens and its link with mermaids would fade away and be forgotten in a matter of days.

As before, the throng, such as it was to date, seemed simply to be spreading out, lazily, along the coastal path and drifting on to the southern and northern tines, in order to watch for seals and seabirds, in the likely absence of mermaids, and enjoy the sunshine and fresh air in the meantime. As soon as the era's endemic cloud and rainfall resumed, as it was scheduled to do within twelve hours, the number of curiosity-seekers would presumably decline sharply. The sky had as much blue as white now, though, and no gray at all; there was every prospect that the spring weather would make the one-mile walk to Morpen quite pleasant. The traffic was light, the hedges were replete with birdsong, and the agricultural odors were not unduly offensive, in spite of the local habit—in frank defiance of EU regulations—of spreading seaweed on the fields by way of fertilizer.

As he walked along the road, Simon checked his watch in order to measure the time he might have in hand once he reached Morpen before his scheduled meeting. He considered the possibility of calling in at Douglas Jefferson's cottage in Morpen before going to the Estate-owned one where he had arranged to meet Thomas Mallory, in order to see whether anyone was there, and if so, who. On due reflection, however, he decided against it, because he wanted to get the negotiations with Father Mallory out of the way before he embarked on an earnest discussion with Douglas Jefferson and made the peace offering of a conducted tour of the vitreous cocoons. What he needed for the moment, he felt—quite strongly—was a peaceful philosophical discussion with the Dominican about their different approaches to the question of the "entity" in Myrddin's Cave and the neider: an hour or two of verbal sparring, akin to his last discussion with Alexander Usher, but without the edge of resentment and hostility that Usher had acquired when he realized that Simon would not, as he had blithely expected, allow him free access to the Abbey's crypt and library.

Simon was still not sure that the refusal in question had not been a mistake, and whether it might have been better, even in the short run, to have given the Reverend what he wanted. Had he known then that another Churchman was about to appear on the horizon, wielding more powerful argumentative artillery, he would probably have thought it worthwhile to have the Anglican onside. But Felicia would not have liked it, and what Felicia did and didn't like had become an increasingly important factor in his calculations, because he had a responsibility to her, and because he needed her. His waking dreams of the previous night had served to make that even clearer than it had been before.

On the other hand, now the sun was shining, brightly and warmly, in a patchily blue sky otherwise replete with beautiful white cumulus clouds, the seeming truths of the darkness did, indeed, begin to seem more like whispered lies than glorious revelations. Simon could feel his depression lifting gradually under the arrows of the sun, and his confidence in the future returning. He hadn't had a dream-slip all morning, and he couldn't help wondering whether it might be over, and whether he might be on the mend.

I can do this, he thought. *At the very least, I can handle Father Mallory. And then, whatever fate throws at me, I'll take the challenges one by one.*

But he knew that wasn't really him, not the Simon he knew and . . . well, anyway, not the Simon he knew.

What I really need, he thought, is to get back to my old routine. I need to get back to work: not snatches of work, here and here, but solid work, obsessive work twelve hours a day, seven days a week. It's not compatible with having a life, of course, but what does it matter? What does having a life offer by comparison? Complication, time-consumption and heartache. Is it worth it?

But he couldn't simply say *no* to that question. Felicia, Megan, Marianne, Zoe, and so on, might be as much as fifty per cent heartache, and Douglas Jefferson, Bernard Pallister and Thomas Mallory were probably a hundred per cent heartache, and all of them put together, like links in a chain, were consuming time on a quasi-cosmic scale, but even so, he thought, life, simply by virtue of being life, had its attractions and its compensations, and an intrinsic worth of its own. Perhaps he could do it, even though the Simon Cannick he knew might not have been able to.

Morpen had not been converted, yet, into an improvised car park. Unlike St. Madoc, and in spite of the fact that it actually had a village shop, it was still virtually deserted. A handful of its cottages seemed to have people in residence, but the majority were still waiting for temporary occupants, ever since the DSS tenants had been moved on before the deadline of their brief tenure. There was, however, one black Mercedes limousine that looked conspicuously out of place, not least because it had a chauffeur sitting patiently in the driving seat.

Simon had aimed to be a little early himself, in order to be inside the cottage when Thomas Mallory arrived. Mallory had apparently decided to be even earlier, although that might have been because his driver had overestimated the time that it would take to reach Morpen from St. Mary's Deanery in Carmarthen, never having driven the route before.

Thomas Mallory climbed out of the back seat of the Mercedes as Simon approached, shook his hand and apologized for seeming over-eager. Simon apologized in his turn. There were still fifteen minutes to go before the time that they had actually arranged to meet.

Simon took a step in the direction of the cottage door, fishing the key out of his pocket, but the Dominican stopped him. "As it's becoming such a pleasant day," he said, "why don't we stay outside? There seem to be paths leading to the south and the north, and woods not so far away across the fields. I spend far too much time indoors, poring over paperwork or in meetings with fellow Churchmen, who are, Lord forgive me, often not the most interesting company. May we walk a little way, at least out of sight of these rather depressing cottages?"

"Of course," said Simon. "There are no hostelries nearer than the Mermaid in St. Madoc, and very few amenities of any sort, except for the local general store—the village is almost a ghost nowadays—but the paths are adapted for walkers; there are benches at intervals, and the woods are pleasant: the last remnants of the ancient forest, where the druids allegedly once carried out the rites of their mysterious worship."

"So legend has it, I believe," said Mallory, lightly, as they began to walk along a northward-leading path, between two hedgerows. "Have you discussed my requests with Miss Murden?"

"Yes, I have," Simon said. "She's agreeable to my giving you a copy of her father's scans and translations of documents in the library, and his notes. She also agrees that it would be interesting and historically valuable to subject the oldest parchments to multispectral analysis, in order to discover whether there are any residual impressions of previous texts that might have been erased, but she's naturally anxious about what that might entail in terms of the displacement of the documents. She has given me permission to speak to you in general terms about the family's experiences, both distant and recent, in regard to the entity's psychological contagions, but she has also asked me to be wary, and to question you as carefully as I can about your opinions and intentions, in order to ascertain, as far as possible, that there will be no . . . repercussions."

"I see," said Mallory. "A certain caution on her part is understandable—especially in view of certain facts that I only learned last night . . . if one can dignify them with the term *facts*."

"What facts are those?" Simon asked, a trifle sharply, not bothering to quibble over matters of definition.

"I had a visit yesterday evening at the Deanery—one of
the gentlemen who were, to use Miss Harwyn's phrase, spying on our meeting yesterday. The one who would have been
spying on it had we stayed in the village just now."

"Douglas Jefferson," said Simon.

"Yes. I gather from your tone that you anticipated that he
might contact me. It wasn't easy to determine exactly what
he wanted from me, or what he hoped that I might be able to
do for him in exchange, but he did volunteer to make available to me the results of research he has conducted into the
inheritance of the Abbey and its contents. He seemed to be
under the impression—or at least entertaining the hope—
that the Church might lodge an objection to your entitlement
to inherit it, and he offered me his full support for any such
objection, should one materialize. He made some vague remarks about his interest in the land still owned by the Estate,
and the possibility of his buying it, or at least coordinating its
usage, but I got the strong impression that his real motives
were . . . more personal.

"I could simply have told him that the Church has no
intention of raising any objection to your inheritance of the
Abbey, but I must confess that I was intrigued by his attempted intervention, and his roundabout mode of procedure, so I
remained vague. Perhaps it's none of my business, but I am a
lawyer, after all, and strange cases are always intriguing, so
I . . . well, I suppose you could say that I led him on slightly.
He seemed a trifle disappointed to find that the revelations
he made regarding the entity under the Abbey—including
the fact that it sometimes changes color—and the entity in
the bay that sometimes sticks a tentacle out of the water,
came as no surprise to me, but I was parsimonious in giving
him more elaborate information."

Simon frowned, and then said, carefully: "It seems that
Mr. Jefferson had prepared an elaborate case entitling him to
at least a portion of the Murden inheritance some time before
my sudden arrival on the scene and the abrupt remaking of
James Murden's will. Since then, he's been making a series of

hasty adaptations to his plan, and trying to improvise alternative approaches, some of them a trifle desperate. He's already mounting a forceful attack on another front, but the possibility of mounting a pincer movement doubtless appeals to his sense of military esthetics. Although he certainly wants to get his hands on as much of the inheritance as possible, if he can, he also has personal reasons—or thinks he has—for wanting to stop me doing so. In coming to you, he might simply have been clutching at a straw, but I think it more likely that he was trying to sound you out in the hope of gleaning information that might be useful to him. He has another candidate in mind as a possible co-inheritor, but there are still practical and political difficulties in the way of his advancement, so he couldn't simply make you promises regarding his alternative candidate's willingness to hand over all the manuscripts in which you're interested, and give you free access to the Abbey's subterrains."

"Indeed," said Mallory. "He did, however, mention that his friend, Mr. Pallister, owns a construction firm, and would find it very easy to arrange the pouring of enormous quantities of liquid concrete into the subterrains at a moment's notice. He seemed to think that the Church might desire that. Naturally, I did not confirm or deny the hypothesis."

"He hasn't yet had Bernard make me the same offer," Simon said, "presumably because he doesn't think that I desire it."

"Which you are neither going to confirm nor deny, being even warier than I am. I do hope that we can make some progress in getting around that mutual wariness, because, quite frankly, I did not like Mr. Jefferson, who has something of the shady lawyer about him, and in spite of your cautious responses to my requests, I would far rather deal with you and Miss Murden in this matter than with him. Has Mr. Jefferson actually been down into the Abbey's subterrains?"

"I don't know for certain," Simon said, "but I think it unlikely. I'm seriously thinking of inviting him to do so, though, in order to clear the air a little. There's a bench just up ahead, if you'd like to sit down and chat—we're well out of sight of the cottages."

Mallory inspected the surroundings; they were in a small patch of woodland, dense enough to either side of the path, although the bench that Simon had noticed was in a clearing, still brightly sunlit at the present hour. He nodded, and they both sat down before the Dominican picked up the last comment that Simon had made.

"It is, of course, your prerogative to invite anyone you please into the caves beneath St. Madoc's Abbey," he observed, "but do you really believe that it is safe to do so?"

"I haven't yet seen anything to convince me that there's a serious danger," Simon said, carefully. "If you can tell me something about the Toulouse entity, or the Jerusalem entity, that will make me think otherwise, I'll be interested to hear it."

"Of course," said the Churchman. "Can you read Latin?"

Simon was unsurprised by the question, even though it had arrived so abruptly. "Not very well, at present," he said, "but if you're going to give me access to your research, I suppose I'll have to try. I taught myself to translate French with a dictionary, and the French I translate is sometimes peppered with Latin quotations, so I've made a start of sorts. Can you read Welsh?"

Mallory uttered a slight laugh. "No, I can't," he said, "and I haven't even made a start." He produced a memory stick out of one of the capacious pockets of his black overcoat. "This contains scans of all the documents I have that are of any relevance to St. Madoc's Abbey, and selected documents related to the Toulouse entity—mostly in Latin, I fear, much of it in rather bad Latin, and I fear that you'll probably have difficulty even with the small fraction in Old French. If you want to make a superficial examination of the contents before reciprocating, I have a tablet computer in my pocket, fully charged." He reached for the other pocket as he spoke.

"No," said Simon, "let's not waste time." He produced a memory stick of his own, and they made the exchange.

"Thank you," said the Dominican. "For trusting me, as well as for the documents. We've already made the point, I think, that working directly from the sources will be tedious and will take a long time, and that it will save us both time and effort if we can at least begin a verbal summary and commentary, provided that we can overcome, or temporarily set aside, the inevitable differences in vocabulary. I have some very important questions that I want to ask you, which I hope you'll be prepared to answer, and I'm sure that you have some you want to ask me. As I'm the supplicant here, however, perhaps I ought to start. What would you like to know?"

"It's a long list," Simon said, "and it's difficult to know where to start, but . . . you referred yesterday to the entity beneath the Abbey as 'blue honeycombs' and you used an analogy of a hydra in describing the Church, presumably to imply that you know about the existence and nature of the neider—that's what James Murden called the hydra-like marine entity—which you've just confirmed. If you'd like to expand on those remarks, I'll be happy to compare my own interpretations with yours."

"Most satisfactory. Obviously, you have the advantage over me of actually having seen the blue entity, and most of my information is doubly indirect. The bulk of it was collected by Dominican inquisitors in the course of their interrogations, but the Toulouse entity had been discovered before the foundation of the Order, let alone the Inquisition with which it became involved. The initial investigations on behalf of the Church were carried out by papal envoys and agents of Bishop Foulque. To cut the story short, the entity beneath a hill outside Toulouse . . ."

"Outside? It wasn't beneath the cathedral?"

"No, it was well beyond the city wall. In Foulque's time there was a shrine on the hill, ostensibly dedicated to the Virgin, but Foulque had it destroyed and obliterated."

"*Ostensibly* dedicated to the Virgin Mary?"

"Yes. You know, and have made the point in your own works, that many Christian religious sites were readapted from pagan originals, and that such readaptations are very numerous in the French Midi. Whether the other entities once existent there were associated with similar readapted shrines, I don't know, but I suspect so."

"There were entities in the Midi other than the Toulouse entity? How many?"

"We believe that there were three in total in the south of France, although the inquisitors were only able to establish the exact location of the one near Toulouse. The others were already undiscoverable, having presumably been hidden."

"Not destroyed?"

"Possibly, but my predecessors suspected that they had been buried in order to conceal and protect them. The references we have to them are essentially legendary. You've explored part of the legendry yourself, before you had any means of connecting it to entities of whose existence you had no suspicion then."

"You mean the legend of the three Maries who supposedly came to the south of France with Joseph of Arimathea and the Holy Grail?"

"Yes. As you know, it isn't only religious sites that were readapted, but religious figures, who became saints, or had their legendary legacy added to and blended with the legends of existing saints. Female figures were usually readapted as the Virgin or Mary Magdalen. Your books examine various such cosmetic adaptations, including the veneration of Clemence Isaure in Toulouse. It's possible—probable, even—that the sites in the south of France, like St. Madoc's Abbey, were only cosmetically Christianized."

"So you think that each of the three entities in the south of France was associated with a mother goddess of some sort, just as the St. Madoc entity was linked to Ceridwen?"

"That is my speculative reading, yes—assisted, I admit, by your work on the legendry of the Midi. The Toulouse entity seems to have been regarded by its associates, prior to the thirteenth century, as essentially benign, and, for that matter essentially divine, as a source of inspiration and revelation: although it was recognized that the people vulnerable to its influence frequently went mad, the madness in question was commonly regarded as divine, associated by Christians with the paraclete, and by so-called gnostics with Ennoia, or Sophia. The entity wasn't always blue, however. Sometimes it turned red, a phenomenon sometimes associated with emanations of darkness . . ."

Mallory stopped, and Simon realized that a change in his expression must have given him away.

"Have you seen that happen, Mr. Cannick?" asked the Dominican. "An emanation of darkness, I mean?"

At the risk of identifying himself as an instrument of the Devil—because it was obvious now where the Churchman's argument was going—Simon said: "Yes."

"And?" Mallory prompted him.

"And I can begin to understand where the Devil comes into your argument," Simon said. "Yes, the occasional redness would probably seem ominous and threatening to an observer, and the impenetrable darkness sometimes associated with it could easily be mistaken for a diabolical phenomenon, being a good deal more absolute than common-or-garden night and shadow."

"Are you absolutely sure, Mr. Cannick, that your use of the word *mistaken* is justified?"

"Absolutely," said Simon.

"Because it's a matter of faith on your part? Because you refuse to imagine the alternative?"

"Yes. So far, you haven't mentioned the hydra. Where does that fit in to your account? Toulouse is a long way from the sea, but it is on the Garonne, I suppose."

Mallory hesitated, but he consented to go where he was now being led. "It is," he agreed, "but that isn't the point. You know, obviously, that the south of France is ridded with cave systems, an enormously rich source of information for speleology?"

"Yes."

"And you know, too, that exploration of almost all the deep systems comes to an end, in practical terms, when the explorers reach water: underground wells, or even lakes."

"I know there's a legend that the cathedral in Toulouse is built on top of one such cave system and underground lake."

"That example has been Romanticized, perhaps by read-aptation. You know, too, that surface lakes are sometimes simply the superficial termini of extensive underground water-filled pits—which are, so far as divers are able to discover, bottomless."

"There's a rich legendry of bottomless lakes and bottomless wells, and they're commonly associated with diabolical legends. You're presumably telling me that the Toulouse entity, and its one-time analogues, were located in supposedly bottomless cave systems, filled to a certain level with water?"

"Yes."

"And that the water in question was inhabited by hydralike beings analogous to the neider of Morgan's Fork?"

"I believe so. And I believe, as you have evidently gathered, that those entities are indeed diabolical, the basis of a vast number of legendary entities that, when seen only partially, are typically represented as worms, snakes or dragons."

"Including the serpent in Eden?" Simon couldn't resist the temptation to suggest.

"Yes," said the Churchman, without hesitation

"You believe in the literal truth of *Genesis*, then?"

"No, but I believe in its metaphorical truth, its truth as a parable. I'm aware that you do not, and that you have strong objections to the apparent misogyny of the parable."

"Only *apparent*? Let's leave that aside, though. Although Christians have always identified the serpent in Eden with the Devil, isn't it true that there's no actual textual evidence for that in *Genesis*? That God speaks to the serpent as if it were merely a serpent, not a spiritual being in disguise?"

"I'm aware of that observation, but it's a distinction without a difference; the serpent plays a diabolical role, and is all the more suited to it if one takes away the notion that it might have been a caricaturish humanoid devil—an uglified fallen angel—in fancy dress. The caricaturing of evil, and the entire mythology of Lucifer and the war in Heaven, often serves evil's cause, by making a ludicrous scarecrow of it. But evil is real, Mr. Cannick, and it very often does take the form of fragmentable hydrae, of swarms of snakes . . . and evil does try to disguise itself, most of the time, as good, as benign. Lies can only function in an environment of truth, and by donning a hypocritical mask; they cannot admit what they are, because that would be self-defeating. That is why your neider appears to you to be benign—and, in fact, goes to considerable lengths to persuade you of that fact. It is not. Beware, above all, of accepting its gifts."

That ship, Simon thought, *has sailed. A long time ago.* But he did not say it aloud.

"Of course," Mallory added, "there is nothing to prevent the serpent from putting on human form occasionally, for deceptive purposes, but it does not appear to be a simple matter, and if the lore of folklore and legend can be trusted, it can be a slow and highly problematic process. As you said a moment ago, reputedly bottomless lakes and bottomless pits are often associated with diabolism—and, of course, with what the Welsh once called morgens."

"Which you regard as inherently diabolical?"

"Is that not what myth, legend and folklore suggest and assume? Sirens and their kin are almost invariably assumed to be agents of doom, are they not? Or is that merely *apparent misogyny?*"

"In fact, yes," said Simon. "Sirens, lorelei, morgens and all manner of supernatural temptresses luring sailors and travelers to their doom are essentially representations of male resentment of their own reflexive lust, and the vulnerability entailed in being attracted to beautiful women."

"A difference in vocabulary, Mr. Cannick. May I enquire, by the way, as a matter of casual interest, how many additional tourists were drawn to St. Madoc yesterday by your great-niece's masquerade?"

"Too many," Simon said. "Are you accusing Krysten of being an agent of the Devil?"

"Doubtless an unwitting and entirely innocent one, but perhaps. I was interested by Miss Harwyn's reaction, by the way, even though she claimed in so many words to have no moral high ground on which to stand—but perhaps she has already confessed her sins, and is seeking repentance in her own fashion. Let's not get into that, though. Is it my turn, do you think, to ask some questions of you, now?

Simon had to concede, in a spirit of fair play, that it probably was. "Go ahead," he said

"Am I right in assuming that you regard the neider as a purely natural phenomenon?"

"Yes. A very odd one, admittedly, involving exotic states of matter, including those that make up the dark matter forming the greater part of the mass of the universe."

"And you think they evolved, in parallel with all other earthly life-forms?"

"Not exactly. I think they do evolve, like everything else, but I suspect that they might have begun their evolution as artificial entities, deliberately created—but not by God."

"By whom, then?"

"By entities living in the earth's core—entities mostly composed of exotic states of matter: radically alien organisms, but nevertheless organisms of a sort, possessed of exotic bodies.. . and exotic minds."

"I see. And the blue entities that sometimes turn red? Are they natural organisms too, in your view?"

"Natural, certainly. I hesitated for a long time as to whether it makes sense to regard them as organisms, although they certainly give the impression of being alive when examined at close range. During my first close contact with the neider I formed the impression that they were a kind of communication device, a means of enhancing and focusing telepathic contacts between unconscious minds. I still think that they have that property, and that the neider's interest in them relates to the possibilities entailed by it, but I'm also inclined to accept the implications of James Murden's characterization, and to think of them as closely analogous to cocoons—cells containing larvae of some kind."

"A pupation extending over hundreds, if not thousands, of years?" Mallory queried.

"Hundreds, certainly, but the larvae contained in the vitreous cocoons beneath the Abbey now might not be the same ones as those contained in St. Madoc's time."

Mallory was an intelligent man, and a man accustomed to examining the implications of counterarguments to his own. "You're suggesting that when the cocoons turn red, it's because some kind of hatching is taking place?"

"It's possible."

"And what, in that case, is the imago of your hypothetical larva?"

"I was rather hoping that you might be able to help me with that, on the basis of the reports your Domincian predecessors made of the . . . termination of the Toulouse entity. Evidently, they would not have been able to identify any metamorphosite as such, but that doesn't necessarily mean that observations weren't made by the people they . . . questioned."

"That's an interesting hypothesis—but it seems to me that if you have actually seen the blue honeycombs turn red, and observed the flow of Stygian darkness, you're in a far better position to make judgments than any Medieval witness. Have you seen anything faintly resembling an imago?"

"No," Simon admitted, "but I'm wary of getting carried too far by the analogy, and looking for something resembling an insect, flying in the atmosphere. To judge by its intrinsically confusing appearances, the entity has far more exotic matter in its make-up than baryonic matter; it's not impossible that the imago, as you put it, is an entity composed entirely of exotic matter . . . an entity akin to the parents of the hydra, whose natural habitat is the Earth's core."

"I think I see what you mean. You're suggesting that they might hatch *inwards*, producing entities that plunge into the earth's interior, returning to what you imagine to be their source?"

"I think it's possible. At one time I thought that the core intelligences designed and manufactured the neider and the morgens with a view to colonizing the earth's surface and establishing communication with human beings. Now I think it more likely that they created the neider with a view to obtaining control over the vitreous cocoons in order to use them as means of communication with other intelligent beings elsewhere in the universe—but that the task of controlling the employment of the cocoons is problematic in more ways than one."

"Because the blue entities react against the attempt to take control of them?"

"Partly—but I don't think it's quite as simple as that. Again, I'm trying to be wary of crude analogies."

"But you don't think that the same entities that created the neider also created the blue entities?"

"Surely not. When I was first persuaded that the vitreous cocoons can function as a communication device, I thought that their origin might be extraterrestrial, but what you've just told me about the neider-analogue in Toulouse, in combination with a suggestion that you made yesterday and the way my own hypotheses had begun to develop, are now inclining me in another direction."

"Which is?"

"When I first imagined the core intelligences that created the neider, I imagined them, as it were, monolithically—all united in a common cause. Now, I think that perhaps they're in competition, perhaps even in conflict. Not necessarily at war, but perhaps, like the Roman Church, fragmented into countless quasi-independent and instinctively secret factions and sects. It's at least conceivable that core intelligences did design and place sets of vitreous cocoons as well as the hydrae, but even if they were, in essence, similar core intelligences, they might have done so without the right tentacle knowing what the left tentacle was doing. It's all pure speculation, of course."

"The Devil finds work for idle tentacles," Mallory quipped. "Interesting, I suppose, but a somewhat peripheral issue. I think I could have deduced all that from your book on dark matter, but I'm grateful to have it spelled out, and supplemented by your recent observations. The more interesting fraction of that book, it seems to me, is the speculative section concerned with dark mind. Its basic argument, I think, is sound—to wit, that the human mind functions unconsciously to a considerable degree, and that its unconscious components are mysterious by definition. I can follow all the arguments about the mechanisms of the unconscious mind being unknowable directly, but knowable via some of their effects, and that their more peculiar effects, including dreams, hallucinations and delusions, constitute a rich resource for attempts to understand. I sympathize, too, with your notion of a collective unconscious maintained, in part, by a kind of inherent means of communication between minds, the ultimate extension of which is universal mind, tacitly present everywhere—although I think your insistent refusal to recognize that the universal mind is God's a trifle perverse. I cannot see any advantage in calling it a *hypermind*, as if that label differed from the notion of God in any meaningful way. Given that you seem to take it for granted, as a rule of your own faith, that the mind in question is fundamentally benign, although working in mysterious ways, I find it even odder that you are so resolute in denying its godliness. Is it simply because you cannot imagine that, if God is as you conceive Him, there can be any purpose in worship, prayer or faith?"

"I can see that faith, prayer, and even worship, do serve a psychological function . . . ," Simon began.

"But as we are agreed that God is essentially a mind, a supreme intelligence," Mallory interjected, too eager in following his own hobby-horse even to let Simon finish his sentence, "what other functions could they have? Surely you're dabbling in pleonasm, if not tautology?"

"But that's surely not the way that the Church imagines them," Simon argued. "The Church doesn't think of them as mere self-help trickery. The Church promises material rewards for prayer, faith and worship: salvation, heaven and resurrection."

"We might disagree about what we can and do mean by material rewards," said the Churchman, "but I would consider that to be yet another argument over terminology. The Church certainly does assert that there are real rewards that can be acquired by the immortal soul if, and only if, that soul repents of its sins and accepts divine dominion and regulation. But your conception of the dark part of the human mind as something that is part of a much larger, undying mentality, is surely fully compatible with the Christian concept of an immortal soul, and unless I am misreading your own moral philosophy drastically, you certainly have a concept of sin, and do not disagree about the possibility, and goodness of repentance.. Your only real objection, it seems to me, is to the concept of priestly absolution, but you are not unaware that the priest is merely an agent, who performs a symbolic ritual, and that the only absolution — the only possible absolution — comes from God."

"It's a fantasy," said Simon, aware that he was being carried away in a direction in which he had promised himself in advance not to go, but unable to resist the pull of the argumentative tide. "There is no absolution, because there is no God: nothing that takes an interest in us, nothing that cares about us, nothing that responds to worship, prayer or faith. All that there is, and all that there can be, is a summation of all the chaotic urges, appetencies and unconscious desires, whose aspect of connectivity and contagion enables such a sum to be made, arithmetically, and individual minds can react to that summation, but the arithmetical calculation of a total doesn't make that total into an active, censorious entirety possessed of power, motivation or morality. There is no God, in the way the Church imagines one; the very idea is absurd. Ditto the Devil.

"Yes, Father, you're correct in saying that I do have a moral philosophy. I think that things are wrong when they do harm, that sin consists of doing harm to others, and that repentance of one's wrongdoing is evidence of psychological and moral progress. But there is no absolution for sins, nor is there any kind of active agency that personifies evil and tempts us to evil, simply because that's its *raison d'être*. People tempt one another to wrongdoing because other people's losses are their own gains, in terms of crude materialistic calculation. And if you think that the neider, singular or plural, is inherently evil, you can't just pretend to explain that by sticking a diabolical label on it. You have to explain what it's doing in terms of some kind of advantage that it could gain from harming the people that it harms—and tempting them away from the dogmas of the church by revealing to them the stupidity, malignity and harmful consequences of those dogmas doesn't count. Heresy is not a sin. Burning heretics is."

"In fact," said Thomas Mallory, mildly, "I have no quarrel with your final statement, except that you're implying that it summarizes and encapsulates your whole argument. Your theology is faulty, but I don't suppose you care about that. You ought, however, to care about the fact that your psychology is faulty. It isn't the case that people only sin, or mostly sin, for the sake of material gain, and it certainly isn't the case that people only tempt others to sin or usually tempt others to sin, for that reason. The roots of hatred go far deeper than that, and are far more complex. Precisely because of that depth and that complexity, they're amenable to all kinds of hypothetical explanatory schemes, but behind all of that smokescreen, if you look carefully enough, with a clinical eye, you'll see the Devil. And you'll also understand that the only possibility there is of defeating the Devil, and the only hope there is of defeating active evil, is the power and authority of God. I can understand why so many people

226

are able to doubt that he exists, but without him, what would we have? Damnation. We have to believe in the possibility of salvation, because there would otherwise be no point to existence, no point to Creation. Because we exist, and are the way we are, God must exist too, and must be the way he is, and salvation must be possible. It's not the existence of God that's unthinkable and inconceivable, but the opposite."

"The limitation of your imagination," said Simon, "is not an argument. And that's why the difference between us isn't a matter of terminology. It's much more fundamental than that."

"I take your point," said the Dominican. "The difference between us is, indeed, more fundamental than I had hoped. Do I take it then, bringing the argument back to the matter of immediate concern, that you are not planning to oppose the entity that you call the neider: that you are going to assume its benignity and do its bidding?"

"Not necessarily," Simon said. "But I'm certainly going to listen to whatever it says, if it can contrive to speak at all, without prejudgment, and also to listen to whatever communications might come through the vitreous cocoons, blue or red, and judge them, so far as I can, on their merits. Do you have any objection to that?"

"Personally, no," said Mallory. "I shall be interested to observe the result, if only from a safe distance—but I'm a lawyer, not a saint, a historian, or an exorcist. I have faith in God and his limitation of the power of evil; but I do urge you, Mr. Cannick, to take into account the fact that what you do will affect others as well as yourself. If you are damned, you might not go to your damnation alone."

"That is a matter that has been preying on my mind somewhat," Simon admitted. "Do you have any more questions to put to me about my theories of dark matter and dark mind?"

"A great many, if we can find the time," said Thomas Mallory, "but for the moment, you might like to draw a little more deeply into this wood, if you want to observe without being observed. Mr. Jefferson, it seems, suffers from the sin of impatience. Rather than waiting for us to return to Morpen, he seems to have hastily improvised a plan to run into us by apparent accident. But he does not have the lady with him; she must still be in his cottage. Shall we move?"

And although he knew that it was utterly unworthy of him, and flew in the face of everything he believed, not to mention his alleged loathing of cliché, Simon could not help his recalcitrant consciousness forming the thought:

Speak of the devil . . .

XIV
In the Wood

Simon had his back to the section of the path that led to Morpen, and his first impulse was to turn round in order to see what had attracted Father Mallory's attention, but the Domincian had already grasped his sleeve and was pulling him toward a dense clump of trees behind the bench. Simon was vaguely amused by the Dominican's almost child-like desire to hide, and meekly allowed himself to be drawn.

On the way, he permitted himself a correction to his former thought, borrowing yet again from Father Mallory: *But he isn't the devil. He isn't even the pettiest of antichrists . . .*

Within a matter of seconds both men had taken up the positions selected by the Dominican, from which they could peer out through a thicket and see Douglas Jefferson strolling along the path, with the careless stride of a man simply savoring the county air and the sunshine, with no hidden agenda in mind—or pretending conscientiously that that as what he was doing.

"I thought he was going back to Swansea today to meet up with Cerys," Simon muttered, pensively. "By *lady*, I assume you mean Jocasta Symonds? She's still here too?"

"I have no idea who she is," said Mallory, "except that she bears an uncannily strong resemblance to Miss Harwyn. If I had not been early for our meeting, I would not have caught a glimpse of them, but they had just visited the shop. They saw the car, of course. I expect that Mr. Jefferson is eager to know what I might have said to you about what I saw—or perhaps he feels that, since his presence here is now known, he might as well be open about it."

"And why, exactly, are we hiding?" asked Simon, although he didn't have the slightest objection to it, for the moment.

"It's my automatic reaction to being pursued," said Mallory, "although it might, of course, be you he's pursuing."

"Oh, it is," said Simon, softly.

"Purely for motives of possible material gain?"

"Touché" Simon conceded. "But not because he's an agent of the Devil, either. He just thinks that I'm his bastard half-brother."

"Thinks?"

"The DNA evidence isn't conclusive, at that degree of consanguinity. So unless his father has actually admitted to the statutory rape of my mother, yes, it can only be a matter of possibility, the likelihood of which he might be overestimating. He didn't mind so much when he thought it was his secret, but since I let him know yesterday, perhaps foolishly, that I know about the DNA evidence too. I suspect that his animosity has increased. He certainly seems to have stepped up his activity. If the lady is staying in the cottage overnight again, that might be a trifle ominous, from my point of view. Either way, though, I need to have a word with Dougie, and I might not get another opportunity as convenient. I'll catch him on his way back to the cottage, if I may?"

"It's not for me to impede your plans, Mr. Cannick," the other said. The Dominican already had enough crumbs of information to take a few inferences, and he continued almost seamlessly. "The lady staying in his cottage is Miss Harwyn's daughter, I suppose?" he guessed. "And she has a son, who therefore has a plausible claim to a portion of James Murden's estate?"

"Yes."

"Interesting. And yet, he still came to me in order to discover whether the Church might make a claim to the whole, and to offer me the assistance of his tiny fraction of gathered evidence in totally unnecessary support."

"That sums it up quite neatly," said Simon, his gaze following Douglas Jefferson, who was now well past the clump of trees, seemingly unaware of any human presence within it.

"A trifle devious. But Miss Harwyn seems to be aligned with you, against her own offspring, unless I'm mistaken?"

"She is. The situation is complicated. Megan had refused to co-operate with Jefferson, twice—again, nothing to do with material gain, just the repentance of old sins—and that became a complicating factor in his plan to press the mother or the son to put in a claim on the basis of evidence he can provide. The relationship between Megan and her daughter, which was non-existent when you met her yesterday, might now be very complicated—perhaps more complicated than she imagines."

"Fascinating," said the Dominican lawyer. "Did I mention that I love complication, in legal matters?"

"You did," said Simon. "If you wanted to involve yourself in this one, on Dougie's side, I'm sure you'd earn his undying gratitude. As you say, Bernard Pallister owns a construction company. If Dougie asked him to do it, and paid the necessary price, he could not only fill Myrddin's Cave with concrete but blow the neider to Kingdom Come with high explosive."

"And why would I want him to do that?"

"Because you think it's diabolical?"

"Did I not mention that if I ever met the Devil, I'd want to sit down with him, and have a philosophical discussion, rather than simply shout *Vade retro satanas?*"

"You also mentioned that you didn't want to come to St. Madoc because you thought it might be dangerous."

"That was before I talked to you."

"And now you think it isn't dangerous?"

"Oh, no. Now I'm absolutely certain that it's not only dangerous but urgently dangerous—but, precisely because of that, it might be worth the risk of confrontation."

"So you don't want to help Dougie try to prove that Anthony Symonds is the rightful heir to St. Madoc's Abbey, in exchange for a cartload of Medieval manuscripts, including at least a few juicy palimpsests?"

"I'm a man of God, not a market-trader. If Mr. Jefferson wants my help, he'll have to prove that his is the side of right and virtue, and yours the Devil's side. Simply telling me that Miss Harwyn and your mother were once prostitutes is not going to achieve that end, given Jesus's own example. My instinct is to consider fallen women more sinned against that sinning."

Simon didn't bother to object that it was his grandmother, not his mother, who had been a prostitute, especially in view of his mother's deathbed confession that she was not in a position to cast the first stone in that particular matter. Instead, he simply said: "You're not at all what I expected, Father Mallory."

"I'm not what anyone expects," said Mallory. "That makes me a more effective lawyer, and, I hope, no worse a preacher. Am I correct in assuming, now, that you're happy to continue our discussion, and to answer more of my questions, when I've had a chance to look at the documents you've given me—and, of course, *vice versa?* I really do think that between the two of us, in spite of our differences, with the aid of the documents now in our joint possession, we might be able to build up a much clearer picture not only of what might be happening in St. Madoc now but what happened in Toulouse in the twelfth and thirteenth centuries."

"Yes," said Simon, without hesitation, resisting the temptation to add any comment about Jerusalem or Mecca. "But I am rather tied up in St. Madoc at the moment, with my family visiting, and I really would prefer it if I didn't have to come to Carmarthen again."

"Of course," said the Dominican. "In fact, in view of the revelations you've made to me in the course of this conversation, I'm now not only willing but eager to visit St. Madoc. Perhaps I'll be a fool rushing in where an angel might fear to tread, but at least I'm an armored fool. May we arrange a time and place to meet again, if you're going to intercept Mr. Jefferson on his way back to the village?"

"I can't specify anything at this moment, but I'll consult Felicia and Megan, and I'm sure I'll be able to find a slot some time tomorrow. I don't have a mobile phone, but I have your number; I'll ring you this afternoon, or this evening, at the latest. If you want to speak to me before then, you have the number of the Abbey landline. If a lady named Margaret answers, though, it might be wise to check later that any message you leave has got through; she's a trifle forgetful."

"I'll remember. And here's Mr. Jefferson again, coming back at a swifter pace than he went, having obviously given up on encountering us on the path. Thank you for the documents. Mr. Cannick—and God bless you."

"Thanks," said Simon. "You too. Excuse me for rushing off."

Having said that, he left the Domincian lurking discreetly in the wood, and emerged into the open. He went to intercept Douglas Jefferson, who feigned silent astonishment at finding him in his path.

"Might I have a word, Mr. Jefferson?" Simon asked, with the utmost politeness.

Douglas Jefferson peered intently at the clump of trees, obviously looking for the representative of the Holy Office, but accepted the latter's invisibility meekly, without making any enquiry as to his whereabouts.

"Of course, Mr. Cannick," he said, smoothly. "What can I do for you?" In spite of his careful self-control, there was a definitive wariness in his gaze.

"It's more a matter of what I might be able to do for you, Mr. Jefferson," he said. "I fear that we parted on a slightly sour note yesterday—entirely my fault, I fear. Certain information had just been brought to my attention which disturbed me slightly, before I had thought it through properly. When I had, I realized that the inference that had been indicated to me might not be correct, and it occurred to me that if the same inference had been indicated to you, you might also not have had a chance to think it through. So, to begin with, I'd like to clear the air."

"I'm afraid that you're talking in riddles, Mr. Cannick. I have no idea what you mean."

"I'm sorry. I mean that I had just been told about a DNA comparison that seems to imply that you and I might be more closely related than distant cousins: that our genetic profiles had a number of common alleles, including a seemingly-significant one in the Y-chromosome, corresponding to the number that might have been expected if we had the same father, but different mothers."

"*Seems* to imply?" Jefferson parried, his wariness increasing markedly.

"Yes. I don't know how much you know about genetics, but as an occasional science fiction writer, I've had occasion to keep up, with intense interest, with the development of genomic analysis and DNA comparison. I know that such appearances crop up more easily than laymen often realize, having been told insistently by TV melodramas about the absolute certainly of such comparisons. No matter what either of us might think about the possibility that we are more closely related than distant cousins, I think, on careful reflection, there it is highly probable that we are not."

Jefferson thought for a few moments, perhaps deciding how best to phrase his question. In the end he said: "The comparison you saw"—he stressed the *you* faintly but precisely—indicated a certain number of what you call alleles in common? But you think that there might be another explanation for that than inheritance from the same male parent?"

"I do. I believe that you've conducted extensive research into the genealogy of the Murden family, in collaboration with Alexander Usher, and are therefore aware of the unusual number of marriages within the family, especially in the nineteenth century, between first cousins?"

Douglas Jefferson was no fool. He saw immediately where that argument might lead. His face brightened visibly. "You think there might be higher levels of apparent consanguinity between the various branches of the family that trace their descent back to Seymour Murden than would be expected if their marriages had been more . . . haphazard?"

"I do. The genealogies, incomplete as they are, offer strong grounds for that suspicion, and further evidence is collectible, at least in theory. I suspect that if we were able to make further comparisons, we might well find several other individuals with the same number of common alleles that you and I have. In particular, I think we might find that the particular anomaly on the Y-chromosome that caught the consultant's attention, might be common not merely to you and me but to most, if not all, of Seymour Murden's male descendants—Bernard Pallister, for example, although the likelihood of either of us having the same father as him is surely remote. I'm not in a position to confirm or refute the hypothesis, but perhaps you could, and thus set your mind at rest."

After a substantial pause for thought, Jefferson said: "That is, indeed, food for thought, Mr. Cannick, and perhaps a useful basis for further exploration. Thank you for bringing it to my attention. You rightly supposed that, as a layman, I have unthinkingly adopted a kind of quasi-religious faith in the implication of DNA comparisons. You really think that the Murdens are exceptional in regard to their common genes, then?"

"I'm sure of it. In some cases, as you know, it goes as far as apparent identity, but even in cases where no such suspicion can arise, there are often evident phenotypical similarities. My half-sister Marianne, for instance, bears a close physical resemblance to James Murden's sister Felicia. It's not impossible, in my opinion, that if my unknown father really was a descendant of Seymor Murden, that he was from James's branch rather than yours."

The brightness disappeared from Douglas Jefferson's face, to be replaced by a sudden anxiety. "Wait a minute," he said. "Are you saying that you think that *James Murden* might have been your father?"

"I think it unlikely—but a DNA comparison in that instance would certainly be able to confirm or deny it. In the case of the likely denial, however, there might nevertheless be sufficient alleles in common indicate a relationship as close as the one implied by comparison of my DNA with yours. I'm not in a position to make the comparison myself, and poor James is dead—but I'm sure that Megan is in a position to make it. No such claim of relationship would stand up in court, obviously, there being far too much scope for reasonable doubt—but I must confess to having been utterly astonished when I discovered that I had been named in James's will as his heir. Do you think that it might be possible that he knew something that we don't?"

Jefferson, as a layman in matters of genetics and genomics, obviously found the possibilities dangled by Simon all too plausible, and worrying. "And Megan Harwyn has a sample of James's DNA for comparison?" he said, anxiously.

"Indeed she does. She obtained it in order to compare it with her own, obviously, just as she wanted to compare mine with Angela Richardson's—but she can probably make the cross-comparison with a few taps on her computer keyboard. I can't help wondering what her reaction might be to the discovery that she might be more closely related to me than she and I initially assumed. Pleased, I hope—but one never can tell, can one, family tensions being what they are?"

Douglas Jefferson took a deep breath, seemingly having just taken in food for thought that would take some time to digest. "It's obviously a matter to which I'll have to give careful consideration when I have time, Mr. Cannick," he said, in a scrupulously even voice. "It's kind of you to bring it to my attention." He took a step in the direction of Morpen.

"Another moment, please, if it's not too inconvenient, Mr. Jefferson. I might be a little premature, but while I'm in your presence, I don't want the opportunity to pass. I'd very much like to invite you to drop in at the Abbey some time tomorrow, if you're not too busy, in order that I can grant the request you made at James's funeral to look at the crypt—and the cave beneath it, which you might know as Merlin's Cave, or the Cauldron of Rebirth."

He paused to savor the expression of astonishment on Jefferson's face—which, he was certain, must be authentic this time—but he continued almost seamlessly: "I'll have to obtain Felicia's permission, but I'm sure that there won't be any difficulty. I realize that James was intensely secretive about the contents of the cave, and I know that Felicia's automatic impulse was to continue that policy, which I naturally supported—but after an embarrassing interview with your friend Reverend Usher, I quickly came to the conclusion that there was no point in the continuation of the dog-in-a-manger attitude. At present, I'm only a guest in the Abbey, but I seem to have acquired a measure of influence there, and as you're a member of the family, who has been kind to both Felicia and Cerys, and there's a possibility that we might have occasion to work in collaboration in the future, I feel quite strongly that you ought to be initiated to the so-called family secret. Cerys might well have described the vitreous cocoons to you already, but a second-hand description is no substitute for seeing them with your own eyes. Don't you agree?"

To judge by appearances, it was perhaps as well that Simon had spun out his speech at such length, because Jefferson might not have been in a condition to reply had he simply issued the invitation and stopped. As things were, the schemer had had time to collect himself.

"That's extremely kind of you, Mr. Cannick," he said, warily.

"Well, I have a reputation to live up to in that regard," Simon said, blandly. "Mrs. Symonds told me yesterday that you'd referred her to me because of my kindness. I was delighted to be of some assistance. Megan was apprehensive at first, but I'm very glad that she took my advice to see Mrs.

Symonds, and whatever difficulties there might be at first, on either side, my own experience gives me hope that something positive might come of it, for which everyone will have cause to be grateful. If so, you will have played a significant angelic role, as was doubtless your intention."

"Of course," said Jefferson, feigning sincerity magnificently, but presumably well aware that he had just been outcompeted in the subtle hypocrisy stakes. "I'll be delighted to accept your invitation. What time would you like me to come to the Abbey?"

"I have to check with Felicia first, for form's sake, May I ring you later this afternoon—or early this evening, at the latest—to fix a time? I have your mobile number."

"I'll look forward to your call," said Jefferson. "I don't think I have any appointments for tomorrow that can't be moved, in view of the importance of your offer, but I'll have to check with my secretary—for form's sake, as you say. But for now, I really must get back to Mrs. Symonds. I promised to drive her to Swansea, in order to catch her train, and I told her that I was only stepping out for a few minutes, while she made some private calls of her own."

"Of course," said Simon "I understand completely"—and he was pleased to judge, from Douglas Jefferson's expression that the other man seemed to believe him. Simon felt a sudden surge of elation, which dispelled the last lingering traces of the early morning's gloom.

Jefferson strode off rapidly. Simon refrained from following him, but walked back into the stand of trees, where, not at all to his surprise, he found Thomas Mallory, O.P., still lurking

"Did you hear all that?" he asked.

"Most of it," the Dominican admitted. "Very interesting—and esthetically satisfying. I gather that you're planning to kill two birds with one stone, as it were, by inviting the two of us to the Abbey simultaneously?"

"The idea had occurred to me," Simon said. "Would you have any objection to that?"

"None at all," the Churchman assured him.

"Even though it will mean that there will be at least one of the Devil's minions in our company? Metaphorically speaking, of course."

"But the two of you seemed to be on the best of terms—superficially."

"So we did. I was careful not to turn my back on him, though, in case he had a concealed dagger."

"I'm sure that the thought of murdering you would have never crossed his mind, Mr. Cannick," said the Dominican. "The spot might be remote, but he must have known perfectly well that I could not be far away, and it is never a good idea to commit a serious crime in the presence of a lawyer employed by the Holy Office."

"Which might be another good reason to have you accompany us down into the cauldron tomorrow. Not that I was being serious a moment ago. I'm quite certain that Mr. Jefferson has no intention of causing me physical harm. Any danger that we might run in going down into the cave beneath the crypt will be common. But as you already know, if we find that the cocoons are red, as they were last time I was down there . . ."

"A confrontation from which you seem to have suffered no harm," the Dominican pointed out, naïvely.

Simon was tempted to add that *seems* was the operative word, but that would have led to an explanation that he did not want to offer, for the present. Instead he said: "Even so, I feel that it's only fair that I should warn you that your fears regarding the danger of proximity to the vitreous cocoons might be fully justified at present. If you would like to change your mind . . ."

For a few seconds, the pensive Dominican gave the impression of a man who thought that the wise decision might indeed be to back out, but he stiffened slightly, as if he were deliberately pulling himself together—as if he were aware that the game had suddenly changed, but could not resist the temptation to play it anyway.

"I see no reason to repent of my decision to accept your generous invitation, Mr. Cannick," he said, carefully, "but, reflecting on our conversation, may I return the compliment that you paid me and say that you're not at all what I expected?"

"I try not to be the kind of writer who finds a successful formula and sticks to it religiously," Simon told him. "I like to keep moving on, re-creating myself. And to be perfectly honest, I haven't been my old self for quite some time—but I feel a great deal better now than I did yesterday, or even early this morning. It would be a drastic overstatement to say that I'm content with myself, but I'm considerably less discontented that I was when we first met."

"I sincerely hope that you have every reason to be, Mr. Cannick," said Mallory. "Now, as time is passing, I think I ought to return to the Mercedes. I'm very eager to look at the documents on your memory stick, as a preparation for seeing the genuine article tomorrow. Please give my regards to Miss Harwyn. Shall I see her tomorrow?"

"Perhaps," said Simon, as the two men shook hands.

Rather than accompanying the Dominican along the path back to Morpen, Simon cut across country, vaguely intending to join the road to St. Madoc further along its course, thinking hard about everything that he had just done, and his reasons for doing it.

As he had told Thomas Mallory, he was, in fact, far short of being contented with himself, although he did feel considerably less self-dissatisfied than he had an hour ago. The moves he had made in the complicated game he had been dragged into playing seemed to him to be both logical and clever, but he was not under the illusion that they improved his position at all. At best, he thought, they had complicated the situation further in a manner that might not work to his disadvantage. The principal object of his thought and his anxiety, however, was the suspicion that the moves, whatever rationalizations he could apply to them and however freely they seemed to have been made, might not have been *his* moves at all.

He had told Megan that the deductions—or guesses—on which his improvised strategy was based, had been inspired by his dreams of the previous night, especially his dream of meeting the Black Bard in Morgan's Cave. The substance of that dream, he knew, had been provided by his unconscious mind, feeding imagery intrusively into consciousness as it had been doing, at intervals, all day long, albeit in a slightly more coherent and sequential fashion. Doubtless he had been in an altered state of consciousness, permitted by the fact that he had been lying motionless, in the dark, still suffering the after-effects of the alcohol he had consumed with dinner. It did not seem to be too far a stretch of the imagination to think that, in a sense, the unconscious part of his mind had been trying hard all day to achieve some such effect, or at least to lay groundwork for the culminating effect when the moment of opportunity finally arrived. Significantly, he had not had a single flash of dream-substance since that long and relatively coherent hallucination had evaporated, as if, now that the task had been accomplished, his unconscious was now prepared to let his consciousness alone for a while, perhaps taking a rest itself.

But if the hypotheses that he had framed in the course of his various writings regarding the possibilities of communication between unconscious minds were justified—and what speculative thinker was ever going to think that one of his hypotheses was unjustified, unless and until a conclusive falsification raised its ugly head?—there had to be a possibility that the prompts delivered to his consciousness, in order to be woven into images and words, had not originated from his own personal unconscious, but from some more distant, more powerful and more versatile source: that what he had experienced was a vision in the strongest sense of the term: a revelation, of sorts.

Such visions, and apparent revelations, were evidently not uncommon in the vicinity of vitreous cocoons, if what Thomas Mallory had told him was reliable. In fact, reading between the lines of Mallory's brief account, it seemed possible that many forceful visions and revelations recorded and treasured in the course of human history might have been associated with vitreous cocoons, and filtered through their communicative portals.

It had occurred to him before, more than once, that he might only be an inept pawn in this game, stumbling as he was pushed or pulled awkwardly around a board he could not see, in accordance with rules he did not know. But the picture that Mallory had painted of a large population of vitreous cocoons planted all over the surface of the Earth, always in caves, perhaps always in "bottomless caves" above exceedingly deep wells, always in association with aquatic hydra-like entities, put those speculations into a different context, which made the idea of distant game-players and complex strategies seem more plausible.

As to what the objective of the game might be, had his doppelganger, the Black Bard, not told him the answer straightforwardly: to prevent "the world from ending"—or, perhaps more precisely, a particular game being played on the board of the collective unconscious from ending in a way that would result in the pieces being reset.

Thomas Mallory, he assumed, might well be able to sympathize with that way of looking at things, given that God and the Devil were sometimes seen, in legend and folklore, as rival chess-players moving human pieces on a board that symbolized the world. In fact, Thomas Mallory, given his belief in God and the Devil, could hardly imagine such a symbolic game in any other way. The Christian Church pretended not to be Manichean, in the crude sense of imagining existence as an ongoing battle between rival principles of good and evil, but its preachers had always had difficulty avoiding that perspective. Simon was, however, very reluctant to do that, being conscientiously resistant to that way of thinking. He preferred to think that, if there was a game of sorts in progress, in which he was caught up, then it ought not to be a zero sum game, in which one side won and the other lost.

He had thought at one time, earlier in his career, that existence might even be a "zero-player" game, like James Conway's then-fashionable Game of Life, so called precisely because its outcome was entirely dependent on its initial state, being simply the rule-determined unfolding of the logical consequences of a primal configuration. But that was surely a drastic oversimplification of existence as observed and experienced, even though it fit in quite neatly with the Newtonian idea of a "clockwork universe," in which the complex pattern of causes and effects was, indeed, seen as a matter of the ineluctable working out of an initial set of conditions, supplied with a primal energetic impulse whose sum could never be increased or diminished, the aspects of which could only be redistributed, in accordance with entropic destiny.

Reality, Simon had subsequently come to suppose, had to be more complicated than that. It seemed to him to be a game in which there was genuine uncertainty as to the final outcome, and which was therefore not only amenable to strategic interference by players, but necessitated some such interference. But there was, he thought, a vast philosophical and metaphysical difference between the necessary introduction of players and their dualistic reduction to such opposed forces as good and evil, order and chaos, or light and darkness. That was crude, simplistic and, in the ultimate analysis, ridiculous.

His present view had been formed before he had come, or had been brought, to St. Madoc, during the long gestation of his years of isolation, latterly living in the flat beneath Eve's, only interrupted by daily constitutional walks, necessary shopping and regular expeditions on high, to hold the old lady's hand: a Murden hand, the hand of Lilith's daughter, the daughter of one of the Murdens' many "rebirths." Existence, he now thought, had to be imagined as a multiplayer non-zero-sum game in which there did not need to be a single ultimate winner and loser, but which might continue to unfold infinitely and eternally, while being continually modified and re-created.

He remembered that games of that sort had become briefly popular and fashionable way back in the seventies, at about the time when he had been teaching English at the College of Further Education—to Marianne, among others, He had even written a handful of pseudonymous novels spun off from one such game, although he had never actually played the game in question. Afterwards, games of that sort had moved on-line, but he had not followed their progress thereafter, even as a distant observer. Although he had bought a dedicated word-processor in the early 80s, and then upgraded to a personal computer, he had continued to use his PC purely as a word-processor, using the internet, when he eventually linked his machine to it, purely as a research tool. He had never played games of any kind on his computer.

Perhaps, he thought, that had been an error of omission. It might have been useful practice, or at least an aid to understanding . . .

But the point at issue was the analogy, the idea of a universe of matter and mind in which, behind the scenes of baryonic matter and conscious minds, there was a more complex universe of mostly-dark matter and mostly-dark mind, a universe in which solidity, rather than seeming to be the bedrock of quotidian existence, the particularity of substance, was something difficult of achievement for the vast majority of its active intelligences, a kind of ultimate paralysis, a deadly crystallization—but a realm that could nevertheless be colonized from the world of dark matter entities possessed of dark minds, invaded and manipulated. And if it could be colonized, surely it *had to be* colonized, perhaps in pursuit of vulgar motives, some kind of dark material gain, but perhaps, and surely more likely, because it posed a challenge—because, like Mount Everest, in more ways than one, *it was there* . . .

In his mental model, therefore, existence included a minor component of matter, and within that matter, a tiny fraction of solid matter—tiny, that is, by comparison with solar plasma, the liquidity of planetary cores and oceans, and the gaseous

substance of giant planets and cosmic clouds—and existence
had a dynamic, which was fundamentally entropic, of necessity, but within which there was abundant scope for limited
and temporary constructions, which could not deny entropy,
but could, in the short term, defy it, could construct locally
within an overall context of eternal decay: in a word, life.

That kind of existence was a "Game of Life" of sorts: not
Conway's elementary game, the game of cellular automata,
but a far more complicated game, in which there were minds
that were not automata, minds that could isolate consciousness within unconsciousness, prisoners at first of that unconsciousness, helpless instruments of primal drives and instincts,
under the tyrannical dominion of the Schopenhauerian "will
to survive," but which had the capacity to mature and evolve.
They would only change gradually—very little in the course
of a petty span of time like a human lifetime—but over a long
sequence of lifetimes, with the aid of tradition, folklore, legend, myth, history and science, could develop intellect, and
culture and imagination. Eventually, perhaps they might
even domesticate dreaming to the service of intellect, to the
service of the maturation of mind.

Perhaps, in fact, that could be regarded as the Grail Quest
of intelligence, the fundamental task of mind, seen as a collective and a collaborative endeavor, but also, and necessarily, reflected in miniature in the individual mind, *Quod est
inferius est sicut quod est superius, et quod est superius est sicut
quod est inferius, as perpetranda miracula rei unius*, as the Latin
version of Emerald tablet actually said; as it is below, so it
is above, the wonder of the whole being thus procured and
perfected: the work of creation and re-creation, but not so
much creation by a God as the slow, painstaking creation of
a universal mind, a universal consciousness, a simulation
of divinity that was probably still in gestation, not yet even
delivered from the existential womb, let alone able to speak.
Except that . . .

Damn it, he thought, *I'm drifting again, dreaming while
awake. I'm back in last night's dream, without the music. I need to*

get a grip, come down to earth, or, at least, down to myself. Focus, damn it.

Except that, in accordance with the principle that he had tried, in his inept fashion, to explain to Marianne, re-creation inevitably involved destruction. Rethinking, reworking and revising required the continual incessant ending of "worlds", to such an extent that the world-seeds that would remain authorial sequences capable of enduring for moments or millennia with only slight modifications, had to be rare, if the existence were to be possessed of any significant dynamism at all — as it surely was.

According to simulacra of Ceridwen and his own alter ego — of whom even Myrddin Wyllt was merely one in a long chain of rebirths, rather than a parent — what the player who had tried to move him last night, and was still moving him today, in spite of the fact that he had a will of his own, a power to act and a power to understand, was trying to preserve its own particular formation within the game, primarily and fundamentally because the whole point of existence was to continue . . . but also, presumably, in the service of some kind of moral or esthetic thesis, a conviction that *this* configuration ought to continue in existence rather than *that* one, because it was better, in either a moral or esthetic sense, or — and perhaps, preferably, if not necessarily, both.

But whatever was moving him could not be God or the Devil, could not be good or evil by definition, could not be unchallengeable in its view of what ought to exist. Whatever was moving him, if something was, or was trying to, could not have any entitlement to define itself, unchallengeably, as the good, the right, or the light. It might be wrong. And if it was, he needed to know. He needed to know what, beyond his own narrow self-interest, he was playing the game *for*. He needed to understand the morality, or the esthetics that he was being urged, or incited, to defend. He needed to know what the story-line was, and what the ending was supposed to be.

He had been asking that question all along, of course, and other people had been asking it of him too—Megan had posed it brutally only twenty-four hours before—but he had only been able to offer speculations in which he could not yet believe himself, and vague evasions that could not yet satisfy himself. He had to do better, if not now, then very soon, because he had just justified his own sense of imminence by taking action—action that could not, in itself, precipitate a climax, but which might very well, and surely would, ensure that if a climax were, in fact, about to blossom, he had just mapped out his own position within it.

Would it prove to be an advantageous position?

He certainly hoped so, partly because, if it turned out not to be, he was going to feel like a perfect fool . . . if he were in any state to feel anything at all, given that the penalty of getting caught up in a significant re-recreation, reworking and revision of the game's evolving scheme would very probably, and perhaps inevitably be non-existence, for himself and all the other people for whom he had now accepted some responsibility . . .

Adrift . . .

Focus, damn it.

XV
Beneath the Wood

Snapping back to consciousness—consciousness of the external world, that is—Simon realized that he was completely lost. He remembered that he had set off through the little wood heading westwards, but inclining slightly to the left, figuring, in accordance with his mental map, that a course drawn in that direction was bound to bring him back to the road from Morpen to St. Madoc. He had walked that road a dozen times before, in the course of his daily routine, as one of three routes that were readily available to him, but he had never been off the road until today. He knew nothing of the layout of the farms to either side of it, or the patches of woodland and uncultivated land by which the cultivated fields were interrupted. He had known, intellectually, that it was not flat, like a map, but contoured, and that, although it was by no means Snowdonia or the Brecon Beacons, it had its ups and downs, its woods and hedges, its ponds and streams. It was not an area in which one could move in a straight line, or see where one was going with any degree of exactitude.

Simon realized that he had completely lost his sense of direction, but he knew that it was mid-afternoon, and that the sun must be in the south-west. It ought, therefore, to be ahead of him to the left, if he had been heading in the right direction to intercept the road. It was not. It was behind him. But he had surely been walking for far longer than it ought to have taken him to reach the road, if he had, in fact, been heading toward it obliquely. He had lost track of time, but Morpen was only a little more than a mile from St. Madoc. Surely, if he had been heading westwards, he should have reached the coast by now. And if he had veered northwards, as the present direction of the sun suggested, he ought to have encountered the stream that fed into the cleft between the central and northern tines of Morgan's Fork. Either way, he ought to be within a few strides of cultivated fields, planted with . . .

He realized that he did not actually know what crops the local farmers grew, or what livestock they kept. They obviously grew something, because they fertilized their fields. Wheat? Barley? Oats? Rapeseed?

But what did it matter, since he was not, in fact, within a few strides of a cultivated field? He seemed to be in a wood, although surely not the same small wood in which he and Thomas Mallory had hid from Douglas Jefferson, and to which he had returned in order to find the Dominican again after issuing his invitation to Jefferson.

This is absurd, he said to himself. *I can't possibly be lost. The area between St. Madoc and Morpen simply isn't big enough to*

He looked around, carefully, trying to find some clue to where he was. He was, indeed, in a wood—obviously a small wood, because he knew for a fact there were no large ones in the area. Most, if not all, of the trees around him were oaks: the shape of last year's fallen autumn leaves, which had not yet decayed into mulch, was characteristic. He listened, thinking that he might be able to hear the noise of traffic on the road if he were in the right vicinity, but all he could hear was the chatter of birds . . . and the faint ripple of a stream.

So, he inferred, he must have veered accidentally to the north, and he was in the vicinity of a stream that would take him back to St. Madoc if he followed it . . .

Except that, with the sun behind him, he must be facing vaguely north-eastwards, and the sound of the stream was coming from his left.

He moved to the left, through the trees. He found the stream, which seemed to be flowing sluggishly southwards. Evidently, he was in a valley, since there was a stream, but there had to be even lower ground in the direction in which the stream was flowing. He followed the stream, and had not gone twenty paces—all slightly downhill, into a kind of gully—when he came to a pond, into which the stream flowed. The pond was only thirty or forty feet across, but its edges were dense with vegetation. He could not see an outflow where the stream, presumably, continued its course, but all he had to do, he assumed, was walk around the pond, and he would surely find it. That was easier said than done, but could not be impossible; this was West Wales, after all, not the Amazonian rainforest.

While thinking, he had reached the edge of the pond. The water was murky and it stank. Simon remembered that Rhys the Engineer—Rhys Two rather than Rhys One—had

248

excavated huge underground cesspits between St. Madoc and Morpen, into which the sewage of the villages had been diverted, instead of being expelled into the sea. Presumably water brought the sewage into the pit, and was then pumped out again, but the hypothetical design of such engineering projects was far beyond Simon's competence or imagination. He presumed, however, that one of the cesspits had to be nearby, and that leakage therefrom—they were well over a hundred years old, after all—had presumably polluted the pond.

In spite of the bad smell, Simon leaned over to peer into the black depths . . .

This isn't real, he suddenly thought. *I'm not awake. I'm dreaming* . . .

And then Melusine surged forth out of the black water, with a flip of her enormous gray tail, reached out with her clawed hands, picked him up bodily, as she had done—or, at least, seemed to do—once before, and dragged him under the surface, down and down, into what was presumably— and how could it be otherwise?—a bottomless pool . . .

Simon had not had time to fill his lungs with air before he sank into the pool. He barely had time to think that he had to hold his breath, knowing that he would not be able to do it for long before he blacked out, and drowned . . . unless the tentacles of the hydra could grab him in time, and draw him into the belly of the monster . . .

Unsurprisingly, he blacked out . . .

Or, at least, the world went black. He might or might not have lost consciousness for a moment, but it seemed to him that he picked up the thread of his thought again without overmuch delay or confusion. He could not see a thing, though. Wherever he was, there was no light.

The sense of touch told him that he was still wearing his clothes, and that, illogical as it seemed, they were not wet. There was, however, a stink in the air, which he hoped was not emanating from his garments, or his person. He had owned his leather jacket for twenty-nine years, and although it had no sentimental value by virtue of its origin, it was so familiar as almost to be a part of him, and its ruination would seem like the end of an era.

There was, he knew, no dry cleaner within ten miles of St. Madoc, and there were some stinks that even the solvents that dry cleaners used could not leech out of fabrics, especially natural fabrics like leather . . .

He felt fingers touch his face, running gently over his cheek—human fingers, not clawed.

"You know who I am, don't you?" said a human voice, speaking from his left, only a short distance away—within arm's reach.

He reached out. The first thing he touched was a naked breast. He moved the hand downwards and sideways, to the waist, the hip . . . except that there was no hip. Beneath the waist, there was nothing but a contoured mass of flesh, which felt as he imagined that the pelt of a seal might feel, slick and smooth, but not actually wet. That seemed odd. So exceedingly odd, in fact, that he kept running his hand over the curious anatomical phenomenon, trying to deduce something—anything sane and sensible—from the strange contours and exotic tactile sensations.

There was no doubt about it, though. Melusine was a morgen. If she was really there, in the flesh, and not entirely the figment of a dream, then she was a morgen, like the one depicted on the sign outside the Mermaid.

"If you're feeling for a vagina," said a sarcastic voice, "forget it. There are no male morgens. Morgen reproduction is . . . different."

But that makes no sense, Simon thought, reflexively. *The entire legendry of sirens and lorelei is saturated with eroticism . . .*

What he said aloud, however, was: "How do morgens give birth, then?"

"They don't," she said. "*Different* means different."

"What are the breasts for, then?" he asked, although he couldn't help remembering Megan's remark that in the shady world she inhabited, naked breasts meant *come and get me*. Sirens and lorelei . . .

"Never mind," she said, seizing his groping hands in hers. "Hold my hand instead. And relax, damn it. Nobody's going to eat you." She laughed: a strange, musical laughter, like the trill of some weird instrument.

"But what's the point of being super-seductive, if you can't actually . . . ?" he began—and then stopped, not because his internal censor had cut in, but because he realized that he was being foolish. "Melusine," he said, instead. "Where the hell have you been?"

"Here, in the underworld," she replied. "But you knew that. You've been here before. It was clever of you to find the pool, though. I wasn't going to come for you until to-night, but then the song would have had to draw you down to the cave, and we'd have had to take the sea route, which is dangerous—for you, that is—as well as inconvenient. This is better. Thank you. Sorry about the total darkness, but it isn't possible to do anything about it here. Just keep in touch. Keep holding my hands."

"This isn't real," Simon said, firmly. "This is just a dream. I've fallen asleep under an oak tree, like a traveler in some old ballad, and I've been transported to the world of Faerie in my dream."

But an inner voice said: *You know better than that by now, Simon. It's not a matter of either/or, hallucination and reality, or even mind and body. You have to get past that dualistic way of thinking, trying to resolve everything into theses and antitheses. The world is far more complicated than that. But make no mistake, this is as real as anything gets. You really are in the underworld, insofar as a creature of common-or-garden flesh and blood like you can enter it. You're cocooned, obviously, surrounded by a complex shell of dark matter, like a chrysalid, although you can't feel it, for obvious reasons. You can still breathe, just as you can still move, and you can still make contact with Melusine's body, but it's not quite as direct as it seems.*

"There's a terrible reek in here," he observed.

"That's true," admitted the invisible but all-too-tangible morgen. "You'll get used to it—but it might linger, I fear, at least for a little while, when you go back up."

"You are going to send me back, then?"

"That's the plan."

Of course it is, said the inner voice, resentfully.

"Now, listen," said Melusine. "We don't have much time."

Of course not, said the inner voice, on the brink of becoming annoying.

"This isn't really happening," Simon insisted. "It's impossible. *You*'re impossible. It's physically impossible for you to have picked me off the bridge the way you seemed to do—and, for that matter, to have metamorphosed into a morgen, in the flesh, in a matter of minutes. It had to be a hallucination."

"Don't be ridiculous, Simon," said Melusine, impatiently. "It happened exactly as you remember it. As I said, the sea route is difficult and dangerous, but there wasn't any ready alternative. The leap was assisted by the surge of the wave— there's a lot of energy in a wave, and even seals know how to capture a useful fraction of it; and it wasn't as if I were lifting a dead weight. You'd lost conscious control of your muscles, but the dark part of your mind still had perfect control. You could have jumped into the water without my help, but that would have been suicide. But for me and Lenore, you'd have drowned for sure. As things were, going out and coming back, you got away with a few bruises. Perhaps I could even have saved you some of those, if I'd been less clumsy, but you have to make allowances. I hadn't been a morgen in the full sense of the word for at least three hundred years. I was a little rusty."

Simon knew that there was no point in protesting that Melusine had only been a fraction over a hundred years old when she disappeared. Felicia and Melusine had both told him, in so many words, that Melusine was a morgen. She had been born human, but in terms of her dark self, she was a morgen reborn . . .

He knew, too, that there was no need to demand further enlightenment regarding the near-immediacy of her metamorphosis. The sea route was difficult and dangerous, but once she had reached the underworld—effectively, plunging within the physical body of the neider—time had become more elastic: not infinitely elastic, by any means, but elastic enough.

But that still left much that was mysterious, much that his imagination could not yet grasp, even with the help that the neider had given him.

"You're talking to me," he said, still protesting on the grounds of implausibility, even though he knew that his standards of plausibility had been shattered some time ago. "But the neider's kind of consciousness doesn't use words, the way that human consciousness does. We create ourselves—or recreate ourselves—primarily by means of words, by personal history, but the neider doesn't. How can it—and you—have learned to talk so loquaciously when it could barely manage *Don't go* less than three weeks ago?"

"Advice that you ignored," Melusine reminded him, "like the stubborn idiot you are—but we mustn't waste time playing the blame game."

"I want to know!" Simon said. "I need to understand. If you can talk now, *talk.*"

He heard a deep sigh, and the darkness seemed to quiver. He had stopped running his hand over Melusine's abdomen the instant that she had suggested that he might be groping for sexual parts with which she was unequipped, and she had taken possession of his hands, but he pulled his right hand away now, in order to touch his own body, to locate his chest, his chin and his forehead.

He could still feel his clothes, but not his face. He was faceless, like the Black Bard. He was a ghost—and he couldn't really move his hand at all, being wrapped up like a mummy in a cocoon of dark matter, so even the feel of his leather jacket must be an illusion, like the Bard's monkish habit.

Madness . . .

He allowed Melusine to take his imaginary right hand again, as she was still clutching his imaginary left, thus providing him with something to hold on to, in some slightly more-than-metaphorical sense.

"You know perfectly well that what I'm doing isn't, strictly speaking, *talking*," Melusine's voice told him. "What I'm doing, siren that I am, is more analogous to singing, although it's only an analogy, since it's a matter of waves of dark energy, not sound waves. This whole process hasn't been a matter of us learning to translate those emanations into words, but a matter of *you* learning to do it—not consciously, obviously, any more than when humans learn to play musical instruments they're training their consciousness to do it rather than the darker fraction of their minds—but still a matter of training, gradually and with difficulty.

"The route to your unconscious is wide open to us now, in a sense, but it's still very hard to follow consciously, while keeping our bearings. It's been a difficult process of education, and we've had to hurry its final phase far more than we would have liked. We'd have needed months, perhaps years, to complete the process in a smooth and orderly fashion, and we didn't have them. It's been a hurried and hectic business, and to be perfectly honest, we still don't think you're really ready. You're just the best we could contrive, in the time we had left—and that *we* includes you, too.

"We're not unaware that you've been doing your best as well, and we're truly grateful for that, because there have been occasions in the past when such human collaborators as we've had have not only been woefully inept but haven't even made an effort. I won't say that you have no idea how rare people of the caliber of Myrddin Wyllt and Owain Myrddin are, because you clearly do, but you only have the barest notion of what that rarity actually amounts to. You've met Glyndwr—not that he was short of effort, but it was all orientated in the wrong direction. He had the will, but not the way, and now he's just a loose cannon.

"There has been a lot of wastage in recent times as well as a lot of failed attempts. If only we could have secured Taliesin, Shakespeare, Newton, or even Shelley . . . but the real geniuses always slip away. They're too conscious, too egotistical, too full of themselves. Not that I'm implying that you're second-rate . . . although, now I come to think about it, that's exactly what I'm implying, if not third-rate. What I mean to say is that third-rate has its advantages. I'm beginning to ramble now, but that's more your fault than mine. You're improvising—which is good, and healthy, and constructive, but you need to retain the melody, because if you lose it, and it turns into the kind of jazz people play when they're stoned out of their skull, you'll never find a crescendo or a coda. There's a balance to be sought here, Simon, and you have to strike it. The words are all yours, but if they don't fit the notes properly, it isn't really a song, and we desperately need a song . . ."

"I can't hear any music," Simon interrupted. "Not a whisper of *Also Sprach Zarathustra*, not a single scrape of a bow across the strings of a crwth."

"Excellent. We knew you could do it. The temptation is so enormous for your conscious mind to translate our music into yours, to use that ready-made analogy, that it requires real progress to avoid it. It takes genuine sophistication to be able to filter that impulse out, to translate the dark music into words instead. I'm not saying that you're doing it well, but the miracle is that you're doing it at all. If you were Shakespeare or Shelley you'd probably have a much better turn of phrase and far more esthetic fluency, but your gigantic ego would also be getting in the way, you'd be feeding too much of your own idiosyncratic darkness into it. They had lives, you see: active, tumultuous lives; and they loved passionately and were loved in their turn . . . whereas you've had the perfect upbringing, from our point of view: minimal life, and minimal love, in pragmatic terms, but all the apparatus necessary to observe, to try to understand.

"There's been a personal cost, obviously, as you've noticed, and a general one. None of the Myrddins, or even the demi-Myrddins, is any great shakes when it comes to living, or loving, and as for being loved . . . well, that's rare for the wholly human, let alone our kind. But for you, for the chosen one, it's been the perfect preparation. And now, as you can evidently hear quite clearly, in your mind's ear, you can sense the silence that precedes the WORD, the human alpha and the omega, the be-all and the end-all of your kind of consciousness. And even though you're a million miles from ready, in the perfect sense of readiness, we think that you're ready enough to stand a chance—and, at any rate, that you're as ready as you're ever going to be, given that there might be only twenty-four hours of hourglass-time to go before they make their last desperate approach . . ."

"Wait a second! Chosen one, you say? Chosen by whom?"

"Whom? Well, if you look at it that way, by Ceridwen and the Other One . . . Myrddin, if you like, although his existential roots go further back in time than that. But that doesn't actually tell you a lot, does it. By what? By the neider, evidently . . . as you've been told more than once, you're neider yourself as well as human, although there's a sense in which all humans are, having been re-created mentally, if not actually created, by the neider, but it's obviously not as simple as that, because as soon as anything buds from the neider, as soon as it separates from the parent darkness, whatever liquid and solid component it has—flesh and blood, that is— it becomes independent, and differentiation always shades into antithesis: not necessarily into opposition, because that's too crudely dualistic a way of thinking, but into . . . friction, abrasion.

"You know from both experience and observation how marriages deteriorate, and you know how generation gaps develop, especially between intergenerational clones, so you have the imaginative apparatus to grasp the principle of the process. There's a sense, obviously, in which the neider and the morgens are one and the same, but there's another sense in which they're not: separated, divorced, and only capable of uneasy collaboration thereafter. And then there's the other classic conundrum to consider. If the neider chose you, what chose the neider? Other intelligences, displaced in spacetime? Probably.

"Ultimately, of course, it must have been a hypermind that provided the initial swerve, the *clinamen*, but by the time you get up to that stratospheric level of definition, it's like trying to define the wispiest of clouds. The particular whole responsible for your push, your choice, might, in fact, be greater than the sum of its parts, but it might not be wise for you to take that for granted. Personally—speaking as Melusine, that is, James Murden's cousin, the foolish virgin—I've always thought that the whole might be far less than the sum of its parts: in this instance, that the Supreme Being might not be greater than Creation but less.

"You can understand that, being a writer. Isn't *Prometheus Unbound* greater than Shelley, *The Tempest* greater than whichever pseudonymously-hidden human being actually penned it, *Le Morte d'Arthur* greater than the probably-imaginary Thomas Malory, the *Odyssey* infinitely greater than the almost-certainly non-existent Homer? You, of all people understand that the creative process is what's important, not the hand that guides the pen, or the individual consciousness that guides the hand, or the personal unconscious of the dark mind that guides the conscious mind. The important thing is the work of art, the result of the growth and blossoming of the seed, the ripening of the fruit.

"So, what I'm trying to say—what *we*'re trying to say, because this is an authentic collaboration—is that the question 'Chosen by whom?' actually doesn't make a lot of sense, in terms of naming a particular individual or entity entitled to sign its work. You were chosen, maybe at random, maybe out of desperation, or maybe by virtue of some design too mysterious for anyone to comprehend. But you're also here of your own free will, and, at the end of the day—the particular day in question being, in fact, today—you've chosen yourself. You've volunteered. You've even sacrificed your life already—which was a criminally stupid thing to do, although, as things turned out, it was only briefly fatal. You're here, at this point in spacetime, because it's where you want to be . . . not that you could ever have wanted anything different, but that's life. It's not a matter of either/or. Now, do you want to hear the urgent advice or don't you? There's only so much stretching that vulgar time can accommodate."

"I'm listening," said Simon. The words would have rung hollow, if they had been able to ring at all.

"Good. We believe that the entities that healed you when you were shot are now ready and eager to take you back, if they can, but that their window of opportunity seems to be disappearing fast. We don't know exactly how they intend to handle it, but they'll presumably need to draw you down to the portal somehow. You have to go, and you have to take one of us with you."

"You in the sense of a morgen? Or an ouroboros round my neck?"

"Neither. I can't do it, and the worm isn't adequate to the task. This time, the collaboration will have to be more intimate. We've been preparing ever since you came back from the dead, just as they have, and we have advantages they don't, just as they have advantages we don't, but we don't know whether it will work, any more than they probably do. All we know for sure is that it's failed before, more than once even within living memory—ours, not yours. But we're hopeful. It will be difficult for you, perhaps painful, certainly dangerous . . . but please don't fight it. You need us as much as we need you—probably more."

"And what will happen if . . . when . . . I go through the portal again?"

"If we knew that, you probably wouldn't have to go. This is exploration, Simon, a step in the dark. To be honest, it might not make much sense to you, but we'll try to enable you to translate as much as possible, and we'll hopefully take aboard enough to be able to help you find more explanations later.

Expect the unexpected, and keep your wits about you. And if it goes well—perhaps even if it goes badly—it probably won't be your last chance. This could be a long-term commitment, especially if the entities weren't being over-optimistic in saying that they'd patched you up well enough to be good for another hundred years. We can't put a probability on that—not yet, at least—but we don't believe that they were lying. We're almost certain that the entities who resurrected you are only in search of information . . ."

"*Almost* certain?"

"That's correct. But be careful. The entities must think that you're valuable, given that they brought you back from the dead last time—but that might not have been necessary if they hadn't also wanted to examine you as intimately as possible, and tinker with you a little . . . although I tried to keep that to a minimum, and will do so again, if I can. Hopefully, if this goes well, you'll be even more valuable, to them as well as us, and they won't want to jeopardize your future utility . . ."

"You're assuming that there will be a next time, after this one?"

"Unless something goes badly wrong, or there's a factor in the situation that we haven't anticipated . . . which is, alas, not unlikely, given our meager legacy of past experience."

Simon already knew that he wasn't the first of his own kind, and already suspected that at least one of the previous attempts at communication had not only gone wrong but catastrophically wrong. And he knew, too, that of three sets of vitreous cocoons that had once existed in the south of France, none was any longer discoverable, and that the others whose one-time existence was known or suspected had also disappeared. Had they died, assuming that they were ever really alive? Had they hatched out, metamorphosed, or merely been hidden? And, in any of those cases, what had happened to the agents pressed into acting as intermediaries between this world and the one beyond the portal, between the curious neider and the seemingly recalcitrant but telepathically talented larvae in the vitreous cocoons?

The question he actually framed consciously, and imagined that he voiced was: "You're not the first neider to have tried to interact with the St. Madoc cocoons, are you? What happened to the others?"

"Dualistic thinking again, Simon, but in crude terms, no, we're by no means the first offspring to have made the attempt. Don't ask how many, because, even if the question made sense, I couldn't give you an answer. As for what happened to my other selves, predecessors, or progenitors, I assume that they were re-created, because the alternative . . . but we'll probably have time to explore that more extensively later, now that you've begun to translate us, albeit crudely. If we survive, things will improve further."

"But we might not—survive, that is?"

"You know that. You've always known that. You're not the only one in danger of losing his mind here, or being lost by his mind. Enlightenment has its costs."

Dazzle, Simon thought. *Blindness. Crack, bang, boom.*

Aloud—or what passed for aloud in the underworld—he said: "There's not much in what you've told me that's specific, and a lot that's still direly enigmatic."

"How could it be otherwise? If I could be more specific and less enigmatic, I would—which is to say that you would, given that you're supplying the words and that much of the vagueness and mystery is inherent in the words. The first law of existence is: nothing is simple."

"How many others are there?" Simon's reflective wit countered.

"An infinite number, obviously—first corollary of the first law. But esthetics and convenience generally reduce the quotable number to three."

"And the second is . . . ?"

"There is no action without reaction."

"Invariably equal and opposite?" Simon queried, although he knew that that was just a Newtonian echo.

"Alas, no—see rule one."

"And the third?"

"If something can go wrong, it probably will."

"Of course." Simon has the distinct impression that another translator might be handling the conversation very differently—but he had always been glib, if not as witty as he wanted to be.

"As strategies of intelligence go," Melusine's voice told him, suddenly seeming more distant, "wordiness is probably not the best—but I'm biased, so I would say that. Remember when you're down there, though, that all that slithers isn't serpentine. We surely aren't the only players in the game, and although we're not really playing against one another, just because it isn't a zero-sum game, and there might well be every opportunity for win-win situations to occur, that doesn't mean that the play can't end with utter disaster."

Melusine fell silent then, but she released his apparent right hand again, and reached out in the Stygian darkness with her left in order to place it on his apparent shoulder, and give it a slight squeeze. The gesture seemed awkward, but affectionate, intended as reassurance, moral or immoral support.

"Is there any chance," he asked, "that you might return to the surface eventually, re-metamorphosed and equipped with legs?"

"No," she said, flatly. "Not practical . . . and not desirable. If all goes well, though, you'll certainly see—or at least hear—me again. All you have to do is hear our song. You don't even have to play it, although it would obviously be better if you could."

"I have to say, Melusine," Simon observed, "that this isn't what I expected—that *you* aren't what I expected."

"I'm not what I expected either. Far from it. Give my love to Felicia, and tell her there are no hard feelings." The faded voice now sounded blatantly insincere.

"Why would there be any hard feelings?"

"Because she won, of course. I was too slow, too hesitant . . . and a morgen. Not built for that kind of intercourse with humans, anatomically or psychologically. The better woman won . . . and that's not a double-edged remark. Forget the rest, in fact, just give her my love. And Simon . . ." The voice was now fading away, as if coming from a vast distance, a vast silence.

"What?"

"Good luck," the morgen whispered.

And with that, the sound of a blaring horn brought Simon back to his senses, and he found himself, abruptly, tottering on the edge of the drainage ditch that ran alongside the northern edge of the road between St. Madoc and Morpen, having apparently just climbed out of it, and seemingly in danger of lurching into the road into the path of a dark blue Subaru XV. His head was reeling with confusion, but he pulled himself together, urgently, and heroically.

He didn't fall.

That was perhaps as well; the ditch had black, stagnant water at the bottom, which reeked vaguely of ordure. In spite of that, neither his clothing nor his shoes were wet. His leather jacket was in no more need of dry cleaning now—although, arguably, no less need—than when he had parted company with Thomas Mallory.

Simon righted his stance, by no means thinking clearly yet, but no longer in danger of lurching, stumbling or falling over.

There was plenty of room for the Subaru to go past, but it slowed down and stopped alongside Simon.

The driver's window slid downwards with an automatic whirr, and Cerys Murden peered out at Simon.

"What the hell are you playing at, Simon?" she asked, petulantly. "What were you doing in that ditch?"

"Just coming back from an excursion to the underworld," he muttered, still disorientated.

"Productive?" she enquired, ironically.

"Not very," he said, groping for sanity. "Quite frankly, I'd expected a lot more from the contact, or at least hoped for more—but perhaps the fault is mostly mine."

"I know the feeling. Are your shoes wet?"

"No, why?"

"Because you're not getting into my new car with muddy feet. It is the ditch that stinks, I hope, and not you?"

"I certainly hope so. Am I getting into your new car? Why?"

"So that I can give you a lift back to St. Madoc, of course. I know it's only half a mile, and that you're as sanctimonious about your daily walk as you are about everything else, but quite frankly, you don't look as if you can make it on foot, and I probably need to update you. There you are, you see—I'm talking like an executive already."

Simon walked around to the passenger side of the car, opened the door and stepped in. He had to grope for the seat belt, not being accustomed to the intricate maneuver, and his hands were more than usually unsteady. He eventually succeeded in fastening it, though. Then he tried to take a deep breath and calm his turbulent mind.

He looked around. Having grown up in the era of the Ford Popular, the dashboard of the Subaru seemed to him to be reminiscent of the control panel of a spaceship. He felt that he was in transit to an alien world, although the vehicle wasn't actually moving yet.

"This is yours?" he said.

"Technically, no," said Cerys. "Company property, just like my new flat in the Uplands. Just like my life, in fact, which, if I got the right impression from the small print in the contract I didn't have time to read in the solicitor's office, is now the property of Douglas Jefferson, at least for the next two years. Did you ever have the feeling that the door closing behind you is that of the proverbial better mousetrap?"

"More than once," Simon said, with a heartfelt sigh. "You can't have seen much of Dougie since then, though—he's been here for the last couple of days, still chasing down possible ways to throw a spanner in the works of probate."

"Oh, once he'd driven me to Swansea he just handed me over to his Human Resources Department. He doesn't train his trainees personally—he has people to do that for him.

Young Mr. Quillery of HR even has an Induction Program, complete with handouts, but we spent most of the time driving around all of Ceredigion and Pembrokeshire in this thing, looking at huge animal sheds, warehouses and food-processing plants." Mention of driving seemed to remind her that that was what she was supposed to be doing, and she finally put the car into gear and pulled away, sedately.

"So Dougie didn't grill you?"

"He already had, intensively. I'd made it crystal clear before I signed the contract that it wasn't going to entitle him to demand that I tell him anything about Felicia and the Abbey, or even you, that James wouldn't have wanted me to tell him." She shot Simon a sideways glance from which he inferred that she wasn't telling him the whole truth, and that the reason she'd invited him to get into the car wasn't so much because she wanted to impart information as to fish for it.

"He didn't ask you what happened when you went down into the cauldron?" Simon asked, fishing himself.

"Oh, he asked me, several times over. I told him the truth: that I blacked out, probably under the influence of a lack of oxygen, as soon as everything turned red, and that when I woke up, you were there too, also woozy. I didn't tell him about the dream I had, obviously."

"But you did tell him that everything turned red—and, presumably, that the light had previously been blue?"

"Yes," Cerys admitted, with a hint of defiance. "That seemed harmless."

"And do you remember the dream you had?"

Her lips pursed before she answered that question. "Not really. Very vaguely. I remember talking to James and Ceridwen, and being angry with you, although I can't remember why."

"Did you tell him about the gun?"

Cerys applied her foot to the brake. The Subaru stopped. They were only a couple of hundred yards from the first cottages of St. Madoc, but somehow, it seemed like a long way.

"What about the gun?" Cerys asked, presumably having got a bite in her angling quest.

"It had been fired," Simon observed.

"I suppose Rhodri told you that. Mr. Jefferson must have seen that I had it, but he didn't mention it. I don't think that he knows that it had been fired. I didn't realize it had myself until Rhodri took it off me, checked the bullets in the cylinder, and found the empty cartridge-case. I told Rhodri that I must have tightened my finger reflexively when I saw red, before falling down, and that the bullet must have hit the floor of the cave. He said that I was lucky that the ricochet didn't kill me. I suppose I was, but I just forgot about it. I figured that it must have been before you came down, so there didn't seem to be any need to mention it."

Again, Simon was sure that she was not telling him the whole truth—but he could understand why there were certain details of her hallucination that she would not want to mention, and he didn't want to harass her on that matter. "Jefferson seems to know that there's something serpentine in the bay as well as something in the cave that can turn red," he observed, instead.

Cerys put the car into gear again and moved it forwards, into the outskirts of St. Madoc. It was already traveling slowly, but now that the vehicle had to weave its way along the cluttered street, it had no alternative but to crawl. "*Everybody* knows that there's supposed to be something in the bay that looks like a sea serpent," Cerys said, warily, "although nobody ever sees it, except when they're dead drunk. If you're asking whether Mr. Jefferson quizzed me as to whether I knew anything more than everybody else, yes he did, but I told him I didn't, because it's true. Did he say any more than that?" Her tone was now becoming resentful as well as deceitful.

"I don't know what he said, exactly," Simon told her, keeping his tone as mild as possible. "Father Mallory knows far more than he does, anyhow, so Dougie's teasing hints went entirely to waste, in terms of bait."

She pounced on the opportunity to change the subject. "Father Mallory? He's the guy from the Holy Office who wrote to the solicitor asking for a meeting? I saw the letter while I was there. Does he want to look around, like the Reverend Usher?"

"He didn't actually make the request, but I have offered to show him round, tomorrow. I invited Douglas Jefferson too. I thought the mystery was now creating more difficulties than it was solving, I expect James is spinning in his grave, though . . ."

He paused, but Cerys was concentrating on her latest maneuver and let several seconds go by before picking up the thread—and when she did, she did not take up the prompt in the way he had intended.

"If he isn't spinning in his grave already, he soon will be," she said, grimly, pulling on to the bridge after completing her tortuous passage. After a pause, she explained: "For as long as I've been at the Abbey, no vehicles except for ambulances, police cars and fire engines have ever been allowed through that gate. For years on end, Rhodri has had to bring the donkey-cart down to pick up deliveries of food, and everything else. Utterly absurd. Well, I'm going to take the Subaru through, and if the sky falls, so be it."

Simon noticed that she had not asked whether he had any objection. Presumably, she felt that, as a mere guest in the Abbey, for the moment, he had no right even to an opinion. "Do you want me to open the gate?" he asked, mildly.

"Please," she said. As he fumbled with the seat belt, trying to unfasten it, she said: "Isn't it a bit early in the season for all those cars to be strung out along the high street like that?"

"You should have seen it yesterday," was all Simon said, as he finally mastered the catch and opened the car door.

He unlocked the gate in order let the Subaru through, and then replaced the padlock, while Cerys drove the vehicle up to the front door of the Abbey.

The sky didn't fall.

XVI

In the Abbey

Cerys waited by the front door for Simon to join her. As he reached the steps, the door opened and Marianne came out. Simon introduced her to Cerys, and Cerys to her.

"I think you'd better come upstairs, Simon," Marianne said. "Felicia's had another bout of fever. It must have started while we were still in the cave. She's over the worst, but I'm worried about her. Zoe's with her."

Simon's heart sank. He ran upstairs and into Felicia's bedroom.

Felicia was sitting up in bed. "Don't panic," she said, immediately. "It was just a glorified hot flush. I've had some honey and lemon and an aspirin. I do *not* need a doctor, so there's absolutely no need for anyone to start running around the day-trippers trying to find one." She looked severely at Zoe.

"I only volunteered," said Zoe. "I'll go now, since Simon's back—but if you need me again, I'll be in Mum's room. If you can't shout, phone."

"Thanks," said Simon. "I'll come along in a minute, when I've had a word with Felicia."

"That sounds ominous," said Felicia. "I'm all right, really. I don't know what came over me—I had such a good night's sleep. Perhaps I overdid it at dinner. Edith did, it seems. Margaret's sitting with her as we speak."

"Cerys is back," said Simon. "Disenchanted, as ever, but if I'm reading between the lines accurately, I don't think it went badly. She now has a flat in Swansea, and a lovely car—which she's parked outside the front door."

"Good for her," said Felicia. "James maintained his fetish about keeping motor vehicles off the island long after it had become absurd, the stubborn old fool. It's about time that

Pamphile was pensioned off and the supermarket delivery truck was allowed to drive up to the house. What's that smell? Is it that filthy old jacket of yours"

Simon reasoned that the reek could not be that bad, as Cerys had let him into the car. "Probably," he admitted. "Two things. Firstly, I've invited Father Mallory to come to the Abbey tomorrow, although I said that I'd have to check it with you first."

Felicia raised her eyebrows. "You're going to show him the library? Let him look at the parchments?

"With your permission, yes. And the cave. He already knows what's down there—in fact, he knows more about it than I do. He's given me a copy of the relevant documents he's scanned, but they're all in Latin, or in gibberish just as bad. We'll learn more, and sooner, if he and I can continue our conversation, hopefully without God getting in the way too much. I said I'd phone him to fix a time. Can I?"

"Yes, of course. You're the heir, legal technicalities not-withstanding. It's your decision. What's the other thing?"

"I haven't quite finished the first thing yet. Douglas Jefferson was in Morpen, and we ran into him. I thought that it might be a good idea to nip our incipient feud in the bud, so I gave him good grounds to suspect, if not quite to believe, that I might not be his father's bastard after all, and I also offered to take him down into the crypt and the cave—again, with your permission."

"With Father Mallory?"

"That wasn't explicitly stated, but yes. I'll invite them both for the same time, if you give me the go-ahead. I won't do it if you don't like the idea, though."

"You really think that will put a stop Douglas's machinations?"

"No, but there's no point in turning a minor conflict of interest into an all-out war, if the matter can be handled in a civilized way."

Felicia was pensive. "And you're not afraid that it might be dangerous to go down there . . . after last time?"

"Mallory already knows that it's dangerous. I'll give Jefferson a warning, for form's sake, but he'll think I'm just playing games. Can I phone him too?"

"Yes, of course. I can't guarantee that I'll be in a fit condition to receive guests, though. You might have to give them my apologies."

"I can do that."

"And the second thing?"

"I saw Melusine."

Felicia sat bolt upright, amazement painted all over her face. "And you wasted time blethering on about Douglas and your inquisitor? Have you no sense of priorities? Where? Where is she?"

"If what I experienced was real—which I very much doubt—she's still in the underworld, and she seems to have every intention of remaining there indefinitely. But when I say that I *saw* her, that's an exaggeration, even if I was dreaming, as I surely was. I heard her voice, and I thought that I touched her, including her morgen tail, and even held her hands, but it was pitch dark, and very probably a hallucination. She sent her love, though."

"To me? Is that all she said? No sarcastic addendum?"

"She said there were no hard feelings—that the better woman won. I don't think she was being sarcastic."

"I do—but that's good, because it makes it more likely that it really was Melusine. What did she tell you? What does the neider want with you—with us? I *knew* it wasn't just a hot flush. Something's happening, isn't it? Or going to happen, imminently?"

"She certainly seems to think so—but she talked almost entirely in riddles, just as the neider's supposed emissaries always do. It was almost certainly a hallucination, a matter of talking to myself, especially given that she didn't really tell me anything that I hadn't already thought, or couldn't have improvised on the spot. I thought I ought to tell you about it, though, even if it's only an indication of the advancement of my insanity."

"Don't be ridiculous, Simon. If you were insane, I'd know, believe me. Perhaps it was a hallucination, but if so, it's like one of grandmother's hallucinations, a revelation. Is the darkness going to come back?"

"I don't know. There was nothing very specific, just an assertion that I'll have to go back to the cave soon, and a vague warning that something might be waiting for me down there, and expecting me—but I already knew that I'd be going down there tomorrow, because I'd just issued the double invitation—provisionally, at any rate. That was more than enough to stir up some anxieties that might come out in a hallucination. I've had rather a lot of them recently. I had another one early this morning, while it was still dark. You were asleep. But it's all coming from inside me, not outside; the words are all mine, even if I am improvising them to fit some alien music. It certainly resembles communication, but it really isn't communicating anything very substantial. Melusine gave me some supposed advice, but it was mostly anodyne, nothing genuinely helpful. Most of what she said was just a continuation of a train of thought I'd begun when I set off to walk back from a wood north of Morpen, and went astray slightly before finding the road."

"But if it was a hallucination, you would surely have visualized her in the sea?"

"Yesterday, very probably—but that was before I'd heard Father Mallory's account of neider living in bottomless lakes and wells underneath Pyrenean and Alpine caves—after which, hearing Melusine decry the sea route as difficult and dangerous, and praise the waters under the earth, was a perfectly natural adaptation."

"Hallucination or not, you need to tell me everything—and what the Dominican said to you, as well. And don't give me any nonsense about your not wanting to tire me out. I'm already in bed, damn it. I know that Marianne and Zoe are just trying to be kind, but their solicitude is maddening. They have an excuse, but you don't. You have to tell me everything. Now."

"Can it wait until I've phoned Father Mallory and Douglas Jefferson? I promised that I would. Is two o'clock tomorrow afternoon, acceptable? Mallory might want to linger in the library, but Jefferson will want to go down into the cauldron at a trot and come back the same way. He has plots to hatch and schemes to manage. With luck, they'll both be out of our hair before nightfall."

"You'll be lucky. Nightfall is still before six—the clocks don't go forward until the end of the month. But yes, two is fine, and if you can get rid of them both before six so much the better. Go—and don't dawdle. Don't bother to send Marianne or Zoe back; I'm not going have a bout of fever while you're making two phone calls."

Simon nodded, and went downstairs to use the new telephone in the drawing room—the one that had replaced the set ruined by the power surge that had triggered James's heart attack. He phoned Mallory first and settled the time agreed with Felicia. Then he phoned Douglas Jefferson, and duplicated the arrangement. He was suitably impressed by the fact that both men had answered their phones instantly, without letting the calls go to voicemail.

When he turned away from the telephone, he found Marianne standing in the doorway to the corridor.

"I wasn't eavesdropping," she said, "but I couldn't help overhearing . . ."

"That's okay," said Simon. It wasn't secret. But before I go back to Felicia, I do need to repeat the advice I gave you this morning. I really think you might be wise to return to Bristol this evening, or, at least, to persuade Zoe to take Krysten back."

"So you're not planning to invite me to join your expedition to Merlin's Cave?" Marianne queried. "You're taking the man from the Holy Office and your arch-enemy, but not me?"

"I'd like to be sure that you're safe," Simon said.

"And you think that the Dominican and Mr. Jefferson won't be?" she parried, deliberately putting him on the spot.

"To tell you the absolute truth," Simon said, "if they turned out not to be, I really wouldn't care very much—but if I endangered you, I would care . . . deeply."

"Very kind of you . . . should I not care, then, that you might be endangering yourself?"

Still on the spot, Simon didn't know which way to jump. In the end, he said: "I think the risk is slight, but real. It's one thing to decide to run it myself, quite another to expose you to it. The last thing I want to do is to spoil things between us, when we've only just met, and seem to be getting along quite well."

"Well, you're in danger of doing exactly that. I don't want to spoil it either, and that's why I want to be let in on the family secret fully, to enable me to be one of the family. If you shut me out now, especially after all the things you told us yesterday, it will be like having the door slammed in my face."

"I can understand your point of view," Simon admitted, "but what about Krysten and the baby? You can't ask me to expose them to any risk, however slight."

"I haven't asked you to, In fact, I'll make a deal: you let me go down into the cave with you tomorrow, and I'll do my best to persuade Zoe to take Krys home tonight. As I said before, she might agree, in order to be near her suppliers . . . just in case, of course."

Simon felt that he was over the proverbial barrel. After wriggling mentally for a moment or two, he said: "Obviously, you're entitled to know the secret if you want to. Everybody does want to, in fact, even though I warn them all that knowing it will probably drive them mad."

"Did you warn the Dominican about that?"

"He already knew—far more than I do. He didn't want to come within twenty miles of St. Madoc to begin with—but in the end, he couldn't resist the temptation. As for Dougie . . . he'll just think I'm trying to put him off.

"And did you warn Megan, before you showed her?"

"Yes. She couldn't resist the temptation either."

"And you think I'm a fragile lily by comparison? How many times has Felicia been down there?"

Simon raised his hands, palms outwards. "You win," he said. "You can come. I should have invited you. I'm sorry. But you'll talk to Zoe?"

"Yes. I can't make any promises—you know how things are between us—but I'll be as subtle as I can."

"Thanks. I'd better go back to Felicia now; she wants a blow-by-blow of my encounter with Father Mallory, and my latest interval of insanity."

For a moment he thought that Marianne was about to demand that she listen to that too, but she apparently made the decision to be content with what she had gained, and to take further confidences one step at a time.

"I'll be in my room with Zoe if you need me," she said.

"Thanks," Simon repeated, and made his way back upstairs.

He found Cerys in Felicia's room, seeking reassurance as to the state of her health. Felicia was in the process of insisting that she would be all right, and approving of Cerys's preemptive decision to bring the Subaru on to the island.

"I can stay in St. Madoc, if you want me to," said Cerys, rising to her feet. "I don't have to go to Swansea tomorrow."

"Don't be silly, dear," said Felicia. "Go and do your packing. Simon and I need to have a long chat, so there's no need to worry about me for the present, and I'm sure that I'll be as right as rain in the morning."

"I'll come back and see you later," Cerys promised, and left.

Outside, dusk was falling.

"She's only going to stay overnight and pack her trunk," Felicia told Simon. "She's driving to Swansea tomorrow—for good, I suspect, although she naturally assured me that she'll pop in whenever she's in the neighborhood. So from tomorrow onwards, it will just be the two of us. Marianne and the girls don't count, as they'll be going back to their other lives the day after."

"I'm sorry," Simon said. "Cerys leaving must seem like the end of the world as you knew it when James and Ceridwen were the presiding deities."

"Oh, she was never really part of it—just a temporary resident, who was always going to move on, like so many others. It was very kind of her to come back for a while, after finishing university. Edith will still be in the kitchen once she gets over her weak spell, Rhodri in the gardens, and Margaret running round with her vacuum cleaner. Anyway, it might seem heartless, but I wouldn't trade you for James, Grandmother and Melusine. If that makes me a flibbertigibbet, so be it. And the village is still there. Do you suppose that Megan Harwyn will want to take up her right of residency in the Abbey when the will is proven?"

"I doubt it," said Simon, "and the probate might take a long time, given that Anthony Symonds now seems certain to put in a claim for some sort of compensation from the will."

"Megan's grandson? He won't get anything, surely?"

"Probably not, especially given that Megan isn't making any claim on the grounds of being James's daughter, and her admission of being Jocasta's mother will block any attempt to use the DNA evidence to further a false claim that Jocasta is James's daughter—but it will slow things down. I'll just be your tenant and toyboy for a while yet."

"Don't be ridiculous, Simon. You're the heir. Everyone knows that, including Cousin Douglas and Cousin Bernard, no matter how much they sulk. Now, before dinner, tell me everything that Melusine said, and everything that the inquisitor said. I need food for thought before I take a little food for the stomach—which you'll have to prepare, I'm afraid; we can't let Marianne do it. Oh, excuse me . . ."

Felicia's mobile phone, which was on the bedside table, had just begun to ring. After looking at the caller ID, she said: "I'll take it, if you don't mind, Simon." She didn't say who it was but Simon could guess; the only person who ever called Felicia—or, at least, the only one she would not have automatically switched to voicemail—was Megan.

Simon drifted over to the window, in order that he could pretend to be not listening to Felicia's side of the conversation, although he would have had to leave the room in order to avoid that. He peered at the clouds, which were thickening again. The window faced eastwards, and the sky above the horizon was still blue, although the shade was already deepening. To the west, he knew, the front moving in from the Atlantic would already have turned that sector of the sky dark gray.

"I'm afraid I'm still not very well, dear," Felicia said to Megan. After a pause, she added: "No, it's nothing serious, although everyone's fussing, as usual . . . Yes, Simon's back . . . Yes, I gather that his meeting with Father Mallory was quite satisfactory, but he hasn't had time to give me the details. I'm sure that he'll bring you up to date tomorrow . . . Yes, I'm sure that's an excellent idea, by all means do that. I'm sure they'll be very grateful . . . Thank you . . . You too . . . goodbye."

When she had broken the connection, Simon did not hesitate to ask: "What excellent idea is that?"

"Megan's with Krysten, who told her that Edith is ill and won't be cooking anything, so she's suggested that she drive Krysten, Zoe and Marianne to town, so that the three of them can get something a little more sophisticated than the fare in the Mermaid . . . what's the matter?"

"Marianne is trying, as we speak, to persuade Zoe that it might be a good idea to take Krysten home to Bristol."

"Tonight? You can't be serious. If they want to go home, it will be far better to go in the morning. And you've hardly had a chance to talk to them. I thought you wanted to get to know them—last night's dinner barely scratched the surface."

"I do, but I'm not sure that another opportunity is going to come up, now that I'm booked up tomorrow afternoon. Zoe will have to get back to work very shortly. Perhaps they can come to stay again when things are a little quieter . . . or, in fact, a little livelier, but without there being so much pressure on my time."

Felicia's eyes narrowed slightly. She knew him too well by now for him to hide anything substantial from her. "You do think there's danger," she said. "What did Melusine say to you?"

"Nothing specific, as I said. She did suggest that tomorrow might be a crucial day, when something important might happen, something that might pose a challenge to me, personally—but I had already invited Mallory and Dougie to the Abbey, and I'm sure that the hallucination was just reflecting my own anxieties in regard to that."

"Or the possibility that the darkness is going to come back."

"That's possible—but if it's confined to the cave and the crypt, as it was before, it won't do any harm to anyone on the surface."

"But . . . ?" she prompted.

"But I thought it might be a good idea to keep Krysten and the baby away, just in case—which involves Zoe driving them back to Bristol. As you say, though, tomorrow morning will probably be a better time to drive than tonight, given that the rain, once it starts, will probably be heavy. In any case, entertaining the three of them will probably do Megan good. She won't admit it, but you must have seen that she was shaken up last night. You're right, it's an excellent idea."

Simon sat down on the edge of the bed, gave her a reasonably full account of what Thomas Mallory had told him, and was just about to launch into a more detailed account of his vision of Melusine when there was a knock on the door. Doubtless assuming that it was Cerys or Marianne, Felicia called: "Come in."

The door opened. Rhodri was standing on the threshold. His gaze rested very briefly on Felicia before fixing on Simon.

"I'm very sorry to disturb you, sir," he said, "but there's something you need to see—urgently." He stopped dead, obviously not wanting to say any more.

Simon looked at Felicia. Her lips were tight, and the fact that Rhodri had addressed him—a mere guest, for the moment, even if he was the heir apparent—with an obvious intention to keep the subject matter of his concern secret from her, the mistress of the house, obviously caused her a sharp resentment. But she did understand that Rhodri would never have knocked on her bedroom door unless he believed, as he said, that the matter was urgent.

"Go," she said to Simon, very simply, leaving unvoiced the demand that he come back as soon as he could, in order to tell her everything.

By the time Simon reached the doorway, Rhodri was already half way to the head of the stairs and moving rapidly. Simon did not contrive to draw level with him until they were at the bottom, and the gardener clearly had no intention of offering a verbal explanation. Whatever he wanted Simon to see would obviously have to speak for itself.

Simon was not surprised when Rhodri went into the chapel, where the electric light was switched on, although the space was too large for the single bulb to illuminate it anything more than dimly; nor was he surprised to see that the other door to the chapel was open, as that must have been the one by which the gardener had entered, probably provoked into an early return to the main building by the darkening of the sky. What made his heart lurch, however, was the fact that the trapdoor at the top of the steps leading down to the crypt was wide open.

"Who's down there?" Simon asked.

"I don't know, sir," said Rhodri. "I saw that it was open, and thought that I'd better let you know immediately, after what happened last time. It wouldn't have been safe to go down anyway, without fetching the other electric lantern— but I'll fetch it for you now, if you want, while you stand guard. It's in my shed."

"Thank you," said Simon. "Please do."

The gardener disappeared through the open door to the tine. Simon sat down on the front bench of the chapel's ancient seating, and waited.

He did not have long to wait. The beam of the electric lantern that had been taken down into the crypt, and perhaps beyond, became visible almost immediately, and brightened as the person holding it came up.

It was Cerys, but Simon had already jumped to that conclusion. Only her head and shoulders had appeared before she saw Simon waiting for her. She hesitated momentarily before continuing to climb and emerging fully from the hole. She was holding the electric lantern in her left hand. In her right hand, she was holding James Murden's revolver, just as she had done last time she had gone down into the cauldron.

Déjà vû, thought Simon.

Cerys did not seem to be in an apologetic mood, or even a defensive one.

"Well, what of it?" she said, standing beside the open trapdoor, after switching off the electric lantern. "I have every right. I live here, unlike you. I'm family; it's as much my secret as yours—more, in fact. I've been down there before. What's the problem?"

"I don't know," said Simon. "What is? After the last time, I didn't think you'd ever want to go down there again. So why? Or is it none of my business, because I'm not James's heir until the probate court says so?"

"I'm not saying that. I'm just saying that it's my business too. And you already told me that you're taking Douglas down there tomorrow, so where's the harm?" She was agitated; her arms were moving, the right one waving the gun.

"Where, indeed?" Simon parried. "Didn't you phone him to ask him whether he still wanted you to go down, given that he'll be going down himself tomorrow?"

"How do you know . . . ?" Cerys began, and then stopped, probably calling herself a fool for giving the game away.

"How did I know? Well, for one thing, I know that Felicia changed the combination lock on the safe, so I know that the keys you've just used aren't James's keys. Thus, I know that either you made an impression of them before she changed the combination, or Douglas Jefferson made one while you and I were having our collaborative hallucination. Either way, Dougie must have asked you to go down while you were here, presumably in order to take some photographs—as a favor to Alexander Usher, he probably said, although he'll doubtless keep a set for himself . . ."

He broke off as Rhodri appeared in the doorway, holding the spare electric lantern. The gardener was wet; obviously, the rain had started falling, and, given that it was only a matter of yards from the chapel door to the shed, it must be falling hard. Rhodri looked at Cerys, who looked back at him with naked resentment, knowing that he must have discovered the open trapdoor and raised the alarm, being the only person on the island who routinely used the chapel door to come into the house, and the only one for whose whereabouts she had not been able to account precisely when she had calculated that the opportunity was too good to miss, even though her initial plan must have been to wait until dead of night before creeping downstairs.

Simon walked over to the doorway where Rhodri was standing, damply, and took the lamp. "Thank you, Rhodri," he said. "I'm very grateful to you. I'll take it from here."

"Are you sure, sir?" said Rhodri, whose gaze was now directed at the weapon in Cerys's right hand.

"Yes, of course," said Simon. "There isn't any problem. You were absolutely right to come and tell me, but everything is fine. "

"Yes, sir," said Rhodri, uncertainly. He turned round and peered outside, where a sudden darkness had fallen. He closed the door carefully, and then went to the other door, which led to the interior of the house. Before he had reached it, Cerys started to follow him.

"Please don't go, Cerys," said Simon, sharply. "Whether I have a right to ask you for an explanation or not, Felicia will surely want one. If you don't give me one that I can give to her on your behalf, she'll ask you for one herself, and she won't take no for an answer. Do you really want to upset her just before you leave?"

Cerys stopped, and turned round. "You already know," she said, with an edge in her voice suggesting that her heart rate and her anxiety were increasing. "Douglas wanted me to take some photographs—and yes, he said that it was for his good friend Alex, for whom I'd already taken so many. And yes, I did phone him to ask whether he still wanted me to go down there, and he said yes—possibly because he doesn't trust you to keep your promise tomorrow, or thinks you have some trick up your sleeve, or possibly because he doesn't want to start snapping away with his own phone while you're watching him."

She was so close to the edge of panic now that it was perfectly obvious that there was something that she was holding back.

"But you had another reason?" Simon prompted, very gently. He couldn't read the expression in her eyes. Fear? Hatred? But why? If she was frightened, why on earth had she gone down there?

"You know," she repeated. "I know you know. I wasn't sure before, but in the car . . ."

"Because I asked you about your dream? You remembered more?"

"Remembered? How the hell can I trust my memory? That's why I had to go down there, although I didn't expect to find anything, and I wish I hadn't. I thought you might have gone down yourself, but you didn't have to, did you? You've known all along, but you've never asked me, just dropped hint after hint: meek, mild queries, inviting me to confess, even though it's absurd, impossible . . . well, I couldn't confess, because I didn't know the truth. And I still don't, even though . . ."

She stopped. This time, Simon was genuinely taken by surprise, to the extent that he couldn't believe he'd followed the chain of reasoning accurately. "You actually found the bullet!" he said "How? Even if it was on the floor of the cave it's impossible to see a thing in that crazy blue light."

"It's not blue," she countered.

A chill ran down Simon's spine. "You mean it's red?" he asked.

"Dark red," she told him, "and no shape at all. Taking the photographs was a complete waste of time—nothing but a blur. But I could see the floor. The stain and the mangled bullet stuck out like a sore thumb. But it's impossible. I can't possibly have shot you. You couldn't possibly have come back up the steps if I had. You couldn't have gone waltzing off with Megan to see your mother."

"But if the bullet was on the floor of the cave," Simon said, still puzzled, "what you told Rhodri . . ."

"The bullet is caked with gunk," Cerys said. "It was lying on the edge of a big dark patch on the pale gray rock. Not red, even in the crimson light, but so what? It can't be anything but blood, and if it is . . . but if I shot you, and you bled, how was the mangled bullet extracted from the small of your back? And why aren't you dead?"

The hand waving the gun was beginning to seem increasingly ominous to Simon.

"I was patched up," he said, quietly. "That's why we were down there for so long. They told me, in the dream, that I did die, but it was obviously just a temporary operating theater death, from which you can come back if the surgeons are clever enough. They claimed to be working from the inside, while I was distracted by another hallucination. But it wasn't your fault, Cerys. Your finger might have pulled the trigger, but it wasn't you. They were inside you as well as inside me. I know that you didn't want to shoot me."

"You know more than I do, then," she snapped. "What makes you think it isn't going to happen again?"

"That wouldn't be wise," said a voice from the doorway—the inner door, not the one through which Rhodri had brought the lantern. Rhodri had left it ajar when he had hurried through it. It had just opened fully, and Marianne was standing there. Her own right hand was raised in a threatening manner, but it was only holding a mobile phone.

"We've telephoned for help," Marianne added. "Zoe's gone to the gate to let it in."

"That won't be necessary," Simon said, swiftly. "Cerys wasn't threatening me, and she has no intention of using the gun. There's no problem here."

"This time," Marianne said tautly, "I *was* eavesdropping — and I heard more than enough to know that there's definitely a problem.

The sequence of events was easy enough to piece together, Simon thought. As soon as he and Rhodri had left Felicia's bedroom, Felicia had phoned Marianne. Then she had phoned Megan Harwyn. Marianne had told Zoe to go to the gate, probably as much to get her out of the way as to let in any hypothetical help — and Marianne had come downstairs to investigate for herself, had heard voices . . . and listened from the other side of the door.

"It really is all right," Simon insisted. "Cerys went down into the cave, as she's perfectly entitled to do. She was slightly alarmed by what she found there — but she has nothing against me and absolutely no intention of using that gun on me."

"Again," added Marianne, succinctly.

"As I was just explaining," Simon said, "it wasn't her fault the first time. She didn't shoot me intentionally.

"And as she was just saying," Marianne countered, "what makes you think it isn't going to happen again?"

"As I was just about to answer," Simon said, a trifle impatiently, "last time, we were hallucinating, and the entire subterrain was full of impenetrable darkness — impenetrable to our sight, at least, if not to that of dark matter entities. Now, we're on the surface, we're not hallucinating, and there's no unnatural darkness."

"But the portal is red," Marianne reminded him, although she couldn't have the faintest idea of what that datum signified. Even Cerys had little or no idea, Simon reflected, because he, like a fool, hadn't explained it to her, when he had had the chance. Too many secrets, too much misleading leakage . . . and did he even know himself what the present dark redness signified?

Cerys suddenly transferred the gun from her right hand to her left. Holding it by the barrel, she extended the butt toward Marianne.

"Take it," she said, harshly, "if it'll make you feel any better. I wasn't going to use it. If anything else is going to use it, better in your hand than mine. I'm all packed; the car's outside the door—I'm going. Give my apologies, and any explanation you want, to Felicia."

Marianne accepted the revolver, holding it rather gingerly, and moved aside so that Cerys could make her exit—but the door was blocked again. Evidently, Zoe had gone to the gate and come back with "help"—to wit, Megan Harwyn.

"Family life, eh?" said Megan, sardonically, her gaze taking in the whole situation—including the open trapdoor—at a glance. "The left hand never knows what the right hand is doing—and sometimes, the right hand doesn't have a clue either. I have no idea what's going on, as usual, but if you want my opinion, Cerys, you're absolutely right. Pick up your luggage, jump into your lovely XV, and drive—all night, if you have to, the deluge notwithstanding. The further away you are from here, the better chance you have of staying sane—or getting back to sanity, if the ship has left port."

Cerys hesitated, apparently having changed her mind. She reached into the pocket of her jacket in order to grasp something within it.

Meanwhile, Megan sighed. "Simon might hate me for saying it, for so many reasons, but take it from me, Cerys, dear, there really are things that it's much better not to know. Go—live your life. Leave this to people who no longer have one."

Cerys took her hand out of her pocket. Simon took a step toward her.

"I'm going," she repeated. "Here." She threw something, which Simon caught in his free right hand, while the left was still holding the lantern that Rhodri had given him. What he had caught was a pair of keys on a key-ring."

"I don't want them," Cerys said and reached into her pocket again, as she added: "Give them back to Douglas tomorrow, or keep them. I don't care."

"It really is good advice," Megan was saying to Marianne, meaning the advice to go and leave the mess at the Abbey to people who no longer had anything to lose. "I know how much it means . . ."

She was interrupted, as Cerys said: "And this," and threw the second item that she had taken out of her pocket. She threw it at Simon's face, presumably in a petty fit of pique. Simon had no free hand with which to try and catch it, and he was too surprised to duck. The mangled bullet hit him on the forehead—and stuck there.

For an instant, the world went red. He staggered, and almost fell, not because of the energy of the impact, which was trivial, but because his brain seemed to be exploding, albeit without any pain. He remained conscious, after a fashion.

Even so, the reaction must have been very obvious indeed.

"Oh God!" said Cerys. "I didn't mean . . ."

Marianne and Megan had both run forward to catch Simon, evidently thinking that he was going to fall. He tried to tell them that he was all right, that it was nothing, but he couldn't. He braced himself, intent on standing up without assistance and Marianne, still inconvenienced by the gun in one hand and her phone in the other, stepped back, helplessly. Megan was not so timid; she actually grabbed Simon's arms, as she turned to Cerys, and said once again: "Go!" considerably more vituperatively than before.

Simon finally managed to say: "I'm . . ." He had intended to say that he was all right, but he wasn't. He could now feel a spot in the middle of his forehead that seemed to be the nucleus of a heat—not a fire, but a strange warmth that was drilling into his brain and stirring its convolutions. But his rigidity held, and he strove with all his might to regain control of his body and mind alike.

Megan stifled an oath. She was looking him directly in the face. He didn't have to ask what had prompted the expletive. He could guess.

His head cleared abruptly, and he recovered the use of speech. "It's okay," he said, in what he hoped was a level voice. "This is what we're going to do. Marianne, please go upstairs and tell Felicia that Rhodri summoned me because Cerys had gone down into the cave, but that she's back now, and quite unharmed. Then stay with her, if you don't mind. Zoe, please go back to Raven. You and Krysten should be perfectly safe there, but please don't come back on to the tine until you hear from me that it's safe. Megan, please wait here. With luck, nothing will happen, but if something does, use your initiative. You and Marianne ought to be able to get Felicia out of the house, in the unlikely event that anything bad does happen. Don't let anyone come down after me, though, until I've confirmed that it's safe. If the worst should come to the worst, and I'm not back by two o'clock tomorrow, explain to Father Mallory what's happened. If anyone can make an expert guess at what might have become of me, it's him. Handle Dougie as you think best. Okay?"

"No, it isn't okay," said Megan. "You can't go down there. A bullet just disappeared into your head, damn it."

"It isn't a bullet," Simon said. "It was just disguised as a bullet, so that Cerys would pick it up. It's where it belongs now. It doesn't mean me any harm, and neither does the neider, but I do have to go down there, and I really don't have time to argue. Please, everybody, just do as I say—and for Heaven's sake, look after Felicia. Tell her that I love her."

And with that, he simply turned away, and went to the open trapdoor.

"Take the gun," Marianne called after him.

He didn't look back, He just raised his arms, to show that he had the lantern in one hand and the keys in the other, and no free hand—although that wasn't the reason why he thought that taking the revolver might be a seriously bad idea. Then he brought the hands together, in order to hit the switch of the lantern.

And, simply assuming that his instructions would be followed, given that he was not only the head of the family but a man risen from the dead, modified by alien surgeons from *elsewhere* in order to make exactly the move he was making in the game he had hardly begin to understand, he disappeared into the crypt, on the way to the underworld.

Again.

XVII
In the Crypt

But it wasn't that easy. First rule of existence: nothing is simple.

For one thing, the crypt was full of sea serpents. Or eels. Or simply worms. Or not. Some of them promptly wrapped themselves around Simon's legs, immobilizing him, but most of them were busy working on the wall of the crypt opposite the one through the fissures of which they had come. They were working with jaws and teeth such as no snake, eel or worm had surely ever had before, chewing their way through the primitive cement that had been used to block one of the cavities in the wall hundreds of years before.

Simon thought he understood what an enormous expenditure of effort the neider had made, to form and release so many fragments of itself and to intrude them into the crypt. He thought he understood that it must be a once-in-a-generation effort, perhaps a sacrifice. But he had no idea what might be behind the cement plug that they were trying to remove, and he had no idea why the squirming neider-fragments had immobilized him when he had yet to use the keys in his hand to unfasten the second padlock and go down into the red unknown.

He did not have to wait long to find out. The lamplight was bright, but the illumination that it was lending to the crypt began to fade rapidly. The unnatural darkness was not coming from below, however; it was coming from above. Nor was it general and all-encompassing; it was localized and targeted. The shadow descended upon Simon's head, surrounding it like a hood, working from the back, leaving his eyes—all three of them, as he now suspected—free.

Simon did not fall over; in fact, he had the impression that the neider-fragments would not have allowed him to fall, even if he had not had the resolution and the strength to stiffen his stance, to remain upright in spite of what was happening to his head. In the meantime, with his two open eyes, he watched the gnawing worms as they continued their mission of excavation.

"That's good," said a voice from the darkness—not Melusine's voice, this time, but the voice of the Black Bard. "Hold hard. This won't take long to establish. It won't last long thereafter, either—but hopefully long enough to bring you back."

"I can't see you," Simon said, looking around the crypt.

"We're past that stage now," said the Faceless Bard. "This is the final phase, of my rebirth and yours, and hopefully, of securing a link with the otherworldly intelligence. In a little while, I won't even be a separable voice; our identities will be fused, with a common consciousness and a much richer collective unconscious . . . but everything takes time. For now, either tolerate it or, if possible, take advantage of the separation, while it lasts. Mistakes in translation should be minimized from now on, between the two of us—in effect, between you and the neider. Let's do what we can, though, to achieve an orderly process of realization."

The shadow that was disrupting the lamplight, Simon knew, was not the entity that was unfolding him, endeavoring to possess him, but a mere side-effect; the entity itself was essentially invisible, dark in a very particular sense of the word. Nor could he feel it, in any literal sense, sinking into his skin like a liquid, spreading out in the dermis equipping his body with a kind of flexible shell, but also intruding, into his flesh and, more significantly, his mind.

The Black Bard had lived, or endured, the liminal existence of a phantom for nearly a thousand years, even less capable of manifestation than the phantom of Owain Glyndwr. Now, he was sacrificing his fugitive sense of identity in exchange for a temporary reincarnation, the privilege of flesh.

Simon hoped that when the poor fellow discovered what a dubious privilege his particular flesh was, he would not regret the sacrifice too much. But he knew, even at this elementary phase of the integration, that the Black Bard had already undergone a preparation that had changed him permanently, and made this destiny not merely possible but uniquely desirable.

As for himself, he could see far more advantages in the deal than disadvantages, whether it was a diabolical bargain or not. Although it had taken him by surprise, effectively by ambush, he felt no resentment. Had the neider contrived to spell out the choice more explicitly in that morning's dream, or his dialogue with Melusine, he would have made the deal instantly. And the neider had known that, ever since the Black Bard had absorbed a dark matter copy of Simon's mind: one of two copies made in the underworld beneath the crypt two weeks before.

Thomas Mallory, Simon knew, would certainly describe what was happening to him as diabolical possession, and he would not be mistaken about the possession, even though the neider was definitely not the devil. As far as Simon was concerned, though, the possession was a two-way process, a win-win situation, not a zero-sum game.

He had a much better idea, now, of who and what the Black Bard was . . . or, to put it another way, and perhaps more accurately, he had a much better idea now of who and what he was himself. He could already feel the song in his blood, and he could already translate the music into words—not precisely, because translation was an inherently entropic process, in which something was always lost, but he understood now, far better than he had before, what the various processes of rebirth and re-creation had to involve, and why there was a sense in which he was a clone, not merely of Seymour Murden but of Owain Murden, the Black

Bard, Myrddin Wyllt and countless others, going all the way back to some hypothetical Adam, whose parable encoded a metaphorical truth in its myth of human creation—creation in terms of the dark mind, but re-creation in vulgar physical terms—by the neider.

In the beginning, he realized, in more ways than one, there had been the hydra. The hydra had been the original form of much, though not all, of material life, prior to single-celled organisms because it had been prior to cells. The hydra had evolved and, in a sense, devolved at the same time. An essentially elastic and immortal entity, it had "reproduced" by fragmentation and differentiation as well as—and initially instead of—self-duplication.

The evolutionary "tree of life" was not, as it was conventionally imagined, a matter of elementary proto-bacteria or some kind of primeval slime gradually building the cell and all its chemical apparatus, inventing bodily structure at a point far removed from the beginning, and then embarking on an elaborate branching process producing different orders of species. The structure had been there from the inception, preceding the evolution, or devolution, of the most primitive cyanobacteria—and the structure in question, or one of the structures in question, had been a hydra, or a dendrite, possessed of a root, a central stem and peripheral branches.

The hydra had not merely been the starting-point of a process of bioyphysical and biochemical evolution, prior to DNA and all of its wondrous works, but the starting-point of the evolution of mind, because the primal hydra had been—and still was—an essentially hybrid entity, compounded out of baryonic matter and dark matter, moved more by dark energy than momentum and electromagnetic thrust, equipped with the most primitive unconscious mentality. Because of that, it had been capable, in the beginning as well as in the fullness of time, of giving rise to far more complex organizations of unconscious mentality, and also to the particular branch of that mentality which constituted consciousness, by virtue of a process perhaps more analogous to an apotheosis than a fall.

It only required a slight modification to the parable of *Genesis*, Simon thought, to bring it into line with his new perspective, which he had inherited from the version of his clone of which he was in the process of gradually taking possession.

The tree of the knowledge of good and evil was, in fact, the hydra, and the "serpent" merely one of its fragmentary fruit. And, having identified a bigger, better and more fruitful brain in one of the multitudinous species that had followed the evolutionary route of DNA genetics, from its humble beginnings in the very distant past, the hydra—which had followed a very different evolutionary route—had tempted that species with the lure of consciousness. Or, more specifically, it had initially tempted the females of the species, because they were more amenable to temptation, more amenable to imagination—to put it crudely, although nothing is ever that simple, superior. More capable, at any rate, of the initial leap, which some of their more stupid counterparts would ultimately choose to describe as a fall.

There is no action without reaction, of course, and if something can go wrong, it probably will. You gift members of a species with the capacity to think, and to dream, and what do they do? Well, for one thing, they don't all do the same thing, because nothing is simple, but in the main, they think perversely. The majority employ reason, in the beginning, to produce such imbecilities as faith, and to create a mental environment, in the personal microcosm as well as the social macrocosm, in which reasoning becomes increasingly difficult, bogged down in a stinking morass of prejudice, always tending to annihilation: immediately, to the annihilation of others, to sin, but ultimately, and inevitably, to self-annihilation.

And what is a poor hydra-creator to do then? Give up and forget the whole thing? Cancel the particular project, the particular evolutionary sequence, and start again? Or re-create more gradually and less apocalyptically, as slowly, as patiently and as painstakingly as the job requires? And in the meantime, obviously, continue its own problematic evolution and development, its own bizarre growth and differentiation, the recomplication of its own strange mentality, while being both one and many: while still being, in a sense, the primal hydra, and yet constantly becoming multiple and different, as the parent mind, like the parent body, continually fragments, producing not merely difference but perversity and antagonism, the foundation stones of all progress.

And the results of that progress, eventually—not ultimately, by any means—were the neider and its analogues, similarly singular and multiple, similarly confused, and similarly still working on the projects of their own re-creation and human re-creation, while, perhaps—and very probably—being the object of external projects of re-creation themselves.

By whom or by what? How could they know? Minds perhaps darker than their own, and probably much stranger. Where were they? In all probability, everywhere, both remote and close at hand: above and below—which is to say, given that the particular world in which the neider and DNA-life operated was roughly spherical in shape and exceedingly thin, extending only a few kilometers above and below the Earth's surface, inside and out. Probably, if the appearances of spacetime are not unreliable, and proximity is something more than an illusion of perception, at least some of the neider's would-be re-creators, like its initial progenitors, were more likely to be in the Earth's interior than the vasty deep of extraterrestrial space. But who could tell?

That, at the end of the day, was the crucial unanswerable question, the ultimate mystery.

Who could ever tell?

Nobody—and yet, in a sense, anybody. There was no way to know whether any of the stories that were told were true, and logically, most of them must be false . . . but that was no excuse for not trying, for not telling, because if no one tried, the story would always remain untold, and the truth undiscovered . . . or uncreated.

That was the story Simon, finally able to produce a more coherent account of neider identity, if not consciousness, told himself, while translating the music that was beginning to possess his soul into words. He was sure that he would be able to tell it better, given time for reflection, but for the moment, exuberance prevailed.

"That's better," said the voice of the Black Bard—which was, in a sense, his own voice. "Let's not forget, though, that we still have a job to do. This is only the first step, and the easiest. We have to take the next one now."

The neider-fragments immobilizing Simon's legs slithered away. He was free to move. His third eye—the alien eye that had intruded itself into his flesh and his inner being much as the clone had done—had not yet opened, but that was not surprising. It was not adapted to see in his present physical environment. He would open it, if he could, beyond the portal.

Would it be able to see? Time would tell. Presumably, if its senders had done their work well, it would be able to register something—but that would still leave his brain and his mind with the problem of translating and interpreting what it saw. There was no guarantee.

However, the excavator worms had finished clearing a path into the cavity where something had been hidden, many years ago.

Simon stepped over to that wall, a trifle gingerly. He held up the lantern at the level of the hole, and leaned over in order to peer in, almost having to bend double in order to do so, but the interior of the hole was too deep and too dark to be usefully illuminated by the lamp. He had to kneel down and reach in blindly with his arm.

His arm went in almost all the way to the shoulder, but his fingers eventually closed on the object, and he was able to draw it out.

It was not the Holy Grail—at least, it was not a cup in which the blood of the crucified Christ had once been collected.

It was in fact, a primitive musical instrument: a crwth. The frame was roughly rectangular, but not flat; it had the distinctive oblique angle part-way along its length, which facilitated the extension of its strings. It had five of them, with tuning-pegs of a sort, by means of which they could be tightened, but there was no bow in the hole, so far as Simon could feel. The relaxed strings were greasy, presumably having been coated with something to prevent the gut from drying out.

"I can't play this," Simon said. "And what earthly use can it be, anyway?"

"I was once taught to play," the Black Bard reminded him, "but even if I haven't forgotten, I was never any good — certainly no Taliesin."

"But you played it in my dream last night," Simon said.

"I'm much better in dreams than in reality — but that's where the answer to your second question comes in. It played in your dream, but it wasn't really us that were playing it. If it plays again, it certainly won't be your fingers doing it, with or without a bow — its purpose, and its particular virtue, isn't to be played but to be capable of a very special kind of resonance. The whole point of this excursion is the attempt to find true players — hopefully players capable of words as well as music, but at least of making the strings vibrate, and communicating that vibration to the dark mind of the individual holding the instrument, of nourishing his dream, not merely of being able to play the instrument, but to compose its melody."

"You think that something beyond the portal will be able to do that?"

"I certainly hope so. If not, we might remain condemned to silence, at least for a time, if not eternally. But it's not our only hope. There's more than one way to strike a harmony."

Simon set the crwth and the lantern down while he unfastened the padlock on the trapdoor to the crypt, and opened it.

The hole seemed completely dark; the red glow, if it were still present in the chamber beneath the crypt, was too far away to be distinguished, even as a faint glimmer. He picked up the lamp and the crwth again, and began to descend the steps, moving very carefully, afraid of falling while the balance of his mind and body were disturbed.

"But we can't take anything for granted," Simon said. "Whatever and wherever the entities that staged the little pantomime for Cerys and me are, it seems that it wasn't easy for them to reach and manipulate the vitreous cocoons once, and it might be even more difficult to do it again."

"We certainly have some reason to think so," agreed the bard.

"Is that because something will try to stop them?"

"That's possible, although it's not the only possibility, and not the likelier one. Either way, though, past failures have been too frequent, and occasionally too catastrophic, for us not to take the inference that some kind of reactive force is at work. It's probably not a conscious mind, and surely nothing that might employ words, although crude violence might be well within its purview."

"Blind discord?" Simon suggested. "The antimusic of the spheres?"

"Perhaps, but it's not that . . ."

". . . simple." Simon finished. "I get that. There are still some slippery matters that I'm having difficulty grasping, though. While you're still able to maintain a distinct voice, explain morgen reproduction to me. Melusine wouldn't."

"You've already worked it out—and if you hadn't, you'd certainly be able to, once I'm fully dissolved within you. In any case, you don't mean the reproduction of morgens, which originate by neider fragmentation and subsequent fragmentary metamorphosis. You mean the morgen role in human reproduction. And you're only having to ask me because you still have inhibitions regarding the unmentionable. You're such a prude that you wouldn't even mention it to yourself until Melusine left you no option."

"Fair enough. I admit to having a squeamish imagination. So take a little of the pressure off. How, exactly, do morgens contrive the cloning of human males?"

"With difficulty . . . but what isn't difficult? As you've already worked out, from the logic of legend, the whole purpose of morgen design is human seduction: the siren song, the breasts, the hair. They can't offer their . . . lovers a reward in what might be considered the conventional way, having no vagina—but they do have mouths."

"And some kind of anatomical apparatus not only for collecting sperm but for filtering it, for selecting out diploid sperm."

"Obviously."

"And the delivery? The succubus turns incubus? The siren song works on women as well as men, who are even more inclined to believe afterwards that it was all a dream—the kind of dream that hardly anyone talks about for reasons of embarrassment?"

"That's one way—more than trifle hit-or-miss, but it works often enough to be worth persistence.

"And the other?"

"Some morgens—rare, but not unknown—are much more accomplished in the art of metamorphosis than others. They can produce offspring themselves. It's very difficult, as they don't have convenient anatomical apparatus, and very messy, but the nature and quality of the rebirth is guaranteed. The mother rarely survives, alas, but even that's not unknown."

"But I'm the product of a morgen incubus."

"Obviously. I tried to tell you that the first time we talked, but you reacted so badly to the idea I was trying to get across that you contrived a massive mistranslation—except, of course, that your mother really was a willing participant in a statutory rape, which was subsequently assumed by everyone, including her, to be the cause of her pregnancy. He was just a schoolboy; he didn't really mean any harm, and didn't really do any. If they'd had DNA tests back then, he'd have been able to prove that he wasn't the father, but no one would ever have been able to prove—or even to imagine—that your mother had actually become pregnant by being sucked down into a pond, just as you were this morning. She retained a vague memory of it, all-but-inaccessible to consciousness, but she could only think of it as having been dragged down to hell. *As above, so below*, she added to the tale her dreams concocted by herself, much later, after overhearing Ranald Jefferson explain the motto on his fake escutcheon to her own mother. Ranald wasn't a clone himself, but he was closely related to more than one. Your mother made the connection between you and him subconsciously, but the intuition wasn't entirely mistaken."

As usual, Simon had completely lost count of the number of steps that he had descended, although he knew that he had to be far below the bed of the bay if topological appearance could be trusted. The red glow was now visible ahead of him, outlining the rectangular opening at the bottom of the staircase.

When he reached the foot of the stairs, he raised the lantern and extended his arm into the cave, curiously. He had not been able to see it very clearly when he had come down into the blue light, or when he had followed Cerys through the portal, but he was slightly surprised by how small, bare and commonplace the space seemed now.

He might have inspected the walls and ceiling more closely had his attention not been drawn immediately to the dark red ellipse marked out in the wall to the left of the bottom of the stairway, which also seemed smaller than he had expected, only slightly more than six feet in height and no more than four feet wide at its maximum diameter. It did not resemble the vitreous cocoons, which had seemed a much more obtrusive and imposing structure, extending beyond the vulgar dimensions of perceptible space into strange infinities.

Was the seemingly flat red ellipse a metamorphosis of the vitreous cocoons, he wondered, or some sort of residue left behind by their disappearance? Vitreous cocoons could disappear, he knew. Thomas Mallory might presume that they were merely hidden, or buried, but Simon suspected strongly that they really could vanish, perhaps withdrawn entirely into one of the other dimensions in which they appeared to exist in part. Had that happened? The cocoons had turned red before, and then blue again, but this time seemed different. Why? Was it because of what had happened last time the communication portal had been used?

The ellipse too he might have studied with more minute care if there had not been someone barely visible standing in front of it, as if he were standing guard there.

Simon recognized the ghost of Owain Glyndwr, manifesting a degree of admittedly-vaporous substance as well as appearance, complete with vaporous leather armor and a vaporous sword. The pale floor of the cave, where he was standing, was marked by a large dark stain, which might or might not have been dried blood. He did not seem pleased to see Simon.

"What are you doing here?" Simon asked him.

"I have more right to be here that you do," said Glyndwr, waspishly. It was, Simon had to admit, a fair point.

"Has anything come through from the other side?" Simon asked, mildly.

"Not since the girl picked up the seed," reported Glyndwr, grudgingly, and added, gratuitously: "I don't like it. I don't like it at all."

"You haven't been through?" Simon asked.

"Never," Glyndwr replied. He did not explain why not, and the Black Bard either did not know or did not care, because no explanation surfaced in Simon's mind.

"Why don't you like it, then?" Simon asked, curiously.

"I've never seen it like this—red yes, three times before, but never like *this*. It's a very bad sign. People go mad, you know."

Tell me about it, Simon thought, but didn't say it, in case the ghost took the comment too literally.

It occurred to Simon that the three previous occasions to which Glyndwr referred could not have produced any very substantial reward for the neider, and that a different circumstance might therefore be regarded as potentially a good thing rather than a bad one, but he was not all sure that

that kind of logic was applicable either to the phenomenon or the situation. "What would you have done if something had come through?" he asked, still curious

"Given a warning," the ghost told him. "You wouldn't have heard it, but the other would. Not that it could have made any difference. We're all wasting our time. Are there any more of you?"

"Yes, but I asked them not to come down, at least until tomorrow afternoon."

"I don't have enough substance right now to stop them," the ghost said, with a hint of resentment in his voice, "and the days when people were terrified when they saw me are long gone. I'm just a curiosity now; nobody ever turns and flees in panic. But I suppose I could contrive a manifestation of this pathetic sort, in order to suggest that it would probably be a bad idea to follow you, if you haven't come back. Sometimes, it only takes a suggestion to license innate cowardice—but they might not be able to understand me, if they're not Welsh."

Simon did not bother to point out that he was English himself, and that Glyndwr was speaking English to him, as Ceridwen had once asked him to do. Nor did he bother to inform the ghost that anyone who did come down would be a Murden, even though it was a relevant issue. One way or another, they were all part of the crazy process of assisted reproduction that the neider had situated in and around St. Madoc's Abbey. One way or another, they all had a little neider in them, or, more specifically, a little morgen. And because of that, he supposed, whatever happened tonight, the story could go on, and presumably would. But was that a good thing? Thus far, he had been operating on the assumption that it was. Now, and not simply because of Father Mallory's insidious input, he was beginning to wonder.

He didn't know whether he was on the side of right or not. Perhaps he never would. But he knew that if he were to make any kind of reasoned decision, he had to follow the story to the end: the end that was still a mystery, even to the

Back Bard, and to all the sons of the neider's chosen people, the strangest of all the descendants of its Adams and Eves. Perhaps then he would be able to decide how his own story, and the story of the Abbey, ought to proceed, if not to a conclusion, at least to the end of a chapter.

To Owain Glyndwr, he said: "I'd be obliged if you did make that suggestion, if anyone does follow me."

"I'm not your servant," Glyndwr retorted, resentfully. "I'm a chieftain, a warrior, and a liberator." He put his ghostly hand on the hilt of his phantom sword, to emphasize the point.

"I know," Simon said, a trifle wearily. "I didn't mean any offense."

And. thinking that the unhappy ghost was absolutely right about their conversation being a waste of time, he stepped past the obsolete warrior and into the red oval—which did not put up the slightest opposition to his passage, exactly as if it were only a sinister figment of a crazy dream.

XVIII
In Myrddin's Cave

"It's not what I expected," Simon said to his invisible and intangible companion.

"Me neither," replied the bard. Although Simon knew that it was not the first time that one of the neider's offspring had been through the portal, he also knew that his second self had not carried any strong expectations forward from his previous experiences. After all, Simon had been through previously himself, but he had certainly not expected to see the same makeshift illusion that his reconstructors had made then, initially for Cerys, albeit out of imaginative fragments of one of his own third-rate novels. He had expected that they would be able to do better this time, with the aid of the ghostly copy they had made for themselves of his consciousness, however crude that sketch of his inner being had been.

He had also expected to be able to open the third eye that they had apparently gone to so much trouble to deliver to him, and he had expected that whatever they had been able to contrive beyond the portal would benefit further from the special sight of that eye.

For the moment, at least, though, he could not open it. Perhaps, he thought, that was his fault rather than any design fault in the eye, but the fact remained that what he could see, for the present, and so far as he could judge, might as well have been mere dull matter.

He could not see a great deal, in fact, by means of his vulgar earthly sight, because the space in which he found himself was very foggy, full of ocher-gray vapor that reflected the light of his electric lantern in a fashion that seemed to him to be rather jaundiced. The fog seemed to be suspended in breathable air, since he appeared to be breathing normally, but he knew from experience that the sensation of breathing might be an illusion; the neider had alternative means of oxygenating his blood, while he was in the grip of its exotic flesh, and he had to presume that any entity that might be trying to reach him now via the vitreous cocoons would be able to do that too. But the space he seemed to be in certainly gave the impression of having a real atmosphere, albeit a murky one, and he could not, as yet, detect anything to suggest that anything was trying to make contact with him, via the thing in his head or by means of any other apparition.

The atmosphere reeked, in a fashion not unlike the black underworld into which Melusine had drawn him; the fog had an odor that had something unhealthily paludal about it, as well as a strong hint of the cesspit.

In spite of the murk, however, Simon could discern the walls of a cave to either side of the red oval, and a vault that arched above it. The floor on which he was now standing was gray rock, not unlike the rock on the other side of the illusory portal, but seemingly even paler, and considerably more uneven. That pallor seemed out of place, though; the cliffs of the three headlands making up Morgan's Fork were not limestone, like so many cliffs on the south coast of England. Most of the Ceredigion coastline, he knew, consisted of mudstone or siltstone, sedimentary rocks going back some five hundred million years, and the tines were no different, unlike the sarns to be found further to the north, which were ridges of rock moved by glaciers during much more recent Ice Ages. On the other hand, he had reason to think that, in terms of earthly topography, relative to his starting point—the cave from which he had just come, and was presumably still only a couple of psychic strides away—was considerably below sea level, in some kind of lacuna whose faces were susceptible to various transformations associated with exotic matter.

How large the lacuna might be in which he now seemed to be standing, he could not tell, but it was not empty, nor were the formations protruding from the floor stalagmites, although they certainly seemed to be stone of some kind. They were dendritic, like some form of coral, but he could not help thinking of them as petrified hydrae. They were not so densely packed as to make it difficult for a human being to walk between them, and it did not require overmuch imagination to conceive of their being disguised as trees by the glamour that had been cast upon him last time he had come through the portal. It seemed to him that he might be able, if he moved away from the portal into the petrified forest, to find a clearing in the location where he had encountered the bewitched Cerys—perhaps even with a spring, as there was evidently water vapor here, and surely ought to be liquid water as well.

"We are still on Earth, aren't we?" Simon said, uncertainly. "We're simply in some exotic space underneath the bay? An underworld of sorts?"

"I don't know," said the bard, "but I agree with Glyndwr. I don't like it. If they summoned you—as they clearly did— why aren't they here? If your other copy is here, where is he? And why isn't the crwth resonating, if that's what it's here to do?"

Simon thought hard, trying to imagine possible answers to those questions. The bard had referred to his *other* copy because the entities that had killed him temporarily, in order to facilitate the process of making copies of his dark mind had not simply made one, apparently but not necessarily to take away, but another, which the ouroboros fragment of the neider had carried back to its parent, prior to its being fused with the fugitive consciousness of the Black Bard. The dark matter and dark energy that was now being reabsorbed into his own flesh and mind was a clone in more ways than one, another self in more ways than one.

That similitude, obviously, was facilitating the fusion process, and perhaps making it possible without excessive disruption. If such a thing was possible, his fusion with the black bard, might also facilitate a further fusion, possession or repossession by the copy that the aliens had made, securing the communication link that the alien had wanted to establish with both the neider and humans. But if that was the plan, where was the other copy? Given that he had apparently been summoned, why was it not here to meet him, if only in the form of a shadow, if it could not contrive anything more material.

"Perhaps it is here," Simon suggested to the bard, uncertainly. "Perhaps it's in the vapor. Perhaps it *is* the vapor, if the vapor is really there. I'm assuming that the empty space is illusory, that we're actually cocooned in dark matter, as I was this afternoon beneath the pond, or on my previous excursion, when Melusine took me down to the neider by the sea route."

"Oh, there's definitely plenty of dark matter around," said the bard. "I can't sense it literally, obviously, but as a dark mind myself, I'm aware of it. As for dark energy . . . that's everywhere and everywhen . . ."

"If we were still beneath the surface of the tine," Simon reasoned, "in an actual cave . . . but surely we can't be. There wouldn't be enough oxygen in the air, or fog. We have to be elsewhere, and cocooned, if we're not within the body of the neider."

"We're not inside the neider's root," said the bard. "If we were, I'd certainly know it. Unless . . ." The voice tailed off.

Simon had no difficulty following that implication. The neider with which the Myrddins had been in liminal contact for hundreds of years, and their ancestors for thousands, was a recent fragment of the primal hydra, only partially differentiated from other recent fragments, and still having a considerable degree of common identity with them. It was at least theoretically possible, however, that much earlier fragmentations, taking place millions or billions of years ago, had given rise to branches of hydra evolution that had been completely alienated from the other offspring of the primal hydra, and it was possible that alienated offspring of that sort were the entities that had duplicated—or triplicated—Simon, rather than extraterrestrials or intelligences from the Earth's dark matter core.

From some viewpoints, that might be the most plausible of the three alternatives . . . if, and only if, the appearances that were presently being offered to them were not deceptive.

Simon set the electric lantern down on the ground. Then he lifted the crwth in order to gaze at the strings. He tightened them, one by one, thinking that the instrument would surely need to be tuned to pick up a resonance effectively. He ran his fingers over the tightened strings experimentally, not entirely sure that they would make a sound at all. They did, but it was far from melodic. Tuning the instrument in such a way as to make it capable of playing a pleasant tune would probably require fingers and ears more expert than his, even with the Bard to aid him.

Who, he wondered, had made the crwth? And who had hidden it in the crypt in that eccentric fashion. He inspected the wood of the crooked backboard carefully. It might, he supposed, be as much as four hundred years old. The instrument might, therefore, have been Owain Myrddin's crwth. That did not necessarily mean, though, that Henry VIII's one-time wizard had been the one who had sealed it away. That might have been a later inheritor: Seymour Murden, or even Rhys the Engineer, perhaps not so much to hide it as to bury it, to prevent its use, to put it away like the mortal remains of the dead . . . of the dead awaiting rebirth, in their own strange fashion.

But the crwth might, in its essence, be a lot older than that. Even if it were only a copy of a previous instrument, Simon thought, a copy or a rebirth, it could—at least in spirit, as it were—be reckoned the Black Bard's crwth, and Myrddin Wyllt's crwth, and so on, not composed of the same material atoms, but nevertheless resonant with their identity.

Absent-mindedly, his fingers continued to tighten the strings. The tuning-pegs, he thought, must be a recent addition. He was no expert, but they seemed to him to have been turned on some kind of primitive lathe. Had there been lathes in the Black Bard's day? He didn't know. Over time, therefore, the instrument and its clones had probably evolved, modified in the interests of improvement . . .

Again, his finger plucked the retuned strings, making them sound their individual notes.

"Is that better?" he asked the passenger in his mind.

"It's just noise," the bard opined. "It's not music, not resonance. Something's wrong. This place reeks of death."

Was that true? Simon wondered. It certainly reeked of something nasty, but he had led a sheltered existence, with very little opportunity to scent death.

"Is it possible?" He asked the bard, "that the vitreous cocoons have faded to dark red because they're dying . . . because they're already dead?"

"If so," said the bard, "it's unprecedented, within the extent of my memory . . . and probably bad. Very bad. They've been red before, but as Glyndwr said, not like this."

Simon turned round, in order to examine the red oval that was still visible in the wall, exactly as it had been from what had seemed to be the other side. Exactly? Wasn't it a darker shade of crimson now than when he had made the symbolic gesture of stepping through it? Wasn't it gradually fading into darkness? What would happen if it did that? Would he be able to get back?

The idea of being trapped somewhere beyond his own world, unable to return, wherever he might presently be located, was a disturbing one.

"We can't just stand here," he said—ostensibly to the bard, but really just thinking aloud. "Either we go back now, or we go into the petrified forest, but we have to do something."

"We're doubtless under observation," said the bard, uneasily. "Everything takes time—often far more than one would hope. Adaptation is never instantaneous. We can't just go back—that would be admitting defeat. You were sent the eye; the intention must be that it will open, and that it will be able to see."

That too, Simon thought, was thinking aloud. He was already beginning to lose any sense of distinction between his own internal monologue and the bard's—and there was no difference at all when they spoke aloud. In a matter of minutes, he thought, he would be alone. He would still be himself, still recognizable, but he would be alone. Perhaps that was necessary. Perhaps the first fusion had to be completed before the other could begin, before the other even became imaginable,

"Forward it is, then," Simon said, turning his back on the red oval and picking up the lantern again. Holding it up, he began to move away from the portal, into the forest of dendrites. He touched the branches of the nearest one experimentally, but they seemed quite inert. He tried to break a slender twig, but could not do it. Nor did it bend; it was stronger than its appearance suggested.

Beyond the dendrite, the fog seemed denser and its yellow hue seemed to be edging toward green.

Suddenly, there was a perceptible movement: something moving through the air, fluttering like a bat; it was only a fleeting impression, but it changed Simon's perspective instantly. If there were life here, then this surely could not simply be a sealed cave mirroring the one he had just left. It must have an issue; it must give access to some vaster space and more complex environment.

"Is that a bird?" he asked the bard.

There was no answer, not even an "I don't know,"

Already? he thought

Already, came the faintest of echoes, which might or might not have been deliberate.

He took several more strides, still moving away from the wall where the red oval was. He sensed more movement: more fluttering, and a different friction, as if something were moving in or under the trees.

All that slithers is not serpentine, he remembered.

Did that actually mean anything, his pedantic self objected? Surely, the concept of "slithering" and the concept of "serpentine" were intricately intertwined, perhaps to the extent that one implied the other. What slithered, except for snaky things? Slugs? Slime-molds? Maggots? Amoebae? Motile hydrae? But did such things not, as soon as they began to slither, become serpentine?

Stop it, he told himself, sternly. *Focus.*

The point, surely, that neider had been suggesting to him, via Melusine, was that wherever he was going, there would be life, but not neider life. The neider's fragments had participated in excursions of this kind before, probably many times, but their journeys had not led to this particular environment, whether it was illusory or real, or to any consistent destination. That was probably why the neider entertained the hypothesis that the vitreous cocoons provided a viewport not to a single other world but to many.

And the neider was also convinced that it could sense intelligences vaguely akin to its own elsewhere in the solar system, and beyond. But if that were the case, why was it so very difficult to establish communication with entities beyond the portal? Why did the portal lead to many different places, seemingly without useful repetition?

Simon did not attempt to pose the question to the bard. He knew that the bard would not answer. He now possessed the bard. The bard and he were now the same.

But he still didn't know how to play the crwth, and he couldn't remember the song that was supposed to summon Melusine. She was out of reach. The neider was out of reach. Everything was out of reach. He was alone, with a vision of fog and a reek of death, surrounded by petrified hydrae, with only the ghosts of bats or birds to provide an evidence of unease.

"This isn't the way it was supposed to be," he said, aloud, as if his inner bard could still hear him, but he couldn't even convince himself.

But repetition had to be possible, he reminded himself. Not only had he been sent the eye that had not yet opened, but it had been sent to him in a fashion surely indicative of the fact that its senders were the same entities who had apparently extracted a bullet from his back only a fortnight before. It had definitely been a summons. So where were they? And why had they suddenly become so discreet?

Simon moved between two more of the strange stone trees, and found himself in what seemed to be a clearing—perhaps the same clearing in which he had found Cerys previously, if this really was the same place that he had visited then, but disappointingly deglamorized. There was no stream bisecting the clearing, but as he took another three steps forward, he saw that there was a pond: a pool of still black liquid, more reminiscent of oil than water. He was tempted to throw a stone into it, in order the see what kind of ripples were produced, but the uneven ground seemed to be far from replete with fragments of stone, and he could not be bothered searching assiduously for something as trivial as a pebble.

He remembered what had happened the last time that he had approached a pool, likewise accompanied by an odor not unlike the one to which his aggravated sense of smell was now beginning to become accustomed, and which did not seem as offensive as it had before.

"But the world still stinks," he said to the bard.

"So what?" he answered, on the bard's behalf, or his own.

"I don't know. But we're not alone here. Something is watching us. It's almost as if it were trying to avoid us, perhaps to deny that we're here, but that makes no sense to me. There's something wrong here. We ought to know what it is, because all this has happened before . . . not exactly, but similar things . . . to me, to us . . . but I don't know what it is. All I know for sure is that when it has happened before, it hasn't ended well . . . ."

But did he even know that for sure. And again, even if it were the case, so what?

"But there must have been progress," Simon said still speaking aloud, to the fraction of the neider that was still inside him, albeit dissolved in his own uncertain identity, his own stream of consciousness. "You haven't given up. *We* haven't given up. We must have made progress. Small victories, perhaps, but we must have believed, and ought still to believe, that one of us, or all of us, will eventually reach the breakthrough point, the point of realization . . ."

He was very reluctant to lean over the dark pool, fearful that something might surge forth and grab him, in order to drag him into an underworld beneath the underworld, where there might well be another pool, and so *ad infinitum*. The only perceptible movement, however, was not in the pool but in the atmosphere, where there were continued flutterings and where he could still catch the occasional glimpse of a fugitive, rapidly moving flyer.

Bats, he thought. *Bats in the belfry. Vampire bats*. If this were a dream, he thought, the bats would probably be symbolic, but bats could be symbolic of so many things. It would be so much simpler, he thought, if the unconscious sector of his mind could simply speak plainly. But that was paradoxical. The mind was essentially divided, bipartite, its dark part mysterious by definition: a challenge to be met without ever being overcome; a puzzle to be solved without ever being clarified.

There was danger here, but perhaps the danger did not lurk in the fog, in the reek of death and decay. Perhaps, as he

had already hypothesized, the danger lay in the other direction: in enlightenment; in the irruption of too much light into
the dark mind, the flooding of consciousness by precisely
what consciousness existed to keep at bay. Perhaps the danger lay in his head, in the eye that had not opened. But if
that were the case, what would be the point of everything
that had happened? What would be the point of what was
happening now?

He looked up, into the strangely tinted mist, and felt a
slight air current on his face, coming from the direction of the
far side of the pool.

The pool was only thirty feet in diameter, easy to walk
around in spite of the unevenness of the ground, its banks being uncluttered by anything resembling bushes. He did that,
and the air current became more forceful.

And suddenly, quite unexpectedly, it began to rain.

That's impossible, he thought. *Unless there's a sky. Or unless
it isn't rain, but something dripping.*

He put out a hand, as if to catch a liquid drop, but he
couldn't seem to intercept one. By the time he had caught
sight of one, it had already fallen too far to be seized by a
reaching hand. The droplets seemed large, easily catchable
if only he could get his hand into the right place, but he
couldn't.

Perhaps the droplets weren't real. Perhaps, even if they
were, they weren't water, but something else, something
strange. If this were a dream, the rain would be symbolic too,
but rain, like bats, could be symbolic of so many things.

If it really is rain, he thought, *then I'm not in a cave any more;
I must be in the open, exposed, able to get wet. I need to seek shelter.
I need to protect the crwth. I need . . .*

He tilted his head back and looked upwards, vertically,
although he did not really imagine that doing so would allow
him to discern whether the droplets falling around him were
falling from an empty sky or dripping from a solid vault.

What the movement did enable to happen, however,
was that a large drop of what might or might not have been

water—but which, on reflection, probably wasn't—hit him directly in the middle of his forehead, precisely where the "bullet" that Cerys had thrown at his face had struck him, burned him, and fused with his flesh in less than a second.

And he stopped fighting, stopped wrestling with his stupid, perverse, conscious thoughts in his ridiculous, pedantic, knotty fashion, and let himself go.

And the world around him—the hallucination around him—began to dissolve. The rain was symbolic, but only in the crudest possible fashion. It was a solvent, and it was dissolving the world, washing it away.

Simon straightened his head in order to watch the end of the world. He stretched out his arms, one hand holding the lantern and one clutching the crwth, and invited the solvent to wet him, to soak him, to reduce him to a soggy pulp and scatter his molecules in fluid disorder.

The rain did not do that, in crude liquid terms; its material component was discreet. It did not even wet his clothing. But in other terms—in terms of its exotic components—it drenched him. It flowed through him, a hot shower for the soul. It dissolved his hallucination—the fog, the stone dendrites, the reek that might or might not be that of death, and the walls of the cave—but it did not dissolve him; rather, it filled him, not as if he were a container, or even something as simple as a sponge; the absorption was more complicated than that, more intricate and more precise. He swelled, internally.

It was exceedingly peculiar, but not at all painful. And although it was a metamorphosis of sorts, he still felt very much himself, perfectly recognizable. He did feel an urge to sit down, though, and did, and he felt the need to say something to himself, just to confirm that he still had the words.

"That's not what I expected," he said. And then, to test his curiosity, he said: "Where am I?"

There was still solidity beneath his feet, but it was invisible. Everything was now invisible; there was no longer any trace of the black pool, and no hint of a red glow in any direction. Logically, it should have been pitch dark, but it wasn't. It wasn't that there was light, exactly, but there was an impression of some sort that substituted for light, and he knew, or felt, that he was capable of sight, if only he could open his new eye.

There was no warning voice, akin to the one that the Black Bard had briefly been able to manifest, but he knew that he needed to be very, very careful.

His startled third "eye"—what he could not help thinking of as an eye because he had no more convenient metaphor—opened, for the merest blink, which lasted no more than a tiny fraction of a second of objective time. Like the dream irruptions that had plagued him all through the day before, it happened too quickly to rupture the apparent flow of consciousness, but it left a trace behind: something that his consciousness could grasp, and cling to, and attempt to process . . .

What his mind reproduced in terms of quasivisual visual imagery was little more than a display of light, a confusion of which his brain could make very little, but it was not blinding light, not even dazzling light; his consciousness was better able to cope with it than that. It was confusing and kaleidoscopic, but as mere light it was bearable. The problem was that it was accompanied by a cacophony of other sensations that added dimensions of complication whose existence and nature he had never suspected, perhaps kinesthetic, or perhaps the result of a surge of energy—the ordinary electromagnetic energy of living flesh—surging through his sensory nerves . . . and other nerves too, for he felt a shock that ran through his entire body, like an internal fire.

Was this, he wondered, what James Murden had felt at the instant of his death, in response to which his heart had stopped?

Perhaps, he thought—but his own heart did not stop. Nor was his brain scrambled, although he suspected that others might have been, in similar, or at least related, circumstances—not merely the predecessors of his own rebirth but others in St. Madoc, and before St. Madoc, and countless others in Toulouse, in Jerusalem, in Delphi, in Mecca and who could tell how many other places.

His own consciousness did not crack, let alone go *bang* and *boom*.

I can cope! he thought, triumphantly.

He knew that all the credit was not due to him, nor even to the fragment of the neider that had possessed him. He suspected, strongly, that it was a true triple effort, in which the seed of the vitreous cocoons, the tiny larva that had burrowed into his brain, had played the major part in assisting him to weather the onslaught.

It was not the shadow of his own mentality that he had been summoned here to encounter, he realized; that was already inside him, because that was what the fake bullet had been. It had brought him here to receive a far stranger shadow than itself, and to serve as the interpreter and negotiator of the encounter, for its own benefit rather than his, if the two could any longer be separated.

In stepping into the red oval he had not been stepping *through* the relic of the vitreous cocoons, but *into* it. That was so obvious now that he could not imagine how he had ever thought of it any other way. But he was no longer inside the array of cocoons. Quite the reverse. One of them—just one, out of the uncountable number that had made up the blue formation—was now inside him. He was possessed—or, looking at it from another angle, he was now a possessor.

More importantly, he was a winner; his consciousness had survived the ordeal, perhaps not quite the same, but recognizable. He was himself—perhaps not entirely sane, but still capable of organized, rational thought. That was victory. He had contrived to remain lucid under the onslaught of sensation. He could still maintain his internal monologue, his flexible ego. He was still able to bring words to his self-defense.

As usual, his first impulse was to borrow the words, to appropriate the inspiration.

"To be or not to be," he began, but immediately rejected that one, out of hand. "We are all in the gutter," he quoted instead, "but some of us are looking at the stars."

And then he laughed, although, as jokes went, it was not merely weak but private, incapable of enabling anyone else to laugh with him.

The few to whom Oscar Wilde had referred had been viewing the stars from a vast distance—a safe distance—through the protective lens of a vast void of darkness. With the aid of powerful telescopes and related optical instruments, astronomers had been able to grasp something of their multitude, their complexity and even a little of their infinite variety, but only at a very distant removal. They could not experience their immediacy.

Simon could, now—but he knew that he had to be exceedingly careful, if he did not want to be blinded by their light.

As soon as that metaphorical eye inside his forehead had opened, just for a flash, he had understood more clearly the vague impression that he had received while he communed with the neider after Melusine had snatched him from the bridge. He had understood that the dormant, dreaming larvae within the vitreous cocoons of exotic matter did, indeed, have a privileged communication with dreaming minds elsewhere in the universe, on planets, in stars, in clouds of interstellar dust and the hearts of suns, and that other dreaming minds had been capable of tapping into that resource, of sensing the realities of those other minds, those other lives. He understood more clearly, too, why the neider had wanted to establish a connection with the vitreous cocoons that would allow it greater access to that resource—careful, controlled, fruitful access—and why that was such a difficult, dangerous and perhaps impossible quest.

"Take it slowly," he advised himself, sagely. "One step at a time. In fact, don't even try to stand up yet. Just sit, for while, and pull yourself together."

And he laughed again, at the private pun, whose irony no one but him could possibly have savored.

The contact was not difficult; what was difficult was the necessary filtration, separation and focus that could reduce the perception, even belatedly, to something intellectually manageable. The difficulty lay in avoiding being overwhelmed and drowned, not so much by the dark energy itself—the black light, as it were—but by everything that came with the dark energy, everything that rode on the black light, like music on a carrier wave. He had an inkling, now, as to why the human brain and mind were so woefully unadapted for that task, and how careful the larva that had invaded him had already had to be, and would have to be in future, if the flood of dark energy that was now perceptible in principle were not to devastate his capacity for rational thought. He felt that he understood how difficult it would be, even though he was possessed of a carefully clarified copy of the particular darkness of his own soul, for him to reach some kind of viable accommodation with the collective imagination to which he now had access.

He felt that he understood, now, why the entities from elsewhere that had triggered the final phase of the process— the entities that had contrived his stupidly melodramatic death and resurrection, in order to take him out of himself and copy him—had not come back, and could not come back, and why they never would be able to come back, although they had been careful to leave something of themselves behind: a gift.

A problematic gift, to be sure, but a gift nevertheless.

Simon realized that a momentary contact of that kind, with that degree of control and orchestration, was only possible at a particular point of a larva's development: the moment of metamorphosis. That was the only moment in the larva's exceedingly long and complex life-cycle that it was sufficiently fluid, in terms of its dark mentality, to be controllable, to be vulnerable to possession, usurpation and perversion. It was the moment in which the dark matter imago shuffled off its baryonic matter skin, its maggoty husk, the moment at which that aspect of its changeable self died, having already begun to decay.

But death, Simon already knew, is only a transfiguration, not only because the dark components of mind possessed an immortality of sorts—albeit none of the preservations of purified identity imagined by various religions—but also in the more vulgar sense that putrefaction is a kind of life, a transformation of dead human flesh into living bacterial flesh. As in that microcosm and macrocosm, in the microcosm and the macrocosm of the vitreous cocoons death was just a link in the chain. The moment of vulnerability was a moment of potential metamorphosis, not merely in accordance with the program incorporated into the larval equivalent of dark-matter genetics, but—potentially, at least—in accordance with the blueprint fed to it by contact with another mind, perhaps one close at hand and perhaps billions of miles away, but linked nevertheless by the chains of the cosmic unconscious, the dark hypermind.

At that brief moment in the life of the larva, the sending of the gift was possible, and distance, although awkward, was negotiable, surmountable, conquerable.

"The gift?" he said, aloud

Could it not also be called parasitism, predation or putrefaction?

Perhaps. But like those seemingly ugly things, it could also be seen as an agent of progress, an addition to the complexity, the variety and the potential of life.

At any rate, Simon figured that he knew, now, which side he was on in the ongoing struggle for intellectual existence, and where he was located within mental life's rich pattern. He knew why, when the time for the collective metamorphosis had approached, the larvae within the vitreous cocoons had become more active: blindly, because, unlike the neider, they had no consciousness, being purely creatures of darkness in mental terms, no matter what kind of radiant display they put on. He understood how he had been caught up in that increased activity—that contagion of madness, if that was the label one cared to stick on it.

And he felt that he knew, too, how the consciousness from elsewhere that had attempted to take advantage of that moment—as the neider, like its predecessors, had been endeavoring to do for millennia, largely impelled by its own unconscious drives and instincts, with little conscious insight into it what it was doing, or even what it was—had co-opted him into the project, and had given him a role to play, before he had been claimed by another player, in order to play a more complex role.

Exactly how that role would play out, he could not know, as yet, because he could only see a tiny fraction of the game, and a single element of its strategy. He knew that there was still danger, but he knew, too, that the possession he now had—for, in the final analysis, he was surely the possessor, not the possessed—was so precious that the renegade larva and the neider would both move heaven and earth to protect him, if they could. He might have been chosen almost at random by the entities from elsewhere, and he might well be grotesquely ill-equipped for the part, but he was a key player now, a vital link in an inordinately complex chain.

He was an alien, now. He was a parasite; or, seen from another and equally valid point of view, which he naturally preferred, he was a gift. He was a potential. But the entities from elsewhere had not lied to him. He was still, essentially and recognizably, himself. And the copy of his dark mind carried by the seed that had burned into his brain would do everything unhumanly possible to preserve that sense of self, and protect it from harm, even including madness. Unlike the copy that the neider had integrated with the Black Bard, it would not seek fusion and dissolution, which would be far too dangerous; instead, it would seek protection and coexistence, careful and fruitful communication.

And the neider would approve, doubtless not seeing it as the ideal or optimum outcome to its own project, but surely seeing it as an outcome that could work within, and perhaps the best hope for its own progress, in the short term, now that the vitreous cocoons were dead and gone, and any further opportunities it might have had, in theory, had slipped through its tentacles . . . as, apparently, they often did.

But he was not out of the woods yet.

He knew that the will and determination were there, on the part of the alienated fraction of himself, but he also knew that the will and determination might not be enough, and that the darker fraction of himself, which lay beyond the cocoon of consciousness, was swollen now by something literally unimaginable.

He had always been in the gutter, and had always tried, in his own feeble way, to catch glimpses of the stars. Now, he had the potential, but it would be an extremely tricky business, playing with mental nitroglycerine.

Something akin to what had happened to him had happened before, perhaps many times, and it had rarely ended well, not because there was any hostility involved on the part of the entities from elsewhere, entities akin to the neider or entities akin to the vitreous cocoons, but simply because of the vast difference between the resources of perception of those various parties.

Sometimes, he supposed, even a modest flash such as the one that he had just been gifted might have killed its recipient, or left them helplessly deranged, but sometimes, he suspected, they had survived, as he had: not quite as they had been before, but recognizable. Some, at least had made intellectual progress: perhaps tiny victories, but all counting, all taking the great quest a little further, in spite of the fact that it was so enormously complicated, and the fact that to every action there was a reaction—not, alas, invariably equal and opposite—and the fact that something always, or almost always, went wrong, simply because it could. Sometimes, inevitably, the things that went wrong had proved fatal

Even though the hallucinatory world had dissolved, casting him back into brute reality, in one piece and sitting quietly, still thinking, still capable of speech, with words at his beck and call, he was not out of the woods yet.

XIX
The Siren Song

Simon had no map, no guide-book. He did not know where to start, or even whether he ought to start right away. He felt, though, that he hadn't succeeded in pulling himself together yet, that he hadn't quite finished the task in hand.

"What else?" he asked himself.

"Isn't it obvious?" he answered.

"No," he retorted.

But he had brought the crwth with him, on the bard's insistence and it occurred to him he must have brought if for a reason. It was supposed to resonate. Even though he did not know how to play the instrument, it was supposed to be a resource. It had been left for him deliberately, by someone who had been through his before. Owain Myrddin? Perhaps, but in any case, someone. Someone who had been through this before, and had had reason to think that it would happen again.

"If music be the food of love," he said, reverting, as he so often did in mental crises, to his Shakespeare, "play on . . ."

Even though he could not play, he had more resources in the dark and bottomless well of his collective unconscious now than he had ever had before, and the crwth, after all, was only a symbol, a talisman, a crooked crutch, even for the likes of a Taliesin. Perhaps he could resonate. Perhaps he did not have to play the music, because, as he had previously dreamed, he *was* the music, and the music was everywhere and eternal. If properly sensed, it filled, soaked and swelled the soul.

He laughed again, at the private play on words.

So he stroked the strings with his fingers.

This time, they played. He heard the music. He was not conscious of being the music yet, but he felt in his head and his heart, that with the right application, and hard work, he might one day acquire the consciousness of being the music, the ability to draw it out of his dreams, and even to translate it into words . . . coherent words, unafflicted by the vagaries of dream illogic.

He felt that, if he could just get the hang of the resonance, he might one day be able to see everything, hear everything, and be everything that he now had the potential to hear, see and be.

"If I live long enough," he added.

Whether he could survive everything, even in the short term, would obviously be a different matter, but it had to be possible, because others had survived, at least in the short term and had managed to bring something back. They had pulled themselves together, perhaps by means of faith, prayer, or some such foolish contrivance, some such mental trickery, but they had done it. Thus, not only could he do it, but he could do it better, because he had a better stock of accumulated human knowledge and thought at his disposal, and the internet to facilitate access to it. And because of that, he was better placed than any of his predecessors, here or elsewhere, to carry the quest forward. But if he was to see further than anyone else, he would have to do what every far seer had to do, and stand on giant shoulders.

It wouldn't be easy.

In order to indulge the hearing and seeing for which the entities from elsewhere and the larva from the vitreous cocoons had gifted him, he had a lot of mental labor to complete. In order to bring the music to consciousness, and translate it, he would have to learn to play. It would take time.

For the present, he carried on strumming, pretending that he knew what he was doing.

"Start at the beginning," he advised himself.

Where was he, really?

That, at least, was an easy one.

He was sitting on the floor of the cave at the bottom of the steps that led down from the crypt in St. Madoc's Abbey. He counted them, mentally. There were thirty steps.

They were steep steps, but there were only thirty of them!

In going down them, previously, he had always lost count. Everybody, in going down them, had always lost count, but not because their arithmetic was so poor that they could not count to thirty. It did not matter whether they had the kind of primitive mind that calculated *one, two, three, many*, or the kind of sophisticated, pedantic, philosophical mind that was capable, in theory, of counting forever, of starting *one, two, three* and going on to *four*, and *five*, and naming every number thereafter, in accordance with an infinitely elastic system of nomenclature, without ever stopping, unless they ran out of patience, or breath. Eventually, everyone lost count, and before reaching thirty! That was a phenomenon. That was supernatural.

People had always lost count, because in going down those thirty steps they had always became disconnected from the unsafe haven of their consciousness. They had always thought that there were many more steps than there actually were, because they really were going much further than a flight of steps of that limited extent permitted, in terms of vulgar topography. They had always seemed to be going far beneath sea-level—much further than the few fathoms by which the floor of the cave must actually be below sea-level—because, in a sense, they really had gone much further than the bed of the sea. Mentally, they had been entering the realm of . . .

Heaven? Hell? Annwn? The vitreous cocoons?

It was necessary, though, not to dismiss those questions as a mere matter of vocabulary, to try to swat them away by saying that one label was as good as another, and not simply because of the evident absurdity of considering Heaven and Hell as alternative nomenclatures for the same thing. The terminology mattered, because the terminology encapsulated the concept, and that was the whole essence of the problem. In the beginning was, indeed, the Word. The words created the world, and, just as importantly, re-created it.

Simon was certain in his own mind, now, of what had happened to the vitreous cocoons, where they had gone, only leaving behind a red stain on the wall, like a symbolic bloodstain, which only offered the illusion of an outlet. The vitreous cocoons had split, and their chrysalides had changed, had gone on to the next phase of their predestined existence, deep inside the Earth's core—all of them except for the perverted one, the outsider, the one gifted with a novel metamorphosis, which had required a host, and not just any host, in the strange, inimical world of the Earth's surface, which even the neider could only reach safely by means of ghosts, neider and the occasional serpentine tip of a tentacle, but one that was pre-adapted to receive it, to possess it. In order to achieve that, the perverted larva, the gift, had become the lining of "bullet" that had been expelled on to the floor of the cave. There, because he had not gone down to the cave and picked it up himself, Cerys had picked up instead, and brought it to him.

Sometimes, Simon mused, even if Mahomet has a trip to the mountain inscribed in his diary, the mountain can't wait. Except that Mahomet had presumably been the brainchild of a different mountain—only *presumably*, because even though the larva was theoretically capable of a great many things, it could not possibly know everything. Nothing could know everything, except the ultimate mind, the mind of the whole universe, and that would not develop consciousness for a long time yet—billions of years, at least—if it ever did. And even then, in knowing everything, that mind would lose any vestige of individuality, any vestige of concentration, any vestige of will. Not a sparrow could fall, even now, without the hypermind compounded out of the collective unconscious of all existing minds, being aware of the sparrow's fall, but there wouldn't be a damn thing that the ultimate mind could do about the individual fall, or even think about it, because it was just an arithmetical total, and not an identity. Even if, or when, it became an identity, a conscious entity, it still wouldn't be able to care, to act, or to judge. It wasn't God, in any meaningful sense of the term, and never would be.

"Steady on," Simon advised himself. "Gently does it."

The entity that had crammed itself into the larval seed, by means of a miracle of metamorphic compaction, in order to soak up and safely store the legacy of the cocoons' collective unconscious must have ambitions beyond the merely godlike. It wanted to be an active mind, a thinking mind, an evolving mind, a mind capable of purpose and progress. The cost of that was that it had to ignore much of what, in theory, it was capable of seeing and knowing. It had to be selective, self-defining and self-limiting, intensive and obsessive.

In much the same way that dark matter, in order to extend the range if its potential existence, in order to achieve the particular potential of the various states of matter, both familiar and exotic, was obliged to specialize and metamorphose, condensing and concentrating itself, in various interesting ways, so dark mind had to do likewise, focusing and refining intention, in order to achieve the potential of the various states of consciousness, familiar and otherwise, harmonic and otherwise, wordy and otherwise, and their various alloys, some doubtless more esthetically pleasing than others.

Why? Because of the logic of the situation, the nature of existence, the rules of which were infinite in number, although they could be reduced to three, for the sake of mental convenience. Nobody ever lost count before getting to three. Even idiots, crows and goldfish can do that.

Simon continued to strum, softly and rhythmically, and he began, gradually, to resonate to his strumming, to sense the music. He had a long way to go yet before he could become conscious of the music, but he thought that he was beginning to get a feel for it, and perception of its chords, a sensibility of its rhythm.

In the beginning, as he had said to himself before, there had been a hydra. But there had not only been a hydra. Nothing is ever simple, and to every action there is a reaction of some sort. As well as the hydra, there had been a . . . what? A pre-larva? An amoeba? Something. Call it an amoeba, for want of a better analogy.

There had not, of course, been only the two kinds of primal entities. Repeat it: nothing is ever simple. But for the convenience of idiots, crows and goldfish, who never like to stretch their arithmetical abilities to the limit, not to mention the esthetic considerations of lovers of symmetry, who are far more common in Nature than lovers of chaos, dualism had inevitable attractions.

And that was understandable, Simon thought, because symmetry is a form of harmony and harmony is more fundamental than wordiness, and capable of a great deal that wordiness is not, although the converse also applies, thank humanity. It was understandable, but it didn't mean that he had to approve of it. Not wholeheartedly, at any rate.

The point was, however, that everyone coming down that flight of thirty steps lost count, and lost themselves, at least to the extent that they were capable of getting lost—and who isn't?—in the mercurial realm of the great amoeba, the amoebic dreamer, unable to avoid a meeting of minds that could not be anything but confusing, but which, by the same token, engendered in any thinking mind the desire to overcome that confusion, the desire to solve the problem, to make sense.

That was not only true of human minds; it would also be true of the individual minds of particular thinking amoebae, and it was certainly true, too, of the minds of particular thinking hydrae—all of which had some degree of connection, but only unconsciously, with one another, with other minds, and with the totality, and all of which had the same innate drive toward progress, toward enlightenment.

Attempts made by the various parties to communicate, and hence to increase understanding, were beset by difficulties; in many ways, the whole thing was a recipe for disaster. But what was the alternative?

Simon knew that he had been on the floor of the cave before, when he had followed Cerys into the darkness. He had fallen down then, just as she had, and they had lain semi-conscious for a long time, becalmed in a dream that the amoeba had contrived with them and for them, under the prompting and with the collaboration of *the others*, the entities from elsewhere. All four parties had made a contribution to the apparatus and development of that dream, and so had an offspring of the neider, which had hitched a ride with Simon, stuck around his neck like a noose.

Like any product designed by a committee, the collaborative hallucination had not turned out exactly the way that any of those capable of wanting had wanted, and had become something of a monster as various instincts, desires and anxieties had overlapped and reacted. None of the active parties had had any evil intent, but the variation of their agendas and resources had produced various conflicts and frictions, which had inevitably escalated, as the collective story they were compiling had run out of control, borne along by the inertia of its own twisted logic.

The ultimate fix, the *deus ex machina* that had attempted unsuccessfully to resolve the climax, Simon saw and understood, had been mostly his, just as his imagination, much of it filtered through Cerys, had provided the initial décor. It had all been rather crude, as he had observed ashamedly even at the time, but it had not lacked a certain ingenuity.

He had assessed that ingenuity at the time, in a rather critical fashion, but he was used to that. He was never entirely satisfied with his creative works, which never seemed, once they were finished, to have lived up to the hopes that he had initially conceived for them. And he very often found, when he finished a story, whether it was fiction—which is to say, honest lies—or "non-fiction"—lies pretending to a more vulgar variety of truth—that the completion he had contrived was itself only an illusion, that if the story were really to edge a little closer to making sense, than it required a sequel, a more satisfactory rounding out, something that looked a little more like a genuine conclusion. So he wrote sequels. His entire life, in fact, had been nothing but an endless series of sequels and re-creations, always searching for a better conclusion, always disenchanted with the conventional conclusions, the climaxes that only provided momentary satisfaction without ever reducing the need to go on, and on . . .

Was any life different? Could it be?

"Focus!" he instructed himself.

Easier said than done, in the circumstances.

He was letting his egotism get the upper hand, he realized. He was becoming monotonous. He needed to broaden out his musical scope. He needed to think about others. Even though he wasn't a saint, and he really did wish that people would stop accusing him of it, in the sneering, sarcastic tone that they always seemed to be using, even when they meant the compliment sincerely, he had to try to give some thought to the bigger picture, and not just the slightly bigger picture of his own meager, trivial, ridiculous life and his pathetic, broken family, but the much bigger picture.

In brief, he had to ask himself, not what the descendants of the primal hydra, the primal amoeba and the entities from elsewhere could do for him, but what he could do for them. He had to ask himself what contribution he could make, as a mere catalyst if not as an active storyteller, to their ongoing quest for progress and enlightenment, their quest to learn to communicate with other minds, especially minds different from their own: wordy minds, and minds whose music was responsible to a different melody, perhaps even a different kind of harmony.

After all, that was what he was here for. He was a free agent, and he had his own motives, but the real reason that he was here was because the real forces that had nudged him across the board on which the board was being played, the forces that had only done him the favor of making him a piece, but had at least done him the favor of making him a piece that didn't have to move in a straight line—a skipping knight rather than a narrowly-diagonal bishop, if it had been a game of chess, which it obviously wasn't. He was here because some alien consciousness hoped that, unreliable monster as he was, he might be of some service to it, some assistance in its own quest for communication, for the possible relief of its loneliness.

Some people, he knew, would have resented that, but he didn't. He was glad of it. He was being rewarded for it, in various small ways, but that wasn't the point. He didn't think of what he was doing as being a vulgar hireling, let alone a slave; he thought of it as being offered a role to fill, a part to play in something bigger—something so much bigger that it had aspects that were infinite, unconscious links with dark entities inside the Earth's thinly-crusted globe and far away in the vast universe of outer space.

In a sense, he had always had that kind of role, simply by virtue of being a writer, a storyteller, especially stories on a cosmological and mythic scale, and it was hardly surprising, in a way, that his writings had so often mirrored and reflected his current mission, in a fashion for more intricate than mere coincidence. But now, at this particular point in time, he had a chance to go beyond that.

Now, he had a chance to help provide a unique and special link between a descendant of the primal hydra, a descendant of the primal amoeba and an entity from elsewhere: between the neider, the entity whose preferred manifestation, in deceptive appearance, was the blue aggregation of the vitreous cocoons, and something even stranger, even more mysterious.

He had wanted to do that—and he still wanted to do it—by teaching them all to talk, by giving them the gift of words, with which to talk to him, and, if only indirectly, to one another, by edging their re-creation in the direction of his own image. But perhaps that wasn't the right way to go about it—at least, not for the time being. In future, the possibilities were still endless . . .

For now, however, by virtue of the logic of the situation and the way it had developed, thanks to the intersection of the interested parties' various agendas, he was in a position at least to provide a conduit through which they could each reach out in their own way. He still could not play the crwth, but he could strum. He knew now that he could resonate. He could allow himself to be played, and in so doing, in a conscientiously self-effacing fashion, he might be able to al-low them to blend their different styles of musical mind, their different species of harmony, in order to forge the beginnings of a new, and perhaps better, symphony.

He was under no illusion as to the difficulty of that project, and he was all too well aware of the number of times that similar attempts must have failed in the past, but after all, he had to try, didn't he?

Didn't he?

Yes, he decided, he did.

He was still only strumming, making no attempt actually to play a tune on the crwth, or make any convincing simulation of so doing, but he didn't feel that he was failing, because, like the universal mind that was still in embryo, he was only at the beginning of his career, his destiny, and the instrument was, after all, only a symbol. He didn't even try to play himself, in the sense of plotting his dream. As the siren song took hold of him more fully, and more insistently, he just relaxed further and resonated meekly, surrendering himself to the whim of inspiration. He drifted with the Muse, knowing, even as he did so, that there might be nothing in his reverie to which his memory might be able to cling and reproduce, for the moment, in any form subsequently graspable by consciousness, but feeling that even if that were the case, he was not wasting his time, that he was making provision for future though. The detail of what he wrought was forgotten as soon as it was formed, but it was not entirely lost.

He let himself go to the siren song.

Was it blissful? After a fashion. Was he in ecstasy? Not really. Was it the culmination of his life's endeavor? He certainly hoped not, because, even at nearly seventy years of age, he had to hope that the best was still to come. Did it make up for all his past disappointments, failures, frustrations and depressions? Absolutely not—but how could it? How could anything?

The dream was sky-blue, as beautiful as daylight. It was serpentine in its graceful flow like a water-snake. It was smooth and it was melodic and it was fabulous. It bore no resemblance to the usual productions of his imagination, and yet, he felt that it was very much his own, that no one else would have dreamed it in the same way. Many might have contrived it better, but no one else would have been able to give it the precise configuration of his own stubborn eccentricity. He was proud of it. Doubtless he could have done better, had he had time for second thoughts, re-appraisal and re-creation, but he hadn't.

He did, however, have time to make progress within the dream-work, to improve it as he went along, and it seemed to last a long time, although he didn't even try to count the minutes. There seemed to be far more than thirty, although he was by no means sure that his arithmetic was reliable, or even applicable. It was, any case, at least in his not-so-humble estimation, the seed of a great dream-symphony, the larva of a masterpiece as great as a naïve human mind could imagine, and although it wouldn't be perfect, or anything near, for a long time yet, when it was complete, it would surely be a towering achievement of the imagination . . .

At least, it might be.

The song was almost within his mental grasp now, and he had the means now, he knew, to get an imaginative grip eventually . . .

But no action is without reaction, and if something can possibly go wrong, it probably will . . .

The neider's mode of reproduction by fragmentation had the inevitable side-effect of generating difference, and sometimes antagonism. Seen as a whole, as a collective, the neider was by no means monolithic, by no means fully harmonized internally. It had its fundamental mission, its essential ambition, and its semi-coherent dream, but among its multitudinous offspring, it also had its pockets of dissent, of resentment, and even of rebellion.

Simon was not alone in the cave beneath the crypt. The artificially-contrived specter of Owain Glyndwr was there. The living warrior had volunteered for the experiment of self-preservation while hiding out in the Abbey from his English pursuers in the early fifteenth-century. The dreams and ambitions that had led him to tempt his conscious preservation beyond death had, however, been thwarted and betrayed by the spectral condition. Not only had he found that he could not further them, but that he no longer wanted to.

He had become an occasional instrument of the neider, most significantly as an agent of its long and awkward communication with the last and longest-lived of the Ceridwens—the lady of the house for more than two centuries, by her own count, and more than a hundred and fifty by any arithmetic—while the two of them had cultivated their own particular varieties of madness.

Glyndwr had never forsaken his initial rage, but he had been bottling it up for six hundred years. And he was still, in spite of his long servitude to his hydra-creator, the neider, a free agent. He had the option, like Simon, of simply going along with the dream that Simon was forging with the collaboration of the neider and the left-over larva from vitreous cocoons. He could, with a little mental effort, have savored its celestial beauty, its slithering smoothness and its innocent ambition.

But Simon's strumming had been getting on his vaporous nerves for what seemed to his phantasmal sense of duration to have been a long time. On him, by contrast with Simon, the effect had been grating rather than soothing. In his day, he had undoubtedly heard crwths played properly, perhaps well, by true Welshmen, who would have considered an Englishman's strumming to be an insult.

Owain Glyndwr could still have done nothing. It would have been easy, as well as rational.

But he didn't. Perhaps he was at the end of his ghostly tether. Perhaps the psychic fallout of the demise of the vitreous cocoons had corroded his perverted existence. Perhaps, like the man of action he had once been, he simply had an irresistible urge to *do something*—which, since he had been the kind of man he had been, was translated into an irresistible urge to do something violent.

He was only a ghost; appearance was easy for him, but vaporousness was difficult, and solidity far more difficult— but even solidity was not impossible. With sufficient impetus and effort, he could achieve a measure of solidity, not merely for himself but for his spectral sword.

And Simon, by virtue of having his own solidity, of having a stubborn body even in the midst of the most fabulous illusion, could be hurt. He could be killed. In fact, he already had been, once. When he and Cerys had been here, enveloped by the dream that had run out of control, Cerys had actually fired the real gun that she was holding, and the real bullet had actually hit Simon. Whether it had killed him or not, in the full meaning of the term, was difficult to determine, a matter of definition, but through the medium of the vitreous cocoons, the entities from elsewhere and the neider had certainly had to work hard, in collaboration—perhaps not for the first time in their history, but certainly more effectively than on any previous occasion—to bring him back, at least from the brink of death, if not beyond it. They had tinkered with him in the process, and had made dark copies of his mentality, but they had brought him back recognizable to himself and others.

Possibly, something present within him might have been able to do it again, even if Owain Glyndwr had contrived to cut his head off with a sweep of his sword, but probably not, given the very different circumstances.

On the other hand, it was entirely possible that, in a typically human fashion, Glyndwr's whimsical ambition far exceeded his actual capability, and the blow would not have been mortal.

But perhaps not. Had the phantom Glyndwr actually been able to deliver the blow, there was certainly a risk that Simon might have been badly injured, perhaps irredeemably.

But the blow did not land.

By the time the Welsh warrior had raised the weapon, in order to strike, he and Simon were no longer alone in the cave. Megan and Marianne had not bothered to count the number of steps on the way down, although it would not have been impossible for them, but they reached the bottom much more rapidly than anyone ever had before. Megan was carrying the lantern that Cerys had left behind when she left the chapel, and Marianne was still carrying the gun that Cerys had handed to her before leaving.

They weighed up the situation in a flash. Neither of them paused to think that it was impossible, to doubt the evidence of their eyes, or even to wonder what on earth was going on.

Megan ducked in order to get out of the way. Marianne, who was behind her, fired the gun.

Owain Glyndwr was solid enough to be hurt by a bullet, but he was not solid enough to stop one. The first one went straight through him, hit the wall of the cave—which was only twelve or fifteen feet away, and ricocheted. Perhaps it had killed Glyndwr on the way through, and perhaps not, but he was a phantom already. He did not fall, and he did not drop his sword. So Marianne fired again, and again.

Crack, bang, boom.

As luck would have it—if luck had anything to do with it—none of the ricochets hit Simon, Megan or Marianne.

Finally, conceivably with more relief than wrath, the Welsh warrior-prince collapsed, and vanished as he did so, belatedly banished to non-existence, by suggestion, or perhaps by overexertion, if not by hot lead.

And it started to rain.

"Oh shit!" cried Megan. "Grab Simon, damn it!"

Marianne dropped the gun, shaking the wrist that the weapon's recoil had sprained, and did as she was told, in spite of the pain.

In fact, Simon did not need to be carried, or even to be grabbed. He too had seen the surface of the cave-wall splinter under the impact of the bullets, and then begin to crack, and then begin to leak, and finally begin to spray water, initially as flying droplets, but a spatter that threatened to turn into a deluge at any moment. He took the time to grip the crwth firmly, so that he was in no danger of dropping it, and he ran, pushing his sister and his friend ahead of him, stumbling and scrambling, up the steps.

One way or another, all three of them got to the top of the staircase. In theory, all three of them could have counted every one, but in the event, the only one who had the presence of mind and the need to check the accuracy of his intuitive count was Simon.

There were, indeed, thirty. He congratulated himself, on the accuracy of his intuition, not the arithmetical feat itself.

The three of them stood in the crypt then, looking down through the open trapdoor, watching the cave flood by the light of Megan's lantern. Down below, the one that Simon had left behind had gone out.

By the time the water stopped rising, there were only four steps visible. Simon estimated that when the tide was at its lowest, there might be as many as seven or eight of the steep steps visible, but at its highest, the crypt might be subject an invasion of several inches of sea-water.

"I didn't mean to do it," Marianne said, her voice on the edge of hysteria. "I saw a man, I swear, who was about to cut your head off. He vanished when I shot him, but I didn't know he wasn't real! I didn't know it was a hallucination!"

"If it was a hallucination," said Megan, putting a comforting hand on Marianne's shoulder, "It was a collective hallucination. I saw him too—and even if he was just a ghost, that doesn't mean that he couldn't have done real damage if you hadn't shot him. If I'd had the gun, I'd have done exactly the same."

Marianne looked at Simon, her eyes pleading for further confirmation. He was still clutching the bulky crwth, but he freed his left hand so that he could match Megan's gesture by putting it on his sister's other shoulder.

"It's okay," he said. "We all saw him. And ghost or not, collective hallucination or not, if you hadn't shot him, he probably could have killed me."

"But why?" Megan wondered. "Wasn't he supposed to be on our side?"

"Perhaps he was," said Simon. "Perhaps the thing inside my head, for all its ability to see into the remotest depths of the universe, and hundreds of years of leeching the minds of the Murdens, really hasn't got much imagination when it comes to directing live action. Cerys was lured into shooting me in the back—perhaps poor Glyndwr, even though he was a free agent, was simply nudged into doing what he did in order that you'd shoot through him, Marianne. Perhaps he was a pawn, sacrificed in the interests of a long game. And perhaps the fact that you were there to fire the shot wasn't entirely your own idea. At any rate, for what it's worth, I'm extremely glad you were there, and you did exactly the right thing."

"But let's keep it strictly between ourselves, shall we?" Megan advised, "We don't want people to think that we're completely mad, do we? Even if we are. Especially if we are."

"We are, aren't we?" Marianne put in, faintly.

"I don't think it matters, any longer," said Simon. "Insane or not, there isn't any way out of the collective hallucination. It's only partly a matter of location; it's in our bodies as well, handed down through the generations. I hate saying it, as I make such a public fetish out of disapproving of clichés, but the truth is that we can run, but we can't hide . . . which isn't to say that those of us who still have the running option shouldn't take it."

"But things will be different now," said Megan, pointing down into the hole, at the sea-water filling the cave where the vitreous cocoons had kept vigil for so long.

"They will," Simon agreed, "but not completely. They'll be a little quieter, for a while, but it isn't over, here or anywhere else. And for me, at least, it's only just begun. But that's good. At my age, nobody needs endings—just beginnings, if it's possible to find them."

Releasing Marianne then, who seemed to have come back a long way from the brink of hysteria, Simon put the crwth down while he lowered the trapdoor back into the horizontal position. After a momentary hesitation, he fastened the pad-lock, and used the key to double-lock it. Then, once again, he looked at both of his companions in arms, and said: "Thanks." He did not think, even for a moment, of complaining about the fact that his express instructions had been disobeyed. He was not the lord of the manor yet.

XX
The Morning After the Flood

By mid-morning, the household was almost back to normal. Edith had recovered from her brief indisposition and had resumed command of her culinary empire. Marianne was sporting a crepe bandage around her right wrist, neatly secured by Megan, who had assured her that, being a Murden, she had no need to see a doctor—a judgment to which Marianne seemed willing to adhere for the moment, in spite of the professed anxieties of Zoe and Krysten, slightly piqued by Marianne's refusal to explain the accident that had caused the injury in any way that they found plausible. Cerys, who had decided to stay overnight after having gone to bid fare-well to Felicia and having been sternly told that she could not possibly drive along the roads of West Wales by night in such shocking weather, finally decided to set off for Swansea and the future shortly before lunch.

The weather, although not as bad as it had been the previous evening, was still not good. The rain seemed steady and patient rather than aggressive, but it was falling from a uniformly gray sky, and did not give the impression that it was going to stop any time soon.

Simon, playing the part of a true gentleman, carried Cerys's bags downstairs for her and loaded them into the trunk of the Subaru, sheltering under an umbrella while he did so.

"I'm really sorry about last night," she said. "I just lost it, I'm afraid. I was just so ashamed when you caught me sneaking down to the cave. It was stupid of me."

"It wasn't your fault," Simon assured her. "You were lured down, just as you had been before. And, just as before, it was a good thing that you went down. I'm truly very grateful that you did."

"You must be crazy, then," said Cerys. "I can't forgive myself for shooting at you, so how you can do it is beyond me."

"It's all part of pretending to be a saint," Simon assured her. "It's just an act."

"But you're not going to tell me what happened when you went down there last night, after that bullet I threw at you disappeared?"

"It wasn't really a bullet," Simon told her, "and it didn't really disappear. But no, I couldn't even attempt to tell you what happened. To say that I was hallucinating is the understatement of the century. But I survived. I came round just as Megan and Marianne arrived to help me, and we all got out as fast as humanly possible when the wall cracked, as you can imagine. All I can really tell you, and all that you really need to know, that there is no family secret any longer. The cauldron is full to the brim with sea-water. The vitreous cocoons had already died—the red blur you saw and photographed was just a kind of residue, a mock-bloodstain. Maybe they were all that was keeping the sea at bay, and when they died the wall couldn't hold out against the pressure any longer. According to Father Mallory, it happens to all of them in the end. Ours might have been the last, but I doubt it. Anyway, there's nothing under the crypt any more. File them away in your long-term memory and forget them. Live your life. Be happy, if you can."

"Fat chance," opined Cerys. "I'm a Murden."

"Indeed you are, so don't be a stranger. You're Felicia's last link with the past. It would be a great kindness if you were to call in and see her sometimes."

"I will. And if you're in a position to offer me a job with the estate two years down the line, I'll give it very serious consideration. And if you can make peace with Cousin Douglas, maybe I can be a useful link between the two organizations. That is, after all, the ostensible reason why Douglas has hired me."

"I'm not at war with him," Simon assured her, "and I have every intention of exploiting the Jefferson expertise to the maximum if I can, and Cousin Bernard's too—and yours. I'm going to need all the help I can get running an estate. I'm really not cut out for it."

"Nor was James," observed Cerys. She collapsed her own umbrella, shook the raindrops off it, and climbed into the Subaru. A few moments later, the vehicle backed away from the perron of the Abbey, and swerved toward the gate, which was wide open, Simon having given Zoe instructions to leave it like that.

When he turned to go back into the house, Simon found Marianne standing in the doorway—something that was getting to be a habit, and for which she was showing a curious talent.

"Could I bring my car on to the tine now?" she asked.

"Of course," said Simon, as he stepped under the porch and folded up his umbrella. "Zoe can bring hers on too, if she wants to, although it's probably fine where it is. The street isn't going to get nearly as cluttered today as it was yesterday, and Dai Mermaid will be congratulating himself on his good judgment in not taking on any extra bar staff before the end of the month. How's the wrist?"

"Nothing serious. I don't know how I managed to get off all three bullets, though. High on the adrenalin rush, I suppose." She hesitated, and then said: "Am I a murderer now?"

"Hardly," said Simon. "He'd already been dead for six hundred years. Even so, 'the woman who shot Owain Glyndwr' has a fine ring to it, don't you think? You can't really brag about it at school, but I suppose you could tell Zoe, if you wanted to."

"You're joking. I stalled when she asked how I hurt my hand. If I told her what I thought I did, she'd probably leap at the chance to have me committed."

"I don't think that's fair."

Marianne sighed. "You wouldn't," she said. "And you'd probably be right. I'm such a bitch."

"I forbid you to say that about the woman who saved my life. You're a heroine now, and you have to try to live up to it."

"Fat chance," she said, probably deliberately echoing Cerys. "How are you doing? You're the one with the bullet inside your head."

"It wasn't a bullet. It threw out a flash to give me a better idea of what it really is, but it's quiet now, and it will probably stay quiet, at least while I'm awake and capable of rational thought. I'm pretty sure that I have it under control, for now. I'm a Murden, after all: we don't need doctors. In any case, it's benign; if it's capable of wanting anything, the last thing it would want is to harm me."

"Are you absolutely sure about that?"

"Not absolutely—how could I be? But it's what I feel, and it's certainly what I'm going to assume, until I have evidence to the contrary. I'm fine—but in view of everything that happened last night, I wouldn't blame you if you never want to see this place, or me, ever again."

"You're joking," she said. "Didn't you listen to anything I said to you yesterday?"

"Every word.

"Well then, you know where I stand. You might get heartily sick of me, once the novelty wears off and I begin to get on your nerves, or vice versa, but I'm hoping it won't. We're brother and sister, after all. We came out of the same womb. If we can't be one the same side, who can? Anyway, that's what I'm going to assume until I have evidence to the contrary. Aren't you?"

"I am. So, hypothetically, assuming that the will is eventually proven, and I end up with all or most of the estate, would you be prepared to give up your job at the school and come and work for me. I'm going to need a good secretary."

Marianne, taken by surprise, hesitated and hedged. "What makes you think that I'm a good secretary?"

"Instinct and fraternal conviction," he replied. "You'd get free accommodation in the Abbey, obviously."

"What about Megan?"

"She'll probably want a secretary too, once she's the operation's IT manager. But I'm getting my offer in first."

Marianne was still hesitant. "You really want me to come and live here?" she said.

"If things work out, yes, absolutely." Simon hesitated himself before adding: "Zoe and Krysten too. I can't promise to find employment for them right away, but the business side of the estate has been inert for a long time, and if I do end up as lord of the manor, I'd like to manage it more actively than James did. I'd like to develop the village too, if I can obtain the cooperation of Bernard Pallister and Douglas Jefferson. It won't be easy, but if we can agree a plan of some sort, I'll need as much help as nepotism can supply. That's a long-term project, though. For now, I'd just like you to consider it, if you will."

"I will," she agreed, a trifle minimally. "For the moment, though, I can't even run, let alone hide. I don't think I'm safe to drive. Can I stay on for an extra couple of days, if necessary? I certainly can't go back to work with a sprained right wrist, although I'll have to get a doctor's note if it's longer than a couple of days."

"No problem," said Simon. "You'll be very welcome. Felicia will be pleased. She liked you even before you saved my life. Now you're in the black in her moral account book forever."

"You told her?"

"I tell Felicia everything."

Marianne nodded, only semi-approvingly, perhaps thinking: *Good luck with that*. All that she actually said, though, was: "The thing in the crypt is gone, but the thing in the bay is still there, isn't it?"

"Absolutely. Somewhat depleted, I suspect, after yesterday's efforts, but still there, and doubtless all the keener to carry on with its projects."

"There's no chance of it letting you alone then?"

Simon laughed. "I hope not," he said. "I still have an awful lot of questions to ask Melusine. Does that mean that you don't want to come to work for me?"

"I haven't made up my mind yet," she said, only a trifle pensively, "but it seems to me that now I'm certifiably insane, it might be better to have company in the delusion. So yes, I'll probably take you up on the offer. Always provided, of course, that the crack in the rock I caused doesn't cause a general collapse that brings the entire Abbey down."

"You didn't cause it," Simon assured her. "Millions of years of slow erosion caused it. At the very most, you supplied that last straw, and there really wasn't any alternative. You did a good deed, and showed admirably quick thinking in doing it."

"That's just flattery," she said. "I wasn't thinking at all."

"Even better," Simon said. "You have good instincts. That's truly precious—and before you deny it again, be kind to yourself, for once. Just play along with the tune, okay?"

She almost accused him of sainthood, but thought better of it. Instead, she said: "I'll try—but it won't be easy, breaking the habit of half a lifetime.

"I know," Simon said. He put up the umbrella again. "I need to go see Megan," he explained. "I'll drop in at Raven on the way back, but I won't be long."

"It's fine," Marianne assured him. "Felicia's still in bed, and she wants to hear my account of what happened—can I tell her?"

"Everything," Simon assured her, and went down the steps, heading for the open gate with what he hoped was a confident stride.

When Megan eventually opened her door to let him in the first thing she did was to inspect his forehead very carefully. "Is it still in there?" she asked. "There isn't even a bump."

"So far as I know," Simon confirmed, "unless the rain in the Underworld flushed it out. It's mostly dark matter, I guess, so it doesn't take up much space. It's been no trouble thus far. I doubt that it's conscious, but if it is, I have no idea what its plans might be. I suppose it would probably want to take a long look around before making any, after being stuck down in that cave for thousands of years—but I suspect that it will be up to me to formulate any plans that need to be formulated, and make any decisions that need to be made."

"And can you do that?" she said, as they sat down in the lounge. She didn't offer him coffee and a biscuit. They were past the need for rituals of that kind.

"Of course."

"You'll forgive me, I suppose, if I'm skeptical. But just so I'm up to date with the madness, the thing we saw before— the blue thing that seemed to go on forever—is gone now, and was mostly appearance anyway? What's left of it is now inside you, in your reckoning?"

"It's not nearly as simple as that," Simon said. "But yes, most of its previous self, both in terms of baryonic matter and dark matter, is gone, metamorphosed."

"Where to?"

"Who can tell? Downwards, I suspect, embarked on the next phrase of its dark biology."

"And why was it ever in the cave? If it came from the Earth's core, and has gone back there, why come to the surface at all. And why not all the way there?"

"Presumably, because that's where it needed to be, for that phase of its life-cycle: because that was the particular gutter from which it needed to look at the stars. I'm not sure . . . yet."

"And where does the thing in your head fit it?"

"Presumably ditto, because that's where it needs to be . . . the particular gutter from which to look at the stars. At least, I hope so."

"You hope so?"

"Of course. It's a gift. It's my chance to look at the stars, if I can just figure out how to look through it without burning out my retinas . . . so to speak. Of course, the entities that put it there probably see the matter the other way around: as their way of looking into me. When you look into the abyss, etcetera. Or, more succinctly, as above, so below. My chance to get a glimpse of their macrocosm is their chance to get a glimpse of our microcosm. It's win-win situation. It won't be easy, because nothing ever is, but I'm hoping that if and when my new possession and I can begin dreaming productively together, the sky won't be any limit."

"So you reckon that you're some kind of superman now?"

"Alas, no; I'm the same wimp as I always was, although I'm hoping to live for a while yet, quietly and virtuously."

"Virtuously? Living in sin with Felicia?"

"Felicia and I are not living in sin, under any sane definition of the word sin. Quite the reverse, in fact: we're living the dream. All last, we will be if we can. Even though she's been a little under the weather lately, I'm hoping that will go on for a long time too, taking us into unexplored territory, gloriously."

Like Marianne, Megan refrained from saying *Good luck with that*. Instead, she said: "How's Marianne's wrist?"

"Bad. She won't be able to drive back to Bristol, let along go back to work, for several days. She might have to go to town to get a sick note—do they still call them sick notes?"

"God knows. Never asked for one in my life. I must say that she surprised me last night. She had to do it—I wouldn't have had the time to grab the gun from her. Didn't hesitate, though: *pow, pow, pow*, even with a wrecked wrist. It was her idea to go down, too, just in case you were thinking of giving me the credit. Foolishly, I had every faith in you. I thought you'd be fine. Mind you, it was only a phantom sword, so it would probably have shattered on impact, even against a scrawny neck like yours."

"I'm glad I didn't have to test the hypothesis," said Simon, dryly. "I didn't even see the crazy bastard until the first bullet went through him—I was a million miles away."

"Which, knowing you, you were enjoying immensely."

"Do you? Know me, I mean?"

"Not biblically, obviously. But otherwise, maybe as well as anyone can. Our acquaintance might be slight, but it's the quality that counts. Once you've seen a man look a sea serpent in the eye and nearly get beheaded by Owen Glendower without batting an eyelid, I figure that you have his measure. You've come over to invite me to the Abbey for two o'clock, I assume? You wouldn't want me to miss the expression on Dougie's face when he finds out that the legendary cauldron of rebirth is underwater forever, would you?"

"Among other things," said Simon. "But can I ask you to be discreet? I want to do my best to make my peace with Cousin Douglas—all the more so as I can now assure him that his father had nothing to do with my conception."

That caused Megan to start. "Can you?" she asked

"Absolutely," he assured her "But that is one of the other things I wanted to talk to you about. Have you had the results back yet? I'm assuming that when I pointed out the possibility that other Murden males might have the same number of common alleles as Douglas and me, and the same Y-chromosome anomaly, you telephoned the lab that does your DNA analyses for you, and asked them to compare my gene-profile with the one you'd provided of James's years ago?"

She smiled wryly. "Well, it seems that you know me. Yes, I did, among other things, but no, I haven't received the email yet. I'll let you know this afternoon, if it's come through. But what's your proof that Ranald isn't your father?"

"It might be stretching a point to call it proof," Simon admitted. "In fact, I dreamed it, and as it has to do with morgens and their role as temptresses . . . it could be that the whole thing is symbolic, and I'm only one of a long series of clones of Owain Myrddin in a purely mystical sense, which has to do with the dark matter equivalent of DNA and not with actual DNA. But I thought it worth checking: you really did obtain a comparison of my DNA with Angela's?"

"Of course. So did Dougie, apparently. There isn't any doubt about her being your mother. She admitted it, anyway."

"She admitted giving birth to me. You're the one who pointed out to me that it's not necessarily the same thing, genetically speaking."

"You have fifty per cent of your DNA in common. That's a fact."

"You have a hundred percent of yours in common with Jocasta Symonds, but she's not you, and James Murden wasn't her father, even though Dougie Jefferson seems to have cottoned on to the fact that appearances might be made to indicate that he was. All that the fifty per cent of common DNA proves is that I have as much DNA in common with her as a brother would have, or a father. And given Murden habits, let alone what I've now been led to think about morgen habits, it might be a mistake to leap even to conclusions that seem to be obvious."

Megan stared at him for a moment, and then said: "Exactly what are you expecting the comparison of your DNA profile with James's to show?"

"I don't know," Simon said.

"And if you seriously think that the comparison of your DNA with Angela's doesn't prove what I assumed that it proved, what does that imply with regard to the comparison of mine and James's?"

"I don't know," Simon repeated. "But a moment ago, when you admitted that you'd requested the additional comparison, you said 'among other things'? What other things?"

Megan blushed. "I asked the analyst to compare your DNA with mine," she said. "I figured that if you had more genes in common with Dougie than would be expected of distant cousins . . . perhaps it was foolish, given that the comparison with my father's would have . . . except that . . . oh, shit. Have I just opened a can of worms?"

"Probably not. Let's wait and see, shall we?"

"I'm an idiot. I should never have started this bloody hare running?"

"You didn't. Dougie had already jumped to the conclusion. It would all have come out eventually. All you did was let me in on the error and enable me to correct it. I owe you thanks for that, and you certainly have nothing to apologize for . . . but I really would be obliged if you didn't start a fight with him this afternoon. We need to make friends with him, to the extent that I can."

Megan shook her head in mock despair, although the pretence seemed a trifle strained. "Unbelievable," she said "But fine—I'll be good, as long as he lays off the snide remarks. One comment about whoredom in front of the Reverend Father, though, and I might not be able to restrain myself."

"Father Mallory believes that fallen women are more sinned against than sinning. He told me so himself, in so many words, after Dougie had told him that my mother was a whore. I didn't bother to correct the misconception, but if Dougie repeats the allegation in front of Marianne, you'll probably have to get in line to kill him."

"And is that what you believe—about fallen women, that is?"

"Oh, no. I don't believe there's any falling involved, no reason for any disapproval, let alone contempt. People do what they need to do. I was a whore all my working life, selling my precious soul instead of my worthless body. I still would be, if anyone were willing to pay me real money for it. As things are, I have to practically give it away and pretend to be a saint—which I'm not."

"Don't overdo it," she advised. After a pause, she said: "I spoke to Jocasta on the phone last night. I'm going to visit her in Gloucester next week, and I'll get to meet the famous Anthony. How do you want me to play it?"

"That's entirely your business," Simon said. "You know already that I have absolutely no objection to either of them putting in a claim against the estate, if they think they have legal grounds. In a just world, without the stupid entail that was invented in another age, you and Felicia would have inherited the Abbey from James, and it would be nothing to do with me. Do you mind me asking, though, purely as a matter of curiosity, which of you made the phone call?"

"Her, obviously. I'm surprised that you have to ask, since you know me so well. I suppose I could have said no, especially as I'm more than half-convinced that it wasn't her idea to invite me, but . . . well, curiosity kills cats, so everybody says. Except you, obviously, being such a stickler for accuracy."

"Nice sarcasm. So how are you going to play it, then?"

"God knows. By ear, I guess. I'll hate the pair of them, obviously, although I've checked out her ex and Anthony for shadiness, so far as I can, and they both seem clean—they're not even living in sin. No grounds for disapproval there."

"How disappointing for you."

"What was that you said about sarcasm? I'll let it pass this time, but be careful. How's Edith, by the way? If she's still laid up, I could renew my offer to drive your sister and her offspring to town for dinner."

"She's fine—but that doesn't mean that the offer wouldn't be appreciated. I'm calling in at Raven on the way back, so I can mention the possibility, if you like."

"By all means. They'll probably be bored half to death by this evening, with all this rain."

"I doubt it—they have their mobile phones, after all. That seems to be all young people need to keep them amused nowadays."

"Especially if they're into porn, gambling, booking whores and ordering designer drugs. Given the way that foolish little girl has been using hers recently, I'm surprised that you can say such a thing with a straight face."

Simon, who had been imagining far more harmless pursuits, frowned. "I don't have one," he observed.

"And if you had, you wouldn't be doing any of the things I mentioned," she said, with a sigh. "Never mind. After the fiasco with the Jefferson/Cannick DNA comparison, I'm a little reluctant to jump any more conclusions, but I did a few calculations last night. Do you realize how far it is from that wall where the crack opened up last night to the edge of the tine?"

"It's approximately ninety feet to the back wall of Morgan's Cave," said Simon, "and a further forty to the cliff face—but there's no reason to think that it was a hundred and thirty feet of solid rock before last night. The rock between Nyder's Cave and the crypt is furrowed by numerous cracks large enough for a sea serpent to squeeze through. Admittedly, that's not much more than forty feet, but . . ."

She raised her arms. "Okay—I should have known that you'd have done the arithmetic. But do you seriously believe that Marianne's bullets caused the wall to open up all the way to the edge of the tine?"

"It's not impossible," Simon said, scrupulously, "but no, I don't believe that the bullet could have caused the rift to run all that way instantaneously, any more than I believe that the vitreous cocoons detached themselves or their offspring from the situation they'd occupied for thousands of years just for the pleasure of getting one of their larvae thrown in my face. Once I found out what the fake bullet actually was, I figured that couldn't be the reason—and when the cave flooded, it didn't take much imagination to suspect that the cocoons must have known that the internal erosion of the mudstone was approaching critical. Marianne's shots were just the final straw that precipitated the inevitable. Naturally, I'm hoping that, as I seem to be presently lodging a friendly alien presence, it will give me fair warning if the Abbey is in danger of collapsing any time soon. For the moment, I'm assuming that it won't—but I'll check the insurance policy, just in case."

"You're going to continue living there, though?"

"I don't live there; I live in Raven Cottage. But if and when I do move into the Abbey, I'll probably commission a proper geological survey. And if the worst comes to the worst, I'm sure that Felicia and I will be quite content to spend our twilight years in Raven, provided that we can save the library."

"Unbelievable," was Megan's judgment, yet again—but more out of burgeoning habitude than censorious judgment.

Simon put the umbrella up again in order to go round to Raven, even though it was only next door. Zoe let him in. The fact that she and Krysten were both sitting quietly in the study with their mobile phones in hand did not seem as reassuring to Simon as it would have done an hour before. Monique was asleep, for once.

"I'm truly sorry to be neglecting you so much," he said, "but my usually quiet life has become ridiculously hectic of late. We can all go over the Abbey for lunch now, but Megan's going to reissue the invitation that she wasn't able to follow through last night to drive you and Marianne to town for a good dinner. I'd come myself, but I don't want to leave Felicia on her own."

Zoe, at least, had little or no interest in such details. "How did Mum really hurt her hand?" she demanded.

"How did she say that she hurt it?" Simon parried, warily.

"I told you he'd play dumb, didn't I?" Zoe said to Krysten, triumphantly. She turned back to Simon. "I saw Cerys hand her the gun, remember. She fired it, didn't she? What at? Or who?"

"Whatever your mother told you," said Simon, carefully, "it wouldn't be polite for you to doubt it, let alone to draw illegitimate inferences from my innocuous question."

"I told you he'd be full of bullshit too, didn't I?" was Zoe's rejoinder to that, again pretending to address Krysten.

"That's a bit unfair, Mum," Krysten suggested, with a polite judiciousness that seemed to Simon to be entirely appropriate in a dutiful daughter—which Zoe clearly wasn't, at present.

Zoe turned her attention to Simon again. Before she could ask another embarrassing question, Simon tried to deflect the assault. "What's the problem, Zoe?" he asked, mildly. "Have I done something to upset you?"

"Only invited us out here, and then spent all day yesterday trying to get rid of us, after teasing us the day before with all kinds of cryptic clues about the family secret, tying yourself in knots in the process, and then not telling us how Mum hurt her hand. What's *your* problem?"

"Ah," said Simon. "I see. Yes, I'm sorry about the suggestion that you ought to go home yesterday, but I was worried about Krysten and Monique. I'd received indications that it might not be safe here—and I was right. You do know that the caves underneath the Abbey flooded last night, don't you? I was still down there when it happened, and your mother hurt her hand helping me get out."

"Crap," was Zoe's judgment. "How did firing the gun help you get out?"

Simon felt caught in a trap, not for the first time. He didn't want to trespass on Marianne's parental prerogatives, although it certainly wouldn't have been the first time, but he couldn't see any alternative.

"She shot the ghost of Owain Glyndwr," he said. "He was trying to cut my head off. She saved my life."

That, at least, had the virtue of taking her by surprise. Yet again, though, she turned ostentatiously to Krysten to say: "Bullshit."

"It's possible that we were all deluded," Simon admitted, readily. "The cave did rather lend itself to hallucination and madness—but that's all over now. It's flooded; there is no Merlin's Cave any more, no Murden mystery. It's finished."

"And it's safe now?" Krysten enquired.

"Probably. Your mother is anxious that the whole structure might be unsound. I'll advise Felicia to commission a proper investigation, just to make sure. Assuming that it does turn out to be safe, I'd like your mother to come and live here, and to work as my secretary. I'll need one, if I do come into the Murden inheritance."

The change of subject, although far from expertly contrived, had the desired effect.

"You want Gran to come and live here?" Krysten said, curiously. "What will happen to the Bristol house?"

"Nothing," said Simon. "So far as I know, it's built on perfectly solid ground, and she won't sell it—even if you decide to follow her here, in due course."

"To do what?" asked Zoe, equally curiously.

"I don't know, but there are a number of people living locally who have expressed an interest in developing the village into something other than a cluster of second homes and holiday lets. In combination with Morpen, it might become an authentic community—with its own primary school. Two of your cousins, Douglas Jefferson and Bernard Pallister, are already holding meetings with a view to resurrecting and revising a development plan that was first mooted way back in the 1970s. If I inherit the estate and receive the money from James Murden's insurance policy, they'll have to bring their plan to me. Being Murden-descended, of course, we're all supposed to hate one another like poison, for hereditary reasons, but that shouldn't stop us doing business. Cerys is already working for Dougie with something of that sort in mind. If . . ."

"Hang on," Zoe interjected. "Isn't Bernard Pallister the guy I tried to brain when I caught him breaking into the cottage? You can still see his blood there on the carpet."

"He has apologized for that," Simon said.

"According to Megan, if I was eavesdropping correctly," Zoe continued, "he was planning to murder you."

"That was an exaggeration—a negotiating ploy, partly intended to protect your incognito. He's not such a bad chap, really. And as I said, old family quarrels needn't prevent us working together, if we have common interests."

"And isn't Jefferson the guy who's trying to stop you inheriting the estate?"

"He certainly would if he could, and he might well be able to cause some difficulties—but again, if and when his interests come to coincide with ours, he has expertise, connections and commercial interests that will be invaluable to us."

"Us?" Zoe queried. "You and who else?"

"All of us," Simon said, as if it were obvious. "The family. I received the inheritance because I'm descended from Lilith Murden and her daughter Eve. So are you. I'd like you to get some benefit from it, if possible—not in terms of vulgar cash, but a more substantial involvement. We're all Murdens, after all, and that still means something hereabouts. Without us, and Megan's descendants, the entire branch would have become extinct. I think that would be a pity. But there's no rush. Just give it some thought, over the next few months."

Slightly quizzical, but evidently not against the idea on principle, Zoe and Krysten agreed to give the possibility some thought. Then Krysten tucked Monique into the carry-cot and they made what arrangements they could to protect her from the rain—which, mercifully, was beginning to slacken even further.

XXI
Beginnings

Megan arrived at the Abbey at quarter to two, only a matter of seconds ahead of Father Mallory. She had time to notify Simon that her genomic analyst had responded to her query, but they agreed with reciprocal nods of the head to postpone that discussion until later. Douglas Jefferson was too eager to be fashionably late, so he arrived in a matter of minutes. Marianne was with Felicia, and didn't come out to be introduced. The party of four went into the library at two o'clock, where Thomas Mallory waxed lyrical over his first sight of the collection of parchments for long enough to bore everyone else, and to cause Jefferson to manifest signs of considerable impatience.

Eventually, the four of them went down to the chapel, where Simon handed the two keys that Cerys had given him to Jefferson, while Mallory made a detour to inspect the ancient depiction of the morgen and the ouroboros.

"Cerys asked me to give these to you," Simon said, in a neutral tone. "Perhaps you'd do the honors?"

Jefferson accepted the keys without showing the slightest hint of embarrassment. Carefully, he unfastened the first padlock, and lifted up the trapdoor, with only slight difficulty. They went down into the crypt, armed with two lanterns, carried by Simon and Megan.

Douglas Jefferson only spared the crypt a brief sweeping glance as he made for the second trapdoor, although his gaze did pause briefly over the recently opened hole in the wall and the cement rubble. He didn't bother to make any remark about it, but simply bent down swiftly in order to unfasten the second padlock. The Dominican, however, made a much longer inspection of the features of the crypt visible from the antechamber, to the extent that the lamplight permitted, and he was still detached from the other three when Jefferson unlocked and removed the second padlock.

Megan made sure that the lantern she was carrying was in the ideal position to give her a clear sight of Jefferson's face as he tilted the trapdoor back. Simon suspected that she was slightly disappointed. Jefferson had practiced long and hard to train his poker face for business purposes. After five seconds of staring at the surface of the water, he simply said to Simon, accusatively: "What have you done?"

"Nothing," said Simon. "It was, if Father Mallory will excuse the expression, what legal terminology used to call an act of God."

On hearing his name pronounced, the Dominican made haste to rejoin his companions. As he looked down at the water, his face too was unreadable; he was a lawyer with many years experience of contrived inscrutability.

"The rock of the tine is Silurian mudstone and siltstone," Simon explained, helpfully. "It's considerably sturdier than the crumbling cliffs on England's east coast, which have been falling into the sea year by year for centuries, but the rocks in the bay take a particularly severe battering from Atlantic storms that seem to zero in on it like a target. Last night, doubtless provoked by the heavy rain, there was a slight landslip—trivial, I dare say, on the Richter scale, but enough to crack the wall of the cave and let the seawater in. The cave is completely submerged, and will remain so even at low tide. It's a matter of immense regret, obviously, but there's nothing to be done about it, unless you'd care to go down in a diving suit, equipped with a powerful searchlight."

"It was still empty yesterday evening," was Jefferson's only comment.

"And you have the mobile phone footage to prove it, I believe," Simon commented. "Alexander Usher will be very pleased, no doubt. I'm not certain, but I believe that they're the only electronic images of the cave in existence. Cerys didn't show them to me, I fear, so I can't comment on them myself, but I imagine they'll constitute quite a treasure on YouTube—at least for connoisseurs."

"They're utterly useless," said Jefferson, frostily. "Just a red blur. It could be anything." He looked at Thomas Mallory. "Is this a miracle, would you say, Father?"

"Certainly not," replied the Dominican. "It seems to me to have been an event of an entirely natural order. I'm disappointed, obviously, not to be able to see the phenomenon, but it can't be helped."

"I thought you'd be pleased," said Jefferson, a trifle suspiciously. "Didn't you deem it to be essentially diabolical?"

"I think you're misunderstanding my position slightly," said Mallory. "But for what it may be worth, I have reason to believe that similar destructive events have overtaken several other entities of the same sort within the last few centuries. They have now become exceedingly rare—or, at least, exceedingly difficult to find. Perhaps that's not a bad thing, given that the entities do seem to have the capacity to . . . well, in layman's language, provoke delusions and drive people insane."

"You'll get no argument from me about that," muttered Douglas Jefferson, not looking at either Megan or Simon. "Cerys said that she might have been knocked out by some kind of hallucinogenic gas the first time she went down—and that she had begun to see things again last night."

Simon made no comment on that assertion.

"What modern parlance would deem to be hallucinogenic effects have apparently been observed elsewhere," Thomas Mallory put in, judiciously, "although the data is, admittedly, very old, and whatever happened was doubtless vulnerable to considerable misinterpretation. I would like to talk to Miss Murden about her hallucinations, though . . . both the Miss Murdens . . . and Miss Harwyn as well, of course."

"Oh, I haven't seen anything at all," Megan put in, "except for the blue light. I never saw it after it turned red. And Felicia's been ill in bed, so she hasn't seen anything either. You can talk to Cerys, I suppose, although she must be in Swansea by now, and I'm not sure that she'll be very helpful . . . or even very co-operative. People tend to be very wary about reporting their dreams, in my experience."

She glanced at Jefferson, as if expecting a cutting remark, but he was pensive, in no mood, for once, for verbal combat.

The Dominican looked at Simon, but his expression did not seem hopeful. Simon didn't say anything, sure that he would have to suffer interrogation anyway, but equally sure that he could maintain discretion regarding all the aspects of his hallucinatory experience that he wanted to keep private.

"Of course, there's a long history of local delusions," Megan supplied, a trifle maliciously. "Everybody in St. Madoc sees ghosts, although it's quite a while since anyone's seen a genuine mermaid."

"What about sea serpents?" the Dominican put in, seemingly taking up the light tone. "Have any of those been seen recently?"

"One or two," said Megan, "but there are all sorts of things in the sea. It's easy to make mistakes, especially at night. And it's surprising how prone people are to jump to erroneous conclusions." She was looking directly at Douglas Jefferson, but he didn't blush, let alone flinch.

Now it was Thomas Mallory's turn to become bored and show signs of agitation. "As there doesn't seem to be anything to see down here any longer," he said, "might I return to the library, Mr. Cannick? I cut my inspection short a few minutes ago, because I realized that I was making everyone else impatient, but I really would like to continue my initial studies there for a little while longer, if I may. Mr. Jefferson, I'm sure, would rather go about his business."

"Actually," said Simon, swiftly, "I'd like a word with you before you go, Mr. Jefferson, if you don't mind. Perhaps, Megan, you can help Father Mallory in the library, while I take Mr. Jefferson to the drawing room?" Addressing Mallory, he added: "Miss Harwyn has been an enormous help to Felicia and myself in the library of late, helping us to go through the family archives. She's now quite familiar with her father's eccentric filing system. She can show you all the parchments."

"Of course," said the Dominican, with the utmost politeness. "I'd be most obliged."

Simon closed the trapdoor while Megan and the Dominican returned to the steps leading up to the chapel. Then he took James's key out of his pocket and resealed the padlock. "I hope you're not too disappointed," he said to Douglas Jefferson. "I did consider ringing you to tell you not to bother coming, but I wasn't sure that you'd be prepared to take my word for it, and I thought it would be better for you to see for yourself—and, as I said a few moments ago, I wanted to talk to you about another matter. Shall we go upstairs?"

"As you wish," said the little man, tonelessly.

Simon took Douglas Jefferson to the small drawing room, invited him to sit down and offered him a cup of coffee from the ready-prepared pot that was standing on the sideboard. The latter declined, and waited to be informed of the purpose of Simon's request.

"Further to our conversation yesterday, Mr. Jefferson," Simon said, thinking that there was no point in beating about the bush, "I've conducted some further research, assisted by Megan and by Marianne, my sister, who is staying with us in the Abbey at present. I have now ascertained, to my own satisfaction—beyond a shadow of a doubt, in fact—my actual parentage. Your father had nothing to do with it, although he does seem to have been kind enough to have lent my grand-mother and great-grandmother some assistance in finding accommodation and establishing themselves in Bristol when they left St. Madoc. I can assure you that you and I are no more closely related than either of is to half a dozen other descendants of Seymour Murden, who would doubtless have a similar number of alleles in common, including the one on the Y chromosome, because of the unusual frequency of those particular alleles in the family."

Jefferson's poker face remained perfect; he did not smile at the news. "It's very kind of you to have cleared the point up," he said. "Given that whatever evidence you have found is clearly of no concern to my family, I won't bother to ask what it is. I'm entirely happy to take your word for it. It only confirms what I always supposed."

"Thank you," said Simon. "I hope that removes any grounds there might have been for hostility between us. I really would like us to be able to collaborate in future, when I inherit all or part of the Murden Estate, all the more so if Anthony Symonds also becomes an interested party."

"I'd like that very much, Mr. Cannick," the little man said. "All the more so as I seem to have come to an understanding with Bernard Pallister, after many decades of needless hostil-ity. It really is time for a new start, after so many quarrels left over from a family schism that occurred nearly a hun-dred years ago. I do hope that the real and potential value of the estate hasn't been depleted too much by last night's . . . accident."

"So far as I can tell," said Simon, "the so-called Murden secret has been causing unnecessary hostilities and jealousies for a great deal longer than a hundred years. I was, as you know, hoping to take a much more open approach if and when I inherited the Abbey, and I'm not entirely sorry that it will now be unnecessary, since there is no longer anything to hide."

"Indeed," said Jefferson, plainly unconvinced. "I do apologize, but Alexander Usher would never forgive me if I didn't ask: would you care to tell me what it was that you took out of that recently excavated hole in the crypt?"

"Certainly," said Simon. "It's behind you, on the dresser."

Jefferson turned round. His gaze had scanned the crwth when he first entered the room, but he had not paid any attention to it.

"This?" he said. "What is it?"

"A crwth," Simon explained. "It's a traditional Welsh stringed instrument, of the lyre family. It lacks a bow, unfortunately, but it's not without interest. Given its antiquity, I'd like to think, of course, that it might have belonged to Owain Myrddin himself, but there's no possible way to prove that."

"Is it very valuable?"

"I really have no idea what it would fetch at auction, but there's no possibility of Felicia ever putting it up for sale. It's a family heirloom, and she takes such matters very seriously. She might, however, allow me to learn to play it. The strings still provide sounds, and I hope that I might be able to get a tune out of it, with a little practice and tuition—which one can get online nowadays. The world wide web is a wonderful thing, don't you think? All the world's accumulated knowledge at one's fingertips." As he spoke, he touched his forehead lightly. There was, as Megan had accurately observed, no bump.

Jefferson had taken out his mobile phone while Simon was speaking, and he took a photograph of the crwth. "Alex will doubtless be fascinated," he said, by way of explanation. "In view of the fact that you have now given Father Mallory the free run of your library, may I tell Alex that you'll doubtless be prepared to extend the same courtesy to him in future?"

"If Felicia is prepared to give her permission, I'll be delighted to welcome him to the Abbey, and take him to visit any part of the building that he would like to study," Simon said. "You'll forgive Felicia for not coming to receive you, I'm sure. She's rather frail, as you know, at a hundred and one years of age, and she's been suffering from a virus of late. Marianne's been very generous in sitting with her and chatting to her. Felicia doesn't have much opportunity to chat. She's quite well, though, apart from the virus. Not a trace of senile dementia. A true marvel."

"Do give her my regards," the little man said, without bothering to pretend that he cared, as he moved toward the door. "I can't stay any longer, I'm afraid. I'm sure we'll be meeting again quite soon."

"And often," said Simon. "Even if we can't be the best of friends, I hope that we can still do business together. That is, after all, what you wanted when you first came to see me a little over a fortnight ago."

"Indeed," said Jefferson, smoothly. "I hope so too."

Simon still thought it worth sticking to his conviction that all that slithered could indeed be reckoned serpentine, *ipso facto*. He showed the little man to the door.

It took a good deal longer to get rid of Thomas Mallory, but he eventually consented to withdraw from the library, full of regrets that Simon was not yet able to make arrangements there and then for the Vatican to take the parchments from the library on loan, for the purposes of multi-spectral scanning. Simon escorted him to his car.

"We still have a great deal to discuss, Mr. Cannick," the Dominican said, as he stood under the protection of a large black umbrella beside the Mercedes, which was parked outside the front door of the Abbey. Simon, who had not bothered to bring his own umbrella, because the rain was much lighter now, looked regretfully at the tire tracks left in the rain-sodden turf beside the gravel path by Cerys's Subaru and Douglas Jefferson's Lexus, as they had made three-point turns.

Perhaps, he thought, there was something to be said for James Murden's obsessive insistence on maintaining the careful isolation of the tine from the world of motorized vehicles, and from so much else. In reply to Mallory's remark, he simply said: "We both have other claims on our time, alas, but we'll certainly make what arrangements we can. I wish I could say that we have the whole future ahead of us, but we both seem to have left our youth far behind, and one can never tell when the foundations of one's existence are likely to suffer a fatal crack, can one?"

Mallory already had his hand on the rear door of the car, and the patient driver had already started the engine, but the Churchman couldn't resist asking one last question.

"Did you go to see the entity yesterday evening, Mr. Cannick, before the cave flooded?"

"Yes," Simon said. "It was hardly more than a dark red shadow on the wall by then—as you'll doubtless be able to see in the pictures that Cerys took for Douglas Jefferson. The blue appearance, I fear, was mostly that: mere appearance. It was already dying, I think, before I even arrived in St. Madoc, and last night's decay was just the completion of the process. I can't believe that it caused the crack in the rock, though." Long experience had taught him that telling the truth was often an excellent means of potential indirection, because men with subtle minds, especially lawyers, never took anything that was said to them at face value.

"You're getting wet, Mr. Cannick," Mallory observed. "If you can obtain the necessary permissions from Miss Murden for the loan of the parchments as soon as possible, I'd be very grateful. As you say, we're none of us getting any younger." He collapsed the umbrella as he got into the car.

The turning circle of the Mercedes was greater than that of the Lexus or the Subaru, and it was a heavier vehicle. The tire tracks it left were even worse.

Megan was waiting for Simon in the small drawing room, having poured herself a cup of coffee.

"You were right," she said, without preamble. "You and James had even more alleles in common than you and Douglas, including the one on the Y-chromosome, but not enough to imply a fraternal or parental relationship."

Simon nodded. "And?" he prompted.

"Ditto the two of us. More DNA in common than would normally be expected of first cousins, but not enough to suggest that we might be siblings. You'll just have to settle for the one sister . . . unless you really think that she isn't."

"Oh, she is," said Simon. "I'm absolutely certain about that."

"So you don't want me to obtain a comparison sample from her to make sure?"

"Of course not. It couldn't tell us anything we don't already know. She and I have the same mother, but different fathers, end of story. And it doesn't matter, either, how much or how little DNA you and I might have in common. We're next-door neighbors, and friends. That's all we want or need to be, isn't it?"

"Suits me," she said. There was still a slight uncertainty in her tone.

"And you really are James's daughter," Simon added. "Sometimes, the obvious really can be taken at face value, even in St. Madoc. And we need to be careful, occasionally, that we don't get carried away by our hallucinations. That way, madness lies—or at least nightmares."

"You seem saner already, I must admit—but I've been party to too many collective hallucinations lately to get back quite that easily. A trip to town will help, though, as long as Zoe doesn't ask too many awkward questions. With luck, we'll be able to use up three or four hours easily talking about you behind your back without forming a conspiracy to have you committed. If you don't like that idea, you can always come with us. The BMW can hold five and a baby without overmuch squeezing."

"I can't leave Felicia. Thank you, though. You and Marianne have both gone beyond the call of duty in the last couple of days. I appreciate it."

"What are friends for?" she said, lightly. "I kept Mallory at bay as best I could. Fortunately, he's too polite to press me too hard, and even at my age, I can still turn on the feminine charm when necessary, for an innocent like him. He won't let you off so easily."

"He still needs to keep me sweet until he can get Felicia's parchments under his multispectral scanner, and he doesn't have the same aids to interrogation that his forebears used to have. I'll blind him with fanciful theories and speculations. All he has to counter them is God and the Devil. He doesn't stand a chance."

Megan stood up to leave, and Simon escorted her to the front door. The rain had finally stopped, although the sky was still a sullen gray, and the lull gave the impression of being a mere hesitation.

"Will you be okay?" she said, before setting off along the driveway.

"Absolutely," he assured her.

"But you haven't found an ending," she pointed out, and added, defensively: "any more than I have."

"We've done far better than that," he assured her. "The point, as I've said before, isn't to reach endings, but to find more beginnings. That's not easy, at our age, but I'd say that we're doing pretty well. I can't guarantee that we'll live to be a hundred, but I'm pretty sure, now, that neither of us will starve for lack of food for thought."

For a moment, Simon thought that she might object that Jocasta Symonds did not qualify as a beginning, any more than an ending, but in the end she simply told him to send Marianne over to Sanderling whenever she was ready and promised to return the whole family by ten o'clock, "in time for cocoa," as she put it.

Marianne came down ten minutes later. "Everything's fine," she reported. The fever's gone, and we had a long chat. I think it did us both good. I like her, a lot—and that's unusual, for me." She held up her right arm to display the crepe bandage. "She might get tired of me, though, if I have to be here for another four or five days."

Simon took her left hand in his. "I won't say that you worry too much," he said, "Firstly because it's a cliché, and secondly, because none of us really worries enough, but you need to be a little kinder to yourself. You're a heroine, remember, a life-saver, and a crack shot."

"Crazy, you mean."

He kissed her hand, and she blushed.

"I mean exactly what I say," he assured her. "That's the joy of pedantry. I'll see you at ten, or thereabouts. I'll tell Edith to have the cocoa ready. She'll be delighted. It'll be just like old times."

After closing the door behind her, Simon went upstairs, feeling oddly weary, although it wasn't late.

Felicia was sitting up in bed, reading a book. It was not one of Simon's. He couldn't make out the title, but the binding suggested that it was old, perhaps nineteenth-century. Pure escapism, he assumed.

Simon sat down on the bed. Felicia set the book down and examined his forehead. He had already given her an exact account of everything that had happened, or seemed to happen, since the moment he had left the room with Rhodri to the moment when he returned some five hours later, but she had a subtle mind, which was very careful indeed of taking even the most sincere statements at face value. She had been living with Ceridwen's visions all her life, and with James's theories for most of it. She was an expert in not taking anything more seriously than it deserved.

"No sign of any recurrence of divine madness?" she queried.

"Nothing new on that front," he confirmed, scrupulously.

"Any further whispers from the Black Bard?"

"Nothing. If he was ever anything more than a hallucination, his feeble matter and dark mind have dissolved into mine now, quietly and unconsciously. I'm still recognizable though, I hope. I won't forget him, though. Conscious minds are all too adept at that, alas, but I'm clinging to the conviction that he's still there, and will retain a certain presence, perhaps not as a voice, but as a hidden treasure, still accessible if I go about it the right way."

"Are you really going to learn to play the crwth?"

"Absolutely. The one from the crypt will probably need restringing, but if so, it will be done as authentically as possible, and I'm already searching online marketplaces for a bow of suitable antiquity. It'll be costly, but it needs to be done right if it's to be done at all, and it's up to me to do it, if I can. It might be vital to the fruitfulness of future communication."

"But what about your writing? You're getting hardly anything done now—which is largely my fault, I fear."

"There's no fault involved, certainly not on your part. I'll try to keep my hand in with research, collation and reportage, but there's no getting around the fact that my life has changed, and I can no longer be the full-time writer I was a few weeks ago. I've changed too. I really do need to learn to make and understand music. The collection of popular classics stored on my computer for use as background music while I bash away at the keyboard won't be adequate to my needs any more."

Simon picked up Felicia's hand, and held it gently in his own. "This might be hard for you," he said.

"The alternative would be harder," she said, bluntly.

"I'm recognizable now, but I'm not sure that I can remain recognizable. In fact, I rather hope that I won't, in the end, although I hope that the metamorphosis is slow, measured and progressive. I can't be sure, yet, that what the vitreous cocoons left behind in the cave—assuming that it's more akin to a spore than to the amoebic equivalent of a memory stick—really is inside me, or what the eventual effects of having it inside me will be, if it is, but I don't believe that what happened was merely a crazy dream. Much of what I think I know is only based on guesswork, but I trust my intuitions."

"It was assisted guesswork," Felicia pointed out. "And I trust your intuitions too, for what that's worth."

"A lot, in fact. If I were alone in this, then I really wouldn't be able to resist the thesis that I'm simply mad. Occam's razor would surely prefer that hypothesis to the notion of alien beings with thought processes radically different from mine, concocting extraordinarily elaborate schemes in the attempt to establish communication with one another, for no better reason than the desire to communicate, and the desire to be sociable, even though they know they probably won't like one another if they ever do. Isn't that idea inherently crazy, in fact, and evidence in itself of profound madness?"

"Perhaps," said Felicia. "But if it's reality, it's what we have to live with, crazy or not. And if it isn't—well, it's still what we have to live with, if we're crazy."

Simon smiled, wryly. "You're right, of course," he said. After a pause, he added: "And if what happened to me last night was real, then it really is crazy. It could have been Cerys. Perhaps it should have been. She's young, vigorous and smart, not to mention beautiful, and she only pretends to be disenchanted, whereas I'm old, broken-down, and as ugly as sin, with a lifetime of marginal autism and clinical depression behind me. If I'd been an alien intelligence ambitious to be a re-creator, and had had the choice between the two of us, I wouldn't have picked me. You'd seriously have to doubt the judgment of a would-be re-creator prepared to follow that game plan."

"No," Felicia told him, "it had to be you. Sane or crazy, Cerys couldn't have saved or re-created the world. Neither could James. But sane or crazy, you're a man who might. That's what I believe."

"The very idea of saving, re-creating or even changing the world slightly, is crazy," Simon said, quietly.

"And the very fact that you're saying that proves that you're not."

Simon shook his head. "I'm too tiny. An ant with delusions of gigantism."

"Maybe so. But so what? If delusions of gigantism are what's needed, that's what it will take. And I say again, it had to be you. I can understand that perfectly, although I think I understand why you can't."

Simon contented himself with shaking his head.

"You don't believe me? Well, I suppose I can't blame you. Since that first night we slept together, I suppose I've given you the impression that I was desperate, that I'd have latched on to anyone. I've even thought so myself, on occasion. But it's not true. I can see that now. It didn't have to be anyone at all, you see. I'd made my life, determined it and sealed it. I don't say that I was happy with it, but I'd certainly settled for it, for seventy years. Believe me, it took more than just anyone to snatch me out of that inertia. And in my wilder moments of unaccustomed optimism, when the fever takes hold of me, I think that maybe I couldn't have been just anyone either, that it wasn't simply out of desperation that you accepted me, and kept me, and kept me alive. When the madness grips me, I tell myself that in some way, however weird, I'm not just a clone of my mother, but a clone of Ceridwen—*the* Ceridwen, not grandmother—and that whether or not it was one of Melusine's kin who spat you out into your mother's womb—which is absurd, by the way, except perhaps in a symbolic sense—you really are a clone of the Murden prototype. Fundamentally, I sometimes tell myself, insistently, you and I are Adam and Eve all over again—or Adam and Lilith."

"No," said Simon, softly, "we're not. We're better than that, you and I. The Black Bard thought in those terms, of continuity and similarity and endless repetition. Most people do, I suppose. But reproduction can't mean simple replication, or everything would be stuck, paralyzed and petrified. The true genius of DNA, as a re-creator, is mutation. It's an extremely messy process, with millions of failures for every success, but that's the only way it can work, at least without the aid of dark minds, inside or out. I can't begin, yet, to speculate what inherent processes of reproduction and re-creation dark matter life might have, and they might be beyond the scope of any feeble conscious imagination, but I'm perfectly sure that they must involve something analogous to mutation, in order to enable progress.

"So no, you and I aren't mere clones of our forebears, either in our genes or, more importantly, in the dark fraction of our minds, where the mystery of the Murdens truly lies. Whatever is happening now, to us, has happened before, not just to our own forebears but in other lines of human descent in other parts of the world. On the historical surface, all those attempts might seem to have been failures, to have come to nothing, or to have produced occasional chimerical monsters like the Roman Church—but that's because the real successes have accumulated beneath the surface, integrated into the dark fabric of the noosphere, taken for granted by the inheritors of the mutation. The few who have changed the world, have left it unaware that it has been changed, unaware that it was ever different, because that's what re-creation involves.

"You and I aren't clones, Felicia, we're mutants, whom no one else can take seriously, let alone understand. And that's why we need one another, and why we really do need *one another*, and why nobody else will do. It's not because we were destined for one another, merely to repeat some age-old pattern, but because we found one another, unexpectedly and out of the blue, and glimpsed a possibility to make something new, to be something new. And that's why neither of us has to be afraid that, because what we have isn't a marriage, or any other kind of stereotyped relationship that other people can recognize and find credible, it can't be real and can't last. Because it *can* be real, and it *can* last, because it only depends on us, and we can do it if we want to. I do. Do you?"

"You know I do," she said.

"It's settled, then. We're mutants. Perhaps we have no reason to be proud of that, and perhaps we shouldn't be proud of it—but perhaps we can and should be content with it, and content with ourselves and content with one another."

Felicia squeezed his hand, as best she could, with her frail fingers, very much as Ceridwen had done in the very brief while that Simon had known her, and in much the same spirit of reminiscence and anticipation. "I hope so," she said. "I certainly hope so." And then, after a pause, as if she too had thought of Ceridwen, whose hands she had surely held and squeezed thousands of times herself, she lay back in the pillow, looked up at the ceiling, and said: "Tell me the truth, Simon: am I dying?"

As she had died, Simon remembered, his mother—the one who had given birth to him, not the one who had tried to love him—had not allowed him to take her hand, and had refused any attempt to take his. Perhaps she had thought that she had forsaken the right. Perhaps she was punishing herself. Or perhaps she had simply lost all sensation in all her limbs, and her arms, and her hands had already turned to soft stone, effectively dead.

Instead of saying, therefore, as he could have said, truthfully: "We're all dying," Simon chose to say, hopefully, if not truthfully in a pedantic sense. "No, Felicia, you aren't dying; you just have a trivial virus, which I probably brought into the house from one of my various excursions to the mainland." And he added, for sentimental reasons: "I won't let you die. I need you far too much to let that happen. Crazy or not, possessed or not, I have a great deal to do if I'm to make any substantial contribution to the macrocosmic unconscious, whether to save the world or re-create it. I'll need help from others as well as you, but they'll be replaceable. You aren't. You're the only one who can actually share my dreams, and help me negotiate a way through them. It won't be easy, and it will probably take a long time, but the two of us can do it, and nobody else could. What I need from you has to come from you."

She smiled. "That's just flattery," she said. "But thanks anyway."

Was it just flattery? Simon wondered. He honestly didn't think so. But he was a person who genuinely thought he was the possessor of an alien gift, a man who thought that he could save the world by dreaming, thus serving as a vital link between various alien intelligences, and perhaps, by so doing, provided that he could learn to play the siren song, assist in the re-creation of the macrocosmic unconscious, so how reliable could his judgment possibly be?

Perhaps not very—but in any case, it was his end and his beginning. It was his WORD.

He remembered then the oft-misinterpreted message that his mother had brought him from her own personal hell, thinking that it might be important, and which, like almost everyone else in the imperfect world of human words, she had carelessly misquoted and left incomplete.

Because he was an eccentric scholar, however, and liked to think of himself as something of a pedant, Simon knew and could recite the whole quote, and even though his Latin was lousy and he knew full well that the document from which the quote was taken was a fake, he did not doubt that the message, if properly translated, had a useful meaning.

Quod est inferius est sicut quod est superius, et quod est superius est sicut quod est inferius as perpetranda miracula rei unius, he recited to himself. *As it is below, so it is above, the wonder of the whole being thus procured and perfected.*

"The wonder of the whole being thus procured and perfected," he repeated, aloud. And, even though he made a public fetish out of disapproving of clichés, he added: "One step at a time."